SHADOWS

OF THE

CASKET EMPIRE

MARK A. EVANS

~~~ For My Family ~~~

CONTENTS

There is a good reason why they say *truth* is
stranger than fiction.

~~~~~~~~~~~~~~~~~~~~~~~~~~~~~~~~~~~~~~

It's been long rumored the great Native American Indians
believed whenever a man lost his own sense of worth and
self-confidence, that he had been stripped of his shadow.
There are those in life who would not hesitate to destroy a
man's shadow to fulfill their own interests. However, they
should fear the man who would suffer their foolishness
until such a point in time, when he will show his true
courage by turning and casting his renewed shadow upon
their ill-fated deeds and selfish motives, regardless of risks.
Except now, in so doing, the man's new shadow will shine
a blinding, harsh light of truth on their shadowed
immoralities and dark corruptions.

INTRODUCTION

Garner McCall had come to love funeral service, not just the business of it, but mostly the tremendous personal societal value that the vast majority of funeral directors delivered for grieving families every day. He saw it up close and personal time after time. He had worked so hard to learn the business and represent the Great American Casket Company as ethically and professionally as he possibly could.

He learned so much about the business, the market drivers, competition, threats, pricing, profit structures, and above all, the people. From amazing funeral home owners and directors, so many of the folks at GAC, to the industry's power brokers, he spent a decade constantly traversing North America becoming intimately familiar with one of the nation's oldest industries, which was intentionally kept quiet and under the radar. Mostly he loved the people in the business, inside and out of GAC. Well, at least most of them. So often, he would see how many angelic-minded funeral home owners would time and again provide a loving memorial service for one of their less fortunate neighbors without ever a mention of a bill being sent. Regretfully, however, there would be others who were anything but charitable and kind, as well as a few more that would prove even worse still, only pretending to be decent human beings. He had those stories too. Over his career he had seen it all and loved every minute of it.

After more than a decade of leading hard-charging sales growth for the Great American Casket Company and turning-around one under-performing sales team after another, Garner McCall was about to get royally screwed out of his career and kicked to the bloody curb without ever seeing it coming. Worse still, his family would be harassed and terrorized, and even his own life threatened if he didn't shut up and go away quietly. There was a much darker side to GAC than McCall had never known, and he was about to find out in a very personal and painful way. But even almighty GAC failed to consider just how McCall was so unlike all the other execs they had destroyed over the years. He had figured out a lot about the deep dark shadows at the Great American Casket Company, especially with certain customers. What Garner McCall knew would prove more worrisome than anything they had ever confronted in protecting their shiny image and profits!

~~~~~~~~~~~~~

GOOD 'OL BOYS CLUB

Being the lone southerner on the senior leadership team, Garner had been hired from outside the industry by the one hundred year old Midwestern casket-maker. He was brought in to intentionally launch a new style of sales leadership, and he did so, by getting his teams to take charge of their own individual results instead of blaming the company or market. After quickly proving he had the Midas touch by hitting almost every challenge thrown at him, Garner McCall was on an unstoppable fast track or so most thought. However, some old timers were none too pleased that an outsider had come in so quickly and raised the stakes on redefining leadership success in the hallowed halls of GAC. Despite amazing success, a natural southern charm, and a sincere proof to bleed the company colors in his tireless ride for the brand, Garner would never be part of the Midwestern company's "good 'ol boys club." Even though he was very well paid and included in some of their haughty corporate brouhahas, he could never quite shake feeling like a hired hand. Later looking back, that was something he'd always known in his gut. He had trusted them and taken too much for granted, and that would prove to be his mistake and ultimate undoing.

After eight long weeks traveling all over North America to ensure that his team would reign supreme once again for the year's top revenue award, it was a Friday that he had been especially looking forward to taking off to help his wife pack for a much needed two weeks at their favorite beach spot. His team had promised the boss that they would let him rest and not constantly bombard his cell with the usual endless calls concerning routine deal-making and customers on edge about this year's exorbitant price increase being impossible to justify, which was the annual norm. Both he and Denise knew this wasn't true of course, and so like every year before, it would ring as it always had. Upon hearing her husband's familiar ring tone, Denise chuckled and said "Well that didn't take long! I think this one's earlier than last year's!" Garner wasn't surprised his phone was ringing either, even at 7AM mind you, but it turned out that the team had kept their promise. This time, the call was from the new CEO, Rick Winther.

~~~~~~~~~~~

Garner, nor any of his veteran colleagues, ever had much regard for Rick Winther privately. Most would scoff at how truly unproven he was, but they knew he would ascend any way. Nonetheless, they did respect the CEO position. Winther had been hand-picked for the top executive spot a long time ago by the family who mostly owned Great American and everyone knew it, though it was never publicized. He was hurriedly run up through the ranks in one after another progressive role, but never for more than a couple of years. As such, his lack of any actual and real accomplishment was never fully apparent. Regardless, that never stopped the board or the soon to retire long-term CEO, who had also been hand-picked, from touting all of the puffed up bull about Winther's "tremendous contribution to the long term viability of Great American." Everyone knew Winther was the older CEO's heir apparent. He'd be good enough at it too. Just the polished, trained pup they needed to keep the tremendously profitable casket maker so dominating in the industry and execute their orders.

Garner could tell from the nervous energy in the junior CEO's voice that his call was urgent. Winther already knew of Garner's planned vacation day, but said he really needed to address something vitally important and wanted to announce it while Garner was "off soaking up the sun." He even asked again where Garner was taking Denise for their time away, even though they'd just chatted about it the prior week, so it seemed odd that he was asking again. Winther said his last minute need to meet was very important, and particularly concerned Garner's future. Using a well-rehearsed disguise of a warm inviting tone in his voice, he asked McCall to make the drive into the office as soon as possible that morning so they could discuss it in person. Of course, Garner would oblige. Always supportive, Denise said she would finish up their packing by the time he got back.

Driving over, Garner thought back to his last serious conversation with the new CEO a few months earlier. Not long after he came on board, Winther had asked Garner whether he was ready to step up and lead the global team. Why else would he be calling today, knowing Garner was scheduled to be out for two weeks? Why not just cover it over the phone? This must be it! What else could it be, but the big promotion? That was the only possible explanation that Garner could surmise, having been on dozens of serious and confidential calls about all kinds of urgently sensitive or legal issues that came up affecting GAC all the time. One thing was always for certain, the casket

9

business was anything but dull, especially for one of the top death care companies that worked feverishly to control the market, threatening unions, and any media attention of funeral service. No doubt, Garner was convinced that the news of today was about to tee up the best vacation he and Denise had ever had!

~~~~~~~~~~~~~~~

There was an extra half step in his gate as Garner glided up to the top floor corner office. "Come on in.", Winther said, keeping his back to the door and with what sounded like an unexpected, fairly tense tone. Without making any eye contact, Garner was instructed to take a seat at the mammoth, hard-carved conference table in the CEO's richly appointed surroundings. Just as he sat down, the hair on the back of his neck stood at high-alert when out of the corner of his eye, Garner saw Jerry Simmons, Vice President of Human Resources, walk in carrying a sealed manila envelope and quietly closing the door behind him. Jerry was a large affable, friendly guy. Instantly it seemed odd that he wouldn't make eye contact either, only looking down at the floor as he would for the entirety of the five minute meeting that would ensue.

No smiles. No thanks for coming in. No chit chat. Worse yet, no coffee...

The rookie runt of a CEO, trying to look ever so concerned and conscientious, immediately straight out asked Garner if he had used the "F" word in front of employees and customers during a customer golf trip several weeks earlier in Palm Springs. Thinking perhaps this was just an awkward attempt at banter by Winther, laughing out loud with a big grin, Garner replied: "Most damn likely, Rick, hell man, you've seen me play golf!"

Upon realizing Winther wasn't smiling at his usual humorous quip, Garner said, "You're kidding right? Hell Rick, you yourself use the "F" word all the time around here and in a meeting just last week in fact! Come on, Rick!" Looking over at Jerry, the super nice barrel-chested HR exec who was prone to quickly nodding off in most meetings was very much tuned into this one, but still with no eye contact. Jerry kept burning a hole in the floor as if he was too damned ashamed to look up and be part of what was taking place. Sadly, his apparent lack of interest and participation in the hit job on McCall didn't please Winther any too much. Little did Jerry know sitting there fixated on the finest floor in Greed County, that less than a year later he would be reaching out to Garner for a job reference as he tried to rebound from his own ass-kick to the curb. Unknowingly, Jerry Simmons was on Winther's take out list too.

"So it's true!" Winther exclaimed. Staring down Garner as if he'd just confessed to a murder, GAC's new panty-wasted CEO took obvious and great pleasure saying, "Today is your last day at this great company McCall! I cannot see any possible way someone with such poor character and judgement could remain with this company, much less in a senior leadership role. Effective immediately, I am terminating you, and just to be clear, you are being *Fired for Cause!*"

In complete and utter shock, Garner could not even wrap his head around what he had just heard, and his mind went into a total daze. He knew that they could fire him at will, but "cause" should require…well, some legitimate cause! Furthermore, Winther had said it with such a noticeable gleam in his eye too! "You called me at 7AM this morning on my day off demanding that I drive all the way over here just so you could fire me, Rick!?! Are you kidding me?" Garner exclaimed. "Cause for what? What the hell do you believe I have done to deserve getting fired? I can tell you for a fact, that I haven't done a damn thing! You can bet on that!!"

What pissed off Garner just as much as getting fired after working himself to death for the last ten plus years was just how much the new wimpy, ivy-league educated, silver-spooned, overly-polished, hand-picked, junior wannabe-now CEO, so obviously enjoyed demonstrating his newly assigned authority by telling him it was with "CAUSE!" Garner couldn't believe what had just been uttered by this obnoxious jerk! Cause! What the hell was he talking about?

Garner knew he hadn't done anything to warrant being fired. What he would learn next was that it wasn't even because of anything he had done at all, but rather what he hadn't done that was getting him fired. Now, Garner was totally confused. When Winther began focusing his line of questioning more on what another senior executive, Tom Pittman, had been accused of on a recent customer golf trip, Garner suddenly realized this was not about him at all. Confirming what had been alleged about his colleague's constant drunkenness and improprieties, especially in the presence of customers, Winther unabashedly and wide-eyed had the outlandish gall to ask Garner why he had not stopped it, or at least called him directly to report it.

"Are you serious, Rick? Hell, everybody knows how Pittman is, especially on these trips or away at business meetings! You especially! Why would I have called you? He wasn't doing anything he hadn't done a hundred times before! You yourself put him in the job knowing full well what he's always been like!" Garner took some delight reaming Winther out right there in front of Simmons, although knowing full well it wouldn't help.

Trying to think of some way to plead his case, Garner told the unscrupulous CEO that all he had to do was talk to any of the guys on the trip. No sooner had the words come out of his mouth, than did Garner realize that a couple of them on the trip probably couldn't be trusted to have his back, but surely they wouldn't outright lie and get a man fired from his job. He told Winther to especially talk to the managers at the golf course or the hotel where they had all stayed to hear numerous stories of how his senior colleague had gotten so drunk and out of line, particularly with the beer cart girls. With a steely, daring look, Winther quickly snapped back, "I did!"

Garner asked, "So did the guys or the hotel manager tell you how one of the client dinners had gotten so crazy and how Pittman was acting? Did they explain how I had tried to take control of everything?" Again, without even trying to pretend a sense of empathy, Winther looked Garner right in the eye and said, "I did Garner. I personally spoke with all of them and they said it was both of you." Crestfallen and confused, McCall couldn't understand why the sales guys especially, or the other people who had witnessed the crap his superior had done, would have accused him of anything. They were there and saw how Garner had maintained his composure and character despite having the other senior executive on the trip behave so out of line. How could they have thrown him under the bus like that? He wondered if any of it was true. Garner knew that Winther must be lying, but what he didn't understand was why.

Garner knew exactly what had gone on in Palm Springs, but it was Pittman, not himself. Nevertheless, he was getting fired because of something done by someone with whom he had only worked with a few months, and indirectly. To hear Winther's version, McCall and Pittman were in total cahoots, like "two peas in a pod" partying out of control like fools. He told McCall that he had "heard enough of the facts after a thorough investigation" to make his decision for termination with cause. Said it was a "closed and shut case." But Garner knew a lot more than Winther had recounted, especially where it concerned specific customers. Too smart than to dare and share any of that, he'd hold his cards on all of that for now.

Garner barely knew Tom Pittman, and had rarely ever interacted with him before the guy had been made the only executive vice president in the company. No one was exactly clear on how Winther had described the role, other than it apparently made Pittman a kind of chief operating officer of sorts. Everyone knew how Winther and Pittman had been lobbying hard for the top executive spot to become the new CEO over the prior year, until Winther was finally named. So, most figured the promotional move was a conceded second-place role for Pittman. Except, the company had never had a COO, and the really weird thing was how every other function in the company already had a high-level senior executive leading it. Regardless, it was a new role that Winther said was needed and created, although many thought it was just so he could bring in one of his friends to take over Pittman's previous position.

Garner had barely ever spoken to Pittman, who had always worked on the back office side of corporate until he became executive vice president, and in effect, becoming everyone's bosses' boss, apparently. All they had in common was working for GAC plus a mutual love for cigars and golf, and those weren't even discovered until just before the golf trip to California. Weirder still was the fact that out of the blue, one of Garner's managers, Steve Josten, who organized the client golf trip, had supposedly been the one to come up with the idea of inviting Pittman along in the first place.

Customer trips went on all the time as a means to win over new accounts, by taking the owners to five star events like the Northern California wine country or big time sporting events like the Kentucky Derby, professional golf tournaments, and other expensive outings. Whatever their fancy, Garner would spend hundreds of thousands each year on "client acquisition." Smaller operators not approved for invite of course.

Garner knew Josten had been sucking up to Pittman like a lot of people, once he became the new EVP. He, as well as his counterpart in Canada, had been pretty crass and careless at trying unsuccessfully to take Garner out of his job for quite some time, and routinely tried to schmooze and hobnob with the GAC powerbrokers above him. However, Garner would later learn that Josten didn't mastermind the original idea to invite Pittman to CA at all. Nonetheless the invite would still serve its intended purpose to take down both Pittman and McCall, and most conveniently at once.

Still, none of this was right, not by a long shot! It was painfully obvious Garner would have no say in the matter or any opportunity to present a defense, at least not that day. The scheme was over and done.

~~~~~~~~~~~~~~~

Security was on high alert in the hallway and moved quickly to the entry when Winther abruptly stood up and opened his new office door. Instantly, the crowded executive wing of admins and VPs froze-frame as Garner was closely led off the floor by the deputy sheriff, whose presence had already commanded everyone's intrigued attention, and notified that something big was going down. That, of course, was another of Winther's moves for public effect as if Garner might pose some sort of a risk to someone in the office. The public image and gossip around the small company town of McCall being escorted off premises was exactly what Winther had premeditated and planned for the morning's big event. Regardless of the fact, that in more than ten years at the company, Garner had never so much as once had a cross word with anyone, much less a single HR issue of any kind. Perhaps the new slick CEO was just afraid that Garner might kick his ass, which certainly would have been

16

warranted. No one ever accused Rick Winther of having a backbone.

A blur of moments later, Garner McCall was standing at his truck outside the locked building without his hard-earned career, any income, and now knowing that thousands of earned but unvested stock grants would be forfeited because he had been fired with "cause." He knew that single word had would radically change life for him and Denise. But, now all he had on his mind was the really tough message he would have to deliver at home, and to spending the next two weeks being pissed off instead of recharging his batteries as planned. What should have been a wonderful vacation, one they both really deserved after all of his tireless time away from home traveling incessantly for the eternal good of the Great American Casket Company, would now be filled with anger and anxiousness. He especially hated it for Denise who had always graciously accepted and supported his career.

~~~~~~~~~~~~

In a total state of shock, as Garner pulled onto the interstate for the forty-five minute drive home that he'd made so often over the years, it hit him that it wouldn't take long before IT cutoff his server access. Quickly he pulled off onto the shoulder to send one last note to his team as the cars and trucks constantly sped by, gently rocking and swaying his silver crew cab. He tried to gather his thoughts and emotions as he quickly typed out what he knew would be the last note to the people with whom he had worked so closely for so many years. He knew each and every one personally, their spouses, their kids, and their

17

hopes and dreams of future plans. To Garner, the people on his teams had become just as much family as colleagues. One final time, he would get to tell them how proud he was of them and how he genuinely hoped for all of their individual and collective successes and well-being.

Choking back both tears and anger, he began the note with the fact that he had been "fired" by the company that morning. Fired was the only truthful way to say it. He thanked them all for their hard work and dedication to his team and moreover to GAC. He reminded them that when he came into to his role, their division had been historically in last place in virtually every category measured. How together, they had all reversed that scenario with an unbeatable track record, regardless of metric, for the last several years. He told them how he would always be so proud of them and sincerely hoped to stay in touch with each and every one. Within seconds of sending his final team email, Garner immediately began receiving replies of disbelief and shock. But just five minutes after hitting the send button, the heart-warming sound of emails ringing in on his phone had finally stopped and he knew his service had been disconnected by IT. Now the email app would only open to a black screen ominously stating *"You Do Not Have Authorized Access!"*

Pulling back onto the highway, his cell began exploding with phone calls and texts. With his head still swimming and eyes tearing, Garner just kept driving and listening to the sound of his ringtone and beeps from calls going to voicemail and text messages filling up his cell. Thankfully, he had always kept his personal cell phone and number versus opting for a company-issued phone. At least that was one thing they couldn't take away.

Before the day was over, Garner McCall would hear from over two hundred and fifty people around the company, including over ninety percent of his direct team. That would always mean a lot to him. The gist from many of the messages kept ringing over and over again. So many had told Garner not to take things personally; saying essentially that, "outsiders like you, not being from Bergholz, rarely ever last long at corporate! They always shoot the good ones down. It's like everyone says all the time about the so-called big, bad company... It's just in their DNA, whenever they decide to take somebody out at the knees!"

A particularly sweet piece of news shared in one of the voicemail messages was how pissed-off Winther had been to learn that Garner had already spoiled the big breaking news of the "Urgent & Mandatory Conference Call" scheduled later that day. He hoped to put his own unseemly version of spin on the senior sales leader's departure, but Garner had beaten him to the punch by acting so quickly. Everyone knew that whatever he had been accused of, that something wasn't right and not by a long shot! At least those who knew and ever worked with Garner, they knew!

~~~~~~~~~~~~~~

Always his rock, Denise was lying there on the beach next to him, on their huge oversized towel, bronzing her tan and dripping with sexy sweat. She looked good as ever with a book in one hand and a second margarita in the other, listening to her favorite pop tunes, which were always much more modern than Garner's. As he laid next her, the usual comforting outlaw songs of his preferred Willie, Waylon, and Merle kept getting drowned out by sound of Winther's voice and lies ringing in his head. He already knew that Winther had outright lied to his face about talking to the hotel and golf course managers, because he and Denise had called and talked directly to them both on their drive to the coast. The golf course guy had even offered his apologies to Garner upon hearing he'd been fired, "because of how that drunk behaved out here", and said to let him know if he could ever help in any way. The man said he'd been unfairly fired before too, and knew how it feels to get screwed over by a dishonest company. He even said he'd be happy to speak with a lawyer on Garner's behalf too, "if it'd help out any." Garner was overwhelmed by the character and generosity of the man he'd only met once. Thank God, there are still good people who know what right is and are willing to stand up for it.

The lawyer idea got him thinking. If they had wanted to fire him for cause, then maybe the thing to do was make them prove it in court, where he could draw up a pretty convincing case of comparisons about what he knew. Like so many unethical goings-on right in the perceived hallowed halls of GAC. Such as, one executive whose still there and married mind you, had an ongoing relationship with a female sales rep down in the Carolinas for years; or about another top level exec, who screwed anything in a skirt out at The Ranch or in funeral service at-large for that matter. Or, what about when Garner and another top, straight-laced executive uncovered firsthand proof that clearly suggested a senior officer along with the former CEO, Bill Statham, had manipulated, perhaps even masterminded, the company's acquisition of a regional competitor, to bilk the company out of millions? And how then, Statham had so smoothly brushed the evidence under the rug as "an unfortunate misunderstanding." There wouldn't even be an investigation or another mention of that matter, ever again! Garner could definitely fill in those details.

Yep, there was so much more Garner knew. A lot of details about unethical and perhaps even illegal behavior and business practices to draw a stark comparison of being fired for simply cursing and not reporting the inappropriate behavior of another executive on a golf trip. He just needed a way to force them to the table to make his case. Yeah he could sue GAC, which would only require a lawyer and a few grand for a retainer. He knew it wouldn't be difficult at all to find a long line of attorneys who'd love to go after Great American's deep pockets. Except the thought of hurting the company's image still turned his stomach. He just kept thinking about all of the wonderful folks he'd come to know and respect. Garner knew that he wanted to avoid a public action if at all possible. But for sure, that option would stay on the table if there was no other way.

As the sun burned down and the ice melted, Garner thought that legal recourse may be the way to go. Like most, he hated lawyers with a vengeance, and always with good reason. Pragmatically, he also knew that GAC could fight a legal action

21

indefinitely, and he really wanted to try and get this all behind him as quickly as possible and just move on. Surely there was something he could do to get them to reconsider compensating him with a semblance of fairness after all that he had done for the company. Then after another sip of his favorite eighteen year old scotch and a single seasoned sliver of ice, it hit him like a ton of bricks what he needed to do and perhaps just who he needed to call.

~~~~~~~~~~~~~

Cause is a convenient little term. In business, it generally refers to when someone is fired for lying, stealing, doing something outlandish to hurt the company, or say cheating on your wife with the secretary, you know stuff like that, unless, of course, you were a certain somebody who owned a big part of GAC. Clearly the new pubescent CEO wanted Garner out for some apparent reason. However without at least the appearance of a solid reason, even if only manufactured, he'd look foolish firing their top revenue leader of the last several years. Now, he could hide behind "cause." You see the high powered GAC lawyers wrote their executive employment agreements to infer that "cause" could actually be interpreted by the company as pretty much anything they wanted it to mean. Still under normal, honorable circumstances, "cause" most always implied direct fault generated by the terminated party. In Garner's case, he had been fired because of what someone else had done and for not reporting it! It was absolutely incredible and ever so convenient too!

When the former CEO, William Statham, had first asked Garner to move up to corporate and take on the task of turning-around their historically, worst performing sales division, Garner had turned him down, twice in fact. Bill Statham rarely took "no thanks" for an answer, especially from those he regularly referred to as his "minions", but nonetheless he appreciated a man who stood his ground and didn't jump at the first offer of anything.

Statham always seemed credible, professional, and polished in mostly good ways. He fancied his own conceited demeanor that of a statesman, and at the very least a senior senator. Like any good politician, he was always smiling. Plus, he was so smooth, one could rarely tell his true feelings or intentions, but either way he generally left you feeling ok about whatever the topic. While at times his tough as nails mentality could be brutally harsh and direct, he was generally regarded above all as a fair and understanding, compassionate person who just happened to be CEO of GAC for the past twenty plus years. That is, unless someone ever got on his shit list. Statham had come up from the sales ranks. As such, he personally appreciated the commercial organization and understood the hyper-competitive challenges they faced in such a dynamic funeral market. More so, he had particularly become impressed how Garner McCall had redefined the leadership bar on leading people and raising profits.

After twice trying to woo McCall to move away from his beloved South to the land of the Big Ten, Statham told Garner to write down what it would take to make it work for him and his family. Thinking he'd get laughed out of the home office and maybe worse than that if they thought he was being obnoxiously obstinate about taking on more responsibility, Garner sent Bill Statham a brief note to the point with five simple bullets:

Bill, ok, you asked...

1.	*150% salary increase to $265K/YR with 5% minimum annual increase*
2.	*Minimum 35% annual bonus guarantee; 2X or 70% if division hits plan*
3.	*5000 stock grants per year guaranteed; 7500/YR if division hits plan*
4.	*Full 2 year salary & minimum bonus payout guarantee if terminated*
5.	*100% of all stock non-vested shares vest immediately if terminated*

Best,

Garner

Garner's cell rang within minutes after shooting his demands to Statham. He thought that such a quick response had to be bad. His mind began to race with the ringing of his phone..."How stupid, you dumbass! You're about to get yourself fired!" Already breaking into a sweat and trying to breathe, Garner knew the worse thing he could do was let Statham's call go to voicemail. So he did his best to sound calm and confident when he answered. He was an absolute nervous wreck though!

With a huge smile in his voice, Statham's friendly tone uttered words Garner never expected... "Alright McCall, how soon can you be here to sign your new contract and get your ass to work?" Laughingly, Statham told Garner how impressive it was that he knew his worth so well. Jokingly saying that he might "just be a little on the high-side", but nonetheless Statham was a man who knew that you get what you pay for, and he knew Garner McCall was the right person to bring in scores of millions in new business and profits each and every year and especially shape up his worst division. Garner had proved to not suffer slackers or quitters, much less give up on the targets. Give him a goal, and he'd hit it every time!

Of course, Statham told him that the lawyers would draw up the new agreement and not to worry that his 4th and 5th bullets would of course be conditional upon any termination _with cause_ scenario. "It's no different than the standard employment agreement like you're on today, Garner", Statham casually added. Ever the salesman, Statham went on to reel in his prized executive catch.

"Garner, I'm agreeing to your terms because I want you here, we need you here! You will have this job until you're ready to retire my boy! Based upon how much money you'll be making that might be sooner than you ever thought possible. I do have one little piece of gray haired knowledge in my back pocket though, your wife! One thing I've learned over my career is that when a man starts bringing in the really big bucks like you're going to be, that the little Mrs. will help you redefine your retirement plans. So, I'm pretty sure I'm going to have you up here for a long time to re-coop my investment. Let me know as soon as you can get into town and we'll celebrate at The Club!" Almost overwhelmed, Garner could barely believe what he'd just heard from the man he had come to respect so much. He was filled with so much pride and commitment to GAC, more than ever before. GAC was home. GAC was family. Garner McCall would be with GAC forever!

With all of the excitement, Garner would never worry or concern himself with a funny little word like "cause." He never dreamed in a million years that it would ever apply to him. No way! But there it was, as big as life, stated about a dozen times throughout his new contract. As for the ever shrewd Statham, he knew full well that none of Garner's little bulleted demands would mean a damn thing if they ever decided that he was no longer useful. It would be a hard lesson for McCall, and one that GAC would have no problem at all delivering if needed. Statham was infamous for such brutal "teaching moments."

Waging a fight with such a big, powerful company like GAC seemed more and more like a damn good recipe for spending a ton of money, at a time when he wasn't making any. More depressingly, the likelihood of winning, much less getting a fair trial, seemed increasingly insurmountable with a review of his employment agreement; which stipulated any legal proceedings involving the company must be tried in the same little backwoods Greed County where GAC had been headquartered for the last century. Good luck getting a fair shake there! After weeks on end of countless email and phone messages being ignored, all professional efforts of trying to get GAC to reconsider their termination rational concerning his severance and unvested stock status, Garner was about to give up hope and slink away, as he tried to focus his time on finding another job. It's funny how the mere mention of the word "casket" can turn off most all prospective employers.

Then one day he realized that Knowledge is Power! He had a ton of knowledge about the goings on at GAC in the funeral industry. He knew he had to fight for what was rightfully his and thought back to his beach epiphany! He knew that he had one last resort to plead his case for some fairness. Perhaps, just one daring call to Renford Kleinmark, the current Chairman Emeritus of the Board and youngest brother of the Founding Kleinmark family, was what it would take to get GAC to finally respond and do what was right. Surely by striking the right tone with Mr. Kleinmark, who always seemed so genteel and conscientious, maybe all of this craziness could be corrected.

Garner was amazed at how easy it was to get a Kleinmark on the phone. A quick internet search on his name, and up popped a direct phone number to Kleinmark Capital Partners, his personal Private Equity investment company out West. The warm, sweet voice of the woman answering the phone was by design to set the intended tone for anyone wanting to speak to Mr. Renford J. Kleinmark. After the mere mention of Great American, instantly Ren Kleinmark was on the end of the line. Garner had only met him briefly at a couple of the board meetings over the past few years, but Kleinmark recognized his name and warmly said hello. Presupposing that Mr. Kleinmark did not waste his time on trivial hellos, Garner got right to the point. He said he was calling because he had some grave concerns to share about the company and involving the board.

~~~~~~~~~~~

It's still funny the mere mention of what he learned had happened in Cabo just months earlier captured Kleinmark's instant attention. When some very top senior GAC execs and another "key associate" took their counterparts from one of their largest customers down to Mexico for an "off-site" meeting, and how it would generate such a quick response. About how some very suspect, and likely illegal, after-dinner activities would wind up getting his immediate serious attention. Garner assured the most senior board chair that he had all of the attendees' names, dates, hotel info, etc. to email if interested. Showing no regard or interest in such details, Kleinmark began to audibly sigh as he became increasingly uncomfortable hearing of such insidious goings-on about how his family's company was being run, or maybe he already knew, but didn't care for having it shoved in his face. Either way, he was apparently above hearing of such trivialities and cut Garner off mid-sentence to try and keep him from telling anymore about it, saying… "Garner, as Chairman Emeritus of the Board, I cannot be in a position to know about any of these kinds of matters. You will need to share them with the company counsel. You understand I'm sure." Apparently this holier-than-thou bullshit line worked on most. Garner listened but didn't respond. He knew he would only have this one chance to move Kleinmark enough to make the company respond and hopefully be fair, so he kept going.

There were other incidents too that Kleinmark wouldn't appreciate having Garner list during the now feverishly hastened, one-sided call. Like concerns of market manipulation; the intentional enormous disparity in some customer's terms compared to most others; the kinds of activities allowed to go on out at The Ranch, where so many customers visit each year;

some of the reasons restricted private back roads between The Ranch and GAC's private airstrip were used at times; how GAC systematically retains some customer monies and uses the annual price increase initiative to unfairly boost profits; and how the misleading, complex customer agreements had become designed to increase its huge annual free cash generation worth scores of millions in pure profits. Garner assured Kleinmark that he had the clear capability and knowledge to go into great detail about all of these matters, of course only, if and whenever necessary. Garner also knew a few nasty little personal secrets about Kleinmark's new wet-behind the ears CEO. He would keep that information to himself for now. Those details would only come out if things ever really got so ugly that McCall needed to expose them.

McCall was shooting it all out as fast as he could before he totally choked or Ren Kleinmark hung up. Except, the truth was that Ren Kleinmark was too smart to hang up. This was most certainly not his first rodeo, especially given all the storied dark history at GAC. Garner could tell Kleinmark didn't like being bothered with this kind of low level nuisance, but it was painfully apparent that his underlings had not effectively dealt with McCall. Kleinmark knew GAC would need to make this go away and the more they understood what McCall knew, the better, so he kept listening, as his secretary secretly recorded the call.

Saving the best for last and what he knew would be his most powerfully, compelling case of corporate public misbehavior, Garner finally made Ren Kleinmark's voice break and bristle. At the mention of his revered oldest brother, David A. Kleinmark, and particularly how everyone knew of his longstanding escapades and even a very public affair that went on for years, never mind the little wife of course. The numerous stories of rampant infidelities by the man known as "DAK" would no doubt raise eyebrows and questions of rumored improprieties at GAC.

It was well known that the industry's revered DAK Kleinmark, who was credited for leading the company during its most prosperous period, regularly used the company jets to "entertain" customers with... well let's just say, his so-called flight attendants, who had their own unique set of "client engagement" skills. Whenever DAK dropped his five-star Falcon jet down into some little, podunk town to smooth over the feelings of a disgruntled, but always sizeable, funeral home owner, or if he ever decided the need to take away a key competitively-held operator, he rarely, if ever, lost. Although, no one ever knew the real secret to DAK's enviable track record for retaining or landing new, huge clients for Great American.

Garner had heard a lot of these stories involving the man called DAK from some of the elder southern, sales statesmen he had become close with after joining the firm, and who had "worked closely" with the high-powered Kleinmark back in the day. There were some hellacious stories too from the good old days, many of which were about customers who were still around! Turns out old DAK was a real legend in more ways than publicly talked about! "Those were different times", Kleinmark whispered, almost as if to himself.

By the end of the call, a noticeably shaken Renford Kleinmark, with his ever present solemn voice, assured Garner that he would hear from the company to "review everything very soon and I'm sure work things out." Garner thought it was only too funny after getting kicked to the curb and being completely ignored for so long, that within a matter of only a few hours after hanging up with Kleinmark, that an email flew in from the company's top lawyer before the day's end. Jed Malish, the company's chief legal officer, sent Garner a very terse email acknowledging the call with Kleinmark and asking to meet as soon as possible in the next few days.

~~~~~~~~~~~~~~~

Garner thought he had finally gotten their attention and that now, maybe just maybe, had them where he wanted them. Surely now they would treat him and his family fairly. Since he'd shared with Kleinmark about why he had been fired based upon being accused of actually not doing something, and how it undoubtedly paled in comparison to so many other questionable activities.

However what he would ultimately learn, in a very hard painful way, was that his family would *get treated* alright! Like nothing he could ever have imagined!! What had always seemed like an honorable and upstanding company was being led by those who would prove to dispatch the thugs and spiders to crawl and scrape among the slime, if and whenever they felt necessary, to deal with someone they needed to coerce or shut up. He never thought for a million years just how low they would stoop to try and intimidate and torment his family, smear his reputation, and even threaten his life, much less WHO exactly would eventually deliver that threat personally. Garner McCall was about to learn a lot of hard lessons about becoming an exiled corporate executive. All of it would come about in a very personal, hard and painful way! Try they did to intimidate and threaten him, anything to make Garner McCall keep quiet and go away once and for all.

But they underestimated Garner McCall, and by a long damn mile!

~~~~~~~~~~~~~~~~

RECRUITMENT SEDUCTION

It was hard for Garner to believe that two weeks had already gone by since he'd been fired and that it was time for him and Denise to head back to Northeastern Ohio. For the first time in all the years they'd visited the tranquil, private coastal cottage, he dreaded the drive and thought of going back home knowing that he'd have so much stress and anxiety to look forward to. There were so many unknowns and uncertainties, and neither had ever been something he dealt with well. As he loaded up the last of their bags into the back of his truck, he knew in his heart of hearts that he owed Denise another vacation before the next year was out. Hopefully soon, whenever he landed his next job.

This year's had been anything but relaxing for either of them. She tried everything possible to try and keep his mind off of the job, money, and GAC. She planned daily activities to the beach, movies, galleries, restaurants, you name it; anything at all, that she could think of to help Garner from focusing on his career and last day at GAC. She knew him better than anyone and appreciated how he'd put up the best false front possible so that their time away together wasn't a complete downer. Still, she knew her husband of almost twenty years. She could see it in his eyes and on his face. She loved him more than ever for trying so hard to look and act relaxed over the last two weeks, when she knew full well that deep down he hadn't yet moved any of it off of the front burner. What she didn't know was just how long it would take before Garner would be able to do that, and finally let it all go.

Just as she had every year before, Denise signed the registry book of their rented vacation home, usually reminiscing about how much they always enjoyed the ocean views and stepping right out to the private pool and daily walks on beach. This year though, her heart couldn't help but to share something personal of how painful their visit had been due to some very bad news about her husband's job. In leaving those one-way little diary notes each year, for Denise, it was as if she had an old, silent trusted friend on the other side. Someone who only listened and would understand, perhaps even pray for them. She didn't tell Garner about her openness to their temporary home's owners or how she wanted them to understand that *Life* had been lived in their beautiful villa over the past two weeks. For some reason to her it was important to be open about it with someone in some way, and this was a safe, private way to finally get a piece of it off of her heart.

For with Garner, ever since he had broken the hard, painful news to her, after getting back home from his last day at the office, she'd never had a chance to even speak about it openly with anyone, to share any of her emotions or fears. She saw how it had all shaken Garner so, and knew she had be his source of strength, support, and encouragement as he coped with the loss of his hard earned career. Also, she didn't want her husband to see just how upset she was after everything they both had sacrificed for the company over the last ten years. She was just as mad and hurt too. But she loved him too much to allow

34

herself to focus on her own feelings, because she knew her husband needed to process, to be angry, and at some point to grieve. It would be his time for all of those emotions to evolve, and for quite some time to come.

With just one more traditional stop to make, Garner and Denise began the drive off of the tiny coastal island they had visited now for seven years in a row. In their own way, without saying a word and holding hands, it was obvious they both wished this year's visit had been better. Still they knew they'd be back, and both quietly wished for their next visit to come faster than ever before, so as to erase the saddened memories from the one they were leaving behind.

~~~~~~~~~~

The best little French pastry shop was one of their fondest vacation memories each year. They had discovered it on their first trip thanks to Denise's eagle-eye, when she spotted the shop with the cute little name and happy logo way off the main highway in one of those tired strip malls planted everywhere, usually full of t-shirt shops and outlet stores. The short statured French chef, with his ever tanned, wrinkled and creviced face, let his widest beaming smile light up as two of his adoring patrons walked in again. True to form, his brilliant silver hair and short European pony-tail were peeking out from under the bright white, tall, mushroom-styled chef's cap, denoting his craft and expertise in the art of pleasing using only the finest ingredients shipped in from his beloved France. This was their third stop in two weeks, an annual arrive/during/depart ritual for the McCalls, now seven years running. *Calories Be Damned!* - was their motto during the annual two week respite.

Che Pieux had been a hit since Monsieur Bastien Pieux opened up his little pastries and coffee shop over 12 years ago, after abruptly leaving behind the high rent district and a fourth wife back in New York. The talented chef figured the remote coastal inlet was the perfect getaway from unpaid landlords and divorce attorneys. Oui (pronounced "Wee") Chef was what Bastien laughingly told all of his new customers to call him. Like always, his whimsical engaging shtick allowed for just the right amount of moments to evaporate until telling all Che Pieux newcomers, using his charming French accent, that "Oui Chef, but of course, means Yes Chef!" And, how all they had to do was ask for whatever their hearts and stomachs desired and he would surely make it for them! All the while, his big, bright blue eyes bursting every time with complete delight were certain to win over all the children, women, and men who visited his tiny delicious shop located at the end of the long commercial strip. Ever the charmer and Frenchmen, the tiny Oui Chef had a very special affinity for all of the ladies in the shop, even those with husbands in tow. Oh how the daringly, devilish little pastry chef was ever so quick with the holding of both hands to pull each woman close, as if they were dancing, and just enough to smell their perfume and quickly peck each cheek.

Garner knew it was coming of course and would tease Denise a little about her pending kisses. As well as the certainty of a special pastry for her, free of course, from the little French man, who was usually spat with flour all over the front of his apron. For Denise, smiling and rolling her eyes at her husband's usual ready quip, what she'd never let on was how she loved that it was just a normal, happy part of their trip. For just a few moments, especially this year, it was another simple reminder of their good life together and reassurance that it would return again one day.

After selecting their usual huge bag of homemade delectables, Denise would receive her two kisses and beaming smile as Oui Chef followed them outside of his very proud shop front to tell them both how special they were to him. "Please return to me when you are hungry again my friends!" were always his parting words for the lucky ones who discovered his tiny, little pasty shop.

After too many of Oui Chef's amazing flaky buttered croissant treats and coffee, and both agreeing they had to stop eating, Garner and Denise talked about some of the slight subtle changes they noticed as they drove through the small, rural towns that led back to the interstate. They had been there so much by now that they even took note if a local diner painted its sign or if a gas station changed brands. Not much ever changed on the peninsula, or at least it never seemed to. Denise noted, as if talking to herself, just how wonderfully peaceful in a way that must be for those who resided on the quiet sleepy coast, knowing that things always seemed to stay the same. Garner knew what she wistfully meant, and agreed.

~~~~~~~~~~~

Merging onto the northbound busy highway, it would be almost three hours before they would likely stop again for more gas and coffee. Denise had been so excited to find a copy of the newest novel, in a long running series by her favorite author, while they'd been out milling around a few days earlier. She had told Garner that she couldn't wait to dig into it on their drive home and see what happened next with her beloved characters in the romantic story set back in 1400's Scotland. She had read the other three prior novels in the wonderfully romantic tale over the past few years, and was as big a fan as one could be of the story about love had, lost, and longing. Already engrossed before the next mile marker flew by and listening to ancient Gaelic instrumentals with her ear buds, Garner knew her attention wouldn't break until they stopped for gas or the coffee kicked in.

Connecting his phone to the truck's audio system, Garner would keep the volume low on as he listened to the old country songs he hoped would keep his mind occupied as they sailed back northward. He told himself to just relax and enjoy the drive and the beautiful sunny, cloud-free day, but honestly, he already knew his mind would quickly wander just like it'd been doing every day for the past two weeks. The shock of everything was still so fresh and bitter, and now for the first time he'd have a good amount of time to just be quiet and think through what he needed to do moving forward.

It struck Garner's mind that the first time they had visited their favorite beach spot was just after he'd been asked the first time by Statham about stepping up to the senior leadership level at GAC. Thoughts of how he and Denise had talked and dreamt about retiring there one day and how that all seemed so unlikely at the moment unless he could find another job that paid as well as his last. He knew he could do well wherever he went, but finding another opportunity that afforded the annual earning potential as GAC would likely prove challenging, especially given how the economy was presently receding. It was as bad as it'd been in the last eight years, with losses in the markets being the usual top news story of the day. There were lots of folks, including at the executive levels, looking for jobs or just trying to make a move to higher ground.

He thought about just how much they had achieved together and how he wanted to maintain the life they had come to know. It was certainly far more than he'd ever dreamed possible, especially given his upbringing. Garner's family didn't grow up poor, but they were definitely on the low-to-mid end of the socio-economic spectrum in their corner of the Deep South. Garner would become the first in his family to go to college, but it would require him figuring his own way there, if it was to ever happen at all. His parents, Jim and Faye McCall, had always stressed to their kids that getting a good education was extremely important and how each should be sure to work hard to get good grades in school and go to college.

Like most parents, they wanted more for their kids than they ever had. Young Garner took his parent's words to heart. Studying harder than ever before, he made an extreme and conscious effort in high school to get much better grades compared to the elementary period of his less than auspicious scholastic career. Throughout the remainder of his life, he'd think countless times about the sheer size of the consolidated high school building that to him, at the time, seemed to look more like a prison. As well as how the overwhelming volume of students had made such a lasting, emotional impact on the eight-grader when his class visited for initial orientation as their eighth grade year neared its end. From wherever his awareness came, young Garner knew instantly that day that "this was the big time" for him and that he'd need to stop being so lazy about studying and try the best he could to do well. Well he did too, even after having a regular thirty hour per week part-time job plus playing both baseball and football all four years, Garner still graduated in the top five percent of his class of more than three hundred and fifty at the high school that combined students across four rural counties. Even Garner was amazed at how well he had ranked overall, especially since he'd barely made it through grade school; and how most report cards he took home in those earlier years required one of his frustrated parents to go meet with at least some if not most of his teachers. He had finally proved to himself a life-long capability to learn, to reason, and to achieve. More than anything it gave him the confidence he would always need in life, to know he was smart enough to make it. All it took was hard work, or so he naively thought.

Getting to college, much less staying long enough to graduate wouldn't be easy for Garner either. But in doing so, he would learn other invaluable things about himself, his grit, and his sheer determination to survive and succeed. After more than six years trying to get his undergrad degree, Garner would ultimately squeak by with grades that he would always be disappointed with and never mention. Still, he got it done and graduated in the end. By working full-time in a very dirty

40

rubber-black compounds factory, on second shift from three to eleven o'clock every afternoon, seven days a week, Garner would fully support himself in the same kind of factory setting like his father had always bemoaned. The factory that made rubberized raw materials for everything from golf balls to car tires would serve its purpose to allow young Garner the opportunity to support himself after high school, until he finally graduated college and landed his first white-collar job. Though he would always struggle emotionally with how low his overall GPA was by the end, his dedicated guidance counselor and biggest fan at the time, would assure him not to. She said when potential employers realized how Garner had worked a minimum of fifty-six hours per week and often more, for six plus years, going to school full-time while commuting over one hundred miles roundtrip to campus, that his GPA result would ultimately mean less than what his character showed. Thank God she was right. Garner would never forget his ever encouraging champion who had made such a difference in bolstering his confidence and building him up about just what amazing things he could accomplish in life.

~~~~~~~~~~~

As the miles and minutes flew by, Garner's mind kept recalling how everything in his past had led to this point in time. He recalled how his first real sales job after college had taught him so much, especially about how to expect and accept rejection and failure, and ultimately to read customers. Of course, he would later learn a harder lesson that reading some particular corporate executives would prove much more difficult.

His mind wandered to all the people he'd known and worked with before GAC, those who helped and promoted him along the way. He thought of so many with whom he had lost touch and how he needed to reconnect. That was something he committed to himself to doing over the upcoming weeks as he looked for a new job.

Perhaps unconscientiously trying to re-instill a self-confidence that would be needed when he got home to once again grab his own boot straps and pull himself back up, Garner's mind ran through all of the prior promotions and successes so far in his career. Like how after he joined a huge, global machinery company prior to GAC, Garner was quickly promoted after his first year and even selected to train and develop all of their new sales rep recruits. Then promoted quickly again after his second year to lead his first team. He thought about the first time he'd ever made more than a hundred thousand dollars in a year and being awarded the number one sales rep worldwide, out of more than three hundred salesmen. Perhaps, he should have stayed with them, but he wouldn't beat himself up about stuff like that. Although now, it was easy to wonder and imagine where he'd be if he had stayed. He knew he had left for his own good reasons.

At the time, Garner knew after a dozen years that he needed a change. While he'd had good success bleeding their company colors, he also knew in his heart that he wasn't personally passionate about the problems being solved by the products provided by the firm. He recalled at the time how he had wondered if staying there indefinitely, nonetheless was the right thing to do since he was doing well and was so highly considered. In the end though, he decided to draft his first ever resume and see what else the sales world had to offer. Garner had never looked for a job before, but a good friend helped him put a basic resume together and gave him a crash course on the world of job hunting and executive search.

One day, soon after initiating his job search process, and within only hours of applying online for a field sales manager role with what was advertised as a "leading consumer products manufacturer", a recruiter from Memphis with the typical slow southern drawl called an excited Garner McCall. Garner was shocked that he'd gotten a call so quickly. Little did he know the recruiter had been striking out for months looking for the right candidate match, and especially someone who would entertain the unique industry of his client. It was the first job he'd ever applied to online; prior to, all other submissions had required the traditional snail-mailed, stamped approach. After almost an hour of initial interrogatories and liking the responses, the recruiter finally told Garner who the firm was and about their industry. Turns out a lot of people are turned off by the mere mention of the word "casket", but to Garner, the mention of the Great American Casket Company made a positive impression.

Throughout his many early formative years in sales, Garner had averaged driving well over fifty thousand miles per year around his beloved South selling his firm's high-end industrial machinery. In doing so, he had seen GAC's trucks running up and down the highways for years and had particularly always noticed just how clean and spotless they were. His firm's sales training curriculum specifically included techniques on how to identify quality-conscious elements of a firm's business, presuming such attributes as leading indicators of a potential client's likelihood to buy based upon quality and value versus price. As such, the GAC trucks had always stood out oddly enough to the astute young salesman. So, when the recruiter finally and cautiously mentioned them by name, Garner had an immediate positive reaction and interest to hear more about the open field sales manager role. The recruiter was quietly delighted to finally have a prospective candidate on the other end of the phone who could appreciate the consumer product need potential and economic long-term benefits of a possible career selling caskets. Both men were mutually excited and interested to further explore the possibility of a good match between Garner McCall and the Great American Casket Company.

~~~~~~~~~~~~

Being careful not to allow his emotions overly influence his right foot, so that he kept his four-by-four running below eighty, Garner thought back on how arduous and exhausting GAC's interview process had been. For whatever reason, it seemed that after numerous trips to their tiny headquartered town in Northeast Ohio, the top brass kept delaying a final hiring decision. He'd made no less than four trips to GAC's home office for various interviews with human resources, different department heads such as marketing, customer service, and product development, as well for a full day in depth detailed interview with the global sales VP, and finally a fourth day to

44

interface with the entire executive team including lunch with the then venerable CEO, Bill Statham.

Despite their delays, the recruiter kept telling Garner that Great American had been so impressed with him and how he was exactly what they'd been looking for in a new field sales manager. Historically like many casket firms, GAC had typically hired family and/or friends of employees or customers. As a result, their prime targets for sales reps were usually funeral directors, who for whatever reason, had grown tired of the service side but wanted to remain in the industry. One of a few ways to do that was to get into sales with any of the hundreds of casket makers around the country.

But time had proven, in general at least, that most individuals with a heart and mind for service would rarely, if ever, become comfortable to actively and competitively sell, meaning intentionally ask for orders and work at taking away competitively-held accounts versus just being on a friendly "hey-how's-it-going" milk-route routine. To be clear, in so many such cases, it was as simple as a funeral home owner who bought enough caskets to leverage his annual purchase volume into a good paying job for one his less than service-minded offspring. In such cases, the brazen funeral home owner would either keep or switch his purchases with whichever casket maker took on Junior as one of their paid reps. GAC had hired scores of funeral directors over the years that promised a great potential to win new business but most would rarely deliver. After decades of this former and ex-funeral director turned sales rep hiring model, GAC, like most casket companies, was left with a very mediocre

45

client-facing organization that was simply inadequately adept at responding to an ever-changing and hyper-competitive market. When Garner McCall came across the sights of the top execs at GAC, it was clear that he was exactly the type of new, driven leadership candidate they were looking for to come in and work with a particularly struggling sales team.

Garner's mind wondered now where life would have led him and Denise if he had just stood by his word to the recruiter in Memphis when he called to say that he was "out." After all the different trips to GAC headquarters, numerous phone interviews, executive assessments, and five months of jostling back and forth about the potential job start date, he'd had enough and told the recruiter to tell them "Thanks, but no thanks!" He figured if they couldn't make their mind up after everything, then perhaps it wasn't meant to be and that he should just walk away.

Despite his pleading to hang on a little while longer, the recruiter relayed the message to GAC for Garner, who decided to keep looking for another opportunity to sink his teeth into. But by the end of that same afternoon, the recruiter called Garner back saying "They really don't want to lose you and if you're still interested to join them, you can start as soon as possible! Plus to show they're serious, they are offering for you to start at ten thousand dollars a year more than what you asked for! The VP of HR also told me to tell you that the CEO, Mr. Statham himself had personally made the decision for you to receive their offer and extends his personal apology for it all taking so long." Needless to say, the recruiter thought this kind of a fast response from GAC to a young, thirty-something year-old would have been it all it would take. Except, Garner McCall wasn't such an easy sell.

There was something that didn't feel quite right about accepting the job now, regardless of the quick response and increased salary offer, since he'd taken his name out of the proverbial hat. Garner told the recruiter to tell GAC, that while he was very appreciative of their generous offer and response, that he would now be uncomfortable to come on board in fear that someone may think he had played them somehow. He said, "Please tell them for me that there's no way I'd ever want to start out that way with a new company. Please let them know that I am humbly honored to receive their offer today, but I think it's best if I pass and keep looking."

The recruiter couldn't believe the poise and chops of this young executive. Though he never said it, of course, wanting to close his own deal for a lucrative thirty percent commission of the first year's salary once the job was filled. Nonetheless, the frustrated Memphian would be forced to deliver the failed declining message back to GAC. Less than five minutes after hanging up with the HR VP, the recruiter's phone rang again from the seven-four-zero area code but not the same number he'd become accustomed to seeing. This time, it was Bill Statham calling directly from his corner office with his top HR exec listening in on speaker.

As always, Statham was to the point. He told the recruiter with the slow, southern Memphis drawl to call the young man back again, this time on his personal behalf, and to ask for one more consideration of GAC. Statham said, to tell

McCall that their team had delayed the decision because of a direct order from him to freeze all hiring, given the current ongoing flat death rate and resulting sluggish average casket sales. You see, when the economy is down, people tend to spend less on everything, even funerals and caskets. Employing his well-rehearsed humility, the Great American CEO went on to say how personally impressed he had been with the young sales leader who had spoken so clearly and expertly on how to turn-around underperforming sales teams, and especially about how he'd go about it if hired. What Statham didn't say was that Garner had reminded him so much of himself when he had joined GAC as a rookie, non-industry field sales manager. Statham said to tell Garner how he understood and respected what he had obviously concluded in his decision to bow out, but that GAC wanted one more opportunity to win him aboard. To do so, Statham would ask for McCall to come back up to Bergholz once more for a full day with himself and his "top sales minion", Ken Powers, the VP of Global Sales.

This time Statham, who knew how to close a deal, would pull out all stops to win over the young sales leader stud to get him on the team, knowing full well that it would send shockwaves throughout his woe-is-me, apathetic sales organization. The latter would ultimately serve as one of Statham's infamous teaching moments to his lackluster team of order takers. Telling the recruiter to ask Garner, as well as his wife, to please make time on Friday the following week to come back up for what would he personally promised would be worthwhile talks and dinner that evening at the local country club with the two top execs and their wives. To cap it off, Statham said: "Tell young Mr. McCall, just to prove how seriously interested we are, that I'll be authorizing one of our private planes to come down and pick them up at a local airstrip not far from their home near Augusta. Plus, a private limo will pick them up and take them back the next day. Let's see if that approach wins him over!"

Sure enough, Garner and Denise McCall didn't see that one coming. He was incredibly wowed by the fact that Mr. Bill Statham had even gotten involved in anything to do with him, much less offered to send a private plane to make a point. Denise, of course, was so impressed already with GAC making such a hospitable offer, and remarked how she and Garner had flown low-end, cramped coach, and even paid for their own lunches, when Garner's current company had brought them both up to the national sales meeting, after he finished first place worldwide a few years earlier. She was so proud for husband to have such a tremendous opportunity with a company that was obviously so successful and interested.

~~~~~~~~~~~

Cruising onwards toward Knoxville where they'd spend the evening on the final leg of the journey home, Garner recalled how the cushy private jet sat down in the middle of the Ohio farm field. He even remembered how the very private airstrip was located in what seemed oddly far away from the tiny town where GAC had been headquartered for a century. That should have been the first clue, he thought to himself. As he thought about the two limos parked just outside the gate, one for him and one for Denise, looking back now, he recalled how they both got sucked into the well-manicured trappings of it all. Denise was whisked away to The Club for an early lunch and spa day with the wives of Statham and Powers. Both lovely well-healed and pampered ladies played their parts to a tee. Dressed to the nines, with almost matching hairstyles and tans, thanks to their frequent jaunts down to south Florida on one of the company planes, the two corporate wives wooed and courted young Denise with The Club's arugula and blue cheese filet mignon salads. With their own brand of well-rehearsed, wink and nod styled banter, the two women noted how nothing paired better with their planned light lunch fare than a couple of blue cheese olive martinis. "Trust us", they said, about how the double martinis were an "essential preliminary part of their upcoming relaxing spa day." Anyone could understand how a young southern girl could be completely won over by such gracious, cat-like hostesses.

As for Garner, his limo would take a different route to his site of seduction for the day. Recollecting how it was definitely the first time another man had ever intentionally opened and closed a car door for him, his black stretch limo left the private GAC airstrip and tooled out onto the gravel roads after Denise's. But where her driver went straight, Garner's made a hard right turn onto a different road that led down a heavily treed path. He could tell this was not an untraveled road, with its well packed, beveled sides and groomed lighted landscaping and planted trees along the way. Later on, of course after he was in too deep to see past the pretense of it all, Garner would realize just what other types of passengers would take those same limos from the private middle-of-nowhere airfield to the place where very special customers and guests were "entertained" for decades by GAC.

One place not previously on his interview agendas from past trips was one of the coolest places he would have ever the chance to visit. It was simply known as "The Ranch." Created by one of the early founders of the company, this place was a meticulously well-maintained working horse ranch, complete with a couple thousand acres, and home to over five hundred horses and fifteen hundred head of cattle, riding trails, ponds, shooting range, and multiple upscale bunk houses for funeral home guests to stay in. For a horse lover like Garner McCall, The Ranch was, no doubt, a huge draw.

A huge western-styled lodge clubhouse housed a team of the best private chefs, ranging from executive to sous to pastry, preparing some of the best meals that customers of GAC would likely ever eat in their lives, much less in such a tiny town in the middle of nowhere. With over ten thousand square feet under roof, customers never had to roam too far before coming up on an open bar at The Ranch. Not only were the bars always open, whether for an early Bloody Mary or a Screwdriver to start the day of some weary-eyed casket-buying funeral home owner, the quality of the liquor and booze on this ranch was always top shelf. Here all the bottles were the best top dollar, reserve quality, and there was always plenty to go around too, just name your poison, day or night!

Their days had gone as planned of course, with both Denise and Garner completely blown away with the seductive side of the Great American Casket Company. It was all so enticing, and of course completely enshrouded in the carefully presented goodwill for mankind's ultimate need and deserving for high quality casket products. After all, as Garner reflected, they were so convincing in their assurances of how quality was richly built-in to each and every casket, regardless of what any family could afford to pay. The real bottom line was, of course, that the margins on every casket that GAC shipped out far exceeded any minimum profit range compared to most other non-technical product manufacturing firms. While there's nothing at all wrong with Great American or its funeral home clients selling good quality caskets, sometimes the means and severity by which GAC would go to ensure a client came on board or remained loyal were anything but noble. Garner wished he'd never learn some of the things he had or worse yet ignored for so long.

By the end of their respective afternoons at The Club and The Ranch, both Denise and Garner were completely hooked. Who wouldn't want to be part of something so successful, and yet almost charitable? The Statham's and the Powers' had seemed so gracious, kind, and genuinely interested in them as people and so encouraging to have them join "The GAC Family." After a quick breakfast at the Statham's personal home, which was so tastefully homey and down-to-earth for the CEO of a large corporation in such a quaint small town, a brief office tour on Saturday morning was completely arranged to throw the final rope around the McCall's necks. That would be all it would take. As the Statham's stood in front of the towering office complex and waved goodbye to their young prey riding off in the back of the long black limo, they knew the McCall's would be hard-pressed to say to "No" to the life and surroundings they'd just been introduced to in the last twenty-four hours. Now, Statham would have his teaching moment message to send his minion sales troops, and young Garner McCall would forever feel the indebted need to prove his hire to be a great decision.

Just like that, Garner would be working with a company with which he had become so impressed and that seemed just as quality conscious as the one he'd be leaving. He and Denise both thought it was a great company and a wonderful opportunity. Just as most people want to believe, both thought they would be part of the GAC family until Garner was ready to retire. With his right foot still pressing past eighty, all of the thoughts and images of how they both had gotten so drawn into the dark Great American web kept running through Garner's mind.

~~~~~~~~~~~

NO PRISONERS

As his truck and mind raced down the interstate, Garner thought about those early years and how he had truly come to love being part of GAC, and especially all of the great people there. Despite what sometimes seemed like the company might have some dark and shady edges, GAC was full of great people and produced some of the very best funeral products known in the industry. He had done well there too, but it was anything but easy right from the start. Turns out that while a bunch of former funeral directors may not have the whole sales thing down pat, they did understand how to ban together and, attempt anyway, to box-out an "outsider." Garner would learn this lesson right out of the gate upon joining GAC and being introduced to his first, new team. Apparently their collective small attempts to distance and deny access to a non-funeral type had worked in the past, but they didn't know Garner McCall.

Garner's first assigned regional team was larger than any he had led up to that point in his young leadership career, with twenty reps in total across five states. As he would often later reference throughout his executive career by what he called the "three-third's syndrome", Garner now realized the same scenario had affectively applied to his first team at GAC. That is to say, that virtually no matter the group or industry, a new leader could routinely expect that people tended to respond and act in three consistent patterns. The first third usually took on the attitude of "just tell us what you want us to do and we'll do it" mentality; whereas the second group would tend to say the right things outwardly but in secret would hold back and say something to the effect of "yeah they think I'm onboard, but we'll see if this new crap sticks and if so, then we'll jump on board"; and finally the third and last group was much more in your face with their obstinate attitudes, usually noting "yeah, well we've been here a long time, a helluva lot longer than you'll last, and what you're proposing isn't new and furthermore it doesn't work, so you have fun with trying it again with the rookies and if you can get it going, then we'll consider following along." Now to most new sales team leaders, these kinds of dissenting factions can be quite off-putting and cause many to never gain the authority and respect of a new team, especially at a new company in a new industry. But sometimes, the right stuff just happens to be baked into certain people, and McCall was one of those people. You see, he had worked too damn hard to let a bunch of strangers keep him from doing the job that he was hired to do, and he'd be damned if it was about to happen right out of the gate at his new company.

～～～～～～～～～～

On his first team wide conference call, Garner used the list acquired from HR about each person, their tenure, current and former titles, areas of residence, and other such factoids to show he'd done his homework before jumping into the inaugural group call. It was a mix too, almost an exact third, third, and a third scenario. He had several rookies with less than a couple of years struggling to figure out the hurdles, several in the three to seven year group who were settled in and getting comfortable, and finally a sect of grumpy-ass, naysaying veterans, who

55

seemed to have coordinated their "good luck" remarks for the new non-industry manager.

One such former manager, now unhappily demoted back to rep status, even had the stupid audacity to tell his new boss right there on the call that it would likely be a few years before he would figure out their business enough to help the veterans on the team, and how McCall would likely be better off just traveling around with the new reps for the foreseeable future. Even most of the wily older vets kept quiet when their arrogant comrade let that obnoxious advice fly in public, obviously attempting to put the new sales manager in his place. After going around the horn allowing for everyone to introduce themselves on the call, Garner shared his own introduction and expounded upon why he'd elected to join GAC. He assured them of his commitment to travel was no less than seventy-five percent of the time each and every week in the field to quickly learn the business, get to know each of them, plus hopefully to do anything possible to help their team succeed. McCall's degree of matter-of-factness about his travel intentions and work ethic even drew a few unidentifiable wows from his new teammates.

To show that he meant business, Garner said that he'd already worked up his first travel schedule and that he'd be calling everyone separately, right after the team call, to make initial travel schedules. As for the first call to be made however, oh that was modified from his original intended schedule. Now the former, arrogant ex-manager would be at the top of the new published list that would go out later that afternoon. Garner wasn't about to let the ex-manager's arrogance go unnoticed and used it to set an immediate tone with the team that there was only one boss. While he was there to help and work as hard as possible, he, and only he, would be setting his work approach and agenda. Rest assured it got everyone's attention.

~~~~~~~~~~~~

Suffice to say that the call with the asshole, former manager went very differently when it was just one on one. Now that that he wasn't grandstanding for his rep mates, he was far more colloquial and friendly. Virtually in suck up mode from the first hello, which Garner didn't understand or like very much, this guy presented himself as the snot-nosed rat all of his former direct reports had said about him for years, and as Garner would later learn what had led to his demotion. The twenty-plus year veteran was speechless and dumbfounded after being asked about his schedule for the upcoming week, and especially when his new boss said how it sounded great and that he would be joining his new senior sales rep. Piling on, Garner puffed him up by saying, "I figured there's no better way to learn quickly about the business and my new role than to quickly spend time with someone so experienced like you, Bob!"

Garner then notified Bob that he'd find the closest hotel to his house and travel in on that coming Sunday evening to be picked up by 7AM the next Monday morning so they could work through the following Thursday. His new veteran rep, already choking back his embarrassment, began to already make excuses how the next week may not go as planned. Which of course, Garner interpreted correctly that the so-called busy agenda the guy had talked about having worked out for the following week was a bunch of bull. Now noon on the Friday before, Bob would obviously have to scramble and start calling every available funeral home owner and/or director on his intended route to try and piece-mill the semblance of a hard-working schedule together. Garner imagined that there would be a bunch of funeral home owners who might be surprised to hear from their man, Bob, so late on a Friday afternoon. Figuring, it might even screw up his tee time too!

In short, the following first week in the field with one of his new reps went as planned in some ways, and far better in others. Garner knew that if he could win over this rep in the last of the one-third's group of naysayers, then it would go a long way to help break down barriers with everyone else on the team. And, that's just what he did. Bob thought he'd pit Garner up against some of the toughest customers in his territory that absolutely hated GAC, mostly because of their ties to the big corporate consolidators and rumors of far better deals than offered to Mom & Pop owners.

The former ex manager told his trusted veteran cohorts, who chided him on to "put it to the rookie", how "it'd be good training" when he planned to set up his new boss for some major league ass-chewing lessons and embarrassment when he arranged a meeting with his largest prospect in the territory. Bob had called on this same funeral home group owner, that had a couple dozen locations doing hundreds of annual casketed services and was the largest non-corporate in the region, but had never sold him a single casket in over twenty years. The owner simply hated everything that GAC stood for and took no punches in saying so. Nonetheless, by the end of the first meeting, by being nothing more than a sincere, interested listener as to why and how the owner felt, Garner had quickly disarmed the his hostilities. Immediately, Garner gained an open invite back anytime to meet with the owner and his family board. Though the man had hardly ever looked at Bob during the whole hour he and Garner were there. That hadn't gone unnoticed by Bob's new boss either.

Amazed, the veteran sales rep could not believe how his new boss had quickly and completely holstered the ever-readied firearm the elusive customer had always previously taken out to draw a fast aim whenever anyone from GAC darkened their door. It was something special for the veteran rep to behold, and quickly he began to think of other hard to reach suspects around his territory, that he now wanted to see if they were available to meet before the coming Thursday. Just like that, Garner had demonstrated the value of connecting with people on a human basis. It was never about caskets, and he knew that as well as anyone.

Unsurprisingly, most of the remaining calls went very much the same way with both existing customers and prospects alike. Mostly, because Garner quickly made them feel heard and appreciated, whether they bought from GAC or not. Further, what the formerly dismissive rep would learn as well was that his new boss was observing him with customers too, both on the phone and in person. When it was time, Garner would have some sage coaching advice for his new senior rep, whether he wanted it or not. Rather than shoving it down the snide rep's throat,

Garner asked Bob if there was any information or feedback that would be of interest before he got out at the airport to head home that Thursday afternoon.

Taking the bait for feedback from his new boss, the veteran rep, who obviously struggled with being humble or thankful for the business that clients considered with him and GAC, learned that his new boss was equally dedicated and interested to help him improve and become more successful. After providing the instructive counsel to just be more friendly, conversational, and to do more listening than instructing, like on his first call with Garner and the team, the arrogant scowl left Bob's face and was instantly replaced with one best described as "pained, truthful awareness." Garner assured his new man that "clearly you know your business, but they don't seem to know you! Just relax, man, and let them come to you!" Just like that the senior casket salesman knew his new boss was right, and above all else, was caringly courageous enough to tell him to his face."

By the time Garner's plane landed back at the Atlanta airport, and he turned his cell phone back on, there were already several messages on it from several of his new team members about their own upcoming trip plans with the new manager. As he began the eastwardly drive home near Augusta, Garner learned that it turned out 'ol Bob, the former scowl-faced know-it-all veteran rep, had burned up the party lines about what a "real deal" he was and how his teammates should all get their toughest big competitive accounts lined up for his visits. It was nice feedback to hear so quickly being circulating through his new team. Even if it had come from of Bob's fellow old, crusty diehards compadres, who was obviously initiating his own up-sucking act in advance of the new boss's first ride-along. Just like that, in one week of simply being his usual, sincerely interested and genuine self with new industry clients and one rep, Garner had begun to break down many of the team-building barriers to turn-around his first team.

~~~~~~~~~~~~~

Unfortunately, however, the reason Garner's theory of the third's scenario tends to hold true is because of the monotonous bullshit from reps bound and determined to uphold their place in last obnoxious group. Garner had one of these idiots on his first GAC team. True to form, Jimmy was a fifteen-year rep whose only claim to fame was how he had been Rookie of the Year a full decade and a half earlier upon joining GAC. He thought he was pretty smart and sly too, twice canceling planned visits from his new boss the day before Garner was scheduled to fly out. 'Ol Jimmy wasn't going to convince anyone that he was a rocket scientist by any means, or even a rock scientist for that matter, but like most bull-shitters, he talked a good game. The problem Jimmy had though, and couldn't hide from, was the fact that he hadn't hit his sales plan in the last seven years. Unlike all of the other reps in territories surrounding his, poor little Jimmy recanted every sad tale about how his territory had been attacked by the big bad competition. He went on to stress how he and the former boss had tried everything possible to fend off the bottom-feeders, but their deals had just been too enticing for customers. Of course, Garner saw right through this when he asked for specifics with a complete list of each account and owner's name, and said how they would start by visiting each and every one of those lost accounts in poor Jimmy's territory.

While 'ol Jimmy continued to conveniently "forget" to provide his new boss with the expected list of accounts, Garner finally just called one of the data analysts back at corporate to help pull the information for him. Then, the following Friday, after getting back into his office after his Plan-B travel schedule, Garner started calling to speak with each of the funeral home owners. After reaching eight of the twelve accounts, it was clear why they had all abandoned Great American. Poor little Jimmy hadn't been to see any of those accounts in over two years. Hell, he hadn't even called them on the phone to say thanks for their business! All he was doing was taking it for granted. Worse yet, was that Garner learned that each and every one of those accounts had been doing sizeable volume with Great American but hadn't received a volume rebate check for the past few years despite each growing their purchases. Several even said that multiple calls left with 'ol Jimmy about the missing rebates were never returned. Garner knew that something didn't smell right at all and promised each owner that he would dig into things and personally follow-up.

It's funny how people get defensive when they've been caught lying. 'Ol Jimmy got pretty damn mad learning that his new boss had called each of his customers "without permission." Quickly reminding his former Rookie of the Year that the accounts belonged to the company, Garner asked about the rebate checks, already knowing the GAC process was that any earned rebate checks were always mailed directly to the account rep of record for delivery. Not surprisingly, Jimmy denied ever receiving them. The crashing sound of the proverbial pin dropping on Jimmy was deafening when Garner told him to be ready for an eight o'clock morning start on Monday morning of the coming week. Trying to deflect a third time, reciting his planned visits to other "buying accounts", Garner quickly and emphatically told him to "Cancel them!" Saying, "Well, I'll be there just the same! Be ready, and bring ALL of your files to the local warehouse. We will start by going through everything for an exhaustive territory review to see how we can get your territory back on track. Then we will go see as many as possible of these accounts who say they're missing a rebate check." As the next several seconds passed quietly over the telephone line, poor Jimmy knew he'd been caught and would surely be humiliated if he and the new boss walked into any of those funeral homes to see customers he hadn't bothered to visit for so long.

~~~~~~~~~~~~~~~

Garner had never received a work call on a weekend since joining Great American. So when his work cell rang on a Saturday afternoon, he was more than surprised when Statham and Larry Travis, the acting VP of Sales at the time, called him at home. Travis had been put over Sales, when the Powers had been so blatantly having an affair with one of the newest female sales reps. Once the news had become widespread enough, Statham demoted the guy a couple of rungs down the ranking ladder. Of course, affairs were nothing new around GAC, so it'd take much more than that to kick a man out. Plus, the rumor out of HR was that 'ol Ken even kept his same salary from the big senior executive level.

It turned out that Jimmy had called Travis at home earlier that morning to resign out of the blue. He and Travis went way back when they both started in the same region that Statham led near the end of his field days. Both Statham and Travis tried to talk their friend Jimmy out of his decision, only to realize that his mind was made up. Worse, they thought, he'd already made a hasty deal with a top competitor and was slated to start on the following Monday. When Statham and Travis asked 'ol Jimmy why, they was not at all pleased to hear how the newly hired sales manager had already pissed him off so much. "Especially before even having a fair chance of getting to travel with the new manager and getting to know him!" their buddy exclaimed. Of course, the little prick had completely lied and threw Garner under the bus big time.

Although, what poor Jimmy failed to consider was how Garner had worked late the night before, doing his own homework and analysis to understand exactly what rebate each of the accounts he'd spoken with should have received. He also reached one of the little blue-hairs at corporate to confirm the amounts and that each check had in fact been mailed to Jimmy but none were ever cashed. So each amount still showed as a pending credit for each customer.

Initially the Saturday morning call was very one-sided, with Statham doing most of the talking and instructing McCall on how Jimmy had been such a highly valued contributor over the years. Travis chimed in too chastising how Garner had just run off one of the company's most longtime, respected reps and how it would likely be a hard thing for his own reputation to rebound from, having most likely lost any and all credibility with the rest of the sales organization, as well as the company, for that matter. Saying nothing until an obvious moment surfaced when the two senior execs expected the new, junior manager to finally explain himself, Garner quickly got their attention with a review of the facts and his call with Jimmy earlier the prior day. Both men were admittedly surprised but still maintained that a reasonable explanation must exist that would exonerate their friend and colleague.

~~~~~~~~~~~~~~

Word of Jimmy's famed departure got around quickly. It was being talked about as if "Elvis himself had left the hallowed halls of the great GAC building", and was being projected as if something from which the company would surely never recover. Oh how the vultures began to circle, thinking they could swarm and chase off the outsider. Immediately rumors formed about the new asshole, rookie sales manager who had just come into GAC on a tear and started shelling out harsh orders, especially when he didn't understand how "their industry" worked. How could anyone have run off such a legend like the great Jimmy? Now all of a sudden Jimmy had developed an instantaneous and legendary reputation for having held a very tough territory together. Just imagine how it would have declined further, the naysayers bemoaned publicly, had the great Jimmy not been in it? The word was out: Garner McCall clearly wasn't a fit in their quiet and proper industry, and certainly didn't belong in the Great American Casket Company!

It's funny though how those little pesky things... called the fucking facts, will blow up a bullshit story faster than you can say "Screw you, Jimmy!" Everyone expected big time heat to come down on McCall, which of course put Statham in somewhat of an awkward spot, having been the one to bring him in. That was, until later the next week, when Garner scheduled another call to Statham to discuss his next steps about the lost accounts and missing rebate checks, but not before doing a couple other key things. First, he confirmed with HR to have Jimmy return all of his sales files and materials to the local warehouse where Garner had been supposed to meet with him the week earlier. Then, Garner would have all of the boxes rushed via FedEx to his home office. Secondly, Garner cleared his travel schedule and placed calls into every account in Jimmy's territory that had spent at least ten thousand dollars on average each year. After making the calls and going through all the boxes, Garner couldn't wait to hold the planned call with Statham. As for Travis, he'd let Statham decide if he wanted him to join. Always the shrewd one, keeping his cards close, Statham wanted to hear the next wave of information first, so he could then decide how to position the McCall issue internally.

Garner prepared a detailed account listing of more than fifty accounts he'd spoken with directly, including names, titles, and purchases over the prior three years, including a compounded average growth rate percent for each, which was usually declining due to Jimmy's routine of ignoring his customers. He also listed how long it had been since each funeral home owner said they'd seen 'ol Jimmy. Statham was shocked to hear that less than ten accounts reported him visiting at least once in the last year, although a couple of those said he had visited more than once. The biggest shocker that Statham couldn't believe was a composite file showing numerous copies of rebate checks that Jimmy had merely thrown into the boxes over the years and never delivered. Given that he'd been stupid enough to actually return all of the missing checks in the boxes that he personally dropped off at the local warehouse, and which were shipped to McCall, it was obvious he had forgotten about even tossing them aside and never making the necessary efforts to deliver them to his deserving customers. Even more carelessly, stupid Jimmy had himself provided GAC with all the proof and evidence they needed of his dishonesty and lack of care for the company and its customers. Garner Xeroxed copies of each check and showed Statham how they matched up with the accounting review he had done the week prior.

There were a total of eighty-one checks, going back over several years, ranging from a few hundred dollars to several thousand; with the largest sums having been issued to the top firms lost in the territory. In total, the checks added up to almost two hundred thousand dollars. Garner closed out his presentation to Statham explaining how he had already spoken with each owner about their undelivered rebate checks and would be personally traveling the territory for the following several weeks to make each delivery himself. After that, Garner would prepare a post visit summary and send it to Statham.

Needless to say, the customers greatly appreciated Garner for showing up with their rebate checks. To a person, not one of the account owners said they had any use for Jimmy, going on to say that he never did much anyway when he did show up. Many shared how he'd show off his latest, new beamer and thousand dollar suits, or talk about the big lake house that he was always working on. As for the biggest lost accounts, Garner won all but one of those back singlehandedly just by showing up, apologizing on behalf of the company, and asking for their business again. Each of the owners said how they thought they should have received a rebate check but that Jimmy would never return their calls, so they had just finally given up chasing him. The sad thing, as Garner later explained to Statham, was how he had so easily picked up over one and a half million in sales by just visiting the accounts and delivering their checks; and detailing how much personal earnings Jimmy lost by refusing to simply do his job. He also told Statham how he had already informed the rest of his reps that he would begin immediately by calling each of the top thirty customers in every territory beginning the following week. Not to catch them doing anything wrong, but just to establish a connection and trust with their team's best customers.

Suffice to say, Statham was more than impressed with his new man McCall and quickly already planned how to use this teaching moment with the rest of the sales ranks, especially the managers. No doubt, this was a huge star in Garner's cap with

Statham. But it still didn't win any points with his colleagues, who had already thought and hoped he was on his way out to the bloody curb. Now, that was far from the case. McCall's reputation only got stronger from there.

~~~~~~~~~~~~~~

Any successful sales organization always has some great reps too, and McCall was fortunate enough to work with many of the talented ones at GAC. Those usually proved to be the ones whose daddy hadn't been one of the bigger Great American customers who'd gotten one of their worthless offspring one of the cushy sales jobs at GAC.

One of those that Garner often recalled had actually sold shoes for living before stumbling into the casket game. On his first joint travel trip with this particular sales stud, Garner recalled when they stopped to see the rep's first planned customer call for their first day together. The customer was one of the rep's biggest in the territory, and one of those third generation lucky-sperm types. In his forties, the man had the softest set of fatty hands that Garner had ever shaken.

As soon as the rep and the boss sat down in the man's ornate personal office for their eight o'clock morning meeting, the operator began to rant and rave about a casket his firm hadn't received, and which he said was "extremely late and overdue." With his face growing redder and redder with his eyes bulging, the owner never once looked at the latest senior executive from GAC but stared a hole right through his rep. Screaming and shouting, the man went on for several minutes how the late casket was going to cause his firm to miss getting some wealthy

69

dead woman's body casketed in time for her funeral service scheduled the very next day. He said he had personally been calling Great American for days looking for the casket, and had yet to even receive a call back.

Garner just sat there observing the mad man as well as his rep, who never once said a word and sat there calmly staring back. Once the man had exhausted his knowledge of curse words and foul language, the rep finally spoke. He simply said, "Are you done, Terrence?" Now he had referred to the man as Terry in all of his pre-call prep discussions with Garner earlier that morning over breakfast, even telling his new senior leader how he and "Terry" were really good friends. Saying, they and their wives spent personal time together at each other's homes and with their children. He said they had even taken a few weekend vacations together. Mostly, the rep had told McCall how the first planned call for their three days together in his territory would be the easiest of the week and how sweet of a guy 'ol Terry was. Funny, 'ol Terry didn't seem so sweet at the moment.

Once Terrence nodded he was "done", the rep calmly raised the cell phone in his hand to eye-level, and with his arm outstretched, pointed it right at Terrence's nose. "Terrence, do you see this fucking phone in my hand?" the rep softly asked. "It's a funny, fucking thing how I haven't heard one thing about your missing casket or not getting any response from our company. Now, here we come to see you and you whip this shit out on me, and with my new boss along, just to try and make yourself look big. I think that's pretty fucking pathetic." By now 'ol Terrence's face clearly had all the blood drain out of it and

70

was beginning to look as though he might have been embalmed right there by the rep's dressing down.

The rep went on to say, "I'm going to call and find your casket Terrence. I'll also find out when it was ordered and promised for delivery. We'll get right to the bottom of this, right here and now!" Stepping away to call the local warehouse, the rep came back after about one quick minute. Apparently it hadn't taken very long at all to find out from the warehouse manager that Terrence's firm hadn't placed that particular casket order until just two days earlier. The manager said he'd taken the order himself from one of Terrence's funeral directors, who had said she had forgotten to place the order the week before and asked if there was any way possible it could be expedited. She said she knew the owner would be so upset with her if it wasn't there in time. The manager went on to tell the sales rep how, after doing a search for that particular model, he knew it would be impossible to have it delivered within the following two days. He said he personally called Terrence to confirm what he'd found and even asked if perhaps another casket would do for his grieving client's family. He then told the rep how Terrence had said to just try and rush it, which of course meant that he'd expect GAC to pay for all the extra shipping costs to get it delivered.

Finally, about the unreturned calls that Terrence supposedly made, the warehouse manager told the rep that Terrence had only left one message with the night service, and just the night before, but that he had already called him back first thing "this morning on Terrence's personal cell phone." Only that Terrence hadn't answered when he called, nor had he returned the call back to the manager yet either.

Returning with the complete story of how Terrence's predicament evolved, now the rep was getting a little red-faced. As he recanted what he'd just learned, 'ol Terry began to get a little red-faced again too. Remaining standing right there in front of Terrence's handsome walnut desk, the rep told Terrence "this whole situation is a sack of shit!" Saying, "First you folks ordered it late, were told it would be impossible to get here in time, and then after you only called one time about it late last night, Charlie called you back and left an update first thing this morning! Have you even listened to the voicemail he left, Terrence?" When Terrence nodded in the negative, the rep demanded, "Well, let's hear it, Terrence. Put your phone on speaker too, so we can all hear it!" Now with his ass cheeks pressed back into a corner, Terrence played the message of Charlie from the warehouse gleefully explaining how he'd sent one of his drivers on an all-night eight-hour drive in his own pickup truck to a neighboring state just to pick up his casket and how it would be delivered first thing that day. Charlie went onto to say how a regular order would have never made it in time, if the casket had been routed back through the distribution hub. Then, Charlie ended the message chuckling with the good news that there wouldn't be any extra delivery charges since there had only been a little gas involved, and how his driver had been arguing a lot with his wife lately and had actually welcomed the unusually late and long working hours away from home.

"What do you bet that fucking casket is sitting out back right now, Terrence? Those boys at the warehouse normally come by here long before daylight. Let's just go see!" With that, the three men, still with McCall never saying a word, went out back of the funeral home and laid eyes on the missing box. There it was, shining like a brand new penny!

"Good, I'm glad its here." was all that Terrence mumbled. Turning and staring at his much larger counterpart, the rep concluded the discussion with, "Terrence, the next time you or your staff get into a situation like this, you should call me, and only me. If you don't, then it's not my fucking problem. And you're not going to rake me over the coals, especially in front of my new boss the first time you meet him, when you didn't even bother to call me about it in the first place. You call me, and I promise you I will fix whatever problem you have. But if you don't call me, then sure as hell don't come bitching to me about it later! We clear?" "Yeah, yeah, I'm clear. Let's go back in the office and get a cup of coffee." That was 'ol Terry's way of putting the subject of the missing casket to rest, though never apologizing of course. Sadly, some customers would prove to stoop that low, regardless of their part in a mix up.

McCall knew he never had to worry about that rep. He was one of the best, hitting his numbers every year, doing everything possible for GAC's customers to keep them happy, while not taking any unnecessary shit in the process. He was exactly the type of rep every manager longs for.

~~~~~~~~~~~~~~~

Over the course of the coming months, Garner would have mostly positive experiences with the rest of his first team members. Customers and prospect meetings went very similarly, most usually resulting in new gained business or at least locking out a competitor. The reps continued to ask for his guidance too on how they could improve, which Garner always honestly provided with both positives and potential improvement areas for his folks based upon what he had witnessed. Realizing their boss took no prisoners and would do anything to help them win, the team's esprit décor quickly reenergized causing everyone to a person to raise their game. Their newly developed focused attitude, on caring about what customers wanted and felt was important, made their jobs of connecting and winning over new accounts not only seem fun again, but very achievable. Just like that, Garner's new team went from almost dead last place to a resounding first after his first year on the job as their leader.

Always mindful of his teaching moment opportunities, the venerable Statham assuredly would not let such a moment pass by to highly praise his new leader and his assigned region troops. Statham's intended bar for leadership contribution had definitely been raised and redefined. What the CEO mostly admired, and had already seen enough to know, was that Garner McCall, much like himself, fearlessly took no prisoners in doing his job or getting results.

~~~~~~~~~~~~~~~

Like many large corporations, nothing much ever stayed the same. In a designed effort to leverage Garner's potential impact on other teams, besides the sheer comparison that

Statham routinely drew to the others' performance, the region team boundaries would be redrawn for the following two years, specifically just to expand Garner's direct oversight with as many of the reps across the adjoining states to his original region. By the end of his fourth year with the firm, McCall would lead three unique teams, which would all exceed their sales plans and delight the CEO, who had absolutely become his biggest and most outspoken fan. Garner's approach with his subsequent two teams had been the same, despite the ever present one-third's mentalities. His game plan and tactics were simple, repeatable, and most of all effective; get focused, be sincere, work hard, be honest, and always-always ask for the business, even if you already have it! Funny how people want to buy from someone who truly wants their business and doesn't take it for granted. The last part, taking it for granted, was the number one issue that GAC had developed over its history, especially with Mom & Pop's. Garner and his teams intentionally changed this paradigm, and that alone made the biggest difference of all of the successes his teams produced.

After turning-around the smaller region teams, Statham had bigger sights for his proven, self-ascribed protégé. Say what you will about Bill Statham, as ultimately McCall would more than ever dreamed, but at that point in his early career with GAC, the astute CEO realized the broader potential impact the new turn-around star could have on their business. Over the course of his short region level tenure, Garner had revitalized the talent quotient of the teams, meaning that he had in due course intentionally weeded out the lazy and don't-give-a-damn reps for people who truly wanted to excel and win. He hired from all walks, not just the same male funeral director types, but also the opposite sex. As he would find, the latter would generate its own unique set of challenges in dealing with a mostly male industry clientele, but Garner would stand his ground there too with any yahoo acting out of line with anyone on his team. In a couple of cases, he even took great pleasure calling one or two such knuckleheads who just couldn't seem to behave appropriately and fired their asses from ever doing business with GAC.

When they bitched and threatened to sue, Garner gave them the direct line to both CEO and the Chief Legal Counsel. When they threatened to never buy another GAC casket, he reminded them that he would help incentivize them in that regard by reducing their purchase discount to a flat rate of only a couple percent off the wholesale price versus the typical double-digit discounts in the high teens they had accustomed to receiving. All of this tough love was only ever issued mind you, after Garner had tried numerous times in every possible way to smooth out the relationship with a problematic patron. But once one customer became inappropriate and/or belittling toward one of his reps, or when another creep tried multiple times to sexually harass one of his female reps, he would pick up the phone or get on a plane to ensure they understood that GAC would no longer do business with their firm, ever. This would be in lieu of legal action, unless they elected to pursue it and have all of his detailed documentation come out. Garner stood up for his folks, and they knew he would. So did Statham, who wanted McCall to have greater reach across their client base.

Besides recreating the talent on his teams, Garner also worked diligently to help anyone motivated enough to pursue their goals. As a result, his teams saw multiple reps promoted time and again to various higher level roles, like corporate accounts sales, product management, and in one particular case even to a sales manager level. All of this, combined with Garner's tremendous successes and client development skills, confirmed Statham's decision to see McCall promoted to leading multiple teams, thus managing managers.

His goal was simple. Get McCall's approach to become adopted across all of GAC. He could barely contain himself in just imagining the combined net effect of having all of the different regions striving to attain McCall's standards. Statham knew that as his own CEO status came to an intentional wind down over the next five or six years that there were a few critical milestones he still desired. Ramping up the top and bottom-line results each year was at the absolute top of the list. He was confident now that Garner McCall would help him fulfil that purpose.

Always mindful of timing, the shrewd CEO would need to find the right moment to pull the young, aggressive McCall upward on the executive ranks ladder, because in doing so also meant taking down one of GAC's respected, longtime senior sales officers, John Smithfield. In Statham's view, Smithfield had become more like an old cantankerous and fidgety grandfather than the executive officer he needed to be. Statham and Smithfield, both the same age, had started the same year at

GAC almost some thirty years ago back in the sixties, cutting their teeth in the casket business in the sales department, when there was only a small team of reps covering the country.

As it sometimes goes with men, these two were always competing hard to get noticed, sometimes too hard. It was back in the day when industry trade regulations were a lot less restrictive for both Statham and Smithfield who were always tirelessly trying to gain the attention of the hard-charging, DAK Kleinmark. Meaning, either would do just about any kind of a deal with some funeral home owner to win a new piece of business. All that mattered to either one of them was to win and impress their unscrupulous kingpin, DAK.

One example of how far a younger and exceedingly creative Statham went one time was to sell what he had quietly coined as "Miracle Caskets." Miracle Caskets weren't available for every customer of course, but with precision-like strategic aim, the clever, younger Bill Statham would personally go visit any funeral home owner that wasn't giving GAC, and moreover him, all of their purchases each and every month. Once he determined just how many more caskets a particular operator could buy, then he would introduce his idea of Miracle Caskets, if he deemed they were worth the trouble and risks.

The way it worked was pretty simple. DAK gave all of his sales managers access to a cash slush fund of sorts. The fund was normally used for buying booze or women for such deserving clients whenever needed to win or retain business. Since only the biggest operators of course would get access to the entertainment and talent on the Falcon, a local casket salesman working for either Statham or Smithfield had to try and get their customers away from home and out of town on "business" for a night, which most wives saw right through. Plus, what most every funeral home operator really wanted was a better deal on what they paid for caskets. So, the sharp and cunning Statham had devised the perfect little payoff plan of Miracle Caskets.

Here's how it worked: For every additional casket an owner purchased in the prior month, Statham or his most trusted rep would come by for an audit in the first week in the following month. The rep's secret audit would be in the showroom without anyone else around, obviously no witnesses and nothing to deny. Then, for every new incremental casket purchase the owner had made, their rep would leave crisp, brand new one hundred dollar bills inside a casket. For each extra basic wood casket, eighteen or twenty gauge metals, it would be one hundred dollars per unit and one-fifty for any extra bronze, copper, or premium wood. Easy-peasy! After the rep had left the funeral home, then all the owner had to do was to open the showroom caskets to find the cold, hard and entirely tax-free cash to slide into his pocket.

Statham's little practice of Miracle Caskets would go on for years with certain customers in order to avoid any of the customer's new found cash stream going to the IRS, sometimes their partners, and most of all in some well-known cases, their wives. However, should the owner develop somewhat of a foggy memory about his new found greedy loyalty to buy from only Great American, then Statham or his hand-picked man would offer to provide a blow-by-blow detailed listing of each and every "promotional payment" made to the account; with a copy going to the IRS. Nothing like the threat of a little thirty-eight percent tax hit to keep people "honest."

As a result, Statham's little secret plan led him to out sell all of his competitors in the sales manager ranks, and most especially Smithfield. Combined with his ability to schmooze and charm old man DAK, he got and kept himself on the short list for promotions that would ultimately lead him all the way to the CEO corner office of the Great American Casket Company. What about poor old "by the book" Smithfield? He'd never rise further than one more rung up on the sales management ladder than where he'd started. The poor old bastard never did figure out how Statham and his reps had always managed to ring the bell year after year, no matter what the competitors or economy was doing.

~~~~~~~~~~~

Fast-forward more than twenty years later, the ever guiling Statham finally saw the perfect time to take out his old nemesis John Smithfield a full four years before his planned retirement age of sixty-five. It couldn't be any sweeter for Statham as he sat and schemed from the balcony of his one and a half million dollar condo south of West Palm. Having arrived to his luxury winter homestead the previous day, after suffering through another annual sales meeting where he'd been forced to hob-nob with the current generation of casket salesmen, he realized that this year's annual event had actually produced something of great interest and value for him. Like most sales meetings, complete with bad hotel food, too much booze, suck-

80

up sales reps, and endless boring speeches, Statham's shining realization had come when, for a third straight year, his protégé McCall was once again named Sales Manager of the Year for still kicking ass and turning-around minds, hearts, and attitudes. Even more impressed, Garner hadn't benefited from the likes of Miracle Casket deals at his disposal either. Mostly, he was just getting his reps to get off their asses, try working a full week, and actually outsell the competition! Statham allowed one brief unspoken moment to wonder how he might have fared back in the day if he'd been going up against McCall versus Smithfield. Quietly he knew that he was glad that he'd never had to.

Statham's *ah-ha* moment at the sales meeting occurred when, once again, McCall distinguished himself in the acceptance speech he gave at the end of the night's festivities. You see when most all folks get up and accept an award, they generally say very little in fact. Regrettably, most who do prepare a statement, seem to endlessly drone on and on about every little damn deal they did all year long to win their paltry plaque, but rarely if ever talk about who helped them succeed along the way. And if they do, say a manager, it's usually something to the effect of "I want to thank everyone on the team...blah, blah, blah..." and quickly re-shifting their focus back to "me" or 'I." But not Garner McCall. He knew the reason he was there on the stage, it was his team and only them. He felt like he'd just been along for the ride all year taking great pride and joy in watching them at work and having fun winning.

One by one, McCall asked his reps to stand up and remain standing as he listed out the accomplishments and sacrifices of everyone on their team for the past year and how each had contributed to the greater good of their group and GAC. By the time five minutes had transpired, Garner's entire team of fifteen reps were standing beaming with pride in the hushed banquet hall when he finished asking everyone to join him in thunderous applause. Then he quietly sat down.

Glancing around, Statham could see the enviable looks on all the faces of the other three hundred sales reps, and even most of Garner's management compadres. He knew in that instant they were all wishing they worked for McCall. That would prove to be the exact energy and perfectly timed envy he needed to capitalize on his next ploy of pushing Garner farther up the responsibility ladder and shoving Smithfield right off of it and out of GAC. It was too perfect! Bill Statham loved it when such little precious details in life came together so beautifully.

~~~~~~~~~~

To set the next phase in motion, Statham shot a quick congratulatory note to McCall, underscoring how meaningful his speech had been the preceding evening. "Impressive speech last night, Garner - one day you may have to get all three hundred standing!" As Garner poured another cup of coffee for him and Denise, he heard the beep of the email come in and like always looked at it in his usual auto-reflex mode. For a moment, he just stood in their kitchen and thought about how Bill Statham had never seemed like a man to waste words without a specific intent. He knew this meant something important. His response was just as terse: "Thank you, Sir - we have one hell of a team!"

The following week, Statham's admin scheduled a one-on-one call with Garner, which he immediately accepted of course and wondered if it had anything to do with their email exchange. As it would turn out, the call would be Statham's first attempt to lure McCall to the home office with the enticement of a big promotion and a huge pay increase. It would also be the first time that he would reluctantly accept McCall's "thanks, no thanks" response to the lucrative offer. Turns out that Garner knew he wasn't yet ready to move up with the company and wanted more time to get his feet well-grounded under him. He'd been working on a really big customer deal with an operator that owned over twenty funeral homes that he felt like he needed to keep his full attention on. Statham could respect his rationale and elected to not push, but the determined CEO decided right then and there that he'd get McCall to Bergholz before the year was out.

Three months later, McCall and his team landed their new biggest client that would generate over fifteen hundred caskets each year and at a very strong thirteen hundred dollar wholesale average. The ten year deal was worth an estimated nineteen point five million dollars in new revenues for Garner's region and GAC. For starters, Garner structured the deal with a two million dollar upfront payment to the family board, plus lucrative discounts and volume rebates and other free merchandising support displays to help increase average casket sales to unsuspecting consumers. The family simply couldn't believe the terms McCall had brought to the table, unlike any other before, regardless of brand. Now the former stand-offish ownership group welcomed Garner McCall into their business like he walked on water.

~~~~~~~~~~~~

In the casket game, like most wholesale channel businesses, the wholesale average and the terms of the deal are everything, the only things actually. Added together, they constitute the bottom-line profitability metrics for every deal and account. The higher the average and volume, the sweeter the potential deal. Except, most Mom & Pop funeral home operators had been sucked into believing that the same deal and discounts applied to all caskets from GAC, regardless of value or quality. Outside of some national account deals that were always secretly set up as "House Accounts" and exclusively negotiated by Statham and his longtime backroom-dealing crony, Larry Travis, the huge account that Garner had brought in gave him even more credibility and clout with the old guard at GAC. Many folks had been trying to land the great white operator for decades but could never get close enough to the family who owned and ran the biggest funeral outfitter in the entire region. Adding more insult to their collective rusty talents, McCall had roped and reined them in after only a matter of months of taking on his third region.

~~~~~~~~~~~~

Once the notice came out, Statham's admin was arranging a second direct call for her boss to engage his star sales executive. As soon as he saw the admin's direct line phone number pop up on his phone, Garner knew it was the CEO likely calling again. He also knew this was it, and that saying no a second time would likely mean that a third would never happen. He called home from the road that night to discuss it all again with Denise, who would of course just tell him to do what he thought was right. Her complete moral support and love would make their future ambitions very accessible and possible. He knew it would not be smart to deny Statham again. After all, he had always known that at some point he wanted to keep going up and take on more responsibility. He just didn't expect it so soon after only being at Great American for such a short time, especially compared to his counterparts.

After Statham's "we need you here" phone call and agreement to the five bullets, the savvy CEO once again whipped out the enticement of the jet to get Garner back into town and quickly to sign the new deal. Once Garner moved his schedule around, Statham's admin assured him that she would handle the details like always, which included when one of the private jets would shoot down and pick him and Denise up. Just like clockwork, Mrs. Statham had her husband's secretary arrange for another memorable two martini lunch at The Club and a private dining room for the four of them later that evening. They were easy trappings and this time with a guaranteed, pre-negotiated deal that was already done and very much in the promised long-term favor of the McCalls. It meant that the McCalls were going back to GAC headquarters for a second time, but now to celebrate what would be for the wonderful "icing on the cake", or so they thought. Finally, Bill Statham won again and couldn't wait to set his careful, convenient plan in motion to oust his old rival, Smithfield. Never the wiser, Garner nor the folks at GAC would realize how their veteran colleague had been forced into early retirement, or exactly what the move had cost him financially in the waning years of his career.

Ultimately, the aggressive advancement of Garner McCall by Statham very much accomplished the exact intended shockwaves throughout the sales ranks at GAC. As predicted, the domino effect caused many of the old guard sales managers to evaluate their position in the proverbial three-third's buckets as McCall became their new boss. They'd learn too, just as previous reps had, that Garner McCall was going to do his job no matter what and that mediocrity was no longer an option. Suffice to say, that many of the old guard had become very comfortable on their old apple carts, which he was about to turn-upside down. All the while as they privately whined to an outwardly empathetic Statham, the scheming CEO tried not to grin too much like the lurking leopard Cheshire cat he indeed was.

~~~~~~~~~~~~~~~

Over two and half hours after pulling away from Che Pieux, Garner felt Denise's hand touch his shoulder and break the thoughts of his early days at GAC. Stretching and grinning ear to ear, it was obvious the coffee had kicked-in hard enough to break her fixation on the Scottish love story she'd been wrapped up in since they pulled onto the interstate. Having had years and years of experience driving thousands of mile each week back in his bag-carrying selling days traversing all over the South, Garner could have made it all the way to Knoxville without ever stopping. His lovely bride, on the other hand, would have no part in that. It was time to stop for some more coffee and

86

fuel as they made their way back northward to much cooler temperatures. If true to form in past years, it was highly likely they'd both be ready for some more of Oui Chef's delicious delectables for the second leg of the day's journey. Either way, Garner knew it was a given Denise would dig back into her beloved fable once they got back on the road. For himself, more thoughts of the history, goings-on, and misdeeds at Great American would consume his brain as they made their way up to Eastern Tennessee for the night.

After the usual fill-ups, Denise was back into her treasured story while Garner's mind reverted to GAC, thinking how he should have been more expecting of the setup, especially after Statham stepped down. After everything he'd personally witnessed and heard about since joining, especially once he got to the top-level, how could he have allowed himself to become so sucked in and blind? Thinking back now, it was clear how different folks had all tried to warn him, especially the trusted older Southern confidants he'd gotten so close to. They had hinted more than a few times to "always watch your back and trust no one at corporate, especially Statham or whoever comes after him." They had told him story after story of how back-stabbing, or much far worse if required, was deep in the DNA and legacy at GAC.

Collectively their stories suggested that it was just how the company operated; all starting back when DAK ruled GAC with a dead-gripped iron hand. Those wise older reps had long forewarned Garner that the company and those who ran it, or ever would, never let anything or anyone stop them from their intended success and profits; no one, ever. His seasoned confidents went on to warn that "even if Statham or those other bastards up there ever sniff a hint that you might get out of line, you can bet your sweet ass that they'll take you down faster than you know what hit you. Hell Garner, there's even been a few execs who really pushed back over the years that no one's ever heard of again to this day." Garner knew these men weren't the type of guys to blow smoke, but still he only listened without saying a word.

~~~~~~~~~~~

LEGACY

By the mid 1800's, most all of Europe had become enchanted with the new distant world called America. Promises of hope, individual freedoms, liberty, and great prosperity enticed millions to immigrate to the fledging country in order to escape dire poverty, crime, and pestilence that swept across many European countries at the time. The Kleinmark family would ultimately join hordes of their continental comrades and risk the arduous voyage to the brave new world.

The original Kleinmark family tree already went back several generations when Adlar Kleinmark came into the world in 1860. Their family name had come to represent more than just another farming family around the beautiful, peaceful town of Vielsalm, Belgium. By the time Adlar was old enough to understand, he heard the great stories from his forefathers of how their family legacy began with Elias Klein, the patriarch eight generations removed.

At just seventeen, young Elias had left his home in Duren, Germany after the tumultuous Cologne War that ensued when the local archbishop declared himself a protestant and refused to abdicate his position, thus causing a religious rebellion with local catholic factions. Ultimately, the triumphant defense of the Holy Roman Empire was mostly comprised of warring Spanish troops and Italian mercenaries who elected to kill as great many defenders of the opposition as possible. Included among the many protestant casualties were Elias's older three brothers and father, who had been an outspoken supporter of the archbishop.

As the only remaining Klein male and fearing for his life, Elias knew he needed to escape Germany at once. So he traveled west into the safer neighboring land, known today as Belgium, to find a new home for his mother and three older sisters. Wary of retaliation, the reverent Elias decided to change his family's surname by forever signifying his particular reverence for the Gospel of Mark. Found in the thirty-eighth verse of the book's first chapter, one of his most favorite teachings of Jesus was "Let us go into the next towns, that I may preach there also: for therefore came I forth." Thus forever from that day forward, Elias, his family, and all future generations would be known as Kleinmarks.

~~~~~~~~~~

Like most families trying to survive widespread economic hardship, the Kleinmarks worked hard to farm the land and raise crops to keep their growing clan fed. Fortunately, they also had a very unique skillset developed throughout their family's bloodline that helped produce a desperately needed second stream of income throughout each year. The Kleinmarks had become regarded for their well-known reputation, and resulting word of mouth clientele, for producing the highest quality handmade furniture. With an extra special attention to detail, their hand-carved pieces were sought out far and wide by those who could afford the premium productions.

Adlar's father Emest, like his father and grandfather before him, knew that people would pay more for a solid quality product they could show off to their rich friends and neighbors. Whereas a lower cost, lessor quality finished product yielded virtually no advertisement or future business worth much profit. Plus, there were already plenty of cheaper products available, especially in the tough times of the late 1800s.

With that ever constant mindset, the Kleinmarks rarely, if ever, had to market their finished goods. Most were sold before they ever cut the first piece of wood. They could build virtually anything out of a good piece of solid, hard wood. From dining tables, chest of drawers, desks, bed frames, to cupboards, their productions could often be found in fine stately homes across the region. More than three generations of Kleinmark custom furniture had been sold throughout their Belgium homeland, Northern France, and Western Germany. The namesake brand had become synonymous for best in class fine furniture available anywhere throughout that part of Europe. The Kleinmark brand was simply stated on each piece as "Kleinmark Co." encircled by a thin, elegant oval.

Emest and his older brother, by two years, Evrard, along with their five older sisters, learned the same craftsmanship from their father, Jacob, and grandfather, also called Elias. However, their business model, employed throughout the late 1700s and early to mid-1800s, had fully relied on their clientele to come and seek them out at their homestead and workshop whenever a piece of furniture was needed. As a result the orders were consistently infrequent and usually resulted in only a few being received in any given year. Still, Emest and Evrard believed they could likely provide more for the family each year from the furniture business than the farm, if they could only make more furniture store owners aware of the Kleinmark premium craftsmanship brand. So the young brothers worked up a daring plan to generate more furniture business, but would first need to convince their elders for permission to pursue it.

Their creative plan was to travel around to established furniture stores in the populated towns and cities across the region and promote their wares and talents. They would take along several drawings and samples of different carvings and stains to generate interest from the owners of the larger furniture stores.

Much to the dismay of the wishful but leery elders, Evrard, then only nineteen, and his younger brother proved their great passion and determination by spending seven straight weeks during the winter of 1844 braving one of the harshest seasons the old men could recall in their lifetime. Enduring the brutal blizzard and difficult terrains, the boys visited dozens of furniture shops in the larger surrounding cities like Brussels, Rotterdam, Antwerp, Ghent, and Amsterdam across their region. To further stretch out their intended market reach, they also traveled as far away as Dusseldorf and Frankfort in Germany, and south into Luxembourg.

Their business model was simple. All the store proprietor had to do was send a letter requesting one of the boys to come and meet with the store's potential customer interested in buying fine furniture. As soon as a letter was received, the boys promised to be at the store in no less than three days to meet with the owner and their client. For any order received, the owner would be paid a twenty-five percent commission on the sale, based upon a fifty percent down payment and the final fifty percent due upon delivery of the furniture. The boys would also look any interested store owner in the eye and pledge their honor not to sell directly to any customer that the store owner had referred to the Kleinmarks, ever.

To the amazement of their elders, after just a single round of introducing the Kleinmark craftsmanship and commitment, the young men had created multiple new retail store clients that would change their family business model and sales volume forever. Throughout the few decades, the furniture business continued to flourish each year bringing increased profits from the expanded awareness and orders of the exceptional Kleinmark brand.

~~~~~~~~~~~~~

Adlar, like many children across Europe, had been stricken with cholera. While Adlar was more fortunate than so many, who had lost their lives to the pandemic, still his small, frail body had been significantly affected. As such, he would always have the lingering ramifications throughout the remainder of his life. Unlike his other six siblings, Adlar would never fully develop physically and would struggle with the long-term effects of muscle aches and a lack of stamina throughout his adult years. Constantly encouraged by his father, Emest, to overcome his physical frailties in other ways, Adlar looked to outperform his brother and sisters at everything he could. What his physicality restricted, his sheer resolve and ambition made up for.

Having a particular affinity for mathematics and business, Adlar would always be the first to help his father size up the exact amount of lumber and stain needed for a job, or the profit yield they could expect from their crops each season. Unlike his siblings, Adlar didn't need a pencil or paper to work out the equations. He could quickly do them in his head and always got them exactly correct, amazing his family.

Where Adlar excelled on the numerical side of things, his brother Helmutt, seven years his junior was just as uniquely skilled in the art of furniture design and craftsmanship. Even their father was amazed at how his youngest son had quickly become so proficient, more than himself or any other Kleinmark who'd come before. Helmutt was simply masterful by the time he reached twelve years of age at creating the most exquisitely beautiful, decorative custom carvings to elevate their family's brand way beyond its prior reputation.

All of the Kleinmark family could see that young Helmutt was in a class by himself. Merely requiring a simple conversation with a prospective furniture patron about how they envisioned a desired décor or motif, Helmutt could quickly sketch out a detailed drawing of the image. Using his natural skill and soft charm, Helmut's talent would always bring an instant smile to the customer's face as well as an immediate close to an order. Where his older, but smaller and frail, brother Adlar had the brain for business, young Helmutt grew into a tremendous strapping and muscle-bound lad who could chop down a tree as fast as any man, and carry twice as much timber to the mill compared to most.

As the boys continued to help work the farm and grow the furniture business with their father and Uncle Evrard, who had never married and always thought of the boys as his own, they not only learned both trades but also how to "hold their own" in doing so. Evrard and Emest both stood six foot and six inches tall. As well, they were as thick across and strong as hundred year old towering oak trees. The two huge men ran the large family farm and trade business with a tight grip and a hard reign just like their forefathers, while the boys learned right along their side, just as their own elders had before them. Like how to squeeze a yield out of a crop in a bad year and how to turn a raw piece of timber into a masterpiece.

They also learned that sometimes there were people who wouldn't think twice about trying to shortchange a man if not right out lie and cheat him out of what was rightfully his. Whenever such annoying situations developed around their tranquil homestead, the boys were never kept away from gaining a tough life lesson that sometimes had to be learned by some fool, stupid enough to wrong the Kleinmarks. The boys' father and uncle were never shy or secretive about having to deal with what they referred to as "an unfortunate circumstance."

This would usually occur whenever a customer refused to pay as promised or stupidly try to renegotiate a previously agreed-upon price for one of their custom wood-working masterpieces. Both young men could tell any number of countless stories witnessed firsthand about holding the horses' reins as their elders would beat the ever living hell out of some slow paying fool with whom they had lost patience. While the

Kleinmark men were usually mild mannered, neither were guilty of an unnecessary waste of words and above all considered themselves by all counts as honest, fair-minded people. But you could bet all calm, reason, and patience would go flying out the door once their last warning to pay up had been ignored.

While their collection methods didn't do much for repeat orders, the resulting one hundred percent effectiveness rate was an absolute damn certainty and would never be denied. It's funny how slugs always find the money to pay when they have the butt-end of a shotgun in their mouth. This would be another critical lesson etched early into the minds of Adlar and Helmutt, and like the rest of the Kleinmark legacy, one they'd go on to hand down as well.

~~~~~~~~~~~~

One such particular time involved a very wealthy farmer who owned and operated several thousand acres just south of Liege, about a four hour ride north of Vielsalm. As was their standard practice, they would take a half payment upfront for any custom furniture order, with the second half due upon delivery. Now, the Kleinmark men had also taught the boys that sometimes a customer may not have the full amount of cash due on hand at the very moment you deliver their new woodcraft, but as long as they brought it by an agreed-upon number of days later, then that was considered a simply, good business practice. However, anytime a customer didn't show as promised, finally causing the two elder men and boys to hitch up their wagon again and hunt them down, it was unlikely to go well if the late payment was not available when they arrived.

In the case of the wealthy farmer, only his wife had been home when the delivery was made, and the Kleinmark men fully understood that she would not have the remaining three hundred francs at her disposal to pay the balance. Most men then wouldn't permit the little wife to worry about such responsibilities. Nonetheless, she of course assured the men that her husband would immediately ride over the following day with the balance in full for their beautiful, new purchase. After another full week and a half had passed without any sign of the land baron, the frustrated elders and boys loaded up their wagon and shotguns and set out for the four hour ride north to the rich man's big estate.

This time the baron was home alright, sitting on his giant porch and smoking a big fat cigar, when the Kleinmarks rode up in front of the huge white two story mansion. Except now, unlike the friendly sort he'd been when they had all first met, this time the baron didn't show the slightest hospitality to invite the men and boys to step down from the wagon for a cool drink of water. Even though he could see how dirty and dusty they were from an obvious long drive in the wretched, hot summer heat.

Worse yet, the over-fed man gave them an immediate look of disdain though he had just met them a few months earlier after traveling to their homestead and shop in Vielsalm. It's pathetic how guiling and charming a man can be when he's trying to wrangle down the price for something his young beautiful wife must have. By now, Adlar and Helmutt, just thirteen and six, could already see the hardening look on their elder's faces as the rich man gazed down from his lofty porch, supported by six of the biggest columns they'd ever seen, each at least four feet in diameter.

Realizing the portly, rich bastard was making a very futile attempt to put them down, Evrard, usually being the one to at least attempt a peaceable resolution, carefully reminded him that they had not been paid in full over a week and a half since delivering the furniture. He also gently explained to the man how his wife had promised that the balance of the payment would be brought to them in Vielsalm the following day. Unfortunately, showing a snide grin, the haughty man made his first grave mistake, saying: "Why in the hell would I take my valuable time to ride all the way back down to your rat trap of a home and shop in Vielsalm to bring you my money? You both must be complete fools, and from the looks of things, it seems like those two boys are learning the same stupid lessons you are today, by coming uninvited to my home and saying such nonsense."

At that moment, both Emest and Evrard slowly stepped down off of their wagon, which immediately caused the man to almost fall backwards out of the rattan wicker rocking chair. Evrard, with his deep rich solemn tone, told the man, "Sir, you owe us another three hundred francs. That was the price we agreed to when you ordered your furniture. Now your wife was more than satisfied when we delivered it almost two weeks ago. So, just go get the money to pay us, and we'll be on our way." Then the rich man's second mistake was what he uttered next: "I don't give a shit what she said. I think that piece of crap you delivered here last week wasn't worth two hundred francs much less six hundred! I'll be damned if I'm paying you another cent more for it. Furthermore, if that's not good enough for you, then you can take that piece of shit back to your little shop and sell it to someone else!"

Before the obstinate man, now red-faced with eyes bulging, could get up out of that rocking chair, Emest was up on the porch with the back of the man's collar clutched as tight as death in the palm of his bear-claw like hand. In no time at all, Emest had leapt up the six steps, each two-foot deep, that led to the beautiful fifty-foot wide airy porch. Except the fat man wouldn't need the use of those granite stone steps to go down to get the ass-whooping he was about to unexpectedly receive. In a split second, Emest hurled the pudgy man about fifteen feet beyond the bottom step where Evrard was waiting with shotgun in hand. Using the butt of the gun and his entire might, which was considerable, Evrard drove the stock end of the weapon down like a jack-hammer until he heard the obnoxious man's left knee cap pop over and over again. When the idiot thought it a good idea to remind the men of just who he was exactly and how they would be sorry, Emest took a direct right kick to the man's mouth. Breaking out four of the man's front teeth, Emest said they'd heard enough of the man's yapping.

Screaming and rolling around in the dirt, the man painfully mumbled his willingness to pay what he owed, if they'd just let him go into the house to get his money. Now, this wasn't their first such episode and both elder Kleinmark men knew better than to let some fresh crippled victim come back out of his house with a blazing hot pistol pointed at them. So they told the man that they would either go in with him, or he could have his wife bring out the money. It turned out she had been standing and observing from the top right front window of the house the entire time as her foolish, tightwad of a husband finally got what was coming to him. And, when the frustrated man screamed harshly at his wife to bring down the money, Evrard dropped the gun's butt down on the man's other knee cap, telling him that none of this was her fault and to stop being so rude. In no uncertain terms, Evrard also instructed the man that their price had now gone up another fifty francs for all of the trouble and having to make a second trip to collect it. Then Emest chimed in reminding the man how none of it would have been necessary had he just done the right thing a week earlier and brought them the final payment as promised.

With their three hundred and fifty francs in hand, the elders got back into their wagon and slowly pulled away, leaving the man, writhing in agony, in the dirt. As the wagon pulled away, neither boy said a word, simply smiling proudly at how their elders had so effectively handled the stupid baron. It was a good lesson learned, and one they'd later deploy many times.

~~~~~~~~~~~

As the years passed, their father and uncle knew that Adlar and Helmutt had become highly capable young men, and able to ensure the Kleinmark family traditions and brand would continue to do very well during their own tenure of responsibility. That is, if they could survive the unending depressed economy that plagued all of Europe. As it was, it had become increasingly tougher and tougher each year to survive, and Emest and Evrard knew something must change as they grew older.

By the time 1889 arrived, Emest and Evrard had finally come to admit that things were unlikely to improve in their homeland to such a point that would allow their large family to survive, by merely farming and trying to maintain their craftsman's trade. Crops were as barren as ever thanks to the annual draughts their homeland seemed to endlessly endure. Because of the economy remaining so weak, especially due to failing banks, the furniture business had also slowed down significantly.

Evrard and Emest carefully studied all available news reports about the rampant growth in the new America. They sought out the best possible counsel from some of the wealthier furniture patrons who would likely be well-informed in such matters. Then the senior Kleinmark men reached a conclusion that would change the course of this family's trademark history forever. As daring as they had been back in the winter of 1844, both now agreed that one of Emest's sons should immigrate to the new land of America and begin building the family's furniture business in the new frontier. From their best research efforts, all reports showed the American economy had been growing by leaps and bounds for several decades at that point and promised no signs of slowing. They knew how each of Emest's sons had their own strengths and decided to engage them both in the matter.

By now, Adlar was almost thirty years of age and had his own family of five, who too struggled daily on the farm and worked in the furniture business when the work came in. Almost twice Adlar's size, and a strapping lad of twenty-three years, Helmutt was still single and did much of the heavy work on the farm as well around the furniture mill and shop.

It was a perplexing dilemma for the aging Kleinmark elders, now seventy-two and seventy-four, but both still with sound minds and strong bodies to hopefully work the farm and furniture business for yet several more years. Emest knew Adlar would be the best candidate to build and navigate the development of a new business practice. Although he feared asking so much of his oldest son to leave his family, plus the physical demands of simply traveling to America, much less all of the hard work and endurance that would be demanded, was simply too great to ask or expect.

Whereas Helmutt was younger, he was certainly not too young and undoubtedly would want to step up to the exciting, adventuresome task. Still they knew, he did so much in terms of the hard, difficult work around the farm and shop that Emest feared the rest of his family would be impacted if he was to leave them full-time. Rather than force a decision, Emest decided to discuss the matter openly with his sons, who both had long talked about and imagined just how amazing the reported new life must be in the place called America.

Not surprising to Emest or Evrard, both Adlar and Helmutt had the same overall assessment and concerns for the family's situation at home as well as the prospects of an expansion to America. While their father and uncle had worried about taxing the young men with such a heavy consideration, they were still so proud of how the boys methodically deduced the situation, just as they had, and came up with a conclusive plan to be set in motion immediately. It was decided that Adlar would remain at home in Belgium and that Helmutt would go to explore potential growth and success in the new land for the Kleinmark family.

All four men would together devise a detailed business plan that outlined how Helmutt would approach developing an expanded furniture market, as well as the financial details required to fund such a venture. Over the following six months, the Kleinmark men would work out every possible detail they could think of in terms of setting up Helmutt, and ultimately their entire family, for success once he arrived in the new land. Presuming their furniture quality craftsmanship would be just as highly regarded in America as it had become over time throughout their part of Europe, all of the Kleinmark men were both nervous and excited to see what the future held for their family and brand.

By the time the year came to an end, the men had worked harder than ever before and were finally able to set aside the equivalent of three thousand American dollars in cash to fund the venture. This included Helmutt's travel expenses and funds to open up a new shop one day. They also made two dozen detailed, sample-sized carvings in various stain colors along with dozens of different furniture drawings for Helmutt to use as he visited furniture stores in the larger towns throughout the Eastern coast of the new United States, showing the unique capabilities of Kleinmark quality furniture. The remaining biggest challenge for Helmutt would be splitting his time traveling around to introduce their trade and custom expertise, as well as having time to actually build the furniture as soon as orders were procured. Clearly he was going to need to hire some help once he got settled in the new land. The biggest unknown still remaining was exactly how and where Helmutt would begin to learn about the new country. He would need to find his way around to locate the larger furniture stores serving the wealthier clientele. They knew they would need to somehow gather this information, but the news reporting in their area was more on the politics and economy of Europe, not America.

~~~~~~~~~~~~~

One of the Kleinmark's best furniture clients was an area physician and his wife from a nearby town, about halfway between Vielsalm and Liege. The Kleinmarks had gotten to know Dr. Desmet and his wife well, after Adlar had been stricken with cholera as a child. The Desmet's had been unable to have children of their own, and over time Mrs. Desmet had come to truly love the Kleinmark's children, especially their youngest, Helmutt. For some reason, lady Desmet felt a special bond with Helmutt and seemed to buy more and more furniture just so her visits to the Kleinmark home could be justifiably more frequent. Feeling great personal empathy for the sweet young bride of the doctor, Ernest's wife often allowed her youngest boy to go and spend a day with the gentle lady whom she knew longed to love a child. Helmutt's visits to the home of Dr. and Mrs. Desmet became increasingly regular from the time he was almost five years old until the age of ten, when his father felt he needed to start working more at their family's farm and workshop.

Mrs. Desmet was from England and attended London University studying the arts. She had met her husband as he studied medicine at the affiliated London Hospital College. This talented and creative woman would teach her native English and love of drawing to the beloved young Helmutt during their precious time together over those five years. As it would be, the life changing lessons Lady Desmet taught young Helmutt would prove to serve the future of the Kleinmark family legacy in meaningful ways that no one could have ever realized.

Years later as the Kleinmark men contemplated their new world venture, Dr. and Mrs. Desmet happened to stop by unannounced one day to check on a new custom dining room suit she had ordered months earlier. The friendly wealthy couple, who were always so open and sharing, told of how they had spent the prior two months traveling abroad to visit the land called America. They told stories of the big, new, bustling cities like New York and Philadelphia. The elder Kleinmarks thought it must be good fate indeed that their longtime clients and friends had just recently visited the new great land and had showed up at that very moment to speak of it all.

As the Kleinmarks shared the news of their family's venturesome plan, the Doctor and Lady became genuinely interested and offered to help in any way possible. Thankfully, they had brought back a copy of a very detailed map of the new land, as well as several current newspapers from the cities they had visited during their stay. They were only too happy to lend all of the materials to help their longtime friends prepare in any way. As it would turn out, the information from the map and those newspaper articles, about the growing land and population explosion in various cities, would prove to make a huge positive impact for the preliminary planning of the Kleinmark westward expansion.

Trying to absorb every possible relevant detail they could as part of their due diligence, Helmut read aloud all of the newspapers numerous times front to back to his brother and elders, who all helped making notes of specific growth markets and population information. The papers were from several different booming American cities, like New York, Buffalo, Pittsburg, Chicago, Philadelphia, Baltimore, and Cleveland where the Desmet's had visited during their circuitous two months-long hiatus.

From their in-depth studies, the Kleinmark men discerned that more than ten million people populated the upper Northeast portion of the new land and how it may be a good place for Helmutt to begin his initial exploration of the potential market. The more encouraging news was just how fast each town and community across the entire new land was growing at a faster rate than most cities could keep up with. Especially after the completion of the great Transcontinental Railroad twenty years earlier, it became far easier and more efficient to move people and goods all over the new great land.

After all their planning and saving, Helmutt would be ready to embark on the family's exciting new venture in the early spring of the next year, 1890.

After saying last goodbyes to his mother and sisters, the day had finally come for Helmutt to leave home for what they all knew might well be his last. The time had arrived for the family's great American adventure to be set in motion. So, the four Kleinmark men traveled three full days to transport young Helmutt and his two large black duffle bags, one full of his personal items and the other stuffed with samples and drawings, in their delivery wagon to the port city of Vlissingen, in their beloved Belgium. Although few words were actually uttered by the proud, stoic men from Vielsalm, watery eyes and repeated bear hugs for their beloved Helmutt were freely shared.

Reminding once more, as they had done many times over the prior weeks, the elders forewarned Helmutt about the harsh realities that they'd had also read about in the newspapers. How New York City especially was already riddled with crime as would be crooks and gangs from all over the world had also made their way there to capitalize on the new frontier. Finally with added special emphasis, they stressed to Helmutt to be always careful with the large sum of money he was carrying, and never to let anyone ever see his cash or even hear of it. The elders reminded the young man of how they had tried to teach the boys that the world is full of slugs who would try to take advantage in any way possible. All of these things would prove to be true in the new land, as Helmut would dreadfully learn.

Finally, they were prayerful as they left the young lad dockside, unsure of how their great plan would work out. It was indeed such a grave risk and one they had put all the family's savings into. Still it was one that they all felt was required and worth taking. Perhaps it would prove to be too much, but Helmutt assured his loving father, brother, and uncle that he would do his best to make them all proud. The agreement was that he would write a letter home as soon as he landed ashore in America and then at least once per month while he explored the new country and executed the detailed plan they had all developed.

Helmutt never took his watery eyes off of his family or the wagon for as long as he could still see even a small glimmer of it in the distance. He never let on just how scared he was to leave his home by himself and go somewhere so unknown and far away from his family. Helmutt knew that they all needed and were counting on him to be successful, and though he was unsure how it would all go, he knew failing was not an option.

Sailing to the place called New York on the Amsterdam Holland America line was expected to take about six days. Along the way, Helmutt's fears and anxieties were somewhat calmed as he met and spoke with countless others who were literally in the same boat as him. Leaving loving ones behind for a new beginning of hopeful dreams was a very common thread seemingly shared among the folks he met. Learning this gave Helmutt a peaceful calm inside. It was reassuring to meet and talk with others about how this place called America welcomed all people courageous enough to embrace her shores and work hard for their place in the sun. Helmutt knew his family had raised him to work hard, plus he had the prospects of promoting the tremendous Kleinmark furniture brand. He was clear-minded on their strategic mission and how he was to go about introducing their company and working to gain customers, just as his family had for centuries.

From the newspapers they had studied so many times, New York had already grown to a population of more than one and a half million by the time Helmutt set sail. While the city's size was only one-fourth of the Brussels population at the time, the obvious difference to the Kleinmarks was that so many new homes and buildings were being built at such a fast pace in America. So, the Kleinmark men figured that several successful furniture stores already existed for Helmutt to call on as soon as he got settled from his voyage. As well, the same explosive phenomenon was similarly occurring in most other cities throughout the new land. One thing was certain, the market potential was real, and now young Helmutt would have to recall the stories of his father and uncle's marketing skills they employed to pull in more orders from surrounding furniture stores in their homeland. The more Helmutt reviewed the plans, samples, and drawings, the more excited he became about beginning the work and finding his first customers in America.

Once Helmutt landed in New York, he immediately set out to find the hotel recommended by the doctor's wife who had so kindly lent his family the map and newspapers. Knowing how much of a penny pincher her husband was, she assured the Kleinmarks of two things about the hotel her husband had picked during their stay in the big, bustling city. It would be sufficiently clean and, by all means, the cheapest in a safe part of town. So that's where Helmutt headed to make his first base camp and plan a route of attack around town over the upcoming weeks to promote the Kleinmark Co. The following Sunday, his first day on dry land in a week, would be used to get his bearings and to find an up to date map of sprawling New York City. Also as promised to his mother, he would mail the first letter home to let them know of his safe arrival and share all the interesting stories of the people he'd met on the voyage to America. True to his word about writing to his mother, her young lad would only write of the wonderful people and stories he'd heard on the huge ship, but would say nothing of already being so homesick and afraid.

In his second week away, young Helmutt quickly learned many things about New York. Especially how tens of thousands of immigrants from so many different countries all over the world were still coming there in droves to create their own new beginning. He would also learn how people from those different countries were informally settling into different ethnic pockets around the city, which was essentially one big island. Understanding how the city was formed and connected helped Helmutt to traverse and make acquaintances with certain store owners who in some cases could help direct him to others who might be a potential prospect for him.

After his first week of going around New York, Helmutt located and met almost two dozen different furniture store operators. But unfortunately, only one or two of them had any interest whatsoever in a product line as upscale as Kleinmark Co. The typical education that the young Helmutt received was how the vast majority of their customers were poor immigrants who simply couldn't afford fine furniture. In the case of the upper crust class, such as bankers, doctors, and big business tycoons, while there was some potential interest for fine furniture, there were also many existing competitors already located around the city that had an established reputation. So getting into the high-end furniture market would be more difficult unless a particular patron happened to already be familiar with the Kleinmark brand out of Europe.

After spending the following two weeks traveling around the rest of New York and upper New Jersey, Helmutt continued to hear the repeated message of challenge and disappointment. He feared the next letter home about their business prospects would not have a great deal of good news unless there was a positive development soon, other than he was still alive. Helmutt knew that he must work harder to find good markets for their brand. One thing he had learned in all of his visits so far was that the market for fine furniture did exist, but also he would need to find areas where the competition was less entrenched. That would be the only bit of good news with honest, encouraging hope in the letter that was mailed as promised, exactly thirty days since he left the loving family he already missed so much.

The second letter that Helmutt eventually sent home would finally have some encouraging words of hope and potential for his family back home in Vielsalm. Over the course of his second month promoting the Kleinmark Co. brand and assessing the market potential, he began to develop a better understanding of the various types of stores and brands of products that were available in the New York. Helmutt became increasingly confident when he talked about the Kleinmark brand and convincingly shared why it would be beneficial for any particular store owner to promote the product's top quality attributes to his patrons. But, he also began to learn that many store owners were themselves fine craftsmen of very nice furniture, and how they had been in the business of furniture-making before emigrating from their own countries. The densely populated New York and New Jersey markets had caused some to choose between either manufacturing or selling, and the fact was there were already a great many providers addressing the available market. After encountering these challenges firsthand for two straight months, Helmutt wondered if he and his family had underestimated the potential interest for such a high quality brand like their beloved Kleinmark Co.

~~~~~~~~~~~~~

The real difference that helped Helmutt was eventually expanding his search beyond the New York and New Jersey areas that were already so big and overwhelmed with any number of offerings for most products, including finer furniture. Thanks to one very special store owner who emigrated from Italy in the past year and had already learned a great deal about the furniture business in the new huge city, the new young salesman was offered some advice that would set Kleinmark Co. up for its eventual success.

The man who had taken such a liking to Helmutt suggested that he should stop wasting his time in the highly competitive New York, New Jersey areas and get out to smaller towns that hadn't grown out of control yet. The man Helmutt would always refer to as "my very dear friend, Mr. Luigi" said, "start with Philadelphia and Baltimore, they're big yes, but not like here. Explore places like Buffalo, Rochester, and the Syracuse area; then go over to Pittsburgh and on up into the newer Northern Ohio towns such as Cleveland and Columbus. Even Detroit is growing and may be a good potential market for you Helmutt!" Everything Mr. Luigi said reaffirmed the plan that the Kleinmarks had actually devised, with the exception of New York which would not be the best place to start, and maybe wouldn't even work at all. At least until they got a foothold with their brand elsewhere in the new country.

As his family read Helmutt's second letter, now three months after leaving home, their emotions were mixed and anxious. The realization set in that Helmutt was finding bigger challenges than they had all anticipated. They had thought and hoped with all of the money and people in the New York area, surely a brand like theirs would have surely been well received. They had not expected to face such competitive challenges from so many other fine furniture makers that Helmutt wrote about who had also emigrated from so many other places. Now all the family could do was pray for their Helmutt, hope that Mr. Luigi's counsel was honest and accurate, and again wait for his next letter to come.

~~~~~~~~~~

GREAT AMERICAN

Helmutt had always heeded the repeated forewarnings of his elders to be ever vigilant about the large sum of money he was carrying. He knew well from all the times he'd watched his father and uncle brutally deal with unsavory characters, who wouldn't think twice about trying to steal or lie about their money, so an automatic caution was wired into him. For the first two months he had been extremely cautious and frugal as possible. But now unsure of when he might ever go to back to New York, unless it was to sail home as a failure, Helmutt decided to convert the rest of the Belgium francs into U.S. dollars to fund his future explorations.

Going back to the portside bank, where he'd first landed and converted an initial fifty francs, Helmutt waited cautiously for a free banker to speak with about converting the rest of his francs. Sadly it turned out what seemed to be a very formal and proper bank and banker was anything but. As soon as the seemingly upstanding gentleman with the tiny, silver wire-rimmed spectacles preening over his nose said goodbye to the young Dutchman, now carrying almost two thousand, nine hundred American dollars, his deceitful character went into motion. Immediately, as soon as Helmutt left the bank's front door had the banker whisked to the back one and began describing his last patron's red plaid shirt, goldenrod pants, dark brown fedora, and calf-high brown leather boots. Barely making it across the street, two huge thugs were already following

Helmutt with the large black duffle bags full of all of his possessions and money strapped across his back.

On his way to search out a quality livery and buy a good horse for his upcoming travels, Helmutt had no idea that he was about to be jumped by the two crooked goons who worked for the scheming banker. As soon as Helmutt wandered off the main street and down an alleyway to cut over to the next thoroughfare, the two thugs snuck up from behind with their pistols in hand and knocked Helmutt almost completely unconscious, grabbing the two duffle bags with everything he owned inside.

However, what they hadn't noticed at the very moment of their cowardly attack was that a huge black man had just ventured into the alley as well, coming right up behind them. Instinctively turning to race back in the direction of the bank to split the loot, the robbers immediately began to run at full speed without realizing the giant man was standing there blocking their path. Having seen everything that had just happened in the previous split second, the big man, who'd been accustomed to his own past beatings as a little boy, grabbed both men to slow them down, snatching away the duffle bags and slinging them towards a groaning Helmutt. True to their nature, the thugs quickly moved to surround the black man on both sides to take him down with their mightiest blows to his face and back. Except, nothing seemed to faze the enormous man, who with just one blow to their faces knocked each of his foes completely unconscious and down into the dirt.

His blurred vision hadn't kept a very groggy Helmutt from seeing just what this man had so quickly done to the men, as he reached out trying to pull the duffle bags to his side. Just like that, Helmutt realized that he had been so stupid and careless, putting everything at risk by converting all of the money at once. Hearing those fateful words from his elders in his head, he now knew that he needed to be far more careful with his family's money and not let anyone ever know how much he was carrying. Helping Helmutt to his feet, the man who seemed larger than life, showed more concern and empathy than Helmutt had felt since leaving home, except perhaps for Mr. Luigi. Wanting to show his gratitude, Helmutt asked the man if he could buy him a cup of coffee to say thank you, plus he needed to sit down for a spell and clear his head. With as big of a smile possible, the man said, "Oh yes, yes sir, I just love some good, hot coffee!" The man knew of a place not too far away that had really good coffee and helped prop up Helmutt, still pretty foggy-headed from the forceful blows he'd taken. "My given name is Isaac Samuelson, but I guess you can see why everybody just calls me Big Sam.", said Helmutt's unexpected new ally.

~~~~~~~~~~~~~

For the next hour, Big Sam told Helmutt of how his father and mother had grown up on a cotton plantation in the Deep South, but escaped in the late 1840's by the Underground Railroad, which Helmutt had never heard of until then. Big Sam told Helmutt how his parents had come as far north as possible to escape slavery and was proud to say that he'd been born a free man. With a smile as broad as his shoulders, he educated

116

Helmutt on how he'd grown up poor but happy thanks to a farmer with a huge spread just west of Newark, New Jersey.

Big Sam went on to share that after his parents had died on the farm, as had his wife a couple of years back, and how he decided to leave and go into New York City to find different work using his strength and might, plus get away from all of his sad memories. Still, while Big Sam could do the work of at least two regular men, he routinely found that so many employers would often take advantage of a black man, by not paying equal wages and often cheating them out of what they'd earned. For a black man in 1890, even a free one, it wouldn't go well with the authorities if he ever used force to take what was rightfully his. If a black man ever tried to exert his own justice, he'd surely get arrested or much worse. So Big Sam would just always opt to move on to the next job, without the money he'd honestly earned and needed to survive.

As fate would have it that very day, Big Sam had been out looking for his next job when he'd turned down that dirty alleyway and saved his new young friend. Helmutt was struck with how open and honest Big Sam was and felt an immediate kinship to the man who had surely saved him, as well his family's hope for a new future. After their third cup of steaming hot coffee, Helmutt told Big Sam about his wonderful family back in Belgium. Helmut even got a bit misty eyed, as Big Sam could see, while he talked of his family's history, including the ancient stories back to Elias Klein, and hopeful future for the Kleinmark brand of fine furniture. The big man was in awe of how brave his new Dutch friend was to come all by himself to a

117

strange new big place, and with such awesome responsibility. As such encounters often go, the two men, who became instantly bonded in a dark alleyway, seemed to sense that perhaps they had been destined to meet.

~~~~~~~~~~~~~~~~

Whether out of obligation or a new found awareness of his exposed risk, Helmutt asked Big Sam if he knew of the towns that Mr. Luigi had recommended. Though not all, Big Sam had been as far north as Rochester and Buffalo, where his former employer's wife had family and sometimes visited. Big Sam would go along to help drive the mule team and of course protect them from any would be bandits along the way. He told Helmutt about one time when three masked men had rode up on their carriage with guns drawn and firing, supposedly to rob them, when the farmer shot one down off his horse and how he had himself quickly shot the other two with a shotgun. Big Sam said that was the first time he'd ever dug a hole and buried a man before. He also went on to say, it wasn't the last time either.

Big Sam also spoke about going to Pittsburgh a few times when the farmer took some of his beef cows to market because of better prices being offered. Helmutt was very pleased to hear of Big Sam's knowledge of the local lands and his skills at self-protection. But it was the hole digging that gave Helmutt the same comfortable sense of being with his elders, and he knew that meeting Big Sam had been fortuitous indeed.

Big Sam's bright, beaming smile seemed to light up the whole world when Helmutt asked him if he'd like to go along, as he explored all the new cities on the list and looked for new

118

possible furniture clients. Helmutt told Big Sam that he couldn't promise anything for sure, but he that could pay fifty dollars up front if Big Sam would spend the next month traveling around with him. Helmut had never before felt like a small man by any stretch, since having the same stature and build of his father and uncle. But now, his own sense of size seemed instantly dwarfed when his hand disappeared into Big Sam's as the two men shook hands for the first time. Both were delighted about the new arrangement. Big Sam had never held fifty dollars before, at least not all at one time. As for Helmutt, he had never felt safer since leaving home than he did now with his new companion.

After a much safer walk over to the livery and picking out two good quality horses, the men went by the shabby, old tenement building where Big Sam had been staying to collect the very few items he owned. The two men were ready to set out for the first of the cities on the list suggested by Mr. Luigi.

~~~~~~~~~~~

Finally, some good news developed for Helmutt. The visits in Philadelphia produced a couple of interested client prospects with store owners, who like most all others made their own furniture. Although, in both cases, what they were used to producing was more basic in design and they didn't have the expertise on the finer end of design and wood crafting. Much to his delight, both stores were interested to do business with Helmutt, if and when an opportunity developed, and of course once he was established with a shop and address so they could reach him. Going up north to Rochester, Syracuse, and Buffalo, a couple more owners took similar interest and promised to contact him with a telegraph message, once Helmutt got settled and let them know where to send the messages.

Thankfully, as the third letter home would proudly report, it was the next two weeks of his travels in America where everything changed for their Helmutt and the family back in Belgium. With his new friend and traveling companion, Helmutt could now report how fortune had finally smiled on the Kleinmark Co. For no sooner had they arrived into the town called Cleveland, had a wealthy woman shopping in one of the stores overheard Helmutt telling the owner about his family's fine furniture brand and asked to see his carving samples. Though he couldn't believe his ears, this wonderful lady said she had never seen such quality hand carvings and how she loved the "absolute silky smooth finish on the wood." She said, gently caressing the sample, "It's as smooth and soft as a rose petal!" Helmut could imagine no better advertisement to the shop owner than to have one of his own customers rave about the distinctive Kleinmark quality, especially having never seen it before.

After walking the lady and the very suspect shop owner through all of the different drawings of furniture that Helmutt and his family had designed over the centuries, the lady, who was of obvious fine etiquette, expressed her firm interest to order a set of brand new matching chifferobes for her and her husband's bedroom. Accordingly the woman instructed the shopkeeper to make the necessary arrangements with his "new young salesman", never once inquiring about price or cost. As the store owner would later explain, any mention or inquiry of money was below the status and dignity of the woman, who just happened to be one of his most prominent patrons.

Understandably, the store owner was nervous about his new, unknown supplier. As well, he was absolutely uninterested in Helmutt's typical fifty percent down and fifty percent due upon delivery terms. No way was the store owner paying anything upfront to someone he'd just met. Also assuring to Helmutt, how the very kind wealthy lady, being his best customer, "would certainly not be asked for a deposit!" The only good news was that the shop owner had agreed to Helmutt's proposed price for the chifferobes as well as a twenty-five percent commission.

With the upfront negotiations finally settled, Helmutt had a big decision to make if he wanted the order. He would have to agree to make the furniture and deliver it to the store owner, while assuming all of the upfront cost and risks of getting paid; which of course was exactly what he would do. After all, he could now report his first sale and the first new American account in his next letter home, although he would leave out the part about the financial risk.

~~~~~~~~~~

As it goes with sales people who are burning both ends of the candle looking for new order opportunities, Helmutt had similar experiences with store owners when he first visited Columbus and Pittsburgh. While in both new cities introducing his brand, store owners had agreed to take Helmutt, and the ever present Big Sam, out to see a couple of their best high-end furniture clients. Miraculously it turned out in both cases, the two stores had been losing business to other competitors who offered their own "fine furniture" line and wanted to regain interest with some particularly wealthy customers. After hearing Helmutt's presentation on Kleinmark workmanship, both store owners became convinced that a trip to see some special customers would be worth the effort.

After the experience in Cleveland, a fast-learning Helmutt carefully planted seeds in both retailers' minds of either bringing their best customers into the store for a private demonstration or even going to see them at their homes. This was of course only whenever Helmutt confirmed neither shopkeeper had their own so-called high-end line. Both times his approach worked like magic, resulting in an ecstatic Helmutt and Big Sam having two more orders to hang their hats on. Incredibly, all three orders had transpired in little over a week, so the timing couldn't have been more perfect.

~~~~~~~~~~~~

Sitting in downtown Pittsburg at the end of their fourth straight week on the road having a hot cup of celebratory coffee, Helmutt and Big Sam realized now that all they had to do was build the furniture and record the first sales for the Kleinmark Co. in America. Helmutt knew that meant they must quickly find some land with a good shop or barn, which needed to be situated close by a stream or river for water like back home. They would also need to source the proper woodworking tools, like saws, planes, hammers and the such, plus stains, and of course, some premium hardwood timber stock.

All of sudden, their smiles turned to more discerned, serious looks as the gravity of everything needing to be accomplished quickly set in. But still, they simply couldn't hide their exuberance about their recent success. The men realized how their eventful short time together had indeed been successful, and that it was surely something to be so proud of for both of them. Now, they couldn't wait to get started!

~~~~~~~~~~~~~

Bright and early the next morning, the two men went in search of a good oversized, reliable wagon suitable for hauling timber and furniture. Once they located the wagon, Helmutt and Big Sam sought out the local land office in Pittsburgh. Helmutt's thought was Pittsburgh might be the most central location for the shop location of Kleinmark Co. in America. It would allow them to reasonably service both Columbus and Cleveland, but also provide similar access to the Northern cities in upstate New York they had visited. As well, Pittsburgh was close to Philadelphia where some of the preliminary interest in Kleinmark furniture had been expressed earlier in the month.

For the next two days using the information about available land for sale posted in the land office, the two men visited the owners of each parcel of land that met their basic criteria of a sturdy building and access to water. Much to their dimay, in each case, the land was far more expensive than what the Kleinmark men had planned for, or that Helmutt knew he could afford. Going back to the land office for some advice and guidance, Helmutt and Big Sam would learn that, for what they were looking to spend, it was unlikely they'd be able to find anything around Pittsburg. Especially given how the city was booming and land prices seemed to be going up every day. Fortunately, the land office manager, understanding Helmutt's situation, suggested they needed to consider farm land much farther out from Pittsburg, where land was much cheaper. Perhaps down in West Virginia to the South, or over in Ohio to the west. Since their first three fortuitous orders had come from the triangle area of Columbus, Cleveland, and Pittsburgh, the new American furniture makers elected to look westward in Ohio but closer to the Pennsylvania border if possible.

~~~~~~~~~~~~~~~

Big Sam remembered a particular spot where they had bedded down one night when they traveled from Columbus to Pittsburgh. He had taken note of it because he'd grown up hearing his parents talk about the area being part of the Underground Railroad and how there had long been a safe house around the little Ohio town for years. All of which simply continued to fascinate young Helmutt.

Back then the little village was called Nebo, but Big Sam knew it was the same place for sure from the vibrant memories of what his parents had shared. Helmutt remembered the place too as Big Sam recalled one particular parcel they had seen for sale. It was in a fairly new town now called Bergholz, where they had camped along the banks of Yellow Creek. They remembered that Bergholz was a really small town and how they had learned while passing through that it had really only been built thanks to a mining company that wanted railroad access to a new mine in the area. Helmutt had also taken particular note of

124

the Northeastern Ohio area and how for some reason it reminded him of his beloved Vielsalm. He recalled how the Yellow Creek cut and flowed around Bergholz so familiarly like the rivers and creeks that ran through his Vielsalm. And how the big beautiful Ohio River they ferried across into Pennsylvania had made him reminisce of the grand Meuse River that dissected his beloved Belgium.

Figuring Bergholz would only be about one day's wagon ride to Pittsburg, where they could get most of the routine supplies that would be needed, and no more than two days to either Cleveland or Columbus, both men agreed that they would go back to check on the land they had seen for sale.

~~~~~~~~~~~~~~

As Helmutt's entire family continued reading the third flowing letter full of the incredible good news they had been hoping for, of course now a month after the fact, Helmutt had already purchased the small fifty acre farm in Bergholz. The land included two sturdy barns and truly wonderful access to Yellow Creek. The small, frail, ninety-two year old widow who sold Helmutt the land reminded him of his own grandmother back home in Vielsalm. Sadly, she said, it was time for her to move up to the south side of Canton and live with her younger seventy-eight year old sister and brother-in-law, a retired judge, who now farmed full-time and ran a huge hog rendering operation. Since her own husband of more than seventy-six years passed away earlier in the year, she could simply no longer work the farm and care for it on her own. Telling Helmutt, "It's been real good land for us all these years and I know it will be for you too young man, if you treat her right."

At that moment, Helmutt and Big Sam knew it was indeed the perfect place. Helmutt's family was so happy to finally have a permanent address for their Helmutt which would allow them to write him letters from home. They knew that Helmutt must surely be missing everyone so much and wondering what had been happening with his family back home. Now they could keep up regular two-way correspondence with him and at least feel connected in that way.

~~~~~~~~~~~~

Now that Helmutt and Big Sam had a place to operate, they hitched the wagon before the sun was up the following Monday morning and headed back to Pittsburgh to buy all of their supplies. Along the way, they would inquire about procuring some premium hardwood lumber for their first orders. Also while in town, like any smart salesman, Helmutt would circle back to all of the furniture stores he'd visited to let them know of Kleinmark Co.'s new official location and especially of their new orders! He would also send wires to all of the other customers he'd met on their routes over the prior month to advise of the same, and to request any order interests for the future. By the end of the day that Wednesday, the two men were back in Bergholz and ready to get to work building their first orders.

Over the next three weeks, Helmutt and Big Sam worked eighteen hour days, seven days a week to get the shop in initial working order and the new furniture work started. Since Big

Sam knew nothing of furniture making, Helmutt entrusted him with setting up the shop with proper direction, cutting timber to spec, and everything else that didn't require technical expertise. Like any busy operation, there was plenty to keep his big friend and protector busy.

For Helmutt, he quickly realized how he had missed the art and craft of making furniture. Most of all, he missed the actual work and feel of lumber in his hands. Simply smelling the fresh cut wood made him dearly miss his family. After all, it had been a part of him since he could ever remember. He knew more than anything that his first pieces had to be better than perfect, not just for the pride of his family's legacy, but more realistically because of how future orders would be hinged on how these first pieces would be received. It also dawned on him, that he and Big Sam could take the newly finished pieces and revisit all the other store owners who had shown some interest before, or not, but didn't have a fine furniture line. This way they could promote Kleinmark premium quality craftsmanship when they went back into each market delivering their first completed orders. This would become standard operating procedure for every future delivery, thus sparking countless other future orders and renewed interest with shop owners.

With the usual process of making fine furniture to Kleinmark standards, Helmutt knew that it would be, at minimum, a few months before their first orders were ready for delivery, and that was if everything went according to plan with working eighteen hour days. The manufacturing process required that one of them would have to sleep in the shop each night and keep the fire going to regulate the temperature so the stain dried faster than it would otherwise. Given how cold it still was near the end of their first April, not doing so would mean many more weeks before the first orders were ready for delivery. Before the break of each new day, both men started up the new American Kleinmark Co. workshop and gave very careful attention to their craft.

~~~~~~~~~~~~

By the end of May, Helmutt would send each store owner a telegraph from the local rail station to advise them of his progress and expected delivery within the next three weeks or so. However when he gave the Bergholz telegraph clerk the name of the store and owner in Cleveland, the older mustached gentleman suddenly realized that a telegraph had been received from a man by the same name two days earlier. The telegraph for Helmutt had been marked "Urgent, Please Read & Respond Immediately!" Regrettably, the note had simply gotten set aside, and consequently, no one realized to notify Helmutt or to take it out to the new Kleinmark Co. farm at Yellow Creek.

Upon reading the note, Helmutt realized that the husband of the fine lady from the Cleveland store, who had overheard him talking about the furniture and asked to see the sample carvings, had tragically lost her husband to a fall from his horse two days earlier. The note simply asked Helmutt to please come back to the man's store in Cleveland at once and to please advise immediately if doing so would be possible. Hearing Helmutt read the note aloud and realizing that it had now been two days since the note came in and three since the man's

128

passing, the old telegraph clerk offered to send an urgent response "at no charge of course", feeling terrible about forgetting to have the first one delivered. They would send the urgent note back over the wires to Cleveland and ask the telegraph office clerk located there to urgently rush it to the store owner and then to please respond back quickly if Helmutt was still needed. Within less than five minutes, the Cleveland clerk tapped out the simple reply, "Yes please come at once if you can, advise if not." Helmutt had the Bergholz line clerk send back the simple confirmation of "Just got your note today and on my way!"

As history would record, the marveled telegraph invention would send and receive messages across America over sixty million times in 1890, up more than ten-fold compared to just thirty years earlier in time. But those three simple telegraph messages in the old clerk's shaky scribble, and sadly never saved, would document the very essence and beginning of what would change the course of history in America for the Kleinmarks, and ultimately the entire funeral industry.

Rushing back to the shop with quick and careful instructions for Big Sam, who would now have to handle the delicate hand sanding and applying the next layers of stain and varnish to the furniture in its final stages, Helmutt knew in his heart that leaving now posed such a huge risk for their first orders, but that he still must go. What Helmutt hadn't realized was how Big Sam had been paying such careful attention to everything that his young new boss had been doing at every step in the process of building the beautiful furniture. Especially, he had been watching carefully as Helmutt hand-sanded the wood from its rough first state over and over again to create the smoothest pieces of wood he'd ever seen in his life. Though an uneducated man, Big Sam realized that he was witnessing art being created. So then, while Big Sam took his turn spending nights in the shop, he also began to practice Helmutt's craftsman techniques by working with scrap pieces of wood, although never saying anything to his new boss and friend.

Seeing the grave look on Helmut's face, the big man knew now was not a time to panic and that his friend needed his help now more than ever, and he would not let him down. Although Helmutt wouldn't be at the shop, his big friend would care for the furniture as if it were a brand new baby trusted in his sole care. Thanks to all of his desire to learn and practice, Big Sam quickly developed his own artful technique of caressing each board with the softest of strokes. All of Helmutt's concerns for their future sales would be quickly alleviated when he would return from Cleveland to see that each piece had not only progressed as needed, but that Big Sam's delicate touch with the finest of sanding papers was as good as Helmutt had ever seen, even from the legacy of Kleinmark. Helmutt felt that God had absolutely smiled on Kleinmark that day and felt more akin to his new ally than ever before.

~~~~~~~~~~~~~

Helmutt rode as hard as he could to the shop in Cleveland. What was normally an eight hour ride one way, only took young Helmutt and his gelding stallion less than six hours, only stopping briefly for the horse to momentarily to rest and take water. Helmutt wondered on his journey just why he had been summoned so urgently but presumed that it must have something to do with the furniture order somehow, since that was his only connection to the elegant lady. Perhaps with her husband's passing, the lady now wanted to cancel the order and the store owner wanted the matter resolved. However when he reached the store and found its owner, Helmutt would be asked to create something he'd never expected.

The store owner told him that the lady had been understandably distraught over the death of her young, loving husband and had realized that there was no way she could bury him in the kind of plain coffin that was typical in 1890. The store owner spoke of how the woman had summoned him to her home and pleaded with him to reach the young man making their chifferobes, and to see if he would make her husband's casket. She knew the exquisite quality like the carvings she had seen in the owner's store would be the only thing she would ever be comfortable enough to place her husband's body in for all eternity.

Not blinking an eye, young Helmutt instantly agreed to make the woman the finest wood casket that he could, but also acknowledged how it would be his first ever. He further explained how he nor his family, in all their years known around Vielsalm, had ever received such a request, and how caskets in Belgium were typically just as basic in style like those he'd seen in some of the furniture stores during his travels around America. The store owner, like most furniture makers and sellers of the day, also built and sold traditional coffins and caskets for grieving families in need. However, he had never had such a request either. Helmutt asked the store owner if he felt the lady in mourning might be willing to let him come to her home to inquire exactly what she wanted in terms of design, stain, and an interior which he'd also never done. Agreeing, the store owner used his horse and carriage, so that Helmut's gelding could rest at the livery, and took him out to see the grieving woman.

With his ever gentle nature and kind eyes, Helmutt offered the lady his deepest condolences for her loss and said how he would be glad to try and create the finest casket for her husband. Asking her to describe exactly what she felt would be most appropriate, Helmutt listened attentively and began to sketch on his pad full of his beautiful drawings, thanks to his ever loving friend and teacher Mrs. Desmet. As the lady spoke about her husband's love for the land, the corn and wheat they grew, his beloved Texas where he'd grown up, and especially his family and faith, Helmutt penciled effortlessly several tiny images of possible carvings reflecting the man's life and what he knew he could carve into wood. For the first time since the tragic fall, the lady smiled though painfully but still sensing a relief from seeing the special images that Helmutt had quickly drawn. Sitting there in the woman's light-filled parlor, the three of them were convinced that such a casket would be more special than any ever seen, and together shared a special, peaceful solace in that moment.

~~~~~~~~~~~~

Once back to the owner's shop, Helmutt knew time was critical. He would only have a few weeks before the lady wanted to have her husband's funeral service as soon as his family arrived from Texas. Unsure how, all he could do was promise to do his best. Finally the store owner told Helmutt to send him a telegraph as soon as the casket was ready, and that he would inform the town's newest widow. He also said not to worry about the interior and told of how his wife was as good of a seamstress and dressmaker as any, and that she would prepare some of their finest silks for the new casket. All he needed Helmut to do was wire the interior dimensions as soon as possible, for his wife to use in crafting the custom interior.

Hating to bring up price, and knowing the lady was one of his very best customers, Helmutt asked if the shop owner planned to charge her in such a sorrowful time. With a devilish, eye-creaking smirk, the man, though soft and gently, said "Oh yes, absolutely there will be a charge, Helmutt. Both of us will make good money here." Somewhat taken back at the man's delight, Helmutt asked the coffin maker what he normally gets paid for his basic boxes, to which the pine box builder replied "Those things, well we usually get anywhere from ten to twelve dollars apiece from most families. Sometimes more if we think we can." "What do you mean by that?" asked Helmutt. Repeating his smirk, the shop owner informed his young furniture crafter about the heart and purse strings involved with the death of a loved one. Explaining how the grieving can often be easily encouraged to "buy one or two levels up", meaning better sales and profits of course.

As for the wealthy new widow, the shopkeeper was convinced she would pay any price they asked after Helmutt's "artful performance" in her parlor. Now Helmutt had been raised to quote a price as high as possible, thinking back to what he'd always learned from his father and uncle about giving folks room to dicker on price. He had no problem with getting paid a premium price in return for providing a premium product, whether chifferobes or caskets.

Wishing at the moment that he had his brother Adlar's quick head for math to figure up a quick estimate, he elected to ask the shop keeper what a fair price might be in his opinion. "At least eighty-five dollars!" said the man. "Eighty-five dollars?!" replied a stunned Helmutt. He knew the cost of materials per foot board wouldn't be near as much as furniture. Especially since the inside boards didn't have to be stained because of how the interior lining would cover it; plus the finish wouldn't need to standup to a lifetime of wear or sunlight, so that too would require less work and materials. He felt that his real time would be into carving the small pieces to be affixed to the casket so as to reflect the personal memories for the lady. As he surmised it all, there would really be very little expense in the casket once the boards were planed and smoothed down. But since it was his first, perhaps he wasn't thinking of everything.

Nonetheless, the two profiteers agreed to a sixty-five, thirty-five split of the price, allowing for the store owner's normal twenty-five percent plus another ten percent to cover the custom interior expense. A twenty-nine dollar and seventy-five cent sale wasn't too bad thought the store owner, for a casket that he didn't have to build and that would only require less than three dollars' worth of silk to wrap the interior. A pretty tidy

134

profit compared to his normal death box sales. Plus, they would charge another fifteen dollars for the travel expense for Helmutt to bring the casket back so quickly. In all, Helmutt would record a seventy dollar and twenty-five cent sale for something he figured he'd have about seven dollars of materials costs. Once agreed, the two businessmen shook hands and agreed it was a really good deal.

The biggest question Helmutt had on his ride home was how he would find the time to build the casket when he'd have to work even harder to catch up on the furniture orders. Especially, after he had just lost the last two days. Little did he know what his associate had been up to during his absence.

~~~~~~~~~~

When Helmutt returned from Cleveland, the first ever letter sent from his family and homeland had arrived after being mailed almost a month earlier. His eyes teared as his heart smiled wider than it ever had before in his life as he read the words of such pride and happiness his family expressed for their loved Helmutt. He couldn't help but think of the mixed emotions from the sad woman he had met with the day before compared to his own sheer joy and love upon receiving the warm, loving message from his family. There were special personal notes too in their native Dutch, one from Adlar and another from his father, Emest, who also shared the pride of his uncle Evrard, still ever true to his scarcity with words. They told how his third letter had brought them all such joy for his success, and that they were so thankful he had found a new friend and protector in the new world. Finally, as the letter closed, his father told his young

135

Helmutt how they all knew that he would never fail and let them down. How they all knew Helmutt would go to the new land and begin a new "Great American Kleinmark Co."

About midnight, as Helmutt had put the finishing touches on the company's first casket ever produced, his heart told him that his family's infamous Kleinmark Co. brand should be reserved exclusively for their line of fine furniture, and that the casket needed its own moniker. As that moment stood still, Helmutt reflected on his father's special note and decided that "Great American" seemed especially fitting. So he drew the fine-lined script onto the lower foot end of the casket and finished it with the same smooth elegant oval line, just like his beloved Kleinmark Co. logo. To Helmutt, in that quiet, solemn moment, it was perfect.

The casket that Helmutt had created for the woman he'd now met twice, once when happy and the other sad, would more than meet her expectations. First, the store owner and his wife could not believe that a casket could be so beautiful. Helmutt had been allowed to spend more time on the casket than imagined, thanks to the impressive new skill of fine sanding and polishing that Big Sam had quickly learned and applied. As a result, Helmutt had worked tirelessly for a solid week on what would be considered the finest and most exquisite casket that any of the hundreds attending the funeral service would say they had ever seen. Most wondered of the sanity of putting such a fine piece of furniture-like quality into the ground. Nonetheless, others, those of means, would seek out the man who sold the woman the casket with the logo on the foot end in the ever smallest and tasteful script, simply listed as "Great American" and encircled with an elegant, thin line.

~~~~~~~~~~~~~

No one was more astonished than both the store owner and Helmutt when almost a dozen people inquired about the most beautiful casket they had ever seen. None flinched at the price, appreciating that it was indeed as nice as any piece of fine furniture and especially fitting for families of means in a time of need. The two men decided that it may be a good revenue stream to make a few of the caskets in advance, since most families would likely not wait three weeks like the last widow. As they did, the shop owner realized that he could leverage the price even more because of what he would present as "limited inventory." Helmutt also shared the news and showed off his "fine caskets" to all of the other store owners around the region as he and Big Sam traveled about delivering all of the new furniture orders that kept coming in. But mostly what ignited the interest in the new prestigious line from the newly formed Great American Casket Company was the word of mouth that came from each and every funeral.

It turned out that more and more of the middle class families wanted to send their loved ones off in something nicer than the typical plain pine boxes of the day. Before 1890 had come to a close, Helmutt and Big Sam had to build a second work shop just to support the casket manufacturing business, which was growing at a far faster rate than the fine furniture business. It turns out, that even though most people might forego the finer things for themselves in life like premium crafted

137

furniture, they will routinely spare little expense to have a worthy casket for their dearly departed loved ones.

Now twenty-four years old, Helmutt had learned that caskets could be extremely lucrative in terms of margins and with much faster turnover, and of course without any future complaints. Turning out ten new fine caskets a month by the time the 1891 New Year rang in, his family was shocked about his new venture discovery and how the new Great American branded company already had twenty-five additional employees working five days a week, every week. Almost one full year after Helmutt had left his beloved Belgium, though now with faded memories, his monthly letters told of more and more sales increases for both the casket and furniture businesses, but especially for caskets. Each month, Helmutt wrote with glowing pride as he listed the monthly sales and profits for both companies in the regular updates, including a wiring confirmation of the certificate of deposit that were made via the company's bank of choice in Pittsburgh to the family bank back in Liege just north of Vielsalm.

~~~~~~~~~~~~

It was daunting to believe that twenty-five years had gone by so quickly. For Helmutt, it seemed like the blink of an eye because of how he'd always been so incredibly busy building furniture and caskets as well as both businesses and brands in the new world. For his family, it had seemed like an eternity since their young man had left home back in the early spring of 1890.

Now producing over one hundred caskets per week being sold all over the Midwest and Northeast regions, including virtually every furniture store and most standalone mortuaries that were becoming more prevalent, Helmutt and his family had become more successful than ever hoped for. The profits being generated by 1915 allowed them to now send a regular monthly transatlantic telegraph messages back and forth, which were quite more expensive and only utilized by wealthiest of immigrants to stay in close and convenient communications with their families back home. So Helmutt was surprised to get another message after having just received the prior one a week earlier.

Sadly, this wire reported of his beloved one hundred and one year old uncle Evrard's passing and how his father was taking it so hard. His family feared too Emest might not last long in the world, now with Evrard gone. Knowing he must now go home to be with his family in Vielsalm, Helmutt and Big Sam spoke of what was important to be done while he was gone for likely the following three to four weeks. As always, Big Sam knew his friend needed to rely on him, and likewise his friend rested completely assured that he could. By now, Helmutt and Big Sam had been there for each other more times than they could remember. Whenever trouble lurked, the two closest of friends had long been resolved to do whatever it took to make it go away. They had decided long ago that they'd be damned if anyone would take their business away without a fight, and sometimes that meant the harshest of measures, which they would employ when and wherever necessary.

He couldn't help but notice how the trip back home on the huge ship seemed to be so much faster than when he'd first come to America. The first sight of his loving brother Adlar's face at the port in Vlissingen was so wonderful to see that Helmutt exclaimed with great euphoric delight "I see you my brother!" For little more than the next three hours as Adlar guided his new fine German-crafted automobile south through their beloved homeland, the two men in many ways still felt like the young boys they had been upon last seeing and talking with each other. For those brief moments, which passed by far too quickly, it was as if nothing had changed, and both men tried their best to soak up how that felt.

However, little did Adlar fully understand or appreciate just what his younger brother had been dealing with all those years to secure their family's great American success. Helmutt had never shared any of those things in his letters, only wanting his family to be happy and have every good thing he could provide. But indeed there had been a big price to pay for all the success and money that resulted over the years, many in fact. With some of those coming at great personal risks and costs to Helmutt that would haunt him for the remainder of his years.

~~~~~~~~~~~

After the funeral and typical running around to catch up with family long since seen that people all over the world do when they're back home after long periods, Helmutt finally had some time to spend with just his father and brother. Adlar proudly showed his younger brother the new furniture making equipment they had purchased for the shop and told of the recent pieces they'd made with it. He was so proud to share how their trademark quality brand was continuing to prosper in their homeland. By now, Adlar had his own two sons who were just beginning to help work in the family business and learn the craft of fine furniture making. David, seventeen, and his five year old little brother, Renford, both spent every day helping their own generation of elders continue the family legacy, just as the Kleinmark men who'd come before them.

David was the spitting image of Adlar, equally small statured but without the frailty his father dealt with in life since surviving cholera as a boy. David was extremely energetic and strong for his size, plus he had inherited Adlar's keen grasp of numbers and business. As for the youngest of Adlar's seven children, baby Renford was as adorable and loving as any child God had ever blessed upon a family. It was easy to see how Renford absolutely idolized and followed his big brother everywhere he went.

One evening after dinner, the elder Kleinmark men went out to the work shop for a smoke and to talk about the American business. Emest had never inquired, especially in front of the womenfolk, about what kinds of hurdles and struggles that his son must have surely dealt with over the years. But he had been on the earth and in business long enough to know that real struggles always come, and so did Adlar. They also knew that Helmutt had never once told of any such matters in any of his monthly wires since leaving home and wanted to know the full truth about what their beloved Helmutt had endured to build such a successful enterprise.

Ninety-nine year old Emest had been bound to a wheelchair for the last several years since falling and breaking a hip, but his mind and sixth sense were as sharp as ever. As soon as they sat down in the shop and he looked into his son's usually kind-hearted eyes, the aged Emest told of how he'd detected a deep and saddened aspect of his son's countenance since his return to Vielsalm. Adlar mentioned too how his brother's nature had somehow seemed harder now compared to the twenty-three year old who'd left so long ago.

Helmutt, trying his best to smile and conceal his heart and truths, would only speak of being so tired from his recent travel home and all the never-ending work back in America. Seeing right through that, his loving father and brother said nothing for the next full minute, wondering if Helmutt might open up and share something of the truth. Realizing that whatever his youngest son was holding inside, Emest began to speak of how he and Evrard had encountered so much hardship throughout their lives to keep their family and business going all those years. He retold stories both boys knew so well about the various crooks and cheats who tried to steal or wrong them along the way, and how he and his big brother had ferociously handled them. "Nothing ever seemed to come easy for us", a very wise Emest said. As Helmutt looked down and away from his father and brother, his eyes began to tear as he tried his best to hold in the painful realities of the huge price he and Big Sam had paid over the years. Immediately, they all knew there was so much more to be shared about Helmutt's full life experiences in America.

~~~~~~~~~~~~~

Over the next three hours, with the womenfolk wondering if the men would ever come back into the house, Helmutt shared everything on his heart. He told them about meeting Big Sam and how his lifelong friend had saved his life and the family's money so early on. He told them about the store owner in Cleveland, who'd introduced the first opportunity to make a casket for one of his wealthy clients who'd lost her husband to a horse accident. But also how he'd later on learn the store owner was overpricing his Great American caskets and selling another line of "nice enough" high quality caskets at cheaper prices because he could get a better discount. While that wasn't illegal, Helmutt had wondered why sales had seemed to stop and sent in one of their employees to pose as a shopper and inquire about the man's offering of fine caskets. Learning that the Cleveland owner was actually using Great American caskets to get people interested in buying a high-end product, he was then slyly talking them into the other line. Their fake shopper had also mentioned how the store owner would even lean on the cheaper casket and rub its finish, as if it was the only right choice for a family.

Then Helmutt told the gruesome details of how he and Big Sam personally showed up one night as the man was closing up his shop, knowing that his wife would have already gone home to prepare his dinner. How they had worn masks and quietly gone in through the back door from the alley and proceeded to beat the man to a bloody pulp, breaking several ribs and both legs, eventually leaving him in the alleyway after torching his store.

He went onto to add how the Cleveland owner and his new supplier partner located north of Bergholz in a place called Youngstown had schemed and coached the same deceptive bait and switch model to several other store owners across the region. About a month later, after the Cleveland beating news had died down enough, Helmutt and Big Sam showed up at the factory of their competitor situated way out of the city center in the middle of a hot summer night to burn it down. However after breaking into the building and starting a huge fire to several huge piles of timber wood they'd soaked in several gallons of oil-based varnishes and lacquers, the owner unexpectedly ran into the building screaming and shooting at the two masked perpetrators. Apparently he had been living at the shop for quite some time as would later be reported. As it turned out, his wife had kicked him out for refusing to stop carrying on with one of the pretty black girls who worked for him.

Always holstered out of fear of being robbed while delivering and collecting, both Helmutt and Big Sam unloaded their six-shooters in the direction of the man and struck him three times, once in the face and twice in his chest. Knowing there could be no body with bullet holes recovered; Helmutt and Big Sam took the man's body, soaked it with the flammable liquids, and then laid it a top of one the big piles of burning timbers. After emptying all of the flammables as hurriedly they could, again he and his partner rode off. The authorities

144

eventually chocked it up to either the wife's family killing the man for his unfaithfulness or an unfortunate accident. Either way, no charges were ever filed, but all of the other store owners were suddenly willing to once again fill their inventories with Great American caskets, which were now higher in price than ever before. Going forward, order volumes would only go up for Great American.

By the time the clock struck midnight, Helmutt had told countless other dark stories of how he and Big Sam had saved the business by one means or another over the years. How they'd fought off would-be robbers on the roads many times, or how stupidly a store owner from time to time would try and short pay them, just as the fat land baron had with his father and uncle Evrard way back when. They'd dealt with each and every one of them along the way, and to whatever degree had been required. Finally with enough of the brutal realities off his chest and heavy heart, Helmutt was finally able to show a relief-filled smile and say "It was all worth it, and I'd do it all again. Of course, I do wish both of you and Uncle Evrard had always been there with me." Feeling the deepest empathy for their son and brother, both men simply pulled close up and put their arms around him. For surely they could understand and appreciate the trials and painful hardships he'd endured in the new America, especially without his family there to be with him.

~~~~~~~~~~~~~

Over the remainder of Helmutt's visit home, the three men would continue to talk about the future prospects of both the Kleinmark Co. and Great American brands in America. It was clear that Helmutt envisioned great growth potential for both lines but desperately needed more help from someone he could rely on to help manage and grow the businesses, and not just from employees. Just as they had considered back in 1889 that a young Helmut would go and seek out a new pathway for the Kleinmark's in the new world, it was now completely clear that such a consideration was once again required.

This time their young, very smart and aggressively ambitious, hard-working seventeen year old David would be sent back with his uncle to learn the American businesses and be counted on to lead them going forward one day. Emest had presumed by now that Helmutt might have his own son to bring into the family business, but life had required his youngest son's attention solely on building the business. Having always been more like his uncle Evrard, Helmutt had never considered marriage and focused solely on his work and fulfilling the promise to his family back home. So now, the elder Kleinmark men brought young David into their discussions and considerations to feel out his attitude and interest in going to America when his uncle Helmutt returned.

The men were brutally honest with David about the hard work and risks that had been endured thus far to build the businesses, and surely how things were unlikely to be any easier in the future. Just as his father and uncle had both impressed Emest and Evrard in their own assessment of such an adventure back in 1889, when the first notion of expanding to America had originally surfaced, David equally proved his keen sense of reasoning and assessment, now that it was his turn to make such

146

a big similar decision. And so, it was decided. David would travel back to America with Helmutt to learn everything about both businesses and to hopefully one day lead the company.

Little could the men have ever comprehended just what vision, capability, and daringness the newest generation of Kleinmark men would prove to achieve for their family's legacy. Moreover, it would be David's tremendous daringness and greedy desire for greatness that would transform the great Kleinmark family name and brand in ways his elders could have never imagined, or certainly hoped for.

~~~~~~~~~~

DNA

Not surprisingly, it was less than six months when Emest passed away, requiring Helmutt and David to return home again to Vielsalm. Once his older brother of two years had passed and knowing the family was in the good care of the future generations of Kleinmark men, Emest finally let go to be with Evrard.

Adlar could already see that his eldest son had changed in numerous, apparent ways. David's father now saw a look of greater maturity and confidence on his son's face. His son had always been very smart about most things he challenged. But now David was obviously more certain of his self than ever and clearly exuded a level of competence that Adlar had never seen before. It was evident that David had jumped right into both businesses. At his uncle Helmutt's direction, the young man focused more on the casket trade while his uncle handled the furniture side exclusively. In the months since getting to America, David averaged twelve-plus hour days working hands-on to learn the craft of casket-making. After spending all day in the factory, David spent hours each evening going over the financial and sales records, giving special attention to their best customers and product sales in the regions they served at the time.

After only a few weeks since his arrival, David's natural mindset caused him to be curious about more than just the products and operations his uncle and Big Sam had developed. David wondered where the sales came from, about the customers, especially repeating ones, and other dynamics. Explaining to his uncle how he would like to gain a broader understanding of the overall business, the bright young man began digging into years and years of files that would tell a very interesting story of what customers purchased and where. What it wouldn't tell was why.

Over the next couple of months, David spent each evening charting out how the casket sales moved by month, species of wood, state, individual accounts, stains, and styles. Something that Helmutt had never considered. He had simply been too busy keeping his arms around both manufacturing businesses and making sure that orders for furniture and caskets went out on time as promised each month, as well as dealing with any unfortunate nonsense that came up. His mind had never worked like that of Adlar and David. However his young nephew had brought a brand new mindset to the business that had never existed before. Within short order, David had astutely figured out multiple insights from the data as to what was going on in the business. Subsequently, he presented his uncle Helmut with a plan to address each one that was concerning, as well to capitalize on those in their favor. As David reviewed his findings with his elders, his father and uncle were both very impressed with their firm's newest business executive.

~~~~~~~~~~~~

David had immediately become infatuated with America and all its glory as soon as he stepped foot in New York. America possessed an energy that he had never sensed before. Growing up and working in the furniture business back home,

149

even as a young teenager, David saw several different opportunities to grow the furniture business. Regardless, Adlar's condition never allowed for taking on many risks or strenuous endeavors, leaving his eldest son routinely disappointed from not being able to ever capitalize on his grand ideas. But in America, David was immediately taken with the industrial and economic booms of the times. He constantly read every newspaper he could get his hands on from the delivery drivers as they went from town to town. Forgetting to bring David any one of his newspapers incited such a cross look at the delivery drivers, those who wanted to keep their jobs, would only need to experience it once to enhance their future memory. Ultimately it was the information he'd learn from the papers about the growing Eastern seaboard population and the booming Southern economies, which caused his mind to wonder of potential market expansion.

David was always on the lookout of news stories of the great industrialists of the early 1900s. He became completely fascinated with the major tycoons who had made their fortunes in America; like Carnegie, Rockefeller, Morgan, and Vanderbilt. It was particularly Carnegie, an immigrant of equally short stature, who would be the one that David would aspire to emulate. The young man was mesmerized that his idol, before becoming one of America's wealthiest tycoons, had worked the very same Western Pennsylvania railroad lines that he and Helmutt had first rode back to Steubenville. Knowing this made David believe with full confidence that he too could find his own great fortune in the new country.

As he read more and more about the men he worshipped, one definite realization became evident and clear. Great wealth and fortune would not come easily or without battles. Though perhaps a pathetic effort to sell newspapers in the day, story after story, most front page center, relayed numerous accounts of how such men not only built their fame and fortunes in America, but took it by force, if and whenever necessary. Becoming increasingly informed to that of an expert in the travails of the powerful and successful men he admired, those reports would provide the sufficient education and clarity of purpose David needed to pursue his own determined destiny.

~~~~~~~~~~~~

This visit home to be with their family and mourn Emest's passing unfortunately would have to be limited to a quick two week stay for Helmutt and David. Back home in America, both businesses were running at full speed when the two Kleinmark men had left, with the busy springtime just around the corner. Needless to say, they were both anxious to return to Bergholz and dive back into the busy daily operations. Back on the huge ship out of Vlissingen, David reviewed his findings again with his uncle and discussed how he'd like to spend his time as soon as they returned to America. Helmutt became more impressed with David's thoroughness and planning as they discussed what the data had shown and how his nephew wanted to further approach the market. By the time they arrived in New York harbor six days later, plus the sixteen hour train ride from New York through Pittsburgh into Steubenville, and another four hours in the wagon back to Bergholz, young David had gained his uncle's agreement on how he wanted to spend his time over the coming months to grow the business; or perhaps, simply worn him down. Either way, the plan of attack that David would begin employing over the remainder of that and the following year would make an immeasurable impact for Great American.

~~~~~~~~~~~

The best part of David's plan was that it was simple. At that point in time, Great American only served clients in its surrounding region of the country. Mostly from the work and travels of Helmutt and Big Sam in the early days, their casket customers ranged from Ohio to most Northeastern states. However, the country had been growing precipitously all down along the Eastern seaboard as well as throughout the South, as David's newspaper education repeatedly showed. Given that the company had no brand awareness or market penetration in those areas, David believed it was worthwhile to investigate in terms of competitors, retailers, and mortuaries servicing the larger populated cities in each state. First, he wanted to spend his first six weeks back home traveling their current customer geography to fully understand exactly why customers bought from Great American.

Armed with that learning and understanding of how to best position their brand with prospective clients, the eager young man would plan to spend the following three months traveling the new targeted areas to the east and south. To execute his plan, David would start with the Maryland and Delaware markets; then down to Virginia, the Carolinas, Georgia and

Florida, and finally over to the rest of the other Southern states east of the Mississippi River. After which, he would complete his discovery in Kentucky before turning back north into the current Ohio market, where he'd see both existing and prospective customers along the way home.

The two men agreed the learning could be significant for Great American to find new customers and gain a larger market share beyond their current position. It was agreed that David would be expected to telephone his uncle every Sunday afternoon, the only day the shop was ever down, to advise of his safety and progress updates. Thankfully, Helmutt had the foresight when the new invention caught on in recent years to have one installed. No more misplaced telegraph messages for Kleinmark Co. or Great American.

Once David mapped out exactly where reliable train access existed, which would be critical to support potential deliveries into the new markets, he was ready to set out. In the days leading up to his nephew's departure, Helmut often spoke of how proud he was of David's vision and courage to take on such a solo mission. He also told his nephew how the daring plan reminded him so much of the stories Emest and uncle Evrard had retold so many times over the years of their own expansion exploits back in the winter of 1844. Both men hoped this Kleinmark excursion would be just as successful.

Helmutt knew all too well how dangerous it could be for a young man traveling alone, thinking back to when he was brutally coldcocked in an alleyway. Furthermore, he was a much bigger man and older than David. So before his nephew would leave, Helmutt and Big Sam wanted to make sure that he was absolutely comfortable using a gun. It was something so far that the men had really never had to speak about since David's arrival, other than the old stories of the early days. But now, this was different and both men knew David could likely encounter any number of bad situations while off traveling on his own. So they wanted to know at least that he was comfortable pulling a trigger if such a time came when he had to defend himself. The more the men inquired of the young man about his experience with guns, the more it obvious that he had little, if any, direct experience using one, especially for any lethal purpose.

By the time David was growing up in the family business, his father, Adlar, was running it because grandfather Emest had simply become too old. Unlike times gone by when Emest and Evrard would deal directly with any problem situations involving a fool trying to cheat or steal the Kleinmark family, Adlar was compelled to outsource such needed heavy-handed skills. While David had always heard the same stories that his uncle Helmutt had, he personally never had to face the same types of confrontations alongside his own father. Now getting ready to set out on his own, all the men could do was caution David on how to protect his money and property while traveling, but also how to use his gun if needed. After sufficient practice and perceived comfort with a new Browning 1900 pistol that Helmutt had purchased during their recent trip home to Belgium, David was finally ready to set out.

The question still remained, whether or not the young eighteen year old man, though wise beyond his age, would truly be ready if serious trouble ever developed. Like most brazen young men throughout the ages, David said he would be of course. But all his uncle could do was hope and pray. Because the thought of sending a wire to Adlar of the contrary and taking the body of his nephew back to Belgium was something he simply could not stand to think about.

~~~~~~~~~~~~~

David could hardly believe that he was already setting out on such a journey for the Kleinmark family business, in just little over a year of arriving in America. In his mind, he would often think that such daring adventures must surely be one of the hallmarks of any would be aspiring business magnate. As his first train ride hurled east toward Washington, DC and Baltimore areas, David spent all available waking hours reviewing all of the newspaper articles he'd collected and organized by city. He constantly rehearsed the prepared talking points of why Great American caskets had become the preferred high-end standard for more than two and a half decades for some of the most prestigious funeral parlors and morticians in the North Central and Northeastern regions of the country. Another benefit was how the young man would have a far better presentation of Great American craftsmanship capabilities, than the mere carving samples and drawings, like his uncle and elders had relied upon in their promotional travels.

It was David's idea to take along an actual display of real caskets to show the funeral operators he would meet with during his circuits. Uncle Helmutt and Big Sam had thought the young man's idea was simply ingenious. Together the three men designed and built a heavy-duty skid pallet, large enough to hold three full size Great American caskets that would showcase the true quality and uniqueness of their brand. The units would be in the bestselling stain colors, cherry mahogany, walnut, and pecan. The unique pallet design incorporated an easy-removal top cover that was hinged in the upper middle so as to open like the wing-span of a large bird. At each of the three hinge points, two industrial keyed locks were used to secure it. Once loaded from the train car onto a flatbed wagon arranged in advance of each stop with local liveries, David would drive the team of horses around to each prospective funeral operator in each market. The anticipated opening of the hinged cover and final removal of a rainproof cover provided David the perfect controlled timing for each presentation about the Kleinmark legacy craftsmanship and Great American caskets.

From the very first presentation David made upon reaching Baltimore, he quickly realized that he had to be ever mindful to contain his own excitement at the response Great American caskets would always receive. He didn't want new customers to all of a sudden realize that he was just as shocked as they were at the response of how Great American's casketed quality matched that of fine furniture standards. This would be one of many new selling skills the budding casket salesman would quickly learn.

The young man was repeatedly awestruck at how each and every presentation went exactly the same way. Every funeral operator, whether in his own parlor or furniture store, had an immediate interest in offering Great American caskets. No matter the location during the entirety of his travels, the response was always the same. Each operator seemingly wanted access to Great American quality, and while price was usually always paramount, it was less so given the perceived select clientele that would likely prefer such high-end funeral products. Once David shared how most of their customers reported how Great American sales volume resulted from middle income families who spent more for such beautiful caskets in which to send off their loved ones, his new prospective customers were eagerly interested to put them on display. Especially once they realized that they would set their own retail price locally. A practice that would continue unendingly with future generations of funeral operators; and would likewise cause significant undue funeral cost increases to consumers, in comparison to almost any other product, service, or industry for decades and decades to come.

~~~~~~~~~~~~~~

David's first phone call home to update uncle Helmutt was overwhelmingly positive, having gone better than either man had hoped. He had already received multiple orders for caskets after his introductory rounds in the first two markets. Plus, the decision to only require a twenty percent advance payment versus the usual fifty percent went over very well. New customers had the added security of only having to wire their deposit to a holding account at a highly respected Pittsburgh bank, which would not be drawn upon until their caskets were ready for shipment. This peace of mind approach gave new customers the added security required to take faith in the new salesman, much less given how the product quality was an absolute testament to that of a highly, reputable company.

Following weekly calls home, after the rounds in Virginia and North Carolina, were equally glowing of how the presentations and receptions had gone. David was so proud how each stop produced new order commitments. There had also been unplanned competitive market learning, particularly in Richmond, when David became familiar with an established casket builder and distributor. As he would learn, it was a firm that had been making and selling low-end to middle tier hardwoods as far north as Baltimore and as far south as Wilmington, North Carolina. Although their boxes were produced to the same, typical basic pine box standard designs of the day.

Actually the firm had gotten wind of David's dog and pony show, and managed to sneak in and attend one of his presentations to see the so-called top quality products they had been hearing so much about around their region. Sure enough, they were equally impressed too. The owner, whose family emigrated from Scotland in the late 1700s, told his new young competitor a story of survival and expansion which sounded very similar to that of David's own Kleinmark legacy. In his early seventies and with only one son in the business, who had not been blessed with the art of wood crafting, the stately gentlemen expressed his firm interest to distribute the young lad's new high-end caskets. Whether being genuine or cunning, the wiser business man spoke of his family's large customer base and brand name recognition throughout the region. Thus stressing how Great American could enjoy much quicker success by partnering with his firm than trying to compete, especially if David could also offer a middle price point line of good quality. Also, it would give the man's firm a stronger mid to upper-end line that was painfully absent, as David's presentations had so obviously highlighted to every one of the man's customers being visited. The man went onto share further how his son, though lacking any woodworking skill, had been fortunately blessed with the gift of gab and a personality that all of the customers just loved. Though, not a businessman or craftsman, his son worked harder than anyone at selling because of much he loved it. Still, the elderly father knew that his son's personality alone would not keep the company going forever.

Intrigued by what the man had to say, young David assured it would be discussed on his next phone call home with his uncle, and that he would certainly hear back regarding a possible proposition from Great American. Meanwhile, the old casket maker knew one thing was certain; his business was about to start declining thanks to the arrival of Great American in his territory, unless he found a way to partner with the young man working so hard to promote his line.

The following fourth week down in South Carolina visiting the two most populated cities, Columbia and Charleston, had equally gone as planned, producing similar results. David was truly enjoying his exciting journey in America and continued to fall in love with the land and people. From seeing the cherry blossoms bloom for the first time in Washington, DC

159

to experiencing the Lowcountry region of South Carolina, the young man's awakening to the new beautiful country continued to make memorable impressions. So far every part of the experience had gone flawlessly, but that too was about to change.

~~~~~~~~~~~~~~

Just as his uncle Helmutt had let his guard down with the conniving New York banker, young David was about to make a similarly grave error. He had become too comfortable and trusting of the new interested patrons on his journey introducing Great American. Just as life will usually provide, David was about to get an education in deathly deceit that would change him forever.

His life education would come at the end of the casket introductions around the Charleston battery, where David fell in love with the architecture and civil war history from not so long ago. As those he met retold the glory stories from the famed peninsula battles, it was as if he could still smell the gun powder in the air over the Ashley and Cooper rivers. The people there seemed more charming and easy-going than any others he had met thus far in his travels. So it was easy to take on a similar, carefree and relaxed attitude. Nonetheless, he would learn the hard way how there are those in life who would suck you in with such adept subversive skill, only to take advantage when your guard is sufficiently down.

As this situation would turn out, it would be the last presentation held late on a Friday afternoon with a funeral parlor operator last on the list for the week. This particular mortician had the most prestigious building located in the city-center confines compared to all David had seen thus far. The owner, adorned in a freshly starched blue seersucker suit, white ruffled chested shirt, and crimson red bowtie, removed his white, fine straw panama hat and invited David to come inside. Directing the young salesman to take a seat in front of his huge oak desk, and in a chair that sat at least a foot lower than his own, the purported genteel man in his late fifties took great effort and time to boast of his firm's prominence and importance in the community. Unlike most others, this mortician exclusively serviced families with purchased caskets, never having the interest or inclination to manufacture.

Given a strictly niched penchant for targeting the wealthiest of families or at least those financially committed to the appearance of such, the owner presented a stronger interest in the Great American caskets than anyone thus far on the journey. He knew that caskets of such unique, high quality would fetch a far better price, which he of course would set very high compared to any other he offered. After repeated but polite efforts to get the young man to sell him the display of caskets, the man became noticeably irritated at his new salesman's persistent decline. Finally, after becoming unexpectedly hostile and threatening, vowing to never purchase a Great American casket and of course claiming to provide "absolutely all of the quality trade in Charleston for decades", David tried professionally as possible to assuage the man's interest for immediate satisfaction. Incredibly, the stubborn, haughty man kept up his chirping for over two more hours, until David sternly suggested a final time that "No, will unfortunately have to be my answer, sir!" Reluctantly allowing the Great American casket wagon to leave his yard, still unfortunately loaded, the man already had other thoughts of how to get his way.

~~~~~~~~~~~

Regrettably, however, the young and trusting, exuberant Great American salesman had foolishly told the obnoxious funeral operator of his coming plans. Detailing how his next stop overnight would be only a few hours away in Walterboro, South Carolina, before heading further south to Savannah, Georgia and then down into Florida to introduce his exciting new line. Arriving much later than planned that evening, just before midnight due to the man's insistent delays, David was completely exhausted and mentally drained from all the non-stop nagging back in Charleston. So he decided to just go straight to the hotel and to bed. Normally his routine was to first stable the horses and wagon with the local livery, but by the time he arrived so late in Walterboro, the livery was closed.

Checking into the hotel, David inquired of the front deskman about when the livery was likely to reopen. "Not till about five o'clock tomorrow morning", said the desk clerk. "If it's an emergency, I can have the livery man fetched if you want. Otherwise, you're welcome to leave your team out front for the night. There's water in the trough and I can throw'em some hay to eat." Worn out, David thought that would be wonderful and asked the night man if he believed it would be safe to leave the team and wagon on the street in front of the hotel overnight for a few hours. "Absolutely!" said the man. "Don't you worry about

162

a thing. I'll be here all night." So David took the man's assurances to heart and headed up to bed, after requesting an early five o'clock wakeup call.

David's room looked out over the front of the hotel. So the last thing he did before climbing into bed was to gaze down below to his team and property on the street. Everything seemed completely calm and peaceful in the small town known as "The Front Porch of the Lowcountry." Like many weary travelers, sometimes the bed doesn't do the trick no matter how tired you are.

After tossing and turning all night, his mind still wrestling with how difficult and challenging the last prospect in Charleston had been, David awakened and got up for a drink of water. A quick glance at his pocket watch indicated it was about three-thirty in the morning. Still feeling as tired and groggy as when he'd gone to bed, almost forgetting about the team out front, David took a quick peek through the slit in the curtains. Suddenly with his eyes darting left and right and then ripping the curtains back, David was startled to see that his horses and wagon were gone. Perhaps he had misunderstood the night clerk who had offered to give them water and feed for the night. Maybe he had moved them, but something didn't feel right in his gut. He recalled the night man to say the horses would be fine on the street "out front" all night.

Throwing on his trousers, David ran downstairs in his nightshirt to find the counterman and his team. Except now, the so-called night man, who should have been called the "good night man" was nowhere to be found. With every pounding

163

ounce he could summon, David banged the heck out of the bell on the counter until the vibrations between each pound overlapped with the next. Hearing that someone was ringing that damn bell to the rafters, the goodnight man lurched from a back room about as stunned and dazed as most would be when startled to death out of their sweet dreams. Seeing David standing there banging the bell, the alarmed clerk asked "What in damn tarnation is the matter, sir?" Immediately, David knew the look on the night man's face was sad confirmation that he had not moved the team or wagon. Now both men raced out front to the street to see if perhaps the horses had pulled loose from the post and merely wandered off.

After running up and down every street in the small, sleepy town, it was obvious that the horses and wagon were gone. Thankfully, the one positive contribution that the hotel clerk did bring to the whole mess of the situation was noticing how there were definite fresh marks of deep wheel tracks leading east out of town; the same direction from which David had entered just hours before from Charleston. In an instant, David's gut kicked into gear. He just knew that asshole in Charleston, who had been so insistent on having his caskets, must have followed him to Walterboro and stolen them in the middle of the night.

Now here he was in a predicament for sure! The livery was closed. It was the middle of the night, and he had no horse to even try and follow the thief. Thankfully, the night man, feeling terrible about the whole situation, had fortunately ridden his best thoroughbred to work that evening and offered to let David borrow the horse to try and chase down his team. Within twenty minutes, David had gathered his belongings and was riding out of town as fast as he could, but this time with only the clothes on his back and the Browning 1900 strapped across his waist.

~~~~~~~~~~~~~~~~

It took an hour and a half less to make the trip back down to Charleston on the clerk's thoroughbred compared to the wagon ride. After pulling up to the backside of the seer suckered man's funeral parlor, still a good hour before daybreak, David saw his wagon still loaded and locked up sitting under a large awning next to the building as rain and thunder started to come down. Tying up the night man's horse at a safe distance down the street, the city was still in the early process of rousing around the funeral parlor's part of town. Seeing the back carriage garage doors were open, which David knew led to the embalming room thanks to man's self-absorbed and exhausting tour, he quietly cocked the Browning and stepped inside.

Once again he heard the owner's annoying voice as he laughed with another man about the stupid salesman who foolishly told them where he'd be staying in Walterboro and "how easy it was to find the casket wagon just sitting right out front of the hotel free for the taking." He stood quietly for a few more moments as he heard the operator tell the other man how they needed to get the new caskets inside and hidden, as well as take the wagon out to his farm, in case the young salesman showed up looking for it. As lightning and thunder continued to get nearer and louder by the second, David peeked around the corner to get a clear view of both men who were only about

165

twenty-five feet away. Listening for what seemed like an eternity, David's blood began to boil as he heard the greedy man laugh at his expense and refer to him as "one of those stupid heathen European clads from up north." Considering his options, and figuring both men were possibly armed, David knew this was one of those times like he'd heard so much about from all of his Kleinmark elders. At that moment, he knew what had to be done. A lesson would have to be learned, and to a grave extent.

David decided that, without saying a word, he would quickly walk right up to the owner, sitting behind the huge mahogany desk, and shoot him in the left chest area. Then he would shoot the other man, standing to the owner's right, in the right shoulder. This was of course if all went well. One shot each and then he'd get out of there. Taking a deep slow breath, David was completely conscious of how calm his heart rate was in the moment even though he was as mad as he'd ever been in his life.

With his pistol raised, David turned the corner and walked straight into the man's office. Without blinking and walking straight at the owner, keeping the pistol pointed directly at the man's shocked face, David's gun was within four feet of the man's chest when he pulled the trigger. About six feet existed between the tip of the Browning and the second man's chest. After firing the second planned shot, David began to slowly back up to leave, intending to only wound the two men. However the owner, though writhing in pain, was obviously trying to open his desk drawer. Seeing a gun come into sight in the man's right hand, David stepped back towards the desk and shot another round, this time into the man's face, killing him

166

instantly. The second man, begging for his life, began to scream and say that he only worked for the man as a grave digger, and how he had been forced to help steal the wagon. Everything inside David at that moment was oddly peaceful and calm. He knew that he had only wanted to send a message to the dishonest funeral operator, but the fool had made a choice by reaching for his pistol that would also force the same price for his employee's life. With all of that considered in just a split second as the man knelt on the floor begging for mercy, David pulled the trigger once more hitting the man between the eyes and killing him instantly as well. Though killing had not been his intention, David knew there could be no witnesses.

Then he realized how someone else could be inside the funeral home, possibly living upstairs. After quickly searching and seeing no one, David went out the back of the funeral home with his weapon drawn again in case needed. Fortunately, no one else was either around or had apparently heard the shooting from within, over the crashing sounds of the lightning and thunder outside. Calm and clear-eyed, as if awakened in some life-altering, purposeful way, David holstered the Browning and drove the wagon team down through the back alleyway as the sun began to slowly rise.

~~~~~~~~~~~~~

Leading his team back out of Charleston, with the clerk's thoroughbred tethered to the rear of the wagon and following along, the daring young man's thoughts went to how such occurrences must be the unfortunate makings of the infamous tycoons he had read so much about. He knew in his heart that he had never planned to kill the men, but given the circumstances, he also realized how he felt no sympathy for the actions they had chosen to act out against him.

After quickly tying the reins of the night clerk's horse to a post behind the hotel, David immediately headed the wagon south out of town towards Savannah. He knew, other than his name, the night clerk had no knowledge of where he had fled off to with his stallion or what had been stolen, and thus it was unlikely that he would be linked in to the funeral home slayings. Assured that no clues existed to link him to the murders in any way, David left Walterboro immediately, not stopping for food or water.

Once he got to Savannah, he would make his rounds the following day before loading the casket pallet onto the next train headed to Jacksonville to begin the Florida leg of introductions. As David rode through the beautiful South Carolina morning and replayed the dark shadowed images he'd left behind in Charleston, two things were now completely clear.

First, he would never again suffer the foolish and endless bloviating nonsense of some obnoxious funeral director; and secondly, no way in hell would he ever again tell anyone where he was staying or traveling to next. David realized now just how careless and stupid he'd been, and how he might not be so lucky the next time. Plus, he didn't have a protector like his uncle Helmutt had so often spoke of having Big Sam to accompany him. Moreover, he knew deep down inside himself, that never again would he allow someone to try and impede, or worse yet destroy, his desires or intentions to be successful. Never! He

168

knew now that he could, and would, do whatever was necessary to claim his success and fortune. It was if the entire episode had unleashed a new, realized authority to do whatever he needed to achieve his own goals and dreams.

~~~~~~~~~~~

Helmutt could tell from the call home the following day that something was different with the way his nephew sounded. David's tone wasn't as gleeful and carefree as it had been in all the prior calls home. Helmutt realized that something was definitely different, noting that David seemed oddly but calmly serious in how he retold how the prior week's visits had gone. Typically, as most do who are hiding their true feelings, David said he guessed the travel was catching up to him and that he was "just tired."

Not fully accepting David's pretense, the much wiser and older uncle decided to point blank ask if there had been any trouble of any sort so far on the trip. Not wanting his uncle to know how he'd let his guard down so badly and almost lost the caskets, or be told to come home, of course David denied it. Only saying, "no, nothing that amounted to much." Still Helmutt could tell that something was very different, that his nephew didn't want to talk about. Helmutt knew well how such a first time adventure, especially in a new land, would hold many awakenings in store for David, which was one reason he hadn't forced the idea of his nephew taking along a protector and companion. Despite the risks, Helmutt knew just how much he had learned himself at a young age while traveling alone, and knew the life experience would be good for David. Of course, assuming he didn't encounter any real trouble. He'd already considered those certainties before agreeing to the young man's travel plans. For now, he would wait and see how his nephew sounded on the next call. Perhaps he was simply tired. After all he had been pushing it pretty hard.

~~~~~~~~~~~~

Over the next six weeks, David made his way through Florida and up to Atlanta; then heading westward to Birmingham and Jackson, Mississippi, before turning up to Tennessee to hit Memphis and Nashville, both already fair-sized and progressive cities by 1916. Uncle Helmutt's concerns were alleviated after hearing his nephew's voice and energy return to the familiar levels from earlier in the trip. David spoke about several more interested customers who had committed to more advance down payments on casket orders. More interestingly, Atlanta and Nashville had produced two additional potential distribution partners, just like Richmond had early on in the journey. He was excited to know that new distributors for Great American would certainly lead to a much faster market introduction of their line to the funeral market in several key areas.

In his final call home, David reported how the two established firms operated funeral homes but also distributed caskets to other operators across their regions. Owners of both firms saw the same strong potential for Great American quality and committed to placing immediate stocking orders to resale the new high-end casket line. Just like the old Scotsman David had met in Virginia, these two new parties also inquired of Great

American offering a slightly less expensive middle price point line.

As David explained, it would be for caskets with the same exterior quality but no carvings and with perhaps slightly less finish quality in lighter stain colors. Uncle Helmutt was very intrigued at the interesting findings his nephew had learned. The other insights shared with Helmutt were about the aspect of segregation, his first sighting of newfangled metal caskets, as well as just how many companies were out there making some sort of a wood casket, usually still the basic pine box variety. Clearly there were already hundreds of firms making and selling some form of coffin or casket in the U.S. by the time of David's trip.

David talked further of how the funeral market was completely segregated. How he had learned that African American mortuaries rarely, if ever, served a white family, regardless of heritage, and vice versa. After a few stops at black-owned mortuaries, it became clear to David that the product quality and price availability was far below what Great American was offering.

Even more impactful to David's awareness and ideological development about his new country was the coincidence of a racially-charged movie that he had heard about while dining out one evening. So he decided to see the film while traveling in Mississippi at a movie house that displayed its title on their marquee. *The Birth of a Nation* was a silent film by D.W. Griffith, who at the time was considered one of his generation's most talented filmmakers. Released the prior year out on the West Coast of the country to very positive reviews, the film eventually became very popular all across the country. It even became the first American film to be screened at the White House, drawing strong praise from then President Woodrow Wilson. Still drawing huge crowds by the time David heard about the picture, although for various reasons depending upon people's perspectives, the young man, still very impressionable and discovering America on his own, was very incredibly moved by the film's intended content and messaging. Ultimately, the picture had a lifelong, profound impact on David and his way of thinking, personally and in business.

Combined, this information caused David to develop a firm opinion of the African American community; and one that would not change much over the course of history for him personally, or the company, as sadly time would prove. Though he would never say it out loud to his uncle, nor certainly to Big Sam, David had firmly concluded that going after the black trade wasn't worth the effort or interest of Great American.

After visiting the famous Nashville Parthenon he had read and heard so much about on the train ride from Memphis, the final new market stop on the itinerary would be Louisville, Kentucky. Once he had visited with several more area mortuaries and heard more of the same responses for his quality caskets, David was more than ready to keep heading northward. Crossing back over the Ohio River, thinking how the watery border outlined the southernmost sections of the state for which it was named, David exhausted his final rounds in the Cincinnati market as originally planned, where he would finally sell the three popular display caskets, now that each had served its purpose. Finally, it would be only one more day's ride until he would be back home in Bergholz to report and capitalize on his most successful first venture in America.

~~~~~~~~~~~~~~~

TYCOON

Helmutt was amazed at his nephew's successful journey. After visiting eighteen unique markets and more than sixty new, prospective funeral home firms, including three potential distributors, David's initial order commitments totaled two hundred eighty-eight caskets; an average of four per funeral home operator and twenty from each of the new distributor partners. Twenty was a new minimum order size that David had quickly established to test the seriousness of any would be distributor, and none had balked to get their hands on Great American quality.

From what David had surmised from the three prospective sales partners, their combined annual orders could potentially exceed four hundred new casket orders per year; and definitely three times that amount if Helmutt agreed to adding a new middle line of high-finish, non-carved models. Even if the new fifty-seven individual funeral parlor accounts averaged only four casket orders every other month, that projected to another one thousand three hundred and sixty-eight caskets annually; for a combined total of one thousand seven hundred sixty-eight added from the trip. David was so proud to review the projections with his uncle, who listened with absolute marveled delight.

As David reviewed his math again with his uncle, still trying to soak up his nephew's tremendous estimates, it was apparent that if fully realized the Great American production volume and profits were about to explode by thirty-five percent!

If that was indeed true, which the impending commitment deposits would prove out, then Helmutt and Big Sam would need to get busy immediately expanding the shop and manufacturing operations. However his uncle ensured his young nephew that nothing would happen until they received confirmation of the wire deposits.

Over the next two weeks, David followed up with each customer and secured every one of the promised orders. As well, he and his uncle reached agreements with the three new prospective distributors, securing their orders for twenty premium carved caskets as discussed, plus another twenty for high-gloss, non-carved middle price point caskets. Helmut marveled at David's ability to sell a concept of a new mid-priced, de-featured line, especially since the customers hadn't even seen one. He had won the orders on his pure skill of presenting the three skidded high-end models. As David had promised to each new prospective customer, all orders were on a first come, first serve basis. While the initial orders would be honored with the twenty percent down offer, all following orders would be for the standard fifty percent down basis.

After receiving the first Great American deliveries and seeing how grieving families reacted to the new high quality line, there would be no mortuary customers unwilling to agree to the Kleinmark standard terms. Within six months, after launching the new middle tier non-carved line, Great American's order volume grew by another twenty-five percent, virtually overnight. David's first route through the Eastern seaboard and Southern states had taken the annual sales volume from the previous rate of five thousand per year to almost six thousand eight hundred. Factoring in the added commitments for the new non-carved line, Great American would increase their annual production to almost eight thousand five hundred.

In all, David's single-handed market excursion had increased the company volume over one hundred and sixty-eight percent. Needless to say, his uncle and father back in Belgium were astounded at the young man's potential for developing business and relationships so quickly.

~~~~~~~~~~~~~

As the next several months passed by and the ramped up production expansion was well underway, David trained a young bright local Bergholz woman with the most pleasant voice to remain in constant phone and telegraph contact with clients. Now realizing how Great American's growth was only limited to funeral operators knowing of their premium quality, he decided to go back on the road once again to further promote their two lines and gain additional share in more new markets. This time his travels would take him to the country's central regions, as far away as Chicago, Minneapolis, Des Moines, Lincoln, Kansas City, St. Louis, Little Rock, New Orleans, Houston and Dallas. He would do everything the same as before, with the mapping approach and casket display pallet. Except this time, he would take along someone to assist with the work and help provide protection on the journey.

Never having mentioned anything about killing the seersucker fool in Charleston, David used the excuse of needing a second pallet for the non-carved models to be taken along. That would mean someone was needed to drive the second team for the additional wagon. While it was an obvious conclusion given how the new mid-price point line was taking off so well, the thought of having someone else along to have his back if ever needed was reassuring. Still, Helmutt suspected otherwise, having noted how much more subdued his nephew had been ever since returning home. There was no doubt that David's personality was very different, and in a darker way. Unlike the jubilant lad so excited to see the famous sites on his first journey abroad in America, like Washington's cherry blossom trees and Tennessee's Parthenon replica, it was obvious a far more serious young man had returned.

~~~~~~~~~~~~~~

Sitting on the front porch in the evenings as was their custom, the American Kleinmark men regularly talked about David's travels, past and pending, and how tremendously the business was growing as a result. Helmutt had been searching for a way to get David to open up about whatever had changed him so. Finally, remembering how his father, Emest, had used the stories of past threats and thieves he and Evrard had dealt with in their time, he thought perhaps the same approach might work with David. One evening when the night summer air was cool with a slight breeze, Helmutt told David that while it was so good to see their business grow, he also wanted to be honest with his nephew about the hard costs that had been paid in the early years. Helmutt spoke in great detail about the back-stabbing furniture store and mortuary operator in Cleveland and the scheming partner who he and Big Sam had killed up in Canton.

177

He told David about how they had burned the body of the bait-and-switch casket maker, as well as many other heavy-handed necessities through the first twenty-five years.

After speaking so openly and honestly for quite some time, Helmutt finally saw the remorse and tension leave his nephew's face. Then, he asked David straight out about his first journey again. "So I'm going to ask again nephew. Did you have any trouble or ever have to un-holster your weapon out of any dire need on your trip? Something inside of me suggests that you had some trouble to deal with."

Overwhelmed with all kinds of feelings, from having been so careless and from not allowing any remorse whatsoever for killing the men who had stolen the wagon, David's eyes looked down and away, like Helmutt's had just years earlier. And just as Emest had comforted his uncle, Helmutt pulled his chair close to David and placed his large, heavy calloused hand on the young man's shoulder. Telling him that no matter what had happened, the important thing was how he had returned safely, regardless of any success. Helmutt reassured David there was nothing to fear or to be ashamed of, and stressed how it would be a relief to get whatever happened off of his chest, sharing how he had done the same with his own father. Despite his heavy embarrassment of having put so much at risk, David ultimately nodded in agreement.

Looking up at his uncle and beginning to speak, Helmutt's usual kind eyes were looking back with heartfelt empathy and emoted understanding. After telling all that had happened down in Walterboro and Charleston, David shared how the most surprising thing was how he had not felt any shame or regret for killing the two men. He spoke of growing up hearing all the stories from his grandfather and great uncle about dealing out harsh punishment on foolish men who tried to steal or cheat them at business, including killing. David explained how he and his father, who was weak and sickly, had always been required to outsource such heavy-handedness to hired thugs when needed. Therefore, he really didn't know how he would react in such a moment, much less feel, until he was forced to deal with the men in Charleston. David told his uncle about being shocked at how it had felt so natural, and how he even felt "right about it."

Hearing David speak so openly caused Helmutt to feel more pride about the great Kleinmark tradition than ever since coming to America. Recently, reaching his own life's half-century mark, it was now clear that his nephew possessed the same Kleinmark grit, courage, and determination as his forefathers. He now knew the young man had it inside himself to do whatever was necessary to defend and protect the Kleinmark family legacy. Helmutt simply offered these words to the young man, which would remain on David's heart forever:

"You absolutely did the right thing, David. Never doubt that! And never let any man take away anything that belongs to you or our family, for any reason! Don't ever allow anyone the first inch of denial or betrayal. Once you ever do, then you will begin a downward spiral into certain failure until you've lost everything for which our family has worked tirelessly, over so many generations. Know that the calm and resoluteness that

lives inside you, which you felt that day in Charleston, is our family's legacy Kleinmark DNA. Never again question it or anything that you ever feel must be done to protect it! Now, I know that you will do so till your dying day. And that, David, makes me and your entire family very proud of you!"

Those words from Helmutt gave David the needed clarity of purpose and justification that would serve him throughout the remainder of his life. It would be those words that David's mind would often harken back to whenever he needed to justify any action or deed he took to get what he wanted or that he thought justified the benefit of the company. Now with a mindset of complete absolution, David would never allow anything or anyone to ever divert his great dreams and plans.

~~~~~~~~~~~~

Given the reported usual, harsh winter weather experienced in the planned Northern states, David elected to travel by train to the southernmost point of the journey, New Orleans. Out of fun, his uncle teased his nephew about how tough his forefathers, Emest and Evrard, had been when they braved the brutal winter of 1844 in their own market expansion efforts. David had hoped by starting out in early March of 1917 that the temperatures and conditions would be at least tolerable once he and his new helper, Vernon, traveled north of St. Louis. Vernon was a young strapping black man, twice David's size, who had the strength of Big Sam and could handle a gun well. Vernon hated cold weather with a passion too and eagerly supported his young boss's idea to head south. So the four month travel plan was set, and like before, weekly call updates would take place on Sunday afternoons.

By the time David and Vernon returned to Bergholz from the second expedition trip, orders from the existing client base had increased another eighteen percent, mostly due to the new non-carved offerings. Now the annual run rate being produced exceeded the ten thousand mark for the first time. The weekly Sunday calls home had continued to report similar findings and promised commitments from the central States territory.

In all, David reported another seventy funeral home operators and an additional five distributor partners located up and down the central U.S. with interest to sell Great American caskets. Based upon the expectations after meeting with each new prospective client, the company would definitely need to expand again. This time it would increase by another fifty percent, just to meet the demand estimated at fifteen thousand per year.

After seeing how the increases were still continuing to grow each month in the new Eastern and Southeastern regions, , Helmutt and David knew that their brand was indeed unique and catching on like wildfire because of the two successful promotional tours. Rather than just try to keep up with demand, they would devise a plan to at least double the current projected volume to thirty thousand wood caskets, with thirty-five percent being premium carved. That would require buying more land around Bergholz, a lot more! It would also mean hiring and

181

training a great many more workers. All of which they began immediately that year.

Another consideration David had gotten his uncle to agree to, after discovering metal caskets on the first trip, was to explore an investment in having some dye molds founded by one of the Pittsburgh steel mills. After evidencing more opportunity and interest in steel caskets on the second trip, the steel initiative would become something on his immediate front burner agenda. The ever astute David could see a tremendous market interest growing in metal caskets, especially with its protective qualities and paint color options that could be afforded to consumers. This would have to take a high priority. Helmutt agreed.

~~~~~~~~~~~~

As history would prove out, America's involvement in World War I would result in over fifty thousand U.S. casualties resulting from the battle. Although, the real impact of the war on the country would be the devastating impact from the Spanish Flu pandemic that occurred between 1918 and 1920, taking over an amazing 675,000 souls in America alone. Regrettably, the U.S. troops had contracted and transported the disease back to all regions of the country, resulting in one of the greatest human tragedies known to mankind.

As for the funeral trade, the business of death that it is, an always welcomed pandemic ignites a boom market for opportunist casket makers and the like. For Great American, having smartly expanded the prior year's production capacity by almost seven hundred percent, the dark Spanish Flu period for the country resulted in what was considered "a glorious windfall" for the Great American Casket Company. That was, at least, in David Kleinmark's opinion.

Thankfully, being situated so close to a railway line meant that Great American caskets could get shipped out quickly. Most manufacturers were remote and first had to haul their plain boxes into town before getting shipped out. The biggest difference that resulted in Great American's boom period stemming from the pandemic, besides available capacity, was the quality appreciation that funeral homes and families appreciated from the brand. Without question, quality and finish set Great American apart from most all others. Whereas a few casket makers had quality, they never had amassed the manufacturing capacity of Great American. Suffice to say, it was a deadly combination that led to major increases in profits for the Kleinmarks.

~~~~~~~~~~~~

While the pandemic created a tidal wave of flooding orders into Great American, it also brought with it an issue Helmut and David had never previously encountered, requests for free caskets, especially for U.S. service members and front-line medical workers who had succumbed to the deadly influenza. Funeral operators seemed to increasingly request with great ease that Great American either provide outright or at least share in helping with "free" caskets for these two groups. Helmutt and David knew this predicament had the potential to create a very difficult and costly precedent for the future, which would surely repeat whenever other similarly difficult scenarios in the Nation occurred. So their response was always quick and swift anytime Great American would be asked to forego its profits to help a particular fallen victim, regardless of the reason or situation. Their decision was that "absolutely no way in hell would they provide free caskets!" "Kleinmarks are not in the business of charity and there is no such thing as a free casket!" the men would staunchly state, although never directly to a customer. Their official, public and very well thought out response was always something to the effect of: "Every life is precious, and therefore Great American cannot place any individual life's value over that of another."

With that simple and well-worded reply, any would be charity case request was easily quashed. Amazingly, the same approach still works to this day. Regardless of the crisis or desperate circumstance, the company is never willing to provide something even at cost, much less free. Anytime something so magnanimous occurs in funeral service, it is far likely because a local, honorable funeral operator stepped up, never the likes of Great American.

By the end of 1920, Great American was consistently producing over four thousand caskets per month, something Helmutt or Adlar could have never imagined. Great American became widely known by funeral operators all over the country for having plenty of inventory and being able to quickly get caskets shipped out. Even new unknown prospective firms were seeking them out to inquire about opening up an account to get access to the high quality line of mid-to-high-end wood caskets.

The following decade would bring its own set of hardships and challenges to America. Especially tough financial times resulting from The Great Depression era that began in 1929 and ran through the late next decade. Always calculating and shrewd, David saw this as another opportunity to capitalize on a down market and struggling operators. With his trusted backup man Vernon in tow, David went back out on the road to see several distribution partners he hoped might be on the edge of going under. If so, that would create a wonderful opportunity for Great American.

Once the trip had concluded, David had reached agreements in principle with over two dozen of the distribution partners to buy them out. The agreement was simple. The principals at each firm would remain employed, essentially as delivery salesmen, while Great American would take ownership of all assets and distribution rights in the prescribed areas served. Each agreement required that the firm's owner and all future dependents must agree to a strict non-compete arrangement, barring them from ever competing with Great American in any way.

By the time The Great Depression was over, Great American had purchased almost all of the casket distributors they had sold through previously, and at just pennies on the dollar. To the Kleinmarks, it was strictly business. Despite all of the business owners begging them for a fair price, it was either sell out or the Kleinmarks would open up against them and refuse to sell to them, at least for the same prices. One way or another, the distributors would go out of business.

In less than a year and a half, Great American had gone from worrying about its distribution partners to owning dozens of warehouses all over their geography. More importantly the company was now able to control distribution and delivery quality, making them a tremendous force in the heavily fragmented casket industry.

When The Great Depression finally concluded in the late 1930s, Great American had begun producing and selling a number of steel casket models. While their clientele base grew substantially for both wood and metal caskets over the decade, the nation's population and corresponding number of funeral homes had increased too. Most were locally owned and operated by a dedicated family who often lived above the funeral parlor, which was on the main level of the building.

Sadly, as the nation's financial crisis era drew to a close, leaving its brutal devastation languishing on America, the sheer workload stemming from the period took its toll on Helmutt. Further complicating his stresses, another World War was about to mire America down into more economic hardships. This time the combined calamities would directly impact Great American at its heart and foundation. Being required by the U.S. government to document their utilization of wood and steel resources, Helmutt and David would be forced, like all casket makers, to produce an alternative style of product, mostly cloth-covered softwood versions. This would mean another huge manufacturing change, especially after everything they had survived in the prior decade.

All of it was simply too much for Helmutt to handle, causing him to have an extremely severe stroke at age seventy-two. For the first time ever since forming, the Great American Casket Company was at risk of going-under like so many other firms that had succumbed to the depression, or possibly now due to the indefinite future prospects of only producing far less profitable caskets. David fully understood this moment was his family's greatest challenge and that he would need to determine an equally great plan to offset the dire risk to Great American.

~~~~~~~~~~~~

It was clear that the only answer now was simple and obvious, volume! With a war looming which most experts feared would last several years, David knew that low-end, low-profit caskets would flood and dominate the market. Solid hardwood and steel caskets were not even allowed to be used for production because of the country's natural resources mobilization legislation passed into law. Whereas before, the company's growth strategy had been solely focused on capturing greater share in the very profitable mid-to-upper price ranges, now the only apparent strategy was to get back out into the market and assure customers of product availability and determine where struggling regional casket makers existed.

After securing in-home, round-the-clock care for his uncle, and ensuring Big Sam, still fit as ever, and the manufacturing teams were ready for the low-end model transition, David headed out for five months straight in the fall of 1939. Keeping his familiar routine, the weekly check-in calls would still take place, now with Big Sam, about key topics like his uncle's health, production, and shipments. David handled any financial matters from the road by telephone.

By the time he returned, agreements in principle had been reached with over two dozen more casket makers to acquire their businesses, of course for pennies on the dollar. Notwithstanding the typical begging would be damned as always before. David signed direct purchase agreements with dozens of the larger volume funeral operators in each state. Although some refused to accept his terms because they saw Great American as taking advantage of their friends and allies, and considered the casket maker and its aggressive owner a deviant opportunist in trying times. In those situations, David always made note of anyone repudiating his offers and silently pledged to get his revenge at some point in the future. Meanwhile, anyone making his shit list saw their prices go up and deliveries slowed down to a snail's pace.

~~~~~~~~~~~

Helmutt finally passed away shortly after David returned home to Bergholz in early 1940. The worse part of it for David and his family back home, given the strains of war, was that it would be impossible to take his body back to Belgium for burial. Speaking on the phone to his father Adlar, now seventy-nine, David shared the sad news and stated the obvious fact of war and how his uncle's body would require interment in America. "Helmutt was our Kleinmark's family first great American, David, so in some way that seems most fitting. It is the Lord's way my son. I hope someday to visit you both there before I die."

188

To pay homage to his late uncle and the contribution he had made not only to the family, but also the company, David would go to great effort and expense for Helmutt's obituary notice and planning. Without his uncle's sheer courage and tenacity, the young man knew none of it would have existed. Hoping one day his father and other family members would visit, David had a huge, expensive bronze monument erected and placed in a specially created family burial plot behind their home. Regardless, other than the attending minister, David would be the only one to attend his uncle's funeral service.

Not even Big Sam would be invited to attend his lifelong friend's service. Once David had talked Big Sam in to a so-called retirement, he was banned from ever coming back to the company. A few years later when Big Sam finally died and news was sent to David, he would never respond or provide any monies for his headstone, despite how his uncle had always cherished his dear friend and often spoke of his great contributions to all of the success realized by Great American. In his eyes, all that Big Sam had ever been was someone fortunate enough to have worked for his great Kleinmark family's company, nothing more.

Adlar would never have the opportunity to see his son again, visit Helmutt's grave, or see the America that had been so good to his family. Less than a year later, David's father would suffer a very bad fall tripping over some lumber on the Kleinmark Co. shop floor. The accident resulted in his head severely hitting the concrete floor, causing a deep hematoma to quickly develop on his forehead. Sadly, he would never recover due to the fact that the physicians were simply too afraid to administer the necessary medications for surgery given Adlar's age and past health history.

Once again, because of a Second World War, now engulfing his own beloved Belgium, David was unable to travel back home to grieve with his own family in Vielsalm. Desperately wanting to attend his father's funeral, David astounded the local pastor when he paid to have a telephone line and speaker system installed in the church so he could be on the phone and listen to the funeral service for his father, as well as address the crowded church over the speaker. Something only a very rich person at the time could have ever entertained. It did not take long for the news of the new telephone in the church to reach the regions around Vielsalm. Now everyone around knew that the Kleinmark family was indeed a very, very wealthy.

~~~~~~~~~~~

That following year of 1941, once the family was settled from Adlar's passing and sales of the furniture business in Belgium to its employees to own and operate, it was finally time for David's only brother Renford to make his own passage to America. The last Kleinmark male of age, Renford had been required to remain in the family's home country to run the family business once his father had become too ill to do so. At thirty-one years of age, twelve years David's junior, Renford spoke fluent English like all of Adlar's children. From his experience running the furniture enterprise for the past few years, like his older brother, Renford equally excelled at finance and business. Indeed he would be a huge help in many ways to David going-forward.

Now David's primary concern would be how to extract his brother out of Belgium and find him safe passage to America. Like all of his fellow countrymen who had emigrated, he read with incredible disbelief the newspaper accounts of how his family's beloved country's King Leopold III had capitulated and surrendered to invading German military forces in May of 1940. Fleeing the country so would be extremely dangerous for Renford to attempt, but equally expensive for David to make happen. After paying one hundred thousand dollars cash to a top government Belgium official, with whom their dear family friend Dr. Desmet had secretly coordinated and who in turn bribed a like top German officer, covert arrangements were made for Renford to escape the country in late summer. The entire plan had been arranged without any shared knowledge or consideration of their mother or sisters, presumably to keep them from knowing or possibly saying anything. As the brothers would later claim, that way their family would hopefully not ever being accused of conspiring.

Leaving their mother and sisters, all now married, back in their homeland, the two remaining men of the Kleinmark bloodline vowed to one day go back for them all. However that would never happen, despite keeping apprised of how the war continually escalated and crept closer and closer to Vielsalm. Even after reported accounts of the infamous Battle of the Bulge war that directly ignited their homeland with major battles occurring just a few miles north and south of Vielsalm, in the

191

towns of Bastogne and Foy, David and Renford Kleinmark remained silent and disconnected from their family until the end of the war.

The two great Kleinmark men never made any effort to establish communications with their sisters, even though they could have easily, given their resources. Despite all of their brother's-in-law losing their lives fighting against the Nazi's, these two men now considered themselves Americans, first and foremost, thus feeling no compunction or guilt for ignoring to help their family or homeland in any way. All that David ever told his brother was how their "patriotic contribution" to the war effort had been by foregoing all of the millions in profits from the steel and hardwoods they in turn "contributed" from no longer using the resources to make and sell quality caskets.

From then forward, all the men ever did was send some monies back to help their family get by. Once their mother died a few years later, the sisters wrote only one letter back to their brothers stating that they no longer wanted anything from them, especially their "greedy money", and to not ever come back or contact them again. The sisters would never forgive their brothers for abandoning the family or for allowing, especially their own mother, to believe Renford had been kidnapped and murdered by the Nazis, when they could have easily communicated otherwise.

~~~~~~~~~~~~

It was incredible to believe it had been almost fifty years ago since the two companies had been formed. It was equally amazing to think that both businesses had been operating as sole proprietorships since Helmutt applied for the first tax licenses way back when he and Big Sam bought the small farm on Yellow Creek. Now almost forty-three years of age, David was wise enough to know that after all of the expansion, investment, and contractual agreements the company had engaged over the prior decades, that serious legal representation would be needed to ensure the firm's long term viability.

Helmutt had always relied on the legal counsel of a local, one-man firm located over in New Philadelphia, Ohio. A good enough lawyer, the man had not come by reputation, but rather by the need of a new dining room suit from Kleinmark Co. His wife had actually sought out Helmutt based upon the recommendation of her local furniture store. After friendly introductions, Helmutt had routinely looked to the learned man for any legal related requirements. But David realized the business now required far deeper expertise in various corporate and legal matters and went to Pittsburgh to seek out a big name firm to represent his family's expanding enterprise.

~~~~~~~~~~~~~~~

While it was important to David that the selected firm was of sufficient high regard, the most important criteria would be that they absolutely understood and embraced the DNA of the Great American Casket Company and, especially of one, David Adlar Kleinmark. Before darkening the first entryway to any of the big Pittsburg law practices, he was decided that the only firm to be ultimately considered would, in no uncertain terms, need to prove their salt in that unsolicited regard.

David spent three full days meeting with a half dozen of the top corporate law practices around "Steel City", as it had been called for decades by then. All of the firms were located in downtown Pittsburgh in huge, tall office buildings. All had dozens of attorneys working for them, and each with gobs of partner level stiffs wanting to get their greedy hands on the Kleinmark businesses once they heard about the firm's annual revenues of almost thirty-five million dollars. The huge boardrooms David sat in to hear each firm's pitch were equally impressive, as were their mandatory retainer fees, which of course were presented as if they were doing any "considered new client" a great big favor. The first five firms met with were essentially carbon-copies of one another. All slick, smooth, polished, and very expensive. The sixth and last firm David met with, however, did prove to be what he had been searching for.

~~~~~~~~~~~

Roseville Black was led by Arthur Black, one of its original founders, who helped establish the firm when he was just thirty years of age. Black, thirty years senior to the new younger man seeking representation, welcomed David into his personal office on the twenty-fifth floor of the gridiron styled building that overlooked the very spot where three rivers crashed together in downtown Pittsburgh.

Drawing the young potential patron over to the thirty-foot wide picture window view behind his desk to see the impressive confluence of the Ohio, Allegheny, and Monongahela Rivers, the slender and stoic Arthur Black explained, "For forty years, Roseville Black has been incredibly successful because of ensuring that same success for our clients, no matter what issues arise, Mr. Kleinmark." Black went on to stipulate how any number of area practices could take care of a client's legal needs of course, but stressed "our firm is very unique in one regard sir."

Turning and pointing to the most beautiful, dark mahogany hand-carved, glass-top case placed on the client-side of his mammoth desk, Black begin to make a finer point to distinguish his firm. As he handed the young business man one of the two famous Colt Model 1860 Army Revolvers, David couldn't help but think how the weapon had been made the same year of his father's birth, and survived all this time. Black was famous inside his firm for using the iconic pistols to make a well-known point of how the right type of force is sometimes needed to fight for good versus evil.

"Every businessman will face not only hardships young man, but evil itself, that is, if you are successful enough. Roseville Black will use whatever force necessary to ensure your problems go away, so that you can remain focused on your business. Just as those three rivers below us, everything looks fine and peaceful from above. But down below the surface of the raging rivers are currents that will take a man under to certain death in less than a minute. Think of my firm as the only protection you or your business will ever need to keep you safe from evils or potentially threatening undercurrents."

Black's eyes never blinked while he spoke. His face was as steely cool and collected as he uttered his well-rehearsed lines. Inviting the younger Mr. Kleinmark to sit down at the private conference table near the long picture window, the two men spent the next two hours together as Black heard the story of the Kleinmark family and businesses in America. Sensing an immediate mutual comfort and trust, the two men agreed the exact, right fit existed between their firms, and more importantly, themselves.

As Black had his secretary bring up the retainer agreement for signature, he noted what a fine and formal family name David indeed had. Although, after hearing the brave story of the family and their triumph in America, Black told his newest client something that would stick for the rest of his life. "I must say David you are a very impressive and driven young man. No doubt, you have a tenacity and determination unlike most I have ever met. As such, I simply cannot envision referring to you as only 'David'." So with your permission, I am going to refer to you as DAK from this day forward! To me, that has the tough tone and tenor of the seriousness by which you clearly purport yourself in life."

David not only liked the newly ascribed moniker, but decided right then and there to refer to himself as the same for the rest of his life. From that day forward Arthur Black would serve as DAK's personal and corporate attorney. More importantly, Arthur would become the most trusted mentor who would help his aggressive client navigate many troubled waters and deep evil currents over the following decades that followed.

~~~~~~~~~~~

Surviving the depressed economic times in the forties proved impossible for many of the hundreds of casket makers.

For debt-free, cash-rich, and volume-capable firms like Great American, it was another tremendous opportunity to expand by taking full advantage of those striving to stay afloat. DAK saw opportunities everywhere around the country, with distributors, manufacturers, and funeral operators.

When the Second World War finally ended, DAK had scarfed up more casket production plants, including several more metal dye molds. He had also expanded delivery routes out to the West Coast by snapping up over a dozen more distributors. This move instantly expanded Great American's sales coverage to a first time ever national platform. In doing so, DAK's latest penny-pinching investments would set the casket maker up for much faster market growth now that the war was over and hardwood and metal caskets were reintroduced to grieving American families. With a national commercial framework in place, the fifties would focus on accelerated growth with several new products fueled by the expanded sales organization, ultimately propelling the company to more than one hundred million dollars in annual sales revenue.

~~~~~~~~~~~~

By the mid-fifties, what had heretofore always been a sleepy little town of a couple thousand folks, with virtually only one industry and a single rail line, had exploded by tenfold. Furthermore, DAK had all but disbanded the furniture side due to steep competition from all the North Carolina based high-end furniture makers plus much lower margins compared to caskets, which better yet required no warranties to speak of. Bergholz had now become a very real manufacturing epicenter, albeit small by comparison to the likes of the neighboring steel city metropolis. DAK continued to have Renford buy up every available contiguous plot of land that bordered Great American's already sizeable land mass. Regardless, that didn't mean that any local fool would get DAK Kleinmark to pay through the nose for a piece of land. Instead the K-boys, as folks sneeringly called them behind their backs, would buy everything else around a particular piece of land they wanted until the fool yelled uncle and gave in to their low-ball price scheme. Truth be said, no one in Bergholz went up against the K-boys.

By the end of the decade, over fifteen thousand acres sat on the company books. When the next decade came and went, the company would triple its manufacturing space. DAK would also add a lavish, resort-styled, horse ranch situated on several thousand acres outside of Bergholz to breed his own bloodline of thoroughbreds and variety of other breeds of horses. The horses were something he had gotten into so as to constantly refuel thoughts of his Charleston epiphany. Not far from the ranch, the company also built a private airport to house and operate multiple private airplanes; mostly for DAK's own personal use. Whenever needed, the planes and ranch trappings would come in handy to entertain and corral a big-time customer prospect, or perhaps the occasional politician.

~~~~~~~~~~~~~~~~~

DAK faced another key loss by the time he reached his sixty-second birthday in 1960. His dear friend and longtime trusted advisor, and attorney, Arthur Black passed way at age ninety-two. Black had helped DAK guide Great American

198

through various legal threats of hostel unions, numerous acquisitions, and creating a formal Employee Stock Ownership Program, commonly known as an ESOP. As part of their ingenious work, Roseville Black had constructed very effective executive agreements that would always entice top-notch corporate-minded professionals to come live out in the sticks of Bergholz.

DAK knew that they had to create a strong package to draw the best talent, because otherwise no executive in their right mind would have ever considered moving so far out to such a small, nowhere town situated in the middle of a lot of nothingness. More importantly, the one-sided contracts ensured if they ever left, by whatever means or circumstances, that they would only escape with as little of the Kleinmark's money as possible. Leave or escape would be defined as such, whenever DAK felt they were out of favor for any little reason and was ready to kick their ass to the bloody curb. During the entire time DAK and Arthur Black were teamed up, Great American never lost a case whenever someone had sued for what was rightfully theirs. As Black often reminded, "The only things that are rightful and just to a former Great American employee, are only what we decide and say they are!"

~~~~~~~~~~~~~

DAK would often think of his very first train ride to see the cherry blossoms in the Nation's capital, and how he read everything he could get his hands about the tycoons of the day like Carnegie and Rockefeller. Sitting at his own private airport, some forty-eight years later, he was getting ready to take

199

possession of another new private plane. This time it was the very powerful Dassault Falcon, a highly advanced jet with blazing speed and range capabilities. DAK and Arthur had used the older Learjet to shoot all over the country fanning flames and putting out fires.

The best times they had usually involved some big-time wannabe funeral home operator who they'd invite out "for drinks on the jet." Whether they knew to expect it or, the stooge would always get conned into promises of hunting trips to the infamous Ranch, where DAK assured that the room maids were far prettier and shapelier than the little cocktail waitresses he had on the plane. The mere thought of that implausible possibility left most mortal men flatly stunned at the notion. DAK's cocktail talent on the jets was always Grade-A Plus!

The standard routine, once the dude was on the plane, was to say "Look, (name here), we're not here to talk business. We just want to get to know you. That's all." Then once the first few rounds of drinks were clearly taking the intended effects, DAK and Arthur would announce how they had to run over to the local airport office for some concocted "really important telephone meeting" that would take about an hour or so. This setup left the suckered funeral home owner dude and his personal cocktail waitress alone on the plane just long enough. Mindful of details, they even closed the cabin ramp door behind as they left and were certain to have the pilot go with them.

Thinking they were on the plane alone with the girl, making it a he-said, she-said situation, it was pretty obvious what would happen next. Rest assured, the batting average those girls

200

maintained for Mr. DAK was, well let's just say, out of the park! Rarely ever did one of those little pretty girls let Mr. DAK down. Even the holiest of most professed men could rarely resist the temptation that DAK Kleinmark put on their silver platter.

For most of the men, the visit to the jet and promises of impending hunting trips was usually enough to get them to switch to Great American caskets. But if for some reason, the occasional foolish man quickly forgot about their bad graces and pushed back on DAK's offer to sign them up with an immediate order, then the cork went back into the bottle faster than you can say "Fuck me!" Which usually was what most of them said when a special courier showed up the following week with copies of the dude's best and worst sides having some fun with the cocktail girls.

Occasionally, some fools even made the mistake of threatening DAK, suggesting they knew where he lived in the little shit town of Bergholz, and how perhaps they might just send him a reply of equal proportion. DAK, with his constant smooth temper in the face of threat, always heard them out before reminding them that the pictures could have been delivered to the fool's home. Then most men would realize that they had screwed up and took DAK's deal, which of course paid less than what had been offered on the jet. As for those who told DAK Kleinmark to go screw himself, well that's where Roseville Black came in.

~~~~~~~~~~

There were any numbers of situations over the years that Arthur Black directed outside his firm to be handled accordingly when needed. Arthur was known to quip to his special clients how Roseville Black was a simple law practice. Although sometimes, when the law didn't work, then "the unlawful would go to work every time", he would often smirk. It was in those times that Roseville Black would prove its salt about respecting the Kleinmark DNA, as DAK had always demanded from day one. Honorable lawyers were not expected or skilled to handle such heavy-handed matters. So Roseville Black had a certain list of "outside associates" skilled in such matters to call upon whenever some dirty work requirements required outsourcing. Whether it was having someone followed, beaten up, or just harassed and scared to death, whatever worked, Arthur's firm had a long list of thugs and slugs to crawl through the slime and make any problem go away, permanently, if necessary.

They didn't show up on an org chart, but Roseville Black employed several former dirty ex-cops who still had ties with many of the cons they had put in jail at one time or another. Whenever things needed to be handled outside the law, the matter would get pushed down the food chain to one of their dirty ex-cops or cons to deal with. This specially-added level of service protection would be used time and again over the years whenever DAK placed a call to Arthur requesting a meeting in Steubenville. Less than halfway to Pittsburgh for DAK, the mere mention of needing to meet for a drink at the longtime river crossing location signaled to let his legal ally know that deep currents in the water required addressing. Once those meetings occurred, DAK never had to hear of the problem or person again, ever.

With sales now reaching well over a hundred and fifty million, Great American had become one of the largest casket makers in America. The industry was also changing and evolving just as the country's population continued to migrate from farms to larger cities. With shifting economic impacts, the result on funeral homes in the day was the same as many other industries. One of the biggest developments began when second and third generation funeral home owners no longer wanted to remain in the business, or in some cases where an owner had no immediate family to keep the business going. In several parts of the country, the funeral home industry saw one firm buying up others in their area. Some operators continued to grow and expand over and over again. When this occurred, there were now beginning to be funeral home operators who controlled larger and larger chunks of the total available caskets purchased in their regions. As DAK saw this development continuing to reoccur he knew that Great American and other large casket makers in the day would be vying aggressively for those large pieces of business and put a strategic plan in place. That meant getting the jet fired up and heading out to see the big time operators who hadn't had their pictures taken yet. In most cases, just like with previous fools, it would be easy to set them up.

In one particular case out west, Great American was hemorrhaging significant volume where one of the new consolidators was buying up several good Great American accounts and switching them over to main brand competitors. Despite DAK's best efforts, the good ol' boy that owned and operated his growing funeral home empire wasn't willing to take a meeting with the great DAK Kleinmark. This son of a bitch told DAK on the phone one time how he'd heard the tails about his famous tarmac meetings and he'd be damned if he'd ever get bamboozled by Great American. Once more, he told DAK in no uncertain terms what he could do with his Great American caskets and whores! DAK knew this guy was going to perhaps be a tougher challenge than expected. With Arthur gone, DAK would now have to meet his lifelong ally's heir apparent for the first time in Steubenville.

~~~~~~~~~~

Before his passing, Arthur had introduced DAK to Dennis Witman. Witman had been hand-picked and groomed by Arthur to personally handle the Great American account, which included being at the beck and call of DAK Kleinmark. As wide-eyed Black put it, "which means any fucking thing in the world!" Witman was a smart enough lawyer, but unlike most reputable sorts, he was willing to handle anything that came down the pike, regardless of which side of the law it fell on. Since joining Roseville Black right out of a second-rate, mid-tier, public law school, Arthur had taken note of Witman's aggressive interest to advance and take on any situation, no matter how ugly it could get. After testing the rookie lawyer for several years, Black knew his protégé would be the perfect fit to step in and take over Great American when it was time. The only problem with Witman was how he tended to take many things a step or two farther compared to what his mentor Black would have. For instance where a good old fashioned beating from one of the firm's ex-con's would suffice, Witman didn't rule out a complete bound and gag job that ended up with a body at the bottom of the Ohio River.

Witman was a scrawny little prick who had clearly been severely teased as a child, enduring nicknames like Dimwit, D-witt (as in none) and Witless. Standing at five-foot, five-inches, balding by the age of twenty-eight, to go along with his coke-bottle glasses and crooked, yellow teeth, suffice to say, Witman didn't make a strong first impression. However, as Black realized the need to have someone willing to push the limits for his old friend DAK, Witman was exactly the type of lawyer who'd never let the law get in the way of "protecting the client."

Now it was time for Arthur's new man to prove his own salt for the first time to one of Roseville Black's wealthiest clients. So a meeting for drinks at the river crossing in Steubenville was set to deal with one of the fastest growing funeral home consolidators out west.

~~~~~~~~~~~~~~~~

GREED

Death Rate and Volume are absolutely the only things that matter in the casket business. Don't ever let anyone suggest otherwise. Every casket company deeply studies all of the available death rate statistics. Anyone who says differently is an outright liar. Each and every year that Garner sat around the stately Great American boardroom table listening to hired experts project the coming year's death and cremation rate forecasts, there was never a question that everyone around the twenty-foot, hand-carved mahogany table was praying for "a really good year." Maybe not a full blown pandemic, which they all greedily thought would be the best case windfall scenario, of course, but at least, they wanted to see the Nation's death rate start finally ticking up as the experts had predicted for years would occur from the Baby Boomer effect of the 1940s.

Several dire ramifications on the precious Death Care Industry stemmed from Americans being better educated on diet and exercise, food manufacturer's being held to higher nutritional labeling standards by the FDA, the Catholic Church's approving cremation in the early 1960s, and a continuing uptick in the American economy, providing more discretionary spending power than ever before. All combined for a huge two-fold negative effect on profiteers from the death business. People were living longer, healthier lives, with more money than ever to spend in their retirement years; and when they did pass away, more and more consumers were choosing cremation over traditional burial, a far less expensive and profitable option.

These impacts left funeral purveyors, both product and service providers, fighting for an overall declining market yielding fewer funerals than expected, further negating overall revenues and profits. The main way for manufacturers to offset declining sales was to grow in volume, which is exactly what DAK and Great American had been focused on for decades.

Funeral home operators needed volume too, but they could also easily manipulate profits by simply buying cheaper caskets and selling them at the same or higher prices than before. Consumers would never be the wiser. All they really knew about funerals or caskets was whatever their local funeral home director told them anyway, because of how the industry was so intentional and successful at avoiding actual cost information from ever getting out. So, whenever the director leaned in and rubbed on a particular casket, as if they were personally polishing it for the family, it was as if to say, that it was the right choice for their lost loved one. Just like back in Cleveland during Helmutt's day, it still worked every time.

~~~~~~~~~~~~~~~~

By the time the later 1990s came around, the domestic casket industry kingpins came to realize that they weren't the only ones regularly studying the pending impacts expected from the Baby Boomer group in the U.S. By complete surprise, a few key industry individuals had conspired with Chinese manufacturers to start duplicating and importing good-looking, low-end, metal caskets, and worse yet, in the most popular styles and colors. In the matter of just a couple of years, new distributors began to setup warehouses all over the country

207

pushing the new bait and switch Chinese knock-offs, of course never disclosing anything to families. Although Federal law required import caskets to be labeled as such, indicating the country of origin, most of the Chinese caskets were rarely marked. And, if they were, the label was usually found on the bottom side of the casket, of course, where no grieving person would ever have seen it.

Creating more problems, the greedy capitalists also began to sell the cheap knockoffs online via the new world wide web called the Internet, as well get them into some major retail box stores. Consumers now had access to more information than ever before and could buy caskets cheaper than the industry had ever seen. It also meant that funeral home owners would begin losing a huge piece of their profit pie when smart consumers had their own cheap caskets delivered straight to the back door of the funeral home. Now, casket makers and funeral operators alike had a brand new set of challenges to deal with, in order to control the availability of information and caskets in their market.

To deal with these new disturbing challenges of more educated consumers and well-financed entrants to the casket market, Great American and other makers knew they had to act. The quickest vaccination casket makers could inject into their own new economic pandemic was to start offering new lines of cheaper, good-looking caskets to keep funeral operators from taking on the Chinese imports. Although this approach generated lower revenues and profits for domestic producers, the move would help stem the tidal wave of import caskets crashing into

208

their business. By the time the import distributors factored in the expensive freight cost to ship a casket, domestic producers were able to successfully mitigate the price differential to a point where many operators chose to stick with the known brands.

As for the consumers or operators who still went for import options, the industry brokers knew they had to mitigate those disruptions as well. To do so, one of the first things that had to happen was the establishment of an industry-wide consortium to produce and publish "information", or misinformation, about so-called Consumer Rights. Top product supplier kingpins invested heavily into the new foundation ensuring whenever anyone searched online for funeral information, only "the right information" about risks and responsibilities was available, at least based upon what they wanted them to know.

~~~~~~~~~~~~

Take for example, stories Garner heard directly from more than one funeral director about how they were "educating" the local clientele considering cremation or buying a casket from one of the big box retailers. Garner recalled being in one well-known Southern funeral home that had been around since the early 1900s when a grieving young man walked into the lobby. Standing there talking to the third generation owner, who upon seeing an obvious prospect walk inside, immediately turned his attention and well-rehearsed, softened, wide smile toward the younger man. Addressing him by name, the owner said his gentle hello, having served his family many times over the years, and said how sorry to hear how the man's mother had been shot to death by a raging, jealous ex-husband. Then the operator asked the grieving man to take a seat there in his stately vestibule.

Acknowledging how he "reckoned" all of his family had been buried by the funeral home, even back when the current owner's daddy ran it, the young man said his family wanted to look at possibly having a cremation service this time around for their mother. He said they heard it was a lot cheaper. As soon as the tearing man uttered those words aloud, the pompous operator leapt to his feet, turned blood-faced red, and said in the harshest raised voice: "Son, if you and your kin want to burn yall's momma, I can promise you that you won't be doing it in my funeral home! If you want someone to do that, then you're going to have to get the hell out of here boy!"

Garner was stunned to hear the obnoxious asshole owner treat the young grieving man, not more than nineteen years of age, so disrespectfully. The young man, now tearing more noticeably, left humiliated, as if he had asked the mortician to murder his dead mother all over again. Turning his attention back to Garner, the asshole director showed no awareness or concern about how he'd just treated the man. All he said was, "Garner, I'll tell you what friend, if those fucking rednecks don't stop all this cremation shit, you and Great American are going to have to start selling me caskets at half-price to make up the difference!" Garner just stood there, stunned and amazed at what he'd just witnessed.

Another time, a funeral home operator up North called Garner to bitch about the new price increase that had recently been announced, complaining how it was higher than any in the past ten years. To support his threat of possibly switching supply away from GAC for cheaper caskets, the operator told McCall the story of how his funeral home had just received their first internet casket, delivered by a direct freight carrier. Now, all caskets delivered to funeral homes all over the country are sent on big eighteen-wheelers, that's nothing new. A longstanding practice, drivers for GAC, et al, always carried their own lifts and dollies to offload the caskets and put them away inside the funeral home. Most drivers even have a key to the back door of the funeral homes on their routes, for any deliveries before or after hours, so as to not disturb the operator during non-working hours.

Now that consumers could shop and buy caskets online from any number of outlets, caskets were being scheduled for shipment to funeral homes as soon as the credit card cleared. Sometimes this meant that caskets showed up way too early or not soon enough before the funeral, to allow for casketing the body and even holding the family service. In the defense of funeral home owners, in some cases, families would try to hold them responsible to store their pre-delivered casket or complain if it was damaged or hadn't showed up in time for their loved one's service. Either way, it wasn't the funeral home's fault or responsibility.

In the case of the bitching Northern operator, his family client had never mentioned they had bought a casket online, and just had it delivered via eighteen-wheeler. When the truck driver backed his rig into the rear lot of the funeral home, and asked the owner to help him offload the casket, the owner reminded him where the sun didn't shine, and said "Do it your own fucking self!" Now the crate itself weighed several hundred pounds, so obviously the driver was unable to unload it, and finally just had to leave and take it back to his warehouse. Later, when the family heard about the owner's refusal and explanation of how he could not accept responsibility for their "property", the operator thought, perhaps, they would just return it to the manufacturer and come buy one of his high priced boxes. But, no sir! Instead, they had the big rig truck return the following day to the funeral home, where two of the family men met the driver. Once they helped the driver offload the huge, heavy, wooden crate and departed, the men thought they had done what they needed to satisfy the funeral home owner.

Then braggingly, the funeral operator said, "Garner, you should have seen the looks on those two bastards' faces, when I told them that they'd have to uncrate it themselves and then bring it into the embalming room. Plus, I told them they'd have to haul off all of the crating and wrapping materials. I'm not running some stupid dumping ground here, man! I bet you when that story gets around town, there won't be too many others interested in buying their caskets anywhere but from a funeral home!" Garner just listened to the idiot, stunned at what he had heard, and wondered if the man was even listening to himself.

~~~~~~~~~~~~~

Stories like these became all too common, as the industry pushed back from both sides in an effort to try and thwart the eventual onslaught of rising cremation and less profitable funerals. Since DAK's heyday as CEO when growth in the numbers of funerals and profits had soared, the later part of the century brought with it more serious challenges to the industry.

For casket makers like GAC, their response and approach was simple: Make it as hard as possible for new entrants to get a foothold in the market and keep taking more market share by signing up new customers. To do that would mean an all-out discount war with their main rivals. Knowing they would have to keep offering higher and higher discounts to take away the best operators,

Renford and Statham ultimately decided in the late eighties that GAC would start aggressively raising their wholesale prices each and every year. In turn, to keep their best customers happy, they would approve deeper discounts each year to help offset the rising costs. Smaller accounts would pay full bore as casket prices kept increasing, and in turn help GAC keep its profits up, just like always.

Like clockwork every year, GAC would announce a huge increase, especially compared to other durable consumer goods industries. As part of their well-choreographed roll-out and assessment process, each GAC sales rep would track and report on how their top buying customers reacted to the annual increase. They were all well trained on how to spin a particular year's bullshit about why GAC had been "forced" to levy such another high increase to their customers' costs. Weekly conference calls with management would highlight any customers they feared were on edge to leave and switch casket brands. That was, if they didn't offer them a better deal.

Although, mostly the calls concluded with huge laughs at how the vast majority of customers were the stupid ones who had pathetically hemmed-and-hawed upon hearing about the latest huge price increase, but ultimately gave in and accepted it. Garner was always amazed at how only a few operators had figured out that they could easily renegotiate a special buying deal each and every year, thereby offsetting, most if not all of, the increase.

Most just went along, never switching brands, and simply raised their local prices to the already overpaying consuming families. More amazingly, this same practice still continues although many industry-watchers report how funeral costs have increased at more than twice the inflationary rate compared to most all other consumer products in America. Even in the worst of times in the Nation's history, like Nine-Eleven, mass killings, or major health pandemics, never a peep is heard out of the casket industry about donations or even selling at cost, at the very least. Just like the great DAK always flatly demanded, "There Are No Free Caskets, Ever!"

The reality of it, is that "death" is a business, and accordingly, consumers will be charged whatever is necessary to keep profits up for the casket empire. To hear the industry powerbrokers and its well-trained minions talk about their "business" usually sounds more like some great, charitable mission that's being bestowed upon society. While that is sometimes true of a local funeral director, mostly the Mom &

214

Pop variety, mind you, that is almost never true of a casket company. Despite the occasional rumors of some small casket maker providing a free casket, there is nothing magnanimous about it. Funeral purveyors are business people, in it to make money, plain and simple. While there's nothing at all illegal with that, the sad reality is true that the so-called leading firms do nothing at all to protect consumers in their greatest grieving moments.

Today especially, there are numerous pressures on casket sales, such as an increasing and escalating interest in cremation, tons of consumer information on the internet, and readily available cheaper imports. Combined with the reduced number of competitors in a fiercely-fought marketplace, the business of selling caskets became increasingly challenged as the twentieth century evolved. To survive and keep growing, Great American would need to address each and every one of these challenges.

~~~~~~~~~~~~~~

When Helmutt and DAK fueled their own volume growth strategy earlier in the century, funeral homes generally paid the same for a casket of a certain model. The only difference being the shipping cost to get it to the funeral home. Funeral homes then set their own retail consumer prices on the caskets, which is still the practice a century later. In and of itself, the lack of a manufacturer standard retail price approach in the industry singlehandedly assures that consumers pay all kinds of different prices for the exact same product. While the industry-inside argument is made to liken it to that of the automobile industry, the fact is that automakers long ago established a standard manufacturer's suggested retail price; ensuring that consumers were starting from the same price point, and thereby, accustomed to negotiating their prices from there. That's not remotely the case with caskets.

As DAK watched metal caskets become more preferable by consumers, he invested heavily into more dyes and built another dedicated plant for the expanded line in Bergholz. This type of expansion effort required significant investment, which many of the longtime wood competitors to Great American simply could not afford. As a result, the industry again reshaped itself into one with fewer and fewer competitors. As the country's population continued to explode and expand all over, the number of funeral homes had likewise continued to grow in number around the country. Now with fewer top competitors and a larger market, another critical transformation would shape Great American.

~~~~~~~~~~~~

Baker Haskins was the "ol son of a bitch" who had told DAK a few years earlier just what he could do with his jet and whores. Like his father Guy and grandfather Hoyt before him, Baker Haskins was a pure breed funeral home operator. Granddaddy Hoyt had gone out west back in the early 1850's during the gold rush like so many other eighteen year olds seeking fame and fortune. Except, by the time Hoyt got on the scene, it was already towards the end of the infamous rush and the sparkling dust was almost impossible to find. Out of money and unable to travel back to Missouri, the young man remained

216

out west and wound up working for a local business man who owned a general mercantile and a furniture store which, of course, like most offered coffins.

Preferring to work with his hands than stock shelves, Hoyt became quite the basic craftsman for furniture and coffins. Nonetheless, Hoyt's real turn of events occurred when his boss recognized his perceived, kind selling spirit with grieving families. Once the owner decided to separate the funeral side of the business away from the general emporium, he asked Hoyt to run the coffin and parlor trade.

To hear Baker talk about how his elders before him had grown the business he was now so honored to lead, was like hearing of truly refined greatness. The real truth, although never mentioned, was that Granddaddy Hoyt had figured out as well how grieving families would pay more than what the store owner had said to price the funeral products. After just a few years running the man's funeral trade, and skimming off of every paying family served, Hoyt bought the business away for himself. Later on his son, Guy Haskins, would add another funeral home location on the other side of their home town that had doubled the business in the late 1950s.

By the time Baker took over from his father, the two funeral homes were handling more than five hundred funerals per year, making it one of the largest in the upper part of the state. Like so many others in the industry, Baker saw the effects of the population growth and how his own funeral service competitors were expanding to take advantage. Likewise, he began to do the same. Within five years of taking the helm of the

217

family business, he had doubled their annual volume for funeral services, which got the attention of every main casket maker around the country. Even more so, Baker had far bigger aspirations that would one day garner even more attention than he ever imagined.

~~~~~~~~~~~~~~

Fitz Edmondson had bought his way into funeral service. He had been a big executive with one of the huge West Coast power utilities, retiring early by age fifty. The idea of buying a small West Coast casket distributorship business had really just fallen into his lap a year or so after retiring, just about the time he was going stir crazy from boredom. He bought the business thinking it would give him something productive to do, but mostly because it would get him out of the house and out of watching those stupid new soap operas his wife was so fixated on. Altogether the business was only moving about twenty-five hundred caskets a year, most were going to Baker's four locations in the mid-1960s. By then, DAK had taken several runs at Baker, but none successful to any avail. Never apologetic for his past dismissive remarks to the legendary Mr. Kleinmark, Baker was always quite clear how his firm remained "very pleased with the current casket supplier and had no desire to change."

Just as DAK had been his whole life, Baker was a very aggressive and driven man. He saw funeral homes up and down the West Coast part of the country where the owners had no good succession plan and were looking to sell. His steadfast intent was to buy as many as possible. After all, his staff sold

218

funeral services that averaged over twenty-five hundred dollars per family by the late 1960's. On average, his firm was generating a consistent forty percent profit margin from each burial service, or about one thousand dollars per. It was easy math by which to figure a great fortune. Buy up as many bigger volume funeral homes as he could, at least in good markets. While he did, Fitz expanded his warehouse and delivery operations to match Baker's business footprint in order to guarantee supply and availability for the models Baker's teams offered. It was easy pickings.

When DAK was about ready to hang up his CEO spurs in the early 1970s, and subsequently hand the head reins over to Renford, Baker was operating more than forty funeral homes all over the West Coast region, consuming more than ten thousand caskets annually. The bigger problem that annoyed DAK so much was how Baker seemed to always be targeting the better GAC funeral homes and picking them off one by one. Month after month as Baker grew his funeral group, DAK and GAC saw their West Coast volume continue to erode and resultantly their operating cost in the region go sky high. No matter how he tried, DAK couldn't get a serious audience with Baker. Now it wasn't like the good 'ol days when DAK and Arthur would have dispatched some of Roseville Black's ex-cons to rough up 'ol Baker to get his wide-eyed attention. DAK knew GAC would have to find another way to get the big operator's attention.

~~~~~~~~~~~

Funeral home consolidation caused some major changes to the death care industry, and especially to casket manufacturers like Great American. Prior, most funeral home operators had been more concerned with offering the best quality caskets, but now larger ones, like Baker Haskins, operated more like stockbrokers than service providers. Buy low and sell as high as possible was the trade of the day. Buying low meant that larger operators like Baker could shop their annual casket purchases out to the lowest bidding casket maker. Whereas in the early days, caskets used to be bought for standard wholesale prices, now funeral homes wanted special discount deals for their annual purchases. As the competition between casket brands heated up, so did the level of the deals, especially for the biggest regional operators like the Haskins Group.

Once Garner McCall got into the casket business, well after Renford's rein as CEO, the standard average discount was already over twelve percent for good-paying, white-owned, funeral homes. Black-owned firms' average discount was about half of what white firms received. Much of that had to do with the fact that Great American's DNA had unofficially precluded their national sales organization from soliciting the less profitable units usually purchased by black firms.

Just as DAK had realized during his first, early travels, the funeral industry was then, and continued to remain, very segregated by choice from both sides. That also ensured neither side of the racial divide fully understood what the other was up to, or getting in terms of deals from manufacturers. Although today, usually due to necessity from continually declining death rates, some funeral homes do welcome families regardless of race or nationality.

By the time Garner got kicked to the bloody curb, the effective average discount rate was about twenty-five percent for white firms, but only around twelve percent for black firms overall. Keep in mind too, that discounts were only applicable for firms with good credit standing, meaning their bill had to be paid in full on a regular basis. If not, then any discounts or available volume rebates were essentially voided and lost, even if the bill was subsequently paid. That is, unless you were a white account owner who knew the right person to call up at corporate at Great American. If so, then you'd most likely get a "special exemption," not usually offered to less significant firms. An inability to recoup lost discounts would be a major issue for many low-end, smaller volume firms, especially for some in the black segment.

Even the larger and more successful, good-paying black firms with good credit-standings were not afforded the same deals as white firms, mostly because the Great American sales staff was directed, ever so discretely, to not call on them. The directive was to respond accordingly if a black firm called Great American, but not to solicit. This aspect of how Great American did business never sat well with McCall. Not because he was an idealist necessarily, but because he had been hired to grow casket sales, and there were several sizeable black-owned firms his team could have possibly won over. From his way of thinking, Garner never understood why GAC management had always seemed to direct the organization towards white-owned firms, when there were numerous, prominent black-owned firms that could be won, if allowed.

Garner couldn't believe some of the deals that he'd seen get approved in order to get a white-owned funeral home operator signed-on or especially to stay with GAC. Most funeral home owners preferred upfront discounts versus a rebate driven program, because it made their regular monthly casket bill less compared to waiting until the buying year was over before receiving a rebate payout. On the other hand, GAC always tried to incentivize them to take a rebate deal based upon increased casket purchases, instead of guaranteed discounts regardless of how many a customer bought. From DAK's day to Statham's, GAC knew an all upfront discount deal was a sure fire way to ensure that too many slippery funeral operators would also buy from their competitors to keep cheaper units on hand; even if it meant hiding them in the back storage rooms, where the GAC sales reps were never allowed.

So the discount was fixed, usually around the ten to twelve percent range, at least in Garner's early days. Then the funeral operator could earn another eight to thirteen percent if they kept their volume up at certain levels, and at a certain wholesale average. The easiest thing in the world for a greedy funeral operator to do was buy cheaper caskets and sell them at the same high prices as before. The net effect being, inflated profits from selling cheaper quality caskets to unwitting families. When GAC did an all upfront discount deal, there would be nothing to hold the funeral operator to his word about the volume expectations. So if one of them decided to buy some no-name knockoff caskets and sell the shit out the backdoor for bigger profits, GAC would be none the wiser while their volume went south.

As casket makers kept ratcheting up all types of deals, the crazier boundaries got in terms of what many operators had the gall to ask for. Just during Garner's tenure alone, there had been deals involving second homes, new roofs, newly paved parking lots, divorces, tax evasion, and always, always big time entertainment trips to all sorts of major events. The margins realized by established firms like GAC on casket sales easily justified considering just about any kind of deal, as long as the funeral home owner would sign up long enough, committing to enough volume over a multi-year deal. The real challenge then was getting the customer to actually honor the intended term length of the deal whenever another greedy competitor came along with a better offer, which was quite regularly the case. This created a frenzied, unending race to steal accounts where casket companies were constantly trading their competitive paint more than racing stock car drivers at Talladega.

~~~~~~~~~~~~

One such big operator out in Oklahoma was a lucky sperm-club, second generation funeral home owner. As for funeral home owners, casket salesmen had long since sarcastically remarked how the first generation built the business, the silver-spooned, spoiled, second squandered it into almost certain ruin, while the third wave of desperates saved the business from decimation to keep from working for a living. It was always funny to Garner how that notion had proved to be so true over the years. The Oklahoma operator had, in fact, made quite the effort to expand his daddy's two home locations into five by the time he and McCall first met. Becoming one of the biggest accounts in the region for one of GAC's top competitors, this guy had learned real quick how to squeeze for bigger discounts by just mentioning "Great American" to his local bottom-feeder casket rep.

After his latest bitch session to the sales rep about his supplier's own big price increase and not being offered any more discounts to offset it, the silver-spooned owner was bound and determined to get his way like usual. Except this time, the guy pressed too hard on the firm's new CEO, who basically told him that his deal was as rich as it was going to get. Clearly that conversation didn't go over too well, with both men yelling certain non-pleasantries before slamming their phones down. Hell bent on getting his pound of flesh one way or the other, the operator called his GAC rep, who he had barely ever given the time of day to before, going back several past years. Now all of a sudden, he was calling to say how he wanted to meet with "one of your bosses from corporate", so the rep went over his own boss's head and called Garner McCall to fly in.

Garner knew this guy was so full of shit within the first five minutes of walking in the front door of his main location. Huge pictures of himself and his daddy hovered over the lobby like an image of Christ and the Archangel descending from the clouds. After hours of hearing this fool go on and on about how "he" built the business and how "he" had huge plans to keep expanding into more than a dozen locations, it was obvious to

224

Garner that junior was expecting GAC to beg him for his business.

Much to the second-sperm clubber's dismay, Garner didn't fall for that lame approach. Instead, he just kept smiling and congratulating the man on his success, wishing him well with future endeavors. Then acting as if he and his rep needed to leave to go see a "good account", Garner pulled the oldest power move in the book; by looking at his watch, as if to signal he was done listening. After spinning the tables, Garner could see the man's face twitch and twist realizing GAC wasn't taking his bait. Finally, after outright asking Garner to stay and talk about the prospects of doing a deal, the man was forced to show his cards.

Garner asked his rep to go outside and call the other client to move their meeting to the next day. Of course, there was no planned meeting to cancel, but the intended effect took just the same. Now the operator had to talk straight about his business and what kind of deal he was looking for or it was pretty clear to him that this McCall guy wasn't hanging around. Once they had gone through the terms of the man's current deal, what caskets he sold, and his general price list, Garner knew GAC could take this account without any problem. More than anything, this guy was obsessed about his own personal standing and prominence in the community. He wanted to be seen by the local bigwig yokels as being one of the grand poohbahs around town, except he needed some major cash flow to make it happen.

The thing he wanted more than any was to join the most prestigious private golf club in the state. It was located less than

225

twenty miles from where he lived, and was where all of the best players and richest business owners in his neck of the woods belonged. The only problem was the one hundred and fifty thousand dollar initiation fee required just to join the club. He could swing the one thousand dollar monthly dues easily enough, but he was already leveraged to the hilt on his businesses, having taken second and third mortgages on each location, plus his home, just to keep acquiring new locations. What he hadn't planned on, though, were how the combined impacts of the price increases, growing cremation preferences in his market, as well how his direct competitors would lower their own prices, thus causing his profits to bottom out. Garner quickly realized what the conceded man wanted more than anything was to join the swanky golf club. Give him enough cash upfront to join, and this guy would sign in a heartbeat on the dotted line of whatever deal GAC put in front of him.

After five more long hours talking with this fool, including watching him suck down five martinis over an exhausting dinner, the deal was finally agreed to in principle. Garner used the typical upfront discounts to fund the golf fees, and then held the man excruciatingly accountable on the volume side through a complex rebate program. In short, McCall had the self-absorbed asshole by his tiny cahonas!

They also say to be careful what you ask for. As in the case with the Oklahoma golfer, that would prove to be particularly true. While he kept expanding his number of funeral home properties alright, every time he did meant that he needed more cash. And that meant he got deeper and deeper into GAC, every time he needed to make another down payment on a new location. Unfortunately, it also meant that Garner had to keep hearing about the man's conceited updates and redoing his deal each and every time.

Finally though, the situation reached the same point that the fool had gotten to with his former casket supplier. He was tapped out on leverage, and Garner knew it, so he tightened the screws. Now GAC was in control, and as select funeral homes in the man's market area became available for sale that GAC wanted to make certain came their way, they could force the indebted operator to buy the firms. Otherwise, their constant renegotiations and support would come to a painfully, expensive end. As his contemporaries continued to watch the man's business grow in excess of thirty firms across multiple states, none were ever the wiser that GAC had such a tight control on him or his life. Now, whenever the overly-spoiled and pampered operator threatened to break the deal with GAC, Garner would remind him that all he had to do was fully repay all of the upfront monies afforded over the years, plus half of the rebates, as their contract clearly stipulated, for early termination. With twelve years remaining on their repeatedly extended deal, it meant the foolish operator would have to come up with more than five million dollars cash all of a sudden, just to break it. Worse yet for the operator, was how Garner knew no other casket company was going to buy that deal out. The man was so leveraged by GAC and his bank, that he couldn't even sell his business. Now, whenever he bothered to call and try to bitch, the conversation went quite differently and lasted only as long as Garner felt obliged.

~~~~~~~~~~~~

Over the eighties and nineties, the main casket brands tried to figure out how to help funeral operators encourage grieving families to spend more time looking at display caskets, and ultimately spend more in the process. Lots of consultants and blind market surveys suggested that consumers hated going to funeral homes alone, much less into the casket rooms; something that surprised no one of course. One thing they did learn, in fact, was very much unexpected. That was, how the vast majority of people considered the funeral arrangement process an actual consumer "shopping experience." In actuality, what shoppers didn't like was the means and confines of how most funeral operators presented their goods and services. Directly put, people thought funeral homes in general and especially the casket rooms were creepy! Naturally, no one ever wanted to think of ever having to go into a funeral home, for obvious reasons. But once they had to, then by any means necessary, they sure wanted to get the hell out of there as fast as possible. Which from a consumerism perspective, meant that funeral shoppers were making the fastest decision possible to get the "experience" of it over with. Bottom-line: When shoppers hate being in your business, they're probably not going to spend a lot of time getting to know what you have to offer or spend much money!

A couple of GAC's main competitors were the first to figure out a unique solution to the negative shopping experience conundrum. Incredibly, after spending millions of dollars with top marketing consultants, it was finally confirmed that people are actually very uncomfortable being around "a real casket." No kidding, millions were spent to throw a rope around that incredible insight! In fact, many of those surveyed, who had actually arranged a funeral for a past loved one, emphatically stated the worst part of the whole experience was literally going into the casket room. Casket rooms had become common place once the mortuary trade officially separated from the furniture store model back in the early 1900s. Usually, they were small rooms with low ceilings and dim lighting, where the caskets were situated so close together, thus requiring onlookers to be physically forced closer than preferred to the death boxes. Over time these types of routine settings created a dreaded, dark, mental image for those who had ever been into a funeral home.

By the 1990s, newfangled consumer-friendly partial-casket display rooms became the rage in funeral service, allowing grieving families to see more options in various colors of metal and wood caskets, but without seeing any awful, full-size caskets. The rooms also had been cunningly and tastefully designed with special color palettes and soothing pastoral images, evoking peace and tranquility. Built with the finest showroom materials and veneer finishes, the rooms were also very expensive. Each room usually priced out around fifty-thousand dollars for a normal size room, or two to three times that for oversized displays. For larger operators, like the spoiled-sport out in Oklahoma, serious investment dollars would be required upfront to buy such a room outright. Of course, most funeral home owners didn't want to upfront the cash expense, but preferred the rooms be installed as part of a renegotiated long-term complex deal, which GAC and other manufacturers were only too happy to consider. By getting a funeral home owner hooked on the idea of the new cut rooms, casket makers knew they would have the operator's purchases locked up in a tight deal for a number of years, ensuring them the profitable volume.

Usually that process went off as planned, but not always. That was, until a competitor came along and upped the ante, offering even better terms and replacing the display room with their own version. This kind of competitive sparring became the norm in the casket industry, causing an endless flurry of constant deal-making, and sending casket margins lower and lower; for which, in turn, of course, meant that wholesale price increases would have to go higher and higher each year to make up the differences in lost profits. In short, consumer prices escalated in order to pay for the enhanced marketing efforts and competitive jousting.

~~~~~~~~~~~~

Garner had gotten a call from one of his team's newest reps about a customer who had recently had a new display room installed and was apparently so unhappy with it that he refused to pay his regular monthly bill for the full-sized caskets he had purchased for several recent burial services. After calling the guy, who proved to be an absolute hothead, Garner decided to fly out and go help resolve the issue by looking at the room in person. The small town hothead had complained how he hadn't received the room on time, as well as, that it had not been designed as he and the former rep had agreed to, despite his signing off on the blueprints and installation. Something was clearly up with this guy, and Garner wanted to understand it firsthand.

After going with his new rep to meet with the operator, it quickly became apparent that the customer had completely left the layout design up to the former rep, who supposedly hadn't listened to what the man had truly wanted. At least, that's what he said now. Once Garner explained that the casket bill was way past due and had to be paid, regardless of the room issue, which he would make sure was made right, the man agreed to pay his bill in full immediately. Once Garner felt the payment issue was satisfactorily agreed upon, he offered to have the entire room redesigned to suit the man. He would also ensure the project was put at the front of the build schedule just to appease the man even further. Then once the new room had been installed, Garner promised to come back to visit personally to make sure everything was satisfactory.

What Garner couldn't tell from his first trip out to meet with this jackleg was how much of a compulsive liar the man was. After getting the man's personal signature on the new room layout, he never did pay the past due bill as promised. Then once the new room was installed, he was still unhappy and unwilling to sign-off on the installation. Further, Garner learned that the renegotiated deal that had been presented to cover the cost of the room in the first place had never been signed and returned by this jerk. After flying back out a second time to reconcile the situation, Garner and the new rep finally became familiar with the man's true personality. The man was an absolute bald-faced liar and a snake, no way around it.

After doing everything they had promised, he was still unwilling to pay his past due bill, much less sign-off on the new room, and still refused to sign the renegotiated agreement to cover the cost of the room. This snake went even further, incredibly suggesting that GAC had essentially shipped and installed the room in his funeral home without his express "written permission." Given his signature on the room proposal, which included the proposed installation date and necessary waivers, Garner informed the snake that he was up shit creek on that one.

Still the man held his ground and threatened to sue, unless GAC sent their crew back out to remove the room. Seeing the crazed look on the man's face and already getting himself and the new rep out of the funeral home, Garner told the man that was not going to happen. Explaining how GAC had acted in good faith, per their agreements and emails, Garner told the man that the only option at that point would be to accept the new room and sign the agreement, which covered its cost. Otherwise, GAC would have the full retail cost of the second room billed directly to his account immediately.

As the month came to a close a couple weeks later, the man sent multiple threatening phone messages and emails to Garner. Hardly his first rodeo, Garner ignored them all. Once the man's account became past due well over one hundred thousand dollars, Garner had the credit department send out a demand for payment letter that indicated next steps would require forwarding

232

the account out to collection. Doing so would destroy the man's credit, plus in those days, the company could have it published in the local newspaper, which the man knew as well. Realizing that he was fighting a losing battle, the man called Garner one last time while he was out on the road traveling.

By this time, the annual rebate period had concluded based upon the operator's old purchase agreement, from which, he had been expecting to receive a big rebate check for his casket purchases over the prior year. Hearing the man's annoying voice on the phone brought a wry smile to Garner. He thought, oh this is going to be a fun exchange! However he didn't expect what the man would say after more threats to sue, which Garner invited him to do, even offering to provide the direct phone lines for GAC's legal counsel and CEO.

The customer was screaming at the top of his lungs into the phone about the fifteen thousand dollar rebate check that he had been expecting and demanded Garner find out where it was and when he would receive it. Almost chuckling, Garner took great delight to tell the man how the check had in fact been forwarded to his office, since the account was so far past due. As well as, further explaining how he had the man's earned rebate applied against his account past due balance, which now of course included the cost of the second room. Hearing this, more wildly inflamed the man that much further, causing him to scream even louder and curse McCall with every known vile word he could summon.

With his back up against the wall, this crazed nut recited McCall's home address and indicated all he had to do was make just one phone call to have him and his pretty little wife taken out. Garner waited a second to see if the man would threaten him more. But when the fool asked McCall if he was ready to deal now, Garner's only response was this: "I'll tell you what you fucking idiot, you just went too far!" and hung up.

As the next two weeks passed, nothing else was heard of from the insane operator. Unless you count the constant calls he made to the local warehouse telling them to come and pick up the consigned GAC caskets he'd taken out of his funeral home and left opened, out in the parking lot during a rainstorm. Once again, Garner told the guys at GAC warehouse to refuse the demand and had the entire list of damaged caskets billed to the idiot's account as well, about which the idiot was also notified.

Then in the third week, the new rep called McCall and gave him the incredible news that the man had been apparently shot and killed inside the funeral home. Rampant rumors flew all over the industry how this guy must have committed suicide, given how he had always been known to be so prone to such erratic behavior. Some of the old timers around the sales force had heard the sorted tails about the nut job from their newest colleague who was so daunted by it all. But the old timers, who knew enough to never ask, still wondered if perhaps GAC had given the man some help in the end. The old guard around GAC knew if they had, it sure as hell wouldn't have been the first time something like that had gone down.

As for Garner, all he would ever say was how the man seemed crazy and tormented inside his own mind and, apparently in the end, couldn't deal with his own dark shadows. Still, he wondered too. Because he had never said anything about the physical threats made against him and Denise, other than when he had followed company protocol and reported the matter to Malish and Statham. After hearing McCall's serious synopsis of the disturbing events, Statham, as calm and cool as ever, assured him, "Leave it with us."

After hearing all the rumors and speculation, something inside Garner's gut made him wonder too if GAC had had anything to do with the man's death. He would never know one way or the other of course. All he would recall was the sound in Statham's voice when he said to "leave it with us" and how the hair on the back of his neck stood up when he'd heard it. Even today, whenever he thinks about the crazy funeral operator who threatened him and Great American, the hair on the back of his neck still stands up.

~~~~~~~~~~~

Over the modern years, GAC would invest millions to train their sales reps and customers on how to manipulate the profit production out of showrooms through meticulous marketing and merchandising programs. Like any major investment, Great American fully expected a hefty return in terms of better casket sales and more loyal customers. One of the primary ways their team led many funeral operators to improve their competitive and market positions with consumers was by shuffling their margin pricing strategies. Most funeral home operators tended to markup most of their products, like caskets, vaults, plots, and services, such as embalming and the like, an average minimum of three hundred fifty percent to sometimes almost double that. Taking that approach across the board meant even low-end, cheap caskets appeared very expensive on the general price sheet that prospective families were entitled to receive. That was, once the Federal Trade Commission finally required them by law to provide it whenever asked.

However, because casket makers had, and still do, always avoid any standardized retail price for their products, funeral operators were free to set their own retail prices and even rename the products themselves. Thus, confused shopping families are left in the dark in terms of how to compare like for like models between funeral homes. This is all by design of course, to protect the profits and restrict competition. Today, a few minutes online shows that funeral operators promoting to price-conscious minded consumers usually do so by offering their cheapest caskets.

GAC reps have spent countless hours working with their top selling customers to publish much lower markups on the casket models they both prefer to sell, and far higher ones on the low-end. This practice makes the targeted units more price-attractive, while giving consumers the appearance of modestly priced casket products from a particular funeral home. Once the need arrives to price out the whole funeral process, with most families wanting just a "basic level of service", they quickly learn that "basic" means anything but. Though some operators were slow to trust the likes of GAC about moving their gross margins off of caskets and onto to other service items, like embalming or using their chapel for instance, the practice ultimately proved out and eventually caught on across the country. It's funny how caskets have never appeared cheaper on funeral home general price lists, yet consumer funeral costs overall have continued to skyrocket year after year.

After all the years at Great American, learning the ins and outs of funeral service, both good and bad, Garner never understood why more grieving families didn't have someone less emotionally affected to shop multiple funeral homes in their area before making a final selection. Unlike most any other expense purchase, involving several thousands of dollars, funeral consumers invariably tend to only speak with a single funeral firm versus getting multiple quotes. It's incredible to believe really.

~~~~~~~~~~~~~

One other method, by which GAC has long helped its more greedy customers increase their profits, is by avoiding paying higher tax rates on their rebate checks. For years, the Internal Revenue Service has only required businesses to report deposits of ten thousand dollars or more, for the purposes of paying taxes. For willing sly participant funeral home operators, suckered into some of those complex rebate deals, getting a huge rebate check meant paying hefty taxes to good 'ol Uncle Sam.

But DAK and his GAC higher ups had long since figured out that if their larger greedy customers, such as the one out in Oklahoma, would set up separate business entities for each of their branch locations, then the company could ensure that the rebate payments wouldn't ever exceed the ten thousand dollar mark. Sometimes this required structuring to a quarterly, or even monthly, rebate schedule to ensure the lower payment mandate, but rest assured it could be worked out. Not to worry of course, thanks to Arthur Black, GAC's boilerplate agreement freed them from any liability, should a money-hungry operator ever get audited. While the evasive practice wasn't necessarily illegal, it was absolutely complicit, and designed to keep customers buying caskets from the boys in Bergholz.

~~~~~~~~~~~~

Statham had almost never before been so proud of McCall, than when he'd heard about how his man had roped and hogtied the golfing Oklahoma cowboy, and especially of working with him to buy out certain non-GAC firms. He readily admitted, privately of course, that the scheme put his own little Miracle Caskets program back in the day to an absolute shame! Taking Garner's idea, the CEO decided to build off of it and take it to a national level.

His idea was very simple. It was perfect too because many operators were always looking to sell their firms, usually because they needed the money to retire. For most who'd spent their life in the business of running a funeral home, the thought of doing dead body removals in the middle of the night into their later years was not the way most envisioned their golden years. Some others either didn't have children to follow in their footsteps of the business or necessarily trusted their offspring, at any age, to keep from effing up the family business and running it into the ground. GAC reps were constantly reporting how many of their customers were on the lookout for a possible sellout opportunity. So, Statham saw an opportunity just as DAK would have seen it. To make his plan possible, he would need

238

Renford, now the Chairman of the Board, to help facilitate necessary financing, so he could get it up and running, but that couldn't be tied back to Great American. Upon hearing Statham's grand idea, Renford agreed to personally setup a private fund with a tidy quarter million dollar investment to seed it. Now that he had the approval and funding for his newest covert "growth strategy", Statham needed to find the right person to run it. They needed to be someone outside the company and a person he could easily manipulate.

Statham would enlist an old Kleinmark family friend, who had been long failing in business as a commercial insurance agent there in Bergholz, after a very brief unsuccessful stint in sales at GAC, to become President of the new funeral valuation firm. Miles Newsom was one of those sorts who went through life like night bugs are to porch lights. He was attracted to those with lots of money and power, always trying to hob-nob and cling his way upward to a success state in life. Using his good looks and toothy grin, Miles Newsom was all flash, but no spark. Having been around Miles at enough events at The Club, Statham knew he'd be the perfect front man for GAC's newest initiative. As for Miles, Statham knew he had his ass at the first mention of the words, Kleinmark and Cessna. Mostly though, Statham knew that Miles only had a couple of grand in his checking account, no savings, routinely stayed months behind in his dues at The Club, and, in his early forties, was still chasing every woman possible. Should the time ever come, of course, Statham knew Miles could be perfectly dispensable. Such that, no one would ever need to wonder too much, if perhaps, 'ol

239

Miles just got tired of chasing tail and money one day and ended it all.

For now, Miles was smart enough to get the job done, but mostly, just smart enough to do what he was told and nothing more. His task would be easy. GAC reps would be on the constant lookout for any and all firms looking to consider a buyout of their funeral home business. Obviously if the firm was already a GAC-selling firm, then keeping it "in the family" of dedicated customers meant the volume was safe for the future of Great American. If lost, then it would mean a net loss to GAC's profits. Although, if a firm was a competitively-held operator, then getting a GAC-allied account to acquire it produced a windfall for the casketed volume. Statham also saw how GAC could map out and target primary acquisition targets around the country to help drive their strategic growth plans and fuel profits. The plan also afforded GAC the potential to pick and choose certain funeral home operators, who they would control just like Garner had with the Oklahoma fool. Statham knew it was simply too brilliant even though he hadn't originated the idea, which of course, was just a merely, inconvenient little detail that the Board would never know.

Once Miles followed up on a target, he would have full use of an unmarked jet, owned by another private equity firm belonging to one of Ren's wealthy buddies, to shoot all over the country and meet with unsuspecting owners. They would have no knowledge of his affiliation with Great American. His ruse of living in Bergholz and working for a time in the funeral industry, plus his "deep financial expertise," would serve to satisfy anyone

240

looking for his credentialed validation. Anyone still uncertain of his prowess was quickly satisfied after stepping foot onto his "personal" jetliner for introductory meetings and drinks. Like back in DAK's day, modern fools hadn't changed much. Statham had coached Miles to be completely professional and polished in the first tarmac meetings. If there was ever a second meeting, especially with a hard target, just like in DAK's time, Miles would step away to "take a call with another client being sold the following day." Thus, leaving the poor sucker on the five-star leathered sofa with little Ms. Cocktail Easy Pants.

If the guy acted right and sold out, then Miles never had the secret videotapes delivered to the little wife at home. If not, then the same old game was played out accordingly. With over twenty-some thousand funeral homes in North America by the late 1980s, most of which still owned by local Mom & Pop operators, it was usually like taking candy from a baby.

The biggest challenge that Statham saw for GAC was DAK's 'ol nemesis, Baker Haskins, who was continuing to assemble a funeral home empire of his own out west. Though not the largest operator in the country, the problem that still plagued GAC about Baker was every time he snapped up a new location, it was usually a sizeable, longtime GAC account. Meaning GAC kept taking it in the shorts, while operating costs increased year after year, as they delivered fewer and fewer caskets. All the while, Fitz was making out just fine, as his biggest customer grew and grew. Thinking back on how DAK often related his longstanding frustration of how the then young Baker had so obnoxiously refused his interest to do business, or even meet,

241

Statham realized that perhaps the target wasn't Baker at all, but Fitz. He knew he'd have to give it more thought but decided to have Travis get to know Fitz and see if there was any possibility of buying him out. Just maybe, if they could get Fitz over a barrel, then perhaps 'ol Baker might just roll on over too. Now that more than three dozen funeral homes and almost ten thousand caskets were at stake, it was time to find out once and for all, by whatever means necessary.

~~~~~~~~~~~~

ENTERTAINING FOOLS

Fitz Edmondson had entertained plenty of fools back in his day as a big shot energy company executive. Mostly the political types, who always expected their palms to be greased, whenever new legislation approvals were needed to support expanding various utilities up and down the coast line. During his tenure, there was little, if ever, any real treachery required since the energy company tycoons and big governmental fat cats had decades long ago already made absolutely certain that consumers would only have one supplier source for a needed utility; such as water, gas, sewer, or electric. By the time Fitz left his energy company days behind, he well knew the old greedy concept of "you give, you get" when it came to growing business. He also knew the best scenario by far was when the other party came to you. That's when you have real leverage!

The deal with Baker barely reassembled anything like in Fitz's energy days. All Baker wanted was a reliable and steady stream of the casket models that he wanted to push, and didn't have to worry about. The last thing he wanted was to get into his own personal distribution business. He also knew that if he'd tried to operate solo distributing his own caskets that his costs would have been much higher than Fitz's. Fitz had the luxury of selling to other operators and spreading his costs, whereas Baker knew he would be unable to, as they would see him as a competitive threat.

Baker had learned the funeral business and the casket game as well as anyone by the time he celebrated owning his tenth location. Now, he owned dozens more, all of which operated at higher than average margins. His master merchandising approach to setting up his showrooms worked as well as any too, getting grieving consumers to spend more than expected to provide a nice funeral for their departed. He always pushed providing the "Lowest Cost Fine Funerals" in all of the markets he entered. With published prices usually being at least a thousand dollars less than what families were used to paying.

However, when those grief-stricken families wandered into one of Baker's locations, they'd soon learn that "fine" only included one of their cheapest, ugliest, putrid brown or baby-shit green, tin-can-flimsy, metal boxes, basic embalming, and a hole in the ground as long as they already owned a plot.

Forget using his chapel, hearse, or anything else. Having a "fine" funeral at a Haskins Group funeral home meant anything but for families. Once the grievers were sufficiently sucked into the painful process of arranging services for their dearly departed, the last thing they ever wanted was to start over. That's where Baker's tried and true version of upselling began. His team of well-groomed, soft-spoken funeral directors knew just how to gently guide each family through all of their profitable options. Things like, hosting a visitation at the funeral home, having directors meet and greet family and friends attending the services, arranging for local off-duty police officers to assist in leading the procession through town and traffic, setting up an impressive tent covering at the cemetery, handling flower deliveries from local florists, creating flyers about their deceased loved one, projecting a photo collage or video to be aired over monitors during the visitation, handling required paperwork for various government agencies and insurance companies, etc. All the typical things most families routinely expected to be priced into published prices proved to add up quickly.

By the time Baker's families had been run through the mill of choices, the vast majority eventually succumbed to the higher costs, which led to his industry-leading profits. Of course, families could always opt to take care of all of the pesky details on their own if preferred, but as Haskins's team would say with the greatest empathy: "We can handle all of that for you, so you and your family can just be together during this difficult time and grieve." There was any number of ways to get families to reconsider a "fine" funeral for one that was more of the norm. In ninety-plus percent of the cases, Baker's team of well-skilled sales people delivered too. Ultimately, Baker's proven approach of low-ball advertising and bait-and-switch selling helped his business to produce an average funeral sales price almost twenty-five percent above the average around the country.

Baker's funeral homes rarely ever ordered one of the putrid brown or baby-shit green caskets for Fitz to deliver. Although, every display room had at least one back in a dark corner when needed for dissuading purposes. The practice is known as defensive marketing, one of the longest-standing reverse sales tricks the casket business has employed for decades in their attempt to get grieving families to shutter and wonder who would ever put their dearly departed in such a heinous-looking ugly box. Casket companies and their high-priced consultants had studied the effect of defensive marketing on consumers for decades by this point. Over time the gimmick had become widespread and common in most funeral homes, and usually resulted in families spending at least two thousand dollars more than the shitty looking containers were priced.

As a result, Fitz made money hand over fist every time his best customer ordered more and more high-dollar caskets. The better Baker's sales average, the more profit Fitz made based upon the net margin realized from every delivery, which was around seven percent. Once his annual sales hit the ten thousand mark, the average casket being ordered had a wholesale average of almost eleven hundred dollars, higher than the norm in the industry at the time. And which, would go up each and every year as the industry kingpins applied their usual inflated price increases to prop up profits, in order to offset a lagging death rate and increasing cremation preferences.

Fitz was absolutely giddy over how lucrative this whole casket business had become for his once considered "little post-career hobby." Since he'd been able to maximize margins by situating warehouse locations around Baker's funeral homes' footprint, his operating costs were far lower than any of his competitors shipping out to the West Coast. He simply couldn't believe he was personally pulling in seven hundred and thirty-five thousand dollars a year in earnings. That is, thanks to his buddy Baker who he kept completely slap-happy, whatever it took or cost. Those efforts included an "annual retreat" to Fitz's condo down in Cabo San Lucas, Mexico, which they'd been doing for years, supposedly to talk shop and future moves. Mostly though, Fitz and Baker had gotten close, real close.

Fitz was no angel, neither was his best client. He had also been smart enough to pick up on why Baker had so harshly repudiated the great DAK Kleinmark's standing offer to attend his infamous tarmac meetings. Relying upon his perceptions, Fitz had always carefully arranged for just the right kind of personal care and treatment for the man, he thought of as his "million dollar retirement client," whenever they hung out down in Cabo. Although neither man ever spoke aloud of the specialized attention. It just happened, as expected and as intended. Both considered the arrangement a mutual and secretive unspoken understanding. Kind of like when two thieves know they have to at least trust each other, even when no one else could be.

~~~~~~~~~~~~~~

Larry Travis had spent his entire career hanging on so tight to Statham's coattails that you could see the ever presence of frayed threads from Statham's silk smoking jacket under the edges of Travis's fingernails. Anytime the term brown-noser was mentioned, 'ol Travis was usually the first to come to mind around GAC. He had his head so far up Statham's ass that he could tell what the man had eaten for breakfast. Whenever Statham bought a new car, Travis took his old one off his hands. Whenever Statham got his teeth capped, so did Travis. Whenever Statham bought his South Florida condo, so did Travis, just not in as swanky a spot. These two pricks were tighter than Dick's proverbial hatband, and had more secrets than Carter's has pills, as they say. Something DAK admired greatly.

247

Travis had been one of the first reps that Statham hired back when he was still a lowly field sales manager just trying to make his mark and get DAK's attention as a wannabe ball-busting ramrod. The two men, ten years apart in age, were both from the upper Northeast and had a lot in common, right down to the cheap gold chain necklaces and slicked-back greaser hair styles. While the future CEO was busy trying to launch his Miracle Caskets scheme, he knew he needed someone he could trust to quickly help get it promoted around his region with select targeted funeral operators, the ones he thought would be greedy enough to take the bait. Once hooked, he would also need someone to help him go around and do the "drive-by audits" to make sure his new "one hundred percenter" accounts weren't forgetting their obligations to buy only GAC caskets from Statham's team.

Travis was just the one Statham thought could pull off leading such an initiative. He knew Travis wasn't a very good technical salesman, mostly because he just didn't work that hard at it. He sold purely on style and relationships, not quality, value, or service. Travis considered himself more of a persuasionist, meaning he went more after the personal interests of his clients than business. His usual approach was to get a client out for golf or drinks, if not both, and then find out what they really wanted. A new car, new girlfriend for a night or weekend, cash, or whatever, Travis knew if he tapped into those motivations, orders always came easily. Once Statham recognized how his new man possessed more invaluable "seasoned" selling skills, despite a lack of true sales experience, Travis would be the

248

perfect rep to assist with his Miracle Caskets program. From there, once the program had catapulted Statham's region to the top year after year, he and Travis both knew they would be tethered for their entire careers.

~~~~~~~~~~~~~

There's a reason consumers never see half-off coupons or "new and improved" stickers on caskets. Since casket companies never have to budget much monies for traditional marketing purposes, unless maybe for their website or to support state and national funeral associations, they have tons of discretionary funding to spend on inordinate amounts of so-called "market development and client acquisition initiatives." As for how they define either, well, those were always the most interesting discussions in terms of who would get access to the monies and how they'd be spent.

Just as DAK had intended when he built The Ranch, it became the defining mark of entertainment for most funeral directors, ever lucky enough to receive an invite to its hallowed grounds. Any receiving such an invite however, would only be due to a very specific reason. There were never any "thank you" trips to The Ranch. All attendees would be required to meet one of two simple criteria: either a new, qualified prospective account with enough annual buying power to warrant the investment or be an existing customer considered at dire risk of being lost to a multi-year competitive offer. As Statham and other field sales managers learned from DAK, both criteria would be closely tracked and monitored to ensure any invited accounts were either won or retained. Lose out too much on either front, and DAK would find someone else who could prove to not waste his money, time, or resources.

By the time Garner McCall joined Great American and began traveling around the country meeting customers, he heard story after story from old timers who had visited The Ranch back in their day. It was especially interesting to him how almost each and every man voluntarily spoke of their visit to the famed stables and resort as the greatest trip they'd ever made in their lives. Forget Europe or Hawaii, or even their own honeymoons or family vacations, for these particular funeral zealots, getting to go and stay at the mecca of the casket world had meant everything to them. Most amazingly to McCall, it still did, regardless of how many years had gone by.

The Ranch was impressive for sure, with its rolling hills and many trails to ride any number of beautiful horse breeds, or zip around in one of several restored WWII Willys Jeeps DAK had acquired after the Second World War. Then there was the amazing food. People still raved and talked about all the wonderful foods they ate at The Ranch. DAK's chefs were as talented as any in the world, and able to accommodate any request or dietary disposition. For the well-heeled drinkers, who knew their alcohol, The Ranch had no equal. Even when compared to the finest five-star restaurants in New York or Paris. Whether wine, whiskey, scotch, bourbon, gin, or even beer, The Ranch always seemed to have plenty of every type and brand, including the rarest varieties, which surely fascinated all connoisseurs and alcoholics alike. Nothing was too good for visitors of Great American Casket Company lucky enough to stay at The Ranch.

There were bars located everywhere around The Ranch, even the horse stables had a bar. With every one of them manned by a beautiful young girl, usually in her early-twenties attending one of the area universities. Even though Bergholz was quite the drive for the girls, the pay was usually double what they'd get anywhere else. So, they gladly made the trek back and forth each night. This particular team of females was all for show to get the word out about The Ranch, so that all the horniest of funeral directors would want to someday get their own invite there. Rest assured however their GAC rep would be more than happy to do a deal big enough to make that happen. Even if a certain operator sometimes brought their wife along, despite it really being a "serious business trip" you understand, their womenfolk usually wound up becoming new motherly best-friends with all those nice, young ladies at The Ranch. After all, they were just trying hard to work their way through school.

For the heavy-hitters, defined solely by their potential casket volume versus so-called funeral industry contribution crap, they received a special access invitation. These were the ones the likes of which Statham and Travis, as well as all their other crony counterpart selling suck-ups, were always on the lookout for. Even the GAC reps' access to DAK was rare and limited, unless they had a specific business related need. Still, they knew, a sure fire way to up their own exposure to the great man himself was to get a new big competitively-held funeral operator to agree to come to The Ranch for a few days. For these special big game accounts, one of the private jets shot out to pick their ass up and touch it back down at the private GAC landing strip. Then via the connecting private back roads, their own personal town car delivered them to a private, back hallway suite at The Ranch. DAK had thought often of how ingenious The Ranch had served to get his GAC targets to actually come to him versus what he used to refer to as "all those fucking tarmac meetings" he and Arthur had suffered through in the early years.

Back when he and Arthur were running things, him inside the lines and Arthur outside, all it took was a quick call to Black, and later Witman, to request "turn down service" for one of their special back hallway guests. The special service was never arranged by anyone at GAC, rather by Roseville Black, who then outsourced it to one of their dirty ex-cops who knew how to make such things happen. Usually the customer never even knew such a service was coming. Unless they had hinted anything of any interest to their rep about whether or not "girls" would be "around" afterhours possibly, the late night soft knock on the door would definitely be a very friendly one. Usually, it was one of several willing college girls from nearby towns who were looking for extra money, but did not work as a bartender at The Ranch. DAK didn't want some bastard embarrassed the next morning when he sat down to order a Bloody Mary, only to see the same girl he'd screwed the night before. Occasionally Black would approve the use of quality strippers to be called in whenever a client was expecting special treatment out of the norm. Regardless, under no absolute circumstances, did Arthur ever permit any outright hookers. Those brought too many pimp issues, and pimps brought trouble, something DAK would have never tolerated.

The turn-down girls they used were in fact absolutely beautiful, and always between twenty-one and twenty-seven years old. DAK and Arthur were always very strict about not wanting them so young, that they'd regret what they done, or too old that they'd already copped a bad attitude on life. They wanted them young, plumb, and dumb.

Most of all, they were from out of town. Whenever a turn-down service, emphasis on "down", was arranged, Roseville Black would have a car with totally blacked-out back windows and a black glass separating the front and rear seats pick up the girl at a designated spot outside her home town. Then, drive her through the backroads to the backside of the lodge at The Ranch, where she would get out and go in through a private entrance to the back hallway. Ranch Security, aka Roseville Black dirty ex-cops, was in the hallway to make sure the girl went in and came out safely before getting back into the blacked-out car for the ride back to her car.

The traditional play went as follows. The beautiful young girl would give a soft knock on the door. Since the room doors had no peep hole, the operator always opened the door to see the scantily-clad beauty standing there with her big, sad, puppy dog eyes. Apologizing how she hated to disturb him, the young vixen would say how she may have dropped something by accident in the room earlier in the day while cleaning. While the girl got down on her hands and knees, crawling on the floor to look under the bed, the man always soon followed to help look.

Seeing the girl's cleavage hanging out of her barely buttoned blouse, the man could now hardly contain himself. Once the girl got up and plopped down on the side of the bed, as if to ponder just where she might have misplaced her bobble, she noticed the man's favorite liquor on the window side credenza, saying how it's her favorite too. Like any polite gentleman, the horny funeral operator of course offers the poor little girl a drink and before you know it, all is forgotten about the lost bobble as the girl soaks up the man's "incredibly interesting" stories about his "big, impressive" business. From that point, the rest was easy and extremely predictable. From all the statistical analysis on the effectiveness rate of the famed "turn-down service", the net pay-off rate ran right at ninety-three percent.

Like always, photos and videos were taken if ever needed. Over all the years that this little "customer satisfaction" practice went on, nothing terribly bad had ever really happened. While there had been a few of the girls beaten up a little bit, whenever a drunken funeral home owner got out of hand and felt like getting his licks in, there had never been anything more than that. But that would change too, but not until on Statham's watch some time later.

~~~~~~~~~~~~~

There was one good 'ol boy operator from down South, whose daddy had been to The Ranch years before, back when DAK himself was the main host in the evenings. Garner recalled this guy would always talk tirelessly about how his daddy just "fucking loved" his time at The Ranch. Whatever his daddy had told him, he was sure as fire, hell-bent on going there one day himself. Every time Garner ran into the man, whether at an industry conference or just out traveling with his newest female sales rep, who somehow managed to keep the horny director in check, all he ever talked about was how he wanted to "go to The Ranch and get the FULL treatment!"

When the man started to show his colors by moving some of his casket purchases over to a competitor, which Garner interpreted as the asshole's power play to make his new young, female rep suck up to him, literally, he would get his wish for the special invitation to the famed stables in Bergholz. Little did the man realize though that his new little bubbly rep was actually the longtime mistress of a top GAC senior executive. Most execs were extra careful around the small town of Bergholz, to be sure and not let things spill out of control. But in this case, the exec was screwing his girl all over town; in the office, at The Ranch, at The Club, hell, they were even seen one time going at it in the GAC parking lot one evening after work.

It didn't take long before word got back to the exec's little wife about his willing playmate, which was one of DAK's steadfast rules not to break. He didn't like that kind of smut talk going around his honorable company, especially not in public. As such, Statham knew the situation needed to be rectified. When he and the exec offered to pay the girl for her "notoriety," she laughed in their faces, saying how she "didn't give a shit what people thought" and how "Powers should grow some balls!" Seeing the girl's brashness and spunk, never one to miss an opportunity, Statham thought that she would be perfect in Sales, of course.

After giving her a couple hundred grand for "moving expenses," Powers and Statham told Garner, right after he'd been promoted up to the senior level at corporate, that they both felt the "hometown, hardworking girl had really proven herself and deserved a shot in the field." Not knowing any better, or wanting to cause waves early on, he consented to have her take an open sales territory down South. Even though, McCall would generally never hire anyone, male or female, who didn't have prior, significant, direct sales experience. This girl had none. In this case, he knew it wasn't his call to make. Still, everything seemed to be worked out. The girl was happy, the wife was happy, and Powers could still keep his girlfriend; which he proved, but making about thirty "field travel trips" down to her territory over the next twelve months!

Once the horny director got to The Ranch, the first thing he started interrogating McCall over was, "Where's the girls, man? My daddy told me this place was just crawling with young, good-looking broads everywhere!" When Garner told Statham how this guy's expectations were so out of line, Statham knew the man had to go home disappointed. It was a simple matter of how he'd been so overly worked up and loud-mouthed about the possibility of getting his junk rubbed, that they knew he was too much of a risk. Figuring he'd just go back home and tell every funeral director he knew about his special treatment. Plus, he only bought a couple hundred caskets a year. It'd take five times that at least to get free turn-down service at The Ranch. DAK had required long ago that "complimentary service" was reserved exclusively for his favorite heavy-hitters and political allies, and must be approved by him personally. So, "Fuck the piss-ant, horny director, let him go home unsatisfied and find his own tail!" was Statham's response.

On his last night at The Ranch, McCall, the rep, and Powers, all took him out for dinner and to gamble over at the Ohio River casinos. The man ate and drank himself into a pure frenzy, while he sat playing slots and gawking at every riverboat slut who walked by his pathetic perch. Once on the way back to The Ranch, as McCall performed the designated driver duties, the drunken director was totally passed out in the front passenger seat snoring, while the two lovebirds in the backseat stayed quiet.

McCall was just as tired. Mostly, he was tired of the drunks, the smoky casino noise, the rag-tag crowd hoping to win it big, and especially his two handsy colleagues. Of course, he figured out real quick that the "young, hard-working girl" in the backseat, was much more than just his newest rep. Cruising down the highway, he could see from the rearview that the two rear-seated silhouettes kept inching closer and closer. For the first several miles, they had kept the appropriate distance, but it didn't take long for that to erode. About halfway to The Ranch, McCall notices the rep's shadowed image had disappeared from the rearview, and the exec's head leaned back in ecstasy on the seat's headrest, a most fitting and appropriate term, given its application in the moment. It was obvious he was getting his own turn-down service right then and there, going eighty miles an hour down the interstate, no less.

Nothing was ever mentioned to McCall about the rep. Although, both Statham and Powers made sure to say something to him about the evening out with the drunken director, and whether McCall felt the lost sales had been effectively retrieved. All Garner said back to them, was "Of course."

~~~~~~~~~~~~~

Invited customers spent the working hours each day on the trip with the likes of a Statham or Travis, whoever called on them locally, to tour them around the offices and various manufacturing plants. After supposedly being impressed with how Great American caskets are made, the salesmen pointed their targets to the corporate offices of GAC. There they would razzle-dazzle them with all of the types of showroom designs GAC could offer, in either full casket displays or the newfangled "cut" rooms, which only showed a slice or sliver of an actual real casket. This approach continued to be most popular with consumers, and most importantly proved year after year to produce the best revenue and profit results based upon what people bought compared to full size casket rooms.

GAC and other casket companies invested heavily in custom design architectural software that they could use to quickly mock up a brand new cut room prototype for the customer to see and dream of owning. The real hook would be when the presented five to six figure exorbitant cost of the custom room proved to be "nothing out of pocket" for them as a "special customer" since they had taken their precious time to visit GAC. That would eventually lead to discussions of a sweetheart, multi-year deal that would cover the cost of the room, and guarantee that GAC would merchandise it for optimum results based upon their sales data for the firm's sales area. There was never any pressure put on the account to take the room or the deal. GAC had become too smooth for that. That power play would come later, just at the right time.

Once the second day of the trip concluded, if the account was almost ready to bleed GAC colors, dinner the last evening was arranged in the very special Kleinmark dining room back at The Ranch. It was DAK's own private room, where he dined with the company's Board of Directors, or power-playing officials and high up politicians, like the governor and state senators. The reps told their unsuspecting guests that DAK had even entertained certain sitting and former U.S. Presidents in the very room. Once the guests were obviously honored to learn how they would be getting to dine in the famous room, as if some divine intervention had endorsed their unworthy presence, the reps would then announce how the man himself, the great DAK Kleinmark, had heard of their visit and wanted to join them personally for dinner.

DAK never met with funeral directors over the pre-dinner drinks portion of the agenda. He always said how he "sure as shit didn't want to waste any more time than necessary with those fucks." DAK never showed up for dinner until everyone in the group was seated, so he didn't get trapped into an unnecessary one on one rock-kicking conversation with some funeral sap. As soon as DAK entered the room, the reps all immediately stood up as if a god had just descended, giving the proper credence to their infamous leader's legend and import. As intended, the impact of the planned moment was significant and meaningful.

While the evening unfolded and DAK directed his conversation exclusively toward the clients, it was obvious he was interested in their visit and if they were considering becoming "valued" customers of GAC. DAK was as gifted in the art of engagement as anyone. By the time he had finished getting the account's principal owner to share his thoughts on what he'd seen at GAC, the poor fool would be ready to sign on the dotted line the first thing the following morning. Whenever they got that far with a verbal commitment over dinner, DAK always promised to either have them back for more time at The Ranch as his personal guest or to fly out and see the customer's place after the room and purchase deals had been finalized. Unsurprisingly, the impact of DAK in those situations paid off about ninety percent of the time.

But heaven help the foolish GAC reps and managers who ever had to report that DAK's time had been wasted when the targeted client had opted for a competitor instead. Statham had always somehow managed to stay off of that particular shit list.

~~~~~~~~~~

Entertaining wasn't limited to The Ranch or Great American for that matter. Most all casket companies spent tons each year trying to wine and dine accounts all over the country in various ways. Entertaining is huge in the casket business. Especially at funeral conventions, competing firms always try to outdo each other when it comes to getting major players out to a five-star restaurant or to play a big time golf course. Whether it's the big annual funeral directors national meeting or any of the state level association conferences, there will be more money spent on fine cuisine, liquor, and women than anyone could possibly imagine. Put mildly, if there's a funeral director not getting lavished with attention and expensive meals, if not their own turn down service, then they are most likely either an idiot, religious zealot, or they just don't buy enough caskets.

GAC always put forth a prim and proper facade at all the state and national conventions. Dark suits, white starched shirts, and tasteful ties were required at all times. Facial hair of any kind was disallowed, at least while DAK was alive. At all times, jackets were required to go out to dinner with a client, even if the restaurant didn't require it. DAK had figured out long before and coached his salesmen that wives come with their husbands to those "fucking conventions," warning "that you'd all better be straight-laced and on the up and up or I'll have your fucking asses the next morning!" You can bet they flew right too! Causing the old wily veteran reps to tease the rookies, attending their first annual convention each year, saying how they'd better sleep in a jacket just in case 'ol DAK knocks on your door in the middle of the night! The old timers could always tell by the severity of the wrinkles in the rookies' jackets the next morning, which dumbass had taken their warning seriously.

Some competitors, though, were not so much known as being "by the book." There was one in particular outfit, the guys from the East Coast. These boys were slick as slick gets. They were more of the vein of bottom well liquor and low-class strip clubs. In their earlier years, Statham and Travis would have fit in there like pepperoni on a slice of pizza. These East Coasters were out front with their macho bravado at all times, funeral home owners' wives in tow be damned. Hell, right in their casket booth at the shows, these guys would have sluttiest-looking broads with big fake boobs and bigger faker hair in skin tight dresses to lure funeral directors in to talk shop. Pushing cheaply made caskets and bogus funeral insurance, this bunch started their happy hour just after lunch to suck in directors already tired of walking around looking at more boring caskets and cremation urns. It was always obvious the next morning when the expo reopened, how only the youngest snot-nosed rookies manned their booth. Because their slickest, senior reps had stayed out all night partying with their top customers, and were still hungover back in their hotel rooms. They didn't usually show back up until happy hour fired back up right after lunch, or breakfast for them.

The truth was, only the industry big shots ever gave a damn about the conventions. That was where they could easily connect and discuss all the impending threats to their profit kingdoms, without fear of any collusion charges. For some of the everyday funeral directors in attendance just wanted to get the heck out of their home town, where they were always on guard to act so upright and proper. Lest anyone ever see them as otherwise, spoiling their clean-cut image in the community. The fastest way for funeral operators to lose a chunk of their market share was to get a DUI or caught cheating on their wife, so they had to mind their proverbial "P's & Q's" back home. Which is exactly why the big meetings have always been held in places like Las Vegas, New Orleans, or Chicago, where there's plenty of access to some good 'ol sin and mischief.

Over Garner's tenure alone, he'd seen approvals to entertain clients all over the country on all kinds of five-star trips. Expensive five-figure golf trips to big time courses like Pebble Beach, Pinehurst, Sawgrass, Kiawah Island, Doral, you name it. If a funeral director liked to play golf, all they had to do was inquire about buying more caskets from GAC or better yet threaten to leave. Either way, they'd get on one of the best trips known to clients in any industry. Even if they weren't a serious player, there were still plenty of invites handed out to major golf tournaments, such as Augusta, The PGA, The U.S. Open, as well as the Ryder Cup and President Cup matches when they were held inside the country. Even casual players rarely passed up big time opportunities like those.

Other trips also commonly utilized were to the Northern California Wine Country or perhaps a shopping and spa weekend in a big city like New York or Chicago. Whatever it took, GAC reps would present their best case scenario to get the manager to sign off and send it into Garner for consideration and approval. Most of the time, it got approved as long as those asking had a good track record of getting the expected sales in return.

~~~~~~~~~~~~~

Garner recalled one such five-star trip in particular where he'd witnessed the most stupid and egregious behavior by some on his own team. It involved a big group of owner operators and their wives, who were all really good friends, from across the country. Over the course of the big, final, fancy dinner

263

at that year's national convention, one of the wives asked McCall if he was "that man from Augusta, Georgia." Replying, "Well, yes ma'am I grew up and lived close to Augusta for most of my life until moving north with Great American." To which the lady responded in her pleasant tone, "Oh, I've just always wanted to go there and see those Master golfers play ever since my daddy and I used to watch the tournament on TV when I was just a little girl. All those azaleas are just so gorgeous to see on television. I'd sure love to see them one time in person. Do you know anyone there who could help get us tickets?"

All of sudden, seeing that his supplier's top casket man was being put on the spot by his wife, and her three friends now also chiming in on what was sounding like a wonderful experience, Garner's biggest volume client seated at the big round top table came to his potential defense. Saying "Now Honey, tickets to the Masters are about the hardest thing on earth to get a hold of. I'm sure Garner would have a tough time just getting a hold of two, much less eight for all of us."

Quickly reading the men's eyes around the table, who were all waiting to see what McCall would say, hoping just as much that he'd announce a miracle, Garner slowly gazed at the men and asked: "So what if I could arrange it? Would you folks like to go see the Masters next year? That would mean you too, Edward." Edward was the only non-GAC account at the table, and regrettably the biggest volume firm too. He bought more caskets a year than the other three operators combined.

Many sales execs from GAC, including McCall, and even Statham, had tried to swoon and win him over for years, never having any success. Thanks to DAK's hardball antics back in the sixties, GAC had refused to sell caskets to Edward's father and grandfather. DAK had already made an exclusive deal in their home town with another firm, who at the time was twice the size of Edward's family firm. As time went on, Edward's father grew and grew the firm until it had fifteen of the largest volume locations in the region, doing almost twenty-five hundred casketed services each year. The problem wasn't that Edward didn't like Great American caskets, he did. Plus his three buddies sitting around the table were all exclusive with GAC, while he was still buying shitty-made caskets from those East Coast scumbags. The problem Edward had was how, after his daddy started expanding his business, the great DAK Kleinmark shot his jet back up their way to entice them over to GAC. Except Edward's daddy told DAK just what his grandfather would have told him whenever he came back calling, which was, "Go Fuck Yourself!" Edward's forefather's figured they had made out just fine never buying one of "Mr. Kleinmark's caskets," and they made Edward promise to always fend off GAC as well.

Now with the possibility of the famous Masters event being on the hook, Edward kind of looked away and said, "No Garner, we appreciate it, but you all will have to go without us. I wouldn't feel right about taking a trip like that and not buying from you." Quickly without pushing, Garner said, "Edward, here's the deal, if I can get the passes, you and Evelyn would have to come. Otherwise the rest of us would feel bad about that. I don't expect you to buy from GAC until whenever you are ready to think about it. But, it wouldn't be the same with you two."

Before another word could be uttered by either Edward or McCall, the little pleasant but pushy lady, who had instigated the entire topic to begin with, gleefully blurted out, "Well wonderful, it's settled then! If Mr. McCall can arrange it, then we are all going to Augusta next spring! I just can't believe that it could actually happen! This would all be so fun, and Garner, I sure hope your wife would be able to come along too." "Absolutely, she would! I can't wait to have fun telling Denise that I'm going to drag her to a golf tournament! Course, I won't say which one yet until she pleads awhile for me not too. I'll have some fun with that…if, of course, I can get ahold of the passes." he said.

Like most things in life, just about anything is possible if you have enough cash. In this case, four sets of customer passes plus four more sets for GAC personnel, which would include the Statham's, since it would require his personal authorization given how much of an expenditure this little outing would cost. All in, it would be over one hundred and twenty-five thousand dollars by time Garner arranged for sixteen weekly passes at thirty-five hundred each, first-class airfare for the customers, plus the usual five-star lodging and dining. Also, a private charter coach bus would be required to shuttle them to Augusta as well as back and forth each day from the hotel to the course.

The local sales rep was understandably over the moon that his bosses' boss had not only agreed to a trip to the Masters, but especially how he'd gotten Edward to agree to join. That in

266

itself was a major coup that even DAK himself had never managed. The area sales manager, under who the rep and the customer responsibilities fell, well, he had a different reaction. He was one of those old guard types who still didn't like having McCall for a boss.

On the surface, he sucked up more than just about all of his colleagues combined, thinking it would throw McCall off of his full of shit scent. It didn't. McCall had his number, but figured it would take time for him to come around like all the other latter "third" groups before him. This asshole was stunned that his boss had apparently gotten so tight so quickly with "his" top customers. He was even suspect as to why McCall had dinner with them at all at convention, especially since he couldn't be there himself. Of course, as full of shit as he was, he wasn't so stupid to tell McCall not to.

To make a big production out of arranging the trip, McCall had the rep and manager call each of the customers and tell them to look out for an invitation to be emailed the following day that would include a link to a conference call dial-in. The title of the email would be "Masters Update." The following day, McCall made the big announcement on the conference call of how the entire group would in fact be going to the famed, Masters golf tournament, plus staying at one of the area's top five-star resorts. The customers learned too that they would be contacted by McCall's personal assistant to gather their pertinent personal information needed to arrange first-class airfare down to Atlanta, where the GAC guys and their wives would be waiting to join them for a private coach bus ride over to Augusta,

Georgia. That was, right after they dined at one of Garner's favorite topflight restaurants in the Atlanta area he knew so well.

Then to top off the week, on Sunday evening after the tournament winner had been awarded the famous green Masters jacket, the final agenda item before heading back to the airport the following morning, would be a very special dining experience at the most prestigious restaurant in Augusta. Most likely, they would see all sorts of famous celebrities, dignitaries, and sports icons there too since the place was infamous for hosting such, especially on the final evening of the tournament; maybe even the champion golfer himself would make an appearance, as was not uncustomary.

In all, McCall proudly promised a memorable trip that all would surely enjoy. As imagined, the customers and especially their wives were exceptionally thrilled with McCall's announcement and efforts to make such a trip happen for them. Immediately, the wives began to talk about holding their own regular conference calls, at their husband's offices and expense of course, to plan every last detail about their upcoming trip and coordinated attires. Garner would always recall what a fun call that was with such wonderfully charming people who were genuinely excited. The best part was how nothing about the trip ever had anything to do with business.

As for the area manager, he was none too thrilled. He had long considered himself the grand king poohbah of his region and customers. He especially had not appreciated his boss for showing him up so much with his top three accounts and number one prospect. Never mind the fact that the manager had never been successful enough to even get Edward out for breakfast or lunch in over a decade. Somehow McCall had whizzed in and charmed the pants off the whole group in just his first time of ever meeting or spending any amount of time around them. He was not about to settle for that and began to scheme how to make his boss look bad.

~~~~~~~~~~~~

Garner thought it would be cute to take them to Chop, his favorite steakhouse in the entire Atlanta area. The named was in reference to a local surgeon who, known for his lighthearted sense of humor, started the restaurant back in forties, but the name worked especially well for embalming, funeral types too. As soon as the customers and their luggage were loaded onto the luxury coach, he got a kick out of telling the big time funeral operators how he "couldn't think of a better place to take a bunch of funeral directors." Chop is one of those places where the likes of Palmer, Nicklaus, and Woods would definitely have dined at, while in town for the Tour's annual championship cup. Plus, with a name like Chop, it was perfect!

Right out of the gate, the bloviating manager was trying to command everyone's attention as soon as they got to the restaurant. Chop is one of those places where the wine list comes in the form of a book about three inches thick, with the rarest, and most expensive, varieties searchable upfront. This guy was one of those types always boasting about their knowledge for fine wines, as though he was a full-throated, classically-trained, sommelier with a personal cavernous home cellar overflowing with the best varietals from Napa to France.

The real truth, as Garner had seen firsthand, was that this dude only had about ten bottles downstairs in his unfinished home basement, laying on some dusty old, rickety wooden racks. A sommelier he was definitely not. A loudmouth blowhard trying his best to look the part just to impress, yes absolutely! After picking out five hundred dollar magnum-sized bottles of wine, which any fool could do, and all his swirling and gurgling, the fool finally sat down and shut up. As he did, Garner glanced around the table and took quick note. He could see all the rolling eyes as if each of his guests were quietly thanking the Good Lord above that the pompous wannabe's show was over.

With the week's first wonderful dining experience complete, the group was ready to make the two and a half hour drive over to Augusta. Not having been on the road for much more than a half hour, the now, well-oiled manager, and self-elected merrymaker, decided to break out more wine and start filling up plastic cups for everyone. Garner tried to suggest that perhaps everyone was tired from traveling, plus tons of wine had flowed at dinner, so maybe a quiet ride might be in order, but the manager would have nothing of it.

He needed to command the hosting duties once again. So he freely poured more of the high-priced juice, which he had incredulously ordered to-go, no less from a five-star restaurant with markups higher certainly than any funeral home, and charged to the dinner bill for McCall to expense. He was the one, compared to everyone else, who had had way too much to drink, probably coping with his fearful nerves of being seen as insignificant on the trip. Regrettably, he couldn't seem to appreciate how Garner's real intention was that the trip would have strengthened his and the rep's relationships with the customers, especially Edward.

Going up and down the aisle on the bus, constantly overfilling cups, the fat ass drunk finally lost his balance and fell over on top of one of the customer's wives. He was so drunk, that he hadn't even realized that her leg and foot were hurt pretty badly. For several minutes, that fuck just wallowed there in the aisle, as if he was the one in pain. It was clear though, he was in fact absolutely feeling no pain. The lady on the other hand, everyone was worried about and kept asking how she was feeling. After several miles, she would say her aches had begun to subside or perhaps she just decided to grin and bear the pain, not letting the incident ruin her Masters experience. Refusing to get her foot x-rayed when they arrived, she told Garner that she would let him know if she felt it was necessary. Otherwise, he kept an eye out and checked on her repeatedly for the next couple of days. The only good thing that came from the whole event was that the resident GAC wino was pretty damn quiet and subdued for the rest of the trip.

News of incidents like that never takes long to circulate. The following day, Garner got a call from Statham who had already heard about the rumored incident and wanted to understand it fully, since he was planning on joining the group later in the week. He didn't want any landmines before meeting these people and called to get the lay of the land from McCall. Hearing how this particular manager had made a fool of himself again with customers, despite Garner downplaying it and saying

271

the lady was fine and uninjured, the CEO was clearly unhappy. Nonetheless Statham directed McCall to "make sure it's blown over by the time I arrive." He didn't want it mentioned when he got there, although he'd take a piece of the manager's hide at the right moment.

Statham knew more than most that such types of drunken missteps by a sales minion had happened dozens of times during his tenure, and usually nothing serious ever really came from it one way or the other. Closing out their discussion on the matter, Statham added, "He's always been a good salesman. He'll survive it. Let's let it go. But Garner, you make damn sure that he knows not to fuck up like that again, you hear!"

On the third evening at dinner, McCall announced to the group that some special guests would be joining them for Sunday at the tournament as well for the very special dinner after the tournament awards ceremony. One of the funnier clients, teasing Garner, said, "What have you gone and done for us this time, Garner? Gotten Mr. Nicklaus himself to join us for dinner? That'd be just like something you'd do!" Hearing that only made the jealous manager fume and stew even more." Laughingly Garner said, "No, I'm afraid that's quite definitely out of my reach. But I can report, our CEO Bill Statham and his wife are flying down this evening to join us first thing tomorrow morning at breakfast and will be with us through dinner tomorrow evening."

While Statham was certainly no Nicklaus, hearing of his effort and desire to be with their group sent the right message

Garner had intended in the moment. As usual, the Stathams would fly down in luxury far better than first class via Great American's flagship jetliner known as GAC-1, the moniker reserved for the newest Falcon in the company fleet. Never mind, of course, the twenty grand it'd cost to fire up the Falcon for the quick jaunt and park it overnight.

Statham's usual introductions were always the same, firm handshakes and manly smiles for the men and kisses for the women. Statham had a reputation for his female introductions, which were legendary around GAC. If the woman was young and pretty, or even a bit older but still exquisitely beautiful, then he would kiss them right at the edge of their lips, always using a little tongue as if to convey his attraction for their beauty. It was really quite something to see how ladies reacted to his not so subtle advances.

Although, for the ladies who failed short of Bill Statham's standards, then the best he could muster would be an air kiss about an inch away from their good ear. It was something he'd often joked about, when slumming with the sales reps at a bar during the GAC national sales meetings; saying how he'd always try to discern their best ear so they could hear his lips smack together to confirm his attempted kiss. As for the women who had ever had to meet and say hello to the self-presumed suave and debonair ladies' man, those like Denise McCall, they had learned how to perfectly time the slightest head tilt to avoid the flabby old man's approaching tongue.

~~~~~~~~~~~~

Once the tournament had finally commenced and the famous green jacket was donned, the group loaded back up on the coach to head over to what Garner had billed as a most special dining experience of the week for sure, and perhaps a lifetime. The historic restaurant was infamous for serving the likes of Mr. Jones himself, most all famous professional golfers, as well as several U.S. Presidents, movie stars, and captains of industry. This is one of those places that don't even have a website, simply because they don't need to. The place only accommodated a total of ninety-six guests, four at each of their twenty-four closely-situated tables. Somehow, Garner McCall had impressively managed to secure sixteen of their place settings on the most sought-after evening of the year.

As the motor coach pulled up along the sidewalk out front, Garner hopped off to notify the restaurant owner that his party was there a tad early. Except, what he would learn and later report was almost heartbreaking, if not downright embarrassing. The woman at the door was the widow of the late founder of the famed restaurant, and the same woman he'd personally spoken with when making the reservations months earlier. She was a sweet and wonderfully pleasant Southern lady, who just happened to be related to one of Garner's best childhood friends growing up not too far away, just west of Augusta. So they had bonded a little on their call when he'd made the reservations.

Garner's heart almost stopped when the woman told him that someone, a lady with a high-pitched shrill of a northern accent, had called in the day before and totally canceled his reservation. Unsurprisingly, she was quickly able to fill it minutes after receiving the cancellation, since the waiting list was always a mile long. He could not believe it and told her that surely there must have been a mistake, that he would have been the only one to cancel and certainly he had not.

Commiserating with Garner, the woman sadly informed him that she had taken the call personally and explained how the lady had specifically stated she was "calling on behalf of Mr. Garner McCall and the Great American Casket Company to cancel their reservations." Then, the woman added how the shrilled voice lady shared as well that "you specifically stated to have us bill your credit card for whatever sixteen guests would typically spend plus a thirty percent tip." Which of course, I would never do, since I could easily refill the reservation." Garner was at a complete loss. Who would have done such a thing? Plus, he hadn't even announced where he was taking the group on the final evening.

Seeing Garner's complete shock and realizing along with him that someone had maliciously intended to cause him embarrassment, the sweet lady said something he would never forget. The gracious and kind woman said, "Now Garner, don't you worry about a thing. We will absolutely take care of your group. Unfortunately, the tables we would have had your party at are no longer available in the main dining room. But, I do have some space in the back section of the restaurant that would accommodate you all. We normally keep it closed off, except for special overflowing occasions. I promise, we will make sure you folks are completely comfortable. I'm sorry to say the tables back there aren't as nice as the main dining room, but the food and the service are the same. How does that sound my friend?" Garner was so elated to hear her most generous, kind offer that he gave her a huge hug around the neck, making the woman blush with absolute pride.

When he got back to the bus, he decided to stand at the front to get everyone's attention, as if to make a formal announcement. Being obvious not to stare at the manager and his fat pug-nosed wife, who did in fact have a most annoying, high-pitched voice, Garner told his group their reservation was almost ready despite a slight mix-up. When he got to the part about some woman oddly calling in and cancelling their reservation, Garner saw the guilty party look down and away, trying not to smile or laugh. Then, he knew. Regardless of the couple's sinister effort, the dining experience proved to be the most amazing dinner these folks, who were accustomed to traveling the globe in style, said they had ever had in their lives. Afterwards, when the two snakes walked back onto the motor coach, Garner was sure to stop them specifically to ask how they enjoyed their dinner. "Oh yes, it was wonderful!" they sheepishly uttered. To which Garner only responded, "Good, I was especially hoping you two enjoyed it!"

Garner figured the jealous manager and his wife must have called all of the best restaurants in town to figure out where he'd planned the last evening's special dining experience. That was the only explanation, since only he and his assistant knew which restaurant they were going to. Even Bill Statham had asked Garner, only to be told, "Bill, you'll just have to wait and see like everyone else!" It's sad how some folks go through life being horrible, pathetic assholes!

~~~~~~~~~~~~~

Back at the hotel, as everyone settled down in the hotel lobby bar for some drinks and talked about the wonderful week, things only got worse for the fat manager and Mrs. Pugface. The four best-of-friends couples invited Garner and Denise over to the huge couches where they were gathered to thank them personally for such a wonderful time. Plus, Edward's wife prodded her husband to tell Garner what he had been saying all week about having him visit their funeral home when everybody got back home, and to business. She went onto to say how "Eddie's father and grandfather were always picking battles with one of their suppliers, and were usually never happy unless they had some kind of consternation going on with somebody." Then, Edward piped in and said, "Yeah, give me a call next week Garner and let's get this set up. I'm tired of selling those shitty caskets. It's about time I get onboard with you guys!"

Then the ladies all told Garner how much they loved Denise and had already shared email addresses with her. Further, the little lady who had instigated the entire Masters trip to begin with said, "Yeah, you don't know it yet Garner, but you two are coming to our cabin this fall when we all get together! Won't that be fun?! Then we're all going to plan our trip for next year!"

Putting his arms around his wonderful wife, who was always his best sales weapon, Garner McCall agreed with his usual southern mild-manners, saying, "Yes Ma'am, that would be fun indeed!"

Travis was surprised that Fitz Edmonson said he'd be willing to meet with Great American. After all, he knew GAC was a force to be reckoned with in the casket world, but he'd never really worried about them, since Baker was his bread and butter. He knew Baker hated GAC since his early day's run-in with DAK. At his core, Fitz considered himself, first and foremost, a business man and figured there was no harm to at least meet and hear what an executive vice president from the almighty Great American Casket Company wanted to talk about with him. He certainly never dreamed it would have to do with anything about buying him out.

Travis still marveled at the title on his business cards, Senior Vice President – Business Development. It was a made up title that GAC never had during DAK's tenure. In reality, DAK had always served that capacity since his very first trip promoting Great American. But, once Statham took over as CEO, he wanted his trusty sidekick close by to help with whatever wrangling would be needed with GAC's top accounts. Larry Travis would never be accused of being that smart. His purported calm, cool, and collectedness were quickly detected by most as a thinly-veiled guise for his clear lack of cognitive or strategic executive capabilities. Effectively, at least in his mind, he usually remained quiet and tried to look cool.

Within the first six months of Statham first getting promoted to CEO, he subsequently promoted his trusted Miracle Casket ally to be his head of sales. The biggest problem there for Travis was that all the reps and managers were expecting him to travel his ass off every week, which to him sounded a lot like work. Regardless what anyone thought of Larry Travis, they would never accuse him of working too hard. So Statham made him an SVP of something fairly indiscernible. Becoming a basic surrogate and go-between for Statham and GAC's biggest accounts, Travis's role essentially amounted to him being the chief entertainment officer for a handful of accounts. The role fit him perfectly to a proverbial tee.

Not too many people turn down an invitation that comes with having a private jet being sent out to pick up your ass, and only you. Fitz wondered why he'd be getting such an offer from Larry Travis, whom he'd never met. Upon hearing Travis explain that he was planning on being out on the West Coast and then flying back to Bergholz in a couple of weeks, Fitz was open to going to "mecca" and seeing the great GAC operations he'd always heard so much about. He figured, why not. The worst thing could be that he'd learn a lot more about the bigger casket business and industry. Boy, would he be wrong.

Like most, Fitz was blown away with the whole treatment of the jet, the private backroads limo ride to The Ranch, and to hear him tell it: "The booze, oh my god, look at all the booze!" Fitz was a big bourbon man. During his energy days, he'd once made a trek down south to the historic Tennessee Valley Authority for a big industry conference. Since he was so close, after the conference, he and his wife drove up to explore the famous Bourbon Trail just north in Kentucky. Ever since then, he'd become a huge fan of the stuff and always joked about his personal lifelong vow to taste every last bourbon known to mankind before he died. Looking at one of the huge bars at The Ranch, he couldn't believe the number of bourbons on display. Ever the persuader-in-chief, Travis had the bartender setup a tasting for each of the bourbons they had on hand at The Ranch. By the time Statham came out to join them for dinner in DAK's private dining room, 'ol Fitz was understandably pretty much hammered.

~~~~~~~~~~~~~~

Statham was a lot like DAK in some ways, especially when it came to dealing with customers and suppliers. He was as smooth as silk and as sly as a snake when it came to drawing in unwitting fools. He and Travis maintained the boring chit chat over dinner about Fitz's earlier career in the energy sector, how he got into the casket distribution business, and of course how he had partnered with Baker Haskins over the last several years. Still sharp enough to keep his cards close, Fitz played along and told the men how impressive everything at Great American was and how it had certainly lived up to all the billing. Especially, what he'd heard about for years from various customers who had been lucky enough to visit The Ranch.

Once dessert and the second cup of coffee were on the table, Statham cut the ice with his infamous line of "OK, now that we've sufficiently bullshitted each other for an hour or so, let's separate the fly shit from the pepper and talk about why we're here, Fitz." As if right on cue, Fitz agreed wholeheartedly, saying "Yes, Bill, let's do just that. You guys asked me here, so I guess you'll take the lead."

Statham continued, "Fitz, we've had a tough time out on the West Coast growing sales and managing operating costs, mostly due to Baker's growth. It seems that every time he expands and buys out another funeral home, Great American loses another good buying firm. This has happened so much, that it has affected our bottom-line fairly significantly. As you may know, or certainly would at least expect I imagine, we have taken numerous runs at Baker over the years. None of which have materialized, of course. So our purpose for inviting you here for a couple of days was so that we could get to know each other and open up a line of discussion about Great American possibly buying your business.

We're not saying we definitely want to, mind you, but we did want to broach the subject just to see if you'd be open to it. If so, I believe like most, you would find an offer from Great American is the best you'd likely get from anyone, and probably by far. Of course, as you would know, offers depend on a lot of things like debt, overhead, existing contractual obligations, etc. For now, we just wanted to meet and get to know you, and for you to know us."

Fitz had already figured it had to do with caskets obviously, since that was all his business had in common with Great American. Still, his presumptions had focused upon whether GAC would possibly want him to distribute for them out west. He knew they had already closed one of their Northwest warehouse locations, plus the market was aware how they had lost several accounts to Baker's acquisitions.

The thought of selling out, though, had never crossed his mind. But he wasn't going to say that to these guys. Fitz opted to hold his cards close and see what else these guys had in mind. While he hadn't necessarily been thinking about selling, it was also true that he'd never planned to grow into such a large operation as supporting Baker had come to require. The initial thought of it didn't sound that bad, but pulling down almost three-quarters of a million dollars each year wasn't something that he was ready to give up anytime soon. He was making out like a bandit in this casket business!

~~~~~~~~~~~~~~~

After the dinner and straight talk Statham said goodbye as planned, leaving Travis to go back with Fitz to the bar and the rest of the bourbon tasting setup line that he hadn't gotten to before dinner. Though not as smooth as his mentor, Travis asked Fitz about his initial thoughts and reactions to what he heard over dinner. Fitz told Travis, "I'm open to anything Larry, and I really appreciate you guys being interested in my little company. I've got to tell you one thing though. I'm probably doing a heck of lot better than you might expect.

With Baker and my other customers, I'm moving over ten thousand caskets a year and at a very healthy margin too." "Are you comfortable to share with me what your average wholesale margin is, Fitz?" Travis asked. Nodding in agreement, Fitz said, "Sure. I have no secrets. Right now I'm holding about a one thousand and fifty dollar wholesale average, with Baker's share holding a little higher than that." Smiling with his widest manufactured grin, Travis feigned a look of impressed surprise as if to show his new target that he was pleased to hear of such high numbers.

After a little figuring on the back of one of the keepsake-worthy cocktail napkins from their bar spot at The Ranch, Travis began to scribble, saying, "Wow Fitz, so you're doing about ten and a half million in sales a year! That's definitely more than we suspected. Depending upon your net margin yield, we'd definitely be interested to hear more about what it might take."

With his chest all puffed out, Fitz couldn't help from blurting out what his net margin was. He knew it well, because of tracking it so closely each month. "After everything, it's right at seven percent, Larry. So my take home is just under eight hundred grand a year, every year!" Feigning insincerity again about Fitz's numbers and success, Travis knew he'd successfully gotten Fitz to cough up the critical information that he and Statham had wanted out of this trip. Much less, he couldn't believe it had taken less than a half hour to get it out of him. No doubt, all the bourbon helped too. Now with the mission for the evening accomplished, Travis wished Fitz a good evening and said goodbye until breakfast the next morning.

Finally, after hanging out and drinking bourbons he'd never heard of before and flirting with his much younger blonde and big-bosomed, bombshell of a barmaid, Fitz finally got to the inebriated point where he needed to head back to his room in the lodge. This time there would be no soft knock or no turn down service offer for Fitz. Perhaps the next time, if there was a next time. Statham had planned the same straight-up first contact approach with Fitz that he had Miles taking with their targeted

283

tarmac, takeover accounts. If the day ever came when they did have Fitz back in Bergholz, then they would pull out all stops to make sure he took their deal, one way or the other.

Either way Statham wanted to be able to tell DAK, now in his early nineties, before he died that he had landed that son of bitch, Baker Haskins, once and for all for Great American. He knew that would make DAK prouder than anything he'd ever done in his career so far and most likely cement his CEO position for life. Perhaps, even set him up to become Chairman whenever Renford stepped down.

~~~~~~~~~~~~~

ENTRAPMENT

One of the perks of flying private is that one rarely misses their flight whenever they oversleep. As exactly was the case for Fitz after fulfilling his impassioned obligation to taste every last one of The Ranch's bourbons offered by his beautiful, buxom, barmaid the night before. Despite his embarrassment and repeated apologies, Travis helped him laugh it off. Assuring Fitz that countless others before, and surely more to come, had or would, become such a victim of the voluptuous young servers at the industry's fabled retreat. Whether the spirits of the booze or the bar girls, there had been hundreds, maybe thousands, over the years who'd overslept just like Fitz. Once Travis finally had his prey's luggage loaded into the back of his Jaguar, another of Statham's hand-me-downs, he drove slowly out to the company airstrip via the private backroads that he knew as well as anyone.

Once they arrived at GAC Field, Fitz was wowed by the number of glistening, powerful-looking jets and hangers. The image hadn't been visible the night he'd flown in, but now it certainly delivered the impression DAK had intended for anyone invited to grace his own personal aviation operation. Fitz couldn't help taking note of the huge Falcon jet prominently cocked and sitting in the middle of the center hanger, twice larger than the others. It was adorned with a huge, bold banner which displayed the company logo and listed GAC-1 over the huge open entry. Stating his presumption that the Falcon must be primarily for Statham's use, Travis quickly acknowledged the hungover's guess, but also took a little delight in clarifying how his boss's use of the mighty aircraft was only ever "when DAK wasn't expected to need it." Otherwise, Travis said, "Statham had to fly one of the older Cessna's like the rest of us." The real truth being however, that Travis' ass never touched down on the leather seats of any of DAK's jets, unless he was ordered or invited to do so.

The flight maid on Fitz's trip home was definitely not one of the cute college girls he remembered on the first flight in with Travis. Rather one of the middle-aged ladies who usually worked in the airfield office. She would, most professionally and appropriately, accompany Mr. Edmondson back to the Northwest Coast on his flight, serving any food or drinks desired, but nothing else. Statham had not detected any outright character flaws in their dinner guest the prior evening. Therefore, he decided to still put forth GAC's best up and up appearance of propriety until the man, most likely as human as any other on earth, proved to take their bait at the right time in the future. Once Fitz was airborne heading westward, Travis headed back to the offices in Bergholz to scheme out the next moves with his mentor and personal used car salesman.

~~~~~~~~~~~~

As the Statham and Fitz had agreed, it would take a few weeks for Great American's law firm, Roseville Black, to draw up the necessary non-disclosures required to supposedly provide both parties mutual trust before disclosing any critical information. Before dismissing the topic after dinner the prior evening, Statham, haughtily as ever, had been unable to keep from suggesting to Fitz how he "should be sure to have his own "firm" review the agreement and recommend any changes deemed necessary back to Roseville Black." As if he and Great American were somehow removed from such minute particulars. Always the penny-pincher,

Fitz, like so many small-time operators, figured surely high-priced lawyers such as those used by an old, prestigious firm like Great American would certainly be above board of doing anything unethical, much less illegal. Figuring, instead of spending several thousands of dollars to have some lawyer read them over, only to offer one or two tweaks to justify their fee, he just signed and sent them back to confirm his exploratory interest. If ever asked, of course, he would say his "firm's team of lawyers" thought everything looked well enough.

Six weeks after Fitz had worn off the lingering effects of the bourbon bar and thoughts of the bar maid, Travis was reaching back out to move things ahead. This time he and Statham wanted to see Fitz's operations and planned a three day visit on the coast where they would pull their prey closer yet. Once the men had visited a sufficient number of Fitz's warehouse locations, Statham and Travis poured on their impressive praise of Fitz's investment and vision for his business. Finally the third day, they would all get down to brass tax on the numbers, at least at a high-level to confirm the potential price park that Fitz's business would likely be worth.

Fitz had taken Travis' suggestion to prepare a two page overview of his business; including sales volumes, operational cost overall and by location, gross and net margins, redacted

287

customer volumes and sales, and of course, the material types, metal versus wood, being sold at various wholesale averages. The businessmen had already agreed to the known understanding of how Baker's business represented the overall lion share for Fitz. Accordingly, Fitz shared his biggest customer's information as unredacted, proving it to be right at the seventy percent mark of the total. They all well understood that whatever Fitz's business would be worth, it would completely depend on successfully converting Baker's account to Great American. Something Fitz knew would be a tough sale based upon Baker's history with GAC. Also, if Fitz had certain contractual obligations that would impact the valuation of his business, Statham assured him the time had come to speak openly about them.

By the end of the day reviewing Fitz's prepared summaries, it was clear enough that the information was consistent with what Travis had jotted down on the back of the fancy cocktail napkin at The Ranch weeks earlier. In fact, Fitz was moving about ten thousand caskets a year, right at a one thousand and fifty dollar wholesale average, with a bottom-line net profit of seven percent.

Fitz didn't buy from just one particular casket company because Baker had always been all over the board in terms of brands and models. As a result, Fitz had to negotiate with each company independently to get pricing levels that kept Baker highly competitive in the markets he served. As a rule, Fitz's negotiated deals that required an average gross margin of forty-percent, which was pretty difficult early on for many of the manufacturers to accept. However, Fitz could guarantee them zero selling costs or delivery costs, since he covered all of those. The other carrot, or stick really, as the chosen casket makers would swiftly learn from Baker, who they all tried to sell directly, was that if they didn't deal through Fitz, then they would be locked out of his business. Further, Baker promised them all, once they were locked out, then that meant forever.

Once the makers knuckled under, Fitz required the standard forty percent gross margin, of which he passed on twenty-six to Baker. From the remaining fourteen points, seven percent covered his operating costs, leaving a tidy net seven percent for his personal take home pay. Meaning, as the business stood, Fitz was grossing out right at seven hundred and thirty-five thousand dollars a year. Not too bad for the former energy executive who, before stumbling into caskets and getting in tight with Baker, had never earned more than two hundred grand a year in his life.

Now that Statham felt comfortable with the numbers, he asked Fitz about his level of seriousness about selling his firm to Great American, and especially how confident he was in delivering Baker's business, which was around seven thousand caskets per year. Trying to appear to be a big-time shrewd dealmaker, Fitz said, "Well, Bill that all depends on your offer. Make it worth my while and I am confident I can get Baker to come along, as well as most all of the other firms."

"That reminds me", Statham added, "we would be looking for you to only bring over sixty percent of the other customers buying the remaining three thousand units. So based upon the numbers today, we would all be looking at seven for Baker and another eighteen hundred for the rest, for a total of eighty-eight hundred out of the ten thousand, or eighty-eight percent of your present casket volume. Does that sound reasonable and doable?" "I think I could easily get eighteen hundred of the remaining caskets to convert, Bill. Baker's the hard part. I'll need some help there!" Fitz replied. To which Statham added, "Don't worry Fitz. If we do this deal, I'm going to put my best sales executive right at your side the entire way. This guy joined us a few years ago and has walked on water ever since, signing up firms we'd never gotten anywhere with before. If anyone can help you win over Baker, it's Garner McCall. Trust me!" "Ok, Bill, then let's talk about what kind of deal you're thinking about, at least for now." Fitz added, with his own best air of smugness.

Taking a breadth to size up the lessor man sitting across from him, Statham had already decided to start the bidding low and see how Fitz reacted. Saying, "Well, Fitz, assuming everything we've discussed checks out, I think we would gladly be willing to consider an offer as high as a six multiple for your business, which would be one hell of a major payout for you. Also, if you wanted, Great American would guarantee you and your wife a lifetime medical benefits package." "By a six multiple, I assume you mean six times my annual net take home, correct Bill? Fitz asked. "Well, it's a little bit more complicated than that, but that's basically right. Essentially, I would estimate that you would be cashing out somewhere around just over four point four million dollars gross, overall, plus whatever value we paid for any of your owned equipment. I think you said that was worth about another half million. So, it would be almost five million dollars you would receive in total. That's one heck of a payday Fitz." Statham added.

Fitz took a moment, slowly sat back in his chair, and crossed his arms. Intentional or not, his juxtaposition was typical posturing body language code for either "I'm tired of talking" or "I don't like what I'm hearing." Seeing Fitz's withdrawal, Statham pressed for his reaction to the numbers. "Well, I thought it would be much higher, Bill, in all seriousness." Fitz lamented, adding, "What you're basically offering is the current value of my business over the next six years, which if it was expected to remain flat, then perhaps it wouldn't be a bad offer. Except that, Baker has plans to double his business in the next three to five years, and if that happens, then I'd be giving it away."

Trying his best to look empathetic, Statham responded with "Well Fitz, all we can go by are the facts as we know them today. While it may be unlikely, it's also possible that Baker could keel over dead and we'd be left holding the bag, so from my perspective, we would be assuming all the risk going forward. Of course, if you keep the business over the next five years, then all the risks are yours alone and Great American would have to go down a different path. Ultimately that's what you'll have to decide. While we could look structuring the deal somehow to make it a little better I suppose, I'm not sure it would be greatly different than what we've discussed here today. For now, I think we covered all of the initial bases to give us both plenty to think about." To which, Fitz agreed.

Almost ready to adjourn for the day, Statham said there was still one more item that he would like to get some confidence around. Before he and Travis could really put a lot of stock in the chances of the deal paying off, the most important element was obviously how Fitz planned to bring Baker over into the Great American fold. Raising his eyebrows to acknowledge the criticality of his largest customer's longstanding attitude toward Great American, Fitz said he'd been giving the matter a great deal of thought. Now feeling more comfortable with Statham and Travis, as well as the idea of cashing out and no longer having to worry about caskets getting delivered on time or trucks breaking down, Fitz decided to show his cards more than he had up to that point.

"Look, Baker and I go way back. Over the years, we've become close, very close in fact. Not as friends necessarily, more like allies and confidants. I can assure you that Baker has no interest in taking on his own casket delivery operation, he never has. He knows the numbers don't work out and effectively it would raise his bottom-line operating cost if he brought it in-house. I've been able to keep his delivery costs low because of selling to so many other operators. So that's not a concern, as he's mentioned it more than once over the years.

He also knows that I don't plan to do this forever. Although, I've never really ever put a hard date in front of him as to when I might get out of the business. All we've ever discussed was that I would come to him first to discuss it whenever that day came. I know he likes your caskets. Hell, he's always gone on and on about how Great American caskets are far better quality than the ones he sells. So, I think that actually plays in our favor. As for his history with Mr. Kleinmark, the one you guys call DAK, that's what I'm not sure about. Maybe as long as he never had to see or hear from him ever again, perhaps he could get past it."

Then, Fitz's eyelids began to get noticeably tighter, like when someone is struggling to say something out loud versus holding it in. Seeing the tightening on Fitz's face, the two GAC men sitting across the table were as skilled as any in the art of selling and reading people. Both men were too sharp to break Fitz's mental anguish, and just kept still and quiet, waiting to let the silence pull the truth out of Fitz that he was clearly struggling to share. When he did speak, what Fitz actually uttered gave Statham more interest and excitement in the deal than he had ever hoped or dreamed of.

Fitz began to carefully talk about the annual retreats he had been hosting for Baker, going on several years by then. Fitz talked about his condo in Cabo, where the two men had met at least once a year, and sometimes twice. The meetings were strictly considered their "business reviews" and thus never included any wives or family. Although Fitz explained how Baker had regularly taken his family down to the condo over the years, but never when they met there for business. As Fitz continued to talk about those sessions, Statham and Travis could tell there was some secret underlying aspect that existed, although Fitz wasn't ready to disclose it. As they kept listening to him talk about Cabo, it was clear that "business matters" had very little to do with the purpose and intent of the trips.

Finally, after seeming to speak in circles without ever saying anything concrete about why the Cabo trips would cause Baker to switch over to Great American, Statham finally interrupted. Asking, "So Fitz, I feel like there's something you want to tell us but aren't for some reason. Am I reading this correctly?" Without answering directly, Fitz simply said, "Let's put it this way, I know Baker Haskins better than anyone on earth, including his wife. So I am highly confident that if I tell him that I am selling out to Great American, that he will go along and support me. He may not like it, but in the end, I am confident that the relationship we have will prove to be the difference ultimately. That's all I'll say for now. But rest assured, I can deliver Baker's business, one hundred percent of it. I'm not concerned about that. All I'm concerned about is getting paid for delivering a client that's going to keep growing like Baker plans to."

Fitz had spoken with such confidence and certainty that Statham was extremely pleased. It was crystal clear that whatever Fitz was unwilling to share was about his personal relationship with Baker was a game changer. It seemed obvious that whatever Fitz had on Baker was enough to make him do what he wanted. Moreover it seemed that Fitz was willing to cash in all his chips to get what he wanted, even against his best client. Not only did the notion of such secretive information satisfy Statham, but the very idea of whatever the juicy truth would prove to be was something he and Travis would have to get out of Fitz, somehow.

Accustomed to always having the last word in such matters, Statham said, "Well obviously Fitz, you seem very confident about whatever it is that you believe will persuade Baker to come our way. I won't press you to tell us for now, since it's not important until we reach an agreement on a deal. However, what I would say just to be completely upfront and transparent, is that any deal we enter into would absolutely require Baker to agree in writing to transfer all of his purchases over to us. Without that, I'm afraid your deal would be worth very little and ultimately not one we'd be interested in." Fitz understood completely.

~~~~~~~~~~~~

Two and a half years had gone by since Statham and Travis last met with Fitz out west. Travis had tried multiple times, although unsuccessfully, to get Fitz back to the negotiating table and continue their discussions. Except that, after his trip to The Ranch and initial what-if thoughts of cashing out had subsided, Fitz came to a conclusion. First of all, until Travis called him out of the blue, he had never before thought of selling his business so soon. Secondly, he didn't feel like it was the right time to hold Baker over a barrel or especially to pressure him into signing with GAC because of what he knew about him. Third and finally, Fitz had always known the best deals occur when the other side comes after you, and far better if they keep coming.

Now that Baker had proven his stated intentions to keep growing locations, his firm's annual casket purchase volume had doubled since Fitz and the two senior Great American execs had last met. As well, Fitz had picked up a few other new clients along the way. He knew the longer he waited, especially while Baker grew and grew, that a potential net payout would continue to increase as well. That is, assuming Great American still wanted to buy his business. Regardless, Fitz also knew the larger and more complex his operation became, the less Baker would ever want to worry with running it himself. He was a funeral man, not a casket shipper. Even if GAC didn't want to buy it, one of the other big firms surely would by now. For Fitz's prospects of cashing out, the best news was that Baker's five year plan had already come to fruition in less than his original window. Also, Fitz understood Baker had no plans to slow down acquiring Mom & Pop locations in his targeted areas anytime soon. He had also come to accept that, if and when he ever did sell, he would eventually be in the position of walking away from Baker's potential future growth, as well as leveraging their so-called close relationship to make it happen.

Perhaps now was the time to finally return GAC's call and restart the discussions. If the same type of offer held true, then the payout should be right at double compared to what they had discussed a couple years back. Thinking about a payout number in the nine to ten million dollar range made Fitz more excited than he had ever been about the idea of selling. Pushing sixty years of age, he could see that kind of cash setting him and his wife up for a superb retirement, far nicer than they'd ever imagined. First things first, he would reach out to Great American. If that went well, then he would invite Baker back down to the condo in Cabo to break the ice about selling out.

~~~~~~~~~~~~~~

Statham had mixed emotions when Travis gave him the word that Fitz was wanting to fire back up past discussions about acquiring his firm. Two years earlier when Fitz had insinuated that he had some apparent dirt on Baker, Statham had badly misread the dialog as a strong closing signal and that a deal would possibly be imminent. Worse yet, like some rookie sales rep prematurely calling his boss to say that a new client had been hooked, Statham had made the grave mistake of subsequently mentioning the high probability of landing Baker Haskins to DAK at a board meeting. Having taken so many runs at Baker Haskins over the prior decades, DAK was absolutely exhilarated with the news and expected quick developments. When those didn't come, Statham was left looking far less than presidential. Something for which he would place the blame on Fitz, and vowed to make sure if he ever got another crack at the man, that he would make damn sure was rectified.

Now over two years later, as Baker's footprint had continued to expand while still targeting the best GAC-buying accounts, the lost volume had more than doubled while operating costs continued to go sky high out west. Opting to keep his eye on the prize, Statham decided to pull out all stops to get a deal done with Fitz. This time when Fitz went to his local airfield to step aboard a GAC jet for the trip back to The Ranch, he would see the huge GAC-1 Falcon sitting on the tarmac. He would also enjoy the company of one the young bombshell cocktail waitresses waiting to keep him "completely" entertained on his private ride. Regardless, much to the surprise of Statham and Travis, once again Fitz didn't take the bait from the willing and bosomy server. Despite how the girl had promised, she'd done her very best to entice him several times.

By the time Fitz touched down at GAC Field and made his way to The Ranch, Statham and Travis were already in DAK's private dining room awaiting his arrival. Except now, the bourbon sampling was limited to Fitz's three favorites, which as with all visitors to The Ranch, had been noted and recorded for future trips, just to impress. The extra little attention to detail worked just as well on Fitz as it always did with any other customer lucky enough to make a return trip to The Ranch.

After Fitz's first drink was in hand, and perfunctory brief chit chat, Statham signaled dinner was ready and that the men should be seated. For this evening's experience, dinner would not include any typical banter or friendly discourse of weather, sports, or markets. Statham got right down to business before the salad forks were ever deployed. By the time the entrees had been devoured, the deal was effectively agreed upon. Statham had cut through the bull-shit faster than the truffle-buttered, filet mignon, confirming that Fitz had reached out and come back to Bergholz to get a deal done.

Essentially their deal would have same term expectations as before, only now the volumes and related payouts would be larger. Like before, Fitz provided the necessary documentation to support the reassessment and offer

298

positions. By the time desert arrived, Statham and Fitz had reached an agreement in principle for the terms of the deal. The following day, Fitz was to meet the two GAC execs at the corporate office to sign mutual letters of intent and cement the essential elements of the deal. From there, Fitz stated his next step was getting Baker back down to Cabo in the coming weeks to break the ice about selling. After which, he would immediately notify Statham and Travis about how the conversation had gone.

Immediately after the dinner meeting was complete, Statham and Travis announced how they both needed to call it a night, as was the plan, thus leaving Fitz on his own at The Ranch. As usually arranged, no other customers or unrequired employees were allowed on property when a target was being hosted. Every detail for his evening activities was planned down to the finest aspect, including having the same voluptuous blonde, bar maid waiting for him at the bourbon bar. She would welcome Fitz with open arms and big hugs just to get his juices flowing, as well as the bourbon. After pouring as much of the best bourbon whiskeys down Fitz's throat, only this time mixed with heavy doses of GHB, the 'ol boy could barely walk back to his room at the lodge. Given the shape he was in, Fitz wouldn't even remember falling onto the bed face first, much less with all of his clothes still on.

~~~~~~~~~~~

The photos were taken from all angles, showing a butt-naked Fitz Edmondson laying bare ass on top of the very young and sexy blonde-haired woman. Blonde, because Fitz's wife was a brunette, just another small important detail that the Roseville Black's dirty ex-cops never missed. There were shots from all different camera angles to assure any onlooker that Fitz Edmundson was one incredibly wild, perverted sex deviant. This time, Statham ordered Witman to make "absolutely fucking certain" that his men went the extra step to make sure Great American would be one thousand percent successful in persuading their victim. True to his wicked character and commitment, Witman relished the authorized license of his assignment. Once it was done, Fitz's setup would prove to be as extreme as anything ever created or ordered by DAK or Statham to make sure Great American prevailed.

Dirty ex-cops always know where to find wayward girls new in town and walking the streets. These girls were routinely getting picked up for turning tricks, usually without a pimp yet or friends in town who would ever be looking for them. Big cities, as dark and dangerous as Pittsburgh, had dozens of these girls every year showing up out of nowhere all the time. This particular time, the girl was a runaway from upstate New York. The tracts on her arms proved a severe cocaine addiction, while the twenty dollar price she quoted for oral sex proved her desperation for cash. Both clues confirmed that the girl was in a very bad state, when she had been found roaming around town like a lost, dead leaf in the wind.

When the white-haired, Roseville Black dirty ex-cop pulled over and picked the girl up, he had told her how pretty she was and that he'd pay her two-hundred and fifty bucks for the night. Already high on coke and almost out of cash, she stupidly asked if he was a nice guy and if she would be ok to go off with him. After providing the desired responses, the zoned out girl got into the dirty ex-cop's dark sedan. As soon as she slid down into the front seat of the car, the girl's third john of the night quickly sped the car away from the dark, dirty curb, noting how beautiful the yellow scarf was that she was wearing.

Not noticing that the white-haired man hadn't even looked or smiled at her when he'd said it, the young blonde was almost out of it again since shooting up after her last trick, who had gotten way rougher than most. Still, even hearing any type of a rare personal compliment made the small town girl smile, although the dulled, hazed look in her eyes confirmed to the dirty cop how easy his task was going to be. That would be the last time anyone would ever see the girl alive again, other than the dirty ex-cop and one of his associates already at The Ranch.

The Ranch outside of Bergholz was only about an hour or so away from where the dirty ex-cop pulled over outside of Pittsburgh and strangled the girl to death. Pulling off the road into an empty dark, desolate parking lot, the dirty ex-cop motioned for the girl to come closer and put her face in his lap. Just as she began to lean down and comply, he quickly grabbed the scarf and yanked her head back with all of his might, stretching the scarf tighter and tighter. Less than a minute later, the girl was dead. As for her beautiful yellow scarf, it would be left around her throat to point out the deep red strangulation marks in the photos with Fitz.

Once the two thugs got the girl's body into Fitz's room, they both took turns punching her in the face again and again, until it was completely bloodied and torn to pieces. They also made several other disturbing marks on the girl's body to show the severity of Fitz's cruelty. Taking Fitz's hands to simulate the blows and strangulation positions, they created scenes that were certain to fully incriminate the drunken fool who remained completely unconscious. By the time an hour had passed, they had made it appear as if Fitz had gone back to his room with the bar maid, for whom the street-walker was a close enough dead ringer, had wild, violent sex with her, and then lost his mind and strangled her to death.

~~~~~~~~~~~~~

It was almost three o'clock in the morning when Fitz finally came to, two full hours after the dead girl's body was taken out of the room. Fitz was freezing from the air conditioner that the two Roseville Black thugs had turned way down to help control the decay and smell in the room. Fitz was instantly scared to death and began yelling out of his mind when he saw himself covered in the blood and the two tough-looking men in dark suits standing over him.

"Where am I? Oh my god, I'm bleeding to death!" he screamed as he frantically looked around the room, seeing blood spattered all over the bed, walls, and ceiling. "Who the hell are you?" he shouted at the men, standing motionless as their victim came to his senses and took in the scene around him. They knew it would take several minutes for the sheer trauma to subside enough, allowing his mind to process what must have taken place. His hands were completely covered in blood, as well as most of his upper torso, face, and hair. Jumping up, the sheet that the men had draped over his freezing body fell off completely, as he ran over to look in a full length mirror across the room. Seeing the bloody image of his reflection, Fitz fell motionless to the floor and began screaming uncontrollably. "Oh my god, oh my god!" was all he said over and over for several minutes.

Once they felt the man was sufficiently beside himself, one of the dirty ex-cops took the bed comforter and wrapped it around Fitz's shaking body. In that moment, Fitz felt the warmth of a human touch and took it for a kindness that he desperately needed. Helping Fitz to his feet and getting him over to the other queen size bed to sit down, the man began to tell Fitz to calm down and that everything was going to be OK. The man told Fitz that he wasn't bleeding anywhere and that he didn't have any wounds, so not to worry. Hearing those words, Fitz could not even believe how that must be true with so much blood all over his body, but then he realized he didn't even know what had happened.

Gaining some sense of composure, still taking in the gruesome images around the room, Fitz asked the men about what happened and who they were. The men explained how they were both former police detectives now working for Great American as security officers. The men explained to Fitz how he and the bar maid had apparently been doing some heavy flirting and kissing for quite some time at the bar the night before, as the video footage from the bar area had revealed. Once they had both gotten so handsy with each other, since no one else was around, the footage showed them both walking back to Fitz's room. Of course, whatever happened inside the room wasn't on tape, the men assured Fitz, who was obviously struggling to recall anything the men were saying. "I don't recall ever even kissing Stacey, much less getting physical." Fitz uttered. Stacey was a sweet and very attractive girl from a nearby town who had been serving bar at The Ranch for the last several years. "Well sir, it wasn't just you. You both were getting pretty roused up based upon what we saw. It looked like you were both getting extremely friendly, especially after doing all those shots." one of the men said in a very stern, commanding voice.

"Well, what in the world happened in my room?" Fitz asked. Standing over him and looking down, the older man with pure white hair continued, "Sir, all we know is that the night janitor called us about hearing some screams. By the time we got here, we found the girl badly beaten to death and strangled around the neck with a scarf. Her face had been so badly beaten that you couldn't even tell it was a face anymore. She also had deep teeth bites on her back and neck, as well as her breasts, which probably explains all the blood that was in your mouth and on your face when we arrived. When we got here, you were passed out cold and covered in blood from head to toe. All we could imagine was that the sex must have gotten out of hand somehow and you two got into a horrible fight.

Either way, the girl is dead and you don't have a scratch on you; only her blood and lots of it." Then one of the dirty ex-cops took his cell phone and began flipping through pictures of what he called the "murder scene" to push Fitz over the edge. After his eyes honed in on a dozen images full of horror, proving he had done the heinous act of murdering the girl, Fitz began to scream out again uncontrollably.

By five o'clock that morning, the men had helped Fitz get into the shower and clean up. They also explained how Mr. Statham was coming out to The Ranch to meet with him at six-thirty to discuss the situation and what would happen from there. When Fitz asked if he was being arrested, the two dirty ex-cops explained how they were not there to arrest him, and how they worked for Great American exclusively, saying, "We will take our direction from Mr. Statham based upon whatever he tells us to do. As of right now, the local authorities haven't been notified."

~~~~~~~~~~~~~

Statham was waiting in a small, dimly-lit conference room when the thugs delivered Fitz, still trembling and consumed with desperation and shock. After going through the planned story, Statham finally asked Fitz what he "wanted to do about it all." Unsuspecting he would have even had a choice in the matter, Fitz looked in total disbelief at the stately, polished man sitting across from him, who he had hoped would make him rich with the deal he had come there to do. "I don't understand, Bill, what do you mean, what do I want to do about it? What can I do? I've murdered a girl, man!" Fitz cried out. Then, Bill Statham went in for the real kill.

"Fitz", he said, "There's no doubt that something went horribly wrong here last night between you and the girl. Who by the way we know had a long history of drug addiction and prostitution ever since she was a teenager. She had come to work

305

here through one of the local church-sponsored rehabilitation ministries we support around the area, but we have had a number of problems with her since she worked here. Mostly drinking on the job and having sex with customers staying here at The Ranch, who she then usually tried to get money out of. Obviously to support her rehabilitation efforts, we got her into counseling, hoping she would eventually get beyond it. My guess is that she had set her sights on you the minute you walked into the bar, especially knowing no one else would be around at The Ranch. Based on her past behavior, you would have most likely been blackmailed in some way.

Fitz couldn't believe what he was hearing and kept telling Statham how he didn't have any recollection whatsoever of ever messing with the girl, much less bringing her back to his room. To which Statham clarified, "Well, you wouldn't have Fitz. Our security team took your blood and did a quick test on it. They're both ex-cops and still have connections with a local crime lab, and get test results back really quickly. Apparently the girl put a drug called GHB in your drinks. They told me it's often called the date rape drug, because of how it quickly sedates the victim and then wears off with a matter of a few hours later. This girl was out to take full advantage of you, Fitz. Plain and simple it seems."

Fitz didn't know what to think. Even if the girl was up to no good, he knew he had still killed her. The two men had even showed him pictures. When he asked about that, Statham assured him that his "guys" had already turned their phones over to him, pointing to the devices lying on a table in the room. "No other photos exist, Fitz, and the room is already being cleaned and refurbished. By lunch time, no one will ever know anything happened in there." he added. Looking completely perplexed at Statham, Fitz asked "So what are you saying Bill, that all of this just goes away?" "That's up to you, Fitz. Whatever happens is up to you. If you feel you should turn yourself into the police, then we can make that call and have them come pick you up. Is that what you want to do?" Statham inquired. Still in a daze and unclear of what he was hearing, Fitz asked further, "Are you telling me I have an option here, Bill? I'm sorry, but I don't understand what's happening or what you're saying."

Leaning in towards his prey, Statham softened his gaze and said, "Fitz, what I'm telling you, is that you are in control of the situation. I hate that the girl is dead too, but that is now a fact. Nothing's going to change that. I also fully believe that girl, and maybe others she could have been working with, were most likely going to take advantage of you, for your money, or whatever. One thing is for certain, she didn't put a ton of that GHB shit in your drinks just to screw you! That girl was up to no good. What I am saying is that we can handle this however you want to, anyway it makes you able and comfortable to go on in life."

Just then Fitz began to immediately think of his wife and children. It was the first time they had even crossed his mind since he'd come to, now some four hours earlier. As his mind and thoughts went to what would happen to them if all of this came out, he began to sob again uncontrollably. Pulling his chair closer so as to seem consoling, Statham placed his hand on the

307

back of Fitz's shoulder and reassured him how he shouldn't worry and how "we can make it all go away as if it never happened." Hearing the confident, calm CEO state those comforting words, Fitz asked, "But Bill, how, how can we make all of this just go away? A girl is dead for Christ's sake. I don't know how to deal with that. Even if she was up to no good, how do you propose we deal with it?" Finally, Fitz had reached the exact, right moment the setup was used for. Now the "VIC", as the dirty ex-cops always referred to their victimized targets, was at the ideal point where they knew they were doomed unless Great American bailed them out and made their troubles disappear. In Fitz's case, his troubles would disappear, plus he'd get rich in the process, if he played his cards right. Now that Statham felt he had Fitz in just the right vulnerable frame of mind, he was ready to fill in the blanks for his future business partner.

Statham pulled his chair back out directly in front of Fitz's, but only about three feet in distance. This allowed him to go from consoler to conspiring confidant, just by positioning his chair. Carefully whispering, to create the illusion of absolute secrecy, Statham assured Fitz there was no way he was not going to allow "a wretched, little tramp like that ruin a good man's life." Telling Fitz, "You know one of the unusual aspects we have access to in our business? That would be cremation, Fitz. That girl was up to no good and had planned to do you in. That's clear to me. Now it's unfortunate that her misdeeds led to her own demise, but at this point, we just need to get rid of the body. Unless you change your mind and decide to turn yourself in, I

308

will have security get the body in lined, cremation casket and load it on the plane you'll be taking home later today. Then your flight will stop off at one of our closest partner accounts in Oklahoma who will immediate cremate the casket, with no questions asked. We sometimes have them destroy returned caskets for us from time, so they won't think twice about it. You can, and should, even go to the funeral home to watch the container go straight into the incinerator, just so you can rest easy that the evidence has been taken care of. From there, you'll fly on home and put all of this behind you, Fitz. How's that sound? If you're OK with that plan, I will call the guys right now and get things rolling."

Looking as guilty as anyone could, but more fearful of being charged with murder for something he knew he would have never done unless he had been drugged out of his mind, Fitz nodded silently to show his agreement. Though, never once considering how preposterous it was to fly caskets so far away just to be destroyed. It's funny how human beings can be so easily convinced to believe something when they need and want to accept it.

~~~~~~~~~~~~~

CONVENIENT ACQUISITION

After trying to get a few cups of strong, black coffee and some food into Fitz, Statham told him that, despite the unfortunate events overnight, there was no reason why they couldn't go ahead and sign their new Intent To Purchase agreement that the GAC legal team had already finalized since their prior evening's discussion over dinner. With his mind hardly focused on the thought of discussing business, Fitz agreed to sign the binding contract without even reading it, saying how he had no problem trusting Statham "at this point."

Except this time, before Statham handed over the pen to a man ready to sign over his life, there was still that one pesky unknown detail that Fitz had never disclosed about Baker. Whatever the secret was and that apparently only came out in Cabo. Now Fitz would be in no position to keep the information close-chested as he had a couple years earlier. Not wasting any time or showing any sensitivity, Statham said, "Now Fitz, despite everything we've had to unfortunately deal with this morning, there's still the matter of what we spoke about a couple of years back when we talked before about doing this deal. I said then how I would need to be absolutely certain why you believe so strongly you can bring Baker over to Great American. I chose not to push you then, but I'm going to have to know everything before we do this deal, which of course is going to make you a very wealthy man."

Fitz didn't have the mental wherewithal or energy to push back on the thought of sharing the secret about his best

310

customer. "Oh that" he said. "Bill, I would need to ask that you keep this to yourself of course, and I know I can trust you so I'm not even going to ask you to acknowledge that request, which is all it is. Obviously, as you and Larry could tell before, it's a very private and personal piece of information about Baker that only I know, and that he would never want to have it get out.

I'm sure DAK told you the stories of inviting Baker, and his dad before that, to some of his infamous meetings on one of his jets, and how Baker, as obnoxious as he can be at times, told DAK just what he could do with his jets and so-called whores. Well, the simple reason for that wasn't that Baker has any moral high ground. The fact is that he doesn't at all; quite the opposite actually. The real truth is that Baker is a closeted-homosexual. He has been for years; although he has a wife and three children, and seems as happily married as most any man. And, when he's down in Cabo, I always arrange to have a young boy, usually around fourteen or fifteen years of age, knock on his door each evening. That's what it's all about Bill. He gets his kicks with boys, not girls. As you can imagine, it's one of those subjects we never discuss, I just make it happen."

Statham was trying to contain his natural shit-eating grin, but Fitz could see the CEO was somewhat enjoying finally hearing what all the suspicion had been about. "So how did you find out, Fitz?" Statham asked curiously. "Well, it was really pretty simple Bill. Any time we were down there, we were surrounded by the beautiful, young girls working at the hotel, restaurants and bars. And I mean spectacularly beautiful, except Baker never looked twice at any of them. But let a young boy ever serve us and his neck would snap around to watch him walk away. You could just see his mind spinning with lust. It really wasn't very complicated. Although, I have to tell you, he and I had been out to dinner hundreds of times, up around where we live, and never once did I see him glance at a boy. Not ever!" "Well, well!" Statham said. "That's really not anything we would ever care about around here. But you can bet your sweet ass, Fitz, that DAK Kleinmark would have never had any young cabin boys flying around with him on the company planes back in his day. Baker would have been bored to death for sure! The main thing is that you're completely confident that knowledge, and of course, mostly your good relationship, will be enough to persuade him to sign over our way." "I absolutely am!" said Fitz, who now seemed to be almost back to his normal self.

~~~~~~~~~~~~

With that important piece of information finally in hand, Statham quickly, but only verbally, reviewed the terms of the deal with Fitz before they both signed the final, binding contract. Now that Fitz's annual sold volume was at twenty thousand caskets, with seventy percent or fourteen thousand units going to Baker, half of the remaining six thousand units would need to be converted. That would a total target of seventeen thousand to reach a full payout on the deal.

The structure of the deal was still pretty simple, although Fitz's net profit margin had changed because of having to enrich Baker's upfront discount another two points to twenty-eight. Still operating on a gross of forty points, Fitz was now left with a net margin of five points versus the seven he'd had a few years earlier. To his credit, he was also working off of twice the revenue, so his payout was significantly increased just the same. The negative metric in the deal calculation was how Fitz's overall average wholesale margin had dropped one hundred dollars, making it now nine hundred and fifty. That result was due to Baker and Fitz's other clients continuing to buy cheaper wholesale units, though still selling them at the same high mark-ups, to offset the growing cremation rate across the country.

Using Fitz's updated numbers, now his annual sales were right at nineteen million dollars, with his annual take home coming in right at nine hundred and fifty thousand per year. However, the evening before, in order to get the dickering and the exhausting dinner over with, Statham had quickly and surprisingly consented to a whopping ten year multiple on the year, a decision he'd already reached, albeit for different reasons, before the Falcon ever took off to go pick up Fitz. After adding in the extra half million for equipment Fitz still owned outright, the deal came to a cool ten million dollars for Fitz, assuming he could get Baker to sign a five year exclusive agreement and convert another three thousand caskets.

Once Fitz brought in Baker's signed agreement, representing a total of seventy thousand strong wholesale units over the minimum five year term, Great American would pay him five million up front in cash. To get the other five million, Fitz would have to bring in enough deals worth another three thousand in the following six months. But, if Fitz failed to get enough contracts signed, representing at least three thousand additional caskets in the first six months, then the second five

313

million was forfeited. If he did get them signed, but the customers' actual aggregate purchases fell short of three thousand after year one, again the full second payment opportunity of five million was lost. Therefore, after one year of signing his deal with Great American, if Fitz signed up enough accounts in the first six months, each with a minimum three year term, and those same accounts bought no fewer than three thousand caskets, a second five million dollars would be paid out in full. Fitz understood and accepted it was an all or nothing deal for the second payout.

As for the great terms offered to get all of Fitz's customers to sign up with Great American, all of those deals had to extend and perform for at least three years. Which meant, that if Fitz's converted customers signed up and took the great discount incentives from Great American just to help their 'ol buddy Fitz cash out in year one, but didn't keep buying in the second and third, the contract expressly stated that all of the first year discount incentives were mutually agreed to be rebilled to the funeral home operator. The contracts also stipulated that in such cases, the rebilled amounts would be due and payable in full within thirty days, no exceptions. Statham knew from his Miracle Casket days how to keep a customer honest and how to punish them if not. As for keeping Baker Haskins honest to uphold his five year purchase agreement, well they didn't expect that to be an issue. Nonetheless, his contract had the same claw back clause in it too, except it extended for five years.

In all, the entirety of the deal was predicated upon Fitz getting commitments for a total of seventy nine thousand caskets over the expected terms of the customer contracts. Once Statham and Travis factored in the than normal price increases over the term, something Fitz had failed to consider, the total topline revenue pick up was north of ninety million, and twenty-five million to the bottom; less the payouts to Fitz. Another huge, accretive financial pick up for Great American in the deal was how their total overall operating costs would decline substantially once they were moving more volume to the West Coast. Statham figured that net pick up to be at least another three million per year; which in itself, essentially paid for Fitz's deal in full, even if he hit on both five million dollar payouts. It was indeed a great deal for Statham and Fitz, and one they both wanted to make succeed. More so, Statham knew what it could mean for him personally with DAK.

Now the results were up to Fitz's relationships and working his ass off to get customers to sign up with Great American. At this point, Statham wanted to make sure that nothing was left to chance given Fitz's state of mind, especially after what he'd gone through at The Ranch and stopping off in Oklahoma to see the dead girl's casket get shoved into the blazing hot fiery crematory. It's one thing to load and ship caskets, it's something totally different to believe you had a direct hand in filling one up. Statham wondered if they had pushed Fitz too far in the process of knuckling him under. Regardless, he was putting his number one ace in the hole on the assignment to ensure the deals got done. To make that happen, he took Garner McCall off of his regular day job and reassigned him to lead the sales conversion and work directly with Fitz.

315

Statham never told McCall that he had only factored in a forty percent conversion rate for the rest of Fitz's customers, outside of Baker Haskins. As usual, he wasn't going to get himself hogtied into an unattainable number that Fitz couldn't hit, and which he'd have to report as another loss to the Board. He knew his best shot of over-shooting the forty-mark, and maybe the sixty, was to quickly get McCall directly involved with Fitz traveling around and winning accounts over.

The only stipulation he put on McCall's authority in doing deals, was that any contract offer including upfront discounts north of twenty points would have to be approved by Travis personally, which seemed highly odd to Garner. To justify the unusual directive, especially given how McCall had always been responsible for approving far bigger deals before, Statham explained to Garner how the deal with Fitz "had been so exorbitantly rich compared to most, and especially with Fitz's number one big client – the Haskins Group." As a result, the clever CEO told his man McCall how Great American needed to get these other firms to sign on the dotted line with "better than normal profit level deals of the day."

Like always, McCall spoke his mind with his CEO, saying how in his opinion it was going to be "unlikely, if not impossible," to get customers to switch over for a mere eighteen to twenty percent offer. Particularly given how GAC and most casket makers were typically doing deals in the mid-twenties by then. Statham told his man to do his best, but to let Fitz pull his weight in the various negotiations; saying "Fitz alone should be worth at least five to eight points. If so, this whole thing should

316

be a slam dunk! Let's see how it goes, Garner, and you keep Travis updated on your weekly progress reports with Fitz."

~~~~~~~~~~~~

By the time Fitz talked Baker into meeting him at the condo in Cabo, a month into the deal had already past. Baker had been pressing Fitz to explain why it was so important for them to go back so soon, since their last rendezvous had just been a few months earlier. Not wanting to spill the beans entirely, Fitz just left it that he was ready to "make some changes" and wanted to speak with Baker first as he'd always promised. Except now, Baker was in the midst of buying another block of funeral homes and didn't want to devote time away just yet.

It was beginning to seem like he was waking up from a dream and a nightmare at the same time, now several weeks removed from flying out of Bergholz. The expectations of the first five million dollar payday, he had thought would be so quick and easy, now seemed like something that was going to be more of a challenge than he realized. While the horrifically vivid images of the bloody and battered bar maid never completely left his mind for long, Fitz was struggling in every aspect of his life, and particularly to get his Great American deal moving in the right direction. Further, Fitz had been less than open and sharing with McCall about his activities, not wanting anyone from GAC corporate looking over his shoulder all the time, and kept putting him off trip after trip. To McCall, the whole thing reminded him of a familiar dumbass named 'ol Jimmy, who he'd seen right through early on after joining GAC. In this case though, Garner knew Fitz had a lot at stake and kept pressing to help.

317

Once Fitz began to start panicking that the clock was quickly starting to spin on his limited time to land the conversion accounts, he finally allowed Garner to come out and start attending the meetings with customers targeted for conversion to GAC. Fitz was amazed at how McCall quickly proved his fluid sales skills, just as Statham had assured. Just as his own sales reps had witnessed, McCall immediately connected and related to Fitz's customers. After the first two meetings where Fitz and Garner met with accounts, both were signed onto three year deals; which of course elated Fitz. It was the first real taste of success he'd had, and helped to spur on his motivation and hope. Now he was wondering whether or not to take McCall directly into see Baker, but his gut said no.

Fitz knew he needed to get Baker back down south of the border to have that one on one discussion on his playing terms. The time had come to get Baker to move, so to make that happen, Fitz decided to tell his main client that he had decided to sell the business and wanted to talk with him about potential buyers. As expected, that got Baker's attention given how whichever firm Fitz sold out to would directly impact his organization so significantly. With that understanding, the two men agreed to meet the following week at the condo.

~~~~~~~~~~~~~

Cabo did not go well, at least for Fitz. Baker left the condo without agreeing on anything, only promising to think about the notion of buying from Great American. Despite even having McCall along to try and bring Baker around to the idea of converting to GAC, Baker had not reacted well to the idea at all.

318

Two days later, Fitz's number one client and his key to a ten million dollar payout had called to opt out of supporting GAC's proposal. Saying how they'd have to find another solution, because he was absolutely not going to buy from Great American. That forced Fitz and McCall to have to call Statham and Travis to announce the deal looked dead unless Baker Haskins had a miraculous change of heart.

Then, astonishingly, just two days after their previous sad news exchange, Baker had called Fitz back and consented to come on board after all. Fitz could not explain what rationalization Baker had come to, only to say that he must have had an epiphany because of how different he sounded on the phone this time. Fitz said Baker didn't sound like himself at all. Regardless, Fitz had emailed the five year purchase agreement to Baker, who signed, scanned, and returned it via email the same day, actually in the matter of minutes. All Baker had asked was that Garner McCall be the one to take the lead converting over his forty-some-odd funeral home selection rooms to Great American's merchandising mix of caskets. He told Fitz that while he wished him well, their personal relationship would not continue in any sense going-forward. He didn't explain further or say another word. After that, the only thing Fitz heard was the sound of the phone line go dead.

~~~~~~~~~~~~~~~~

Now the deal with Baker was done, even though he couldn't understand what had changed his best client's mind, especially after he had been so clear and certain when he'd first said no so matter-of-factly. Either way, Fitz accepted his good

319

fate and decided to look forward to converting the remainder of the needed three thousand other caskets. To do so, he reached out to his new senior sales ally, Garner McCall.

McCall was busy back at GAC corporate in Bergholz, studying the knowns and unknowns of all of Fitz's targeted accounts in a dedicated war room he had established. The walls of the war room were covered in all sorts of stats and information about each account; their orders, metal VS wood sales, wholesale mix, discount and rebate terms had with Fitz, etc. Each account record was assessed and used to determine what kind of a GAC deal it was going to take to get every account to switch over. The challenge was however, as Garner continued to surmise, that the deal levels that Statham and Travis were approving would clearly not get the customers to switch brands.

From what Garner had seen, while traveling around with Fitz, was the reality that Fitz didn't have close selling relationships at all with any of his customers. His approach to signing them up, while Baker's business grew in their areas, had been to win strictly on a price approach in the low to mid-twenties; which was certainly a lot higher than what the firms had been receiving from their former suppliers. That was the only reason any of the customers had ever really signed up with Fitz. Worse yet, he had never even gone back once to visit any of his other funeral home customers since signing them up originally. As a result as Garner witnessed time and again, Fitz had proved repeatedly how he was in no position to leverage his so-called "relationship," as Statham had suggested should be worth enough to make up the difference in terms and help him achieve the goal. No doubt, Garner knew he and Fitz had a huge uphill challenge ahead.

~~~~~~~~~~~~~~~

As more months had passed, only a couple more accounts switched over to GAC. Despite Garner's best efforts traveling with Fitz out west each and every week, being gone for months on end away from home, customers were simply unwilling to compromise and sign up. Weekly war room reviews and updates with Travis confirmed the all-out likelihood that Fitz was going to lose out on the possibility of a second five million payout. Finally, Garner went back to Bergholz, thinking they had done all they could do, but regrettably falling short. The only good news was that the Haskins's firms had been successfully converted and were buying regularly as expected, with their average wholesale mix increasing nicely, immediately after Garner converted their rooms over to GAC.

Then, with only two weeks left in the initial six month critical window, Fitz showed back up in Bergholz unexpectedly. His next scheduled trip in wasn't for another week yet, in which he was to meet with Garner and another executive responsible for converting over the back office aspects of the business, such as inventories, payables and receivables, billing, computer systems, HR, etc. When Garner had last seen or spoken with Fitz, the man had almost been distraught about the possible thought of losing out on the second half five million dollar opportunity of his deal. Garner recalled how Fitz was virtually apoplectic at how his customers kept refusing his offers.

However now, as Garner and his colleague met with Fitz about the more mundane aspects of converting his business to Great American, there was absolutely no mistaking the fact that his whole attitude and demeanor were completely different. All of a sudden, Fitz was smiling from ear to ear and completely carefree, at least seemingly, which to Garner, seemed really curious.

After the boring aspects about inventory levels, computer systems, and the like had been sufficiently reviewed, Garner began his segment of the review meeting by apologizing for how it looked like they were going to fall short of the three thousand unit target by almost a third. He also asked Fitz if any other clients had followed up about possibly accepting the offers from GAC. To which Fitz, who suddenly began to grin like a hungry housecat that just spotted a trapped mouse in a corner, said "No." Amazed at how Fitz's attitude had changed to one of such casualness, Garner, always one straight to the point himself, said "Ok, so what gives Fitz? You clearly don't seem very concerned about your deal anymore. I don't understand. Have you resigned yourself to the fact we're going to miss hitting the three thousand unit mark or what?" Waiting on his response, Garner and his colleague waited with bated breath to see what was up with the man who previously had been entirely and anally fixated on nothing else in all their previous meetings.

All Fitz said was, "Look, all I have to do is move another one thousand caskets, right?" To which McCall, agreed, still looking confused and waiting for clarification. A good salesman knows the power of silence, and Garner said nothing,

322

knowing Fitz would be forced to continue speaking and explain himself. "After talking with Travis over dinner last night, I came to realize that my contract "only" says I have to move "caskets." It doesn't say which kinds or price points. So basically, I can even get my customers to buy the cheapest ones offered by Great American. Just as long as I hit the three thousand mark, I get the extra five million. I could even buy them myself and give them away if I wanted to. So basically, I could buy a thousand of your cheapest two hundred and fifty dollar low-end cremation caskets and give them away if I wanted to hit the target. Meaning, I could spend two hundred and fifty thousand dollars to make five million! Of course, I'm going to do that! There's no way, I'm going to miss out on another five million dollars guys!" With those words out of his mouth, Fitz looked and acted as if his second payoff was already in the bank.

Just then, McCall and his colleague looked immediately at each other, completely stunned by what they had just heard. Garner persisted and asked, "Fitz, who told you that, Travis? I don't believe that's correct. I read your agreement early on, and it clearly stated the wholesale average would have to be at or higher than nine hundred dollars. To do that, you'd have to keep your sales average pretty much where it's been for the last few years, in order to not fall below that required target." "Travis explained it to me last night over dinner at his house. I guess I had missed it in the contract, but it's clearly stated right there in black and white, plain as day. It only says I must generate sales of three thousand "units" over and above whatever Baker's firm buys, but it doesn't stipulate any kind or wholesale average whatsoever." Fitz said, "Even better still, if, for any reason, Great American can't ship them all before my contract due date, that doesn't count against me either."

Now Garner and the colleague were really perplexed and called for an immediate break in the meeting. As soon as they left the war room, they went straight up to see the general counsel of the company and review the agreement. Sure enough the agreement's wording had been changed since he and his fellow exec had read it originally. Even the lawyer was stupefied, saying he hadn't remembered seeing that clause worded that way in the agreement either, although perhaps he just misread it. Regardless of what the agreement stated, McCall and his colleague knew the spirit and intent of the agreement was not what was written. Nor had it ever been what was discussed in any of the previous meetings and reviews with Fitz, Travis, or Statham. So the three senior execs decided to find Statham and bring him into the discussion to get his position on the matter.

Literally minutes after Statham had arrived and became informed of the dilemma, which if allowed would cost Great American five million dollars for the sale on a thousand of their cheapest two hundred and fifty dollar caskets. In total, at a twenty-eight net profit margin, the whole order would only produce a net profit to GAC of sixty-two thousand five hundred dollars. Surely there was no way Bill Statham would allow something like that to go through, regardless of what his man Travis had suggested to Fitz.

Moments after detailing the situation to Statham in the lawyer's office, all of a sudden, Travis made a single knock at the door and attempted to glide inside, in his usually calm, egotistical manner. Except, most uncharacteristically this time, Statham quickly blocked the door's opening with his hand, pushing back on the thick, solid wood barrier, saying with a peculiar toned emphasis, "Later!" Seeing the two men make eye contact that was oddly meaningful, Garner waited to see what happened next. He and his other colleagues in the room kind of looked at each other with raised eyebrows, seeing how Statham had just shut out his trusty man Travis like that. Obviously, he'd had no reason to do that based upon anything they had said. Garner, the lawyer, and the other exec all immediately wondered why Statham had shut out Travis. Especially, when it would have made more sense to have him come in and explain things from his understanding, although none of them said anything of the sort to the defiant CEO.

After more discussion on the topic, Statham finally said that surely there must have been an "unfortunate misunderstanding." Further he emphatically stated that "No way in hell is Fitz going to be allowed to get away with this kind of bullshit! Not on my watch! Regardless of what he may have thought he heard from Travis!" Funny though, still none of them knew what Travis had actually said. But it was obvious that Travis had immediately learned from Fitz how Garner and his colleague reacted to what he'd said, causing him to rush upstairs and try to shut it down just minutes afterward. Except, Garner and the other two top execs had already found Statham first.

Travis's biggest problem now was that he'd failed to forewarn Fitz from spilling the proverbial beans about the revised loophole. Most of all, he'd failed to realize how ecstatic 'ol Fitz would be to learn about the tiny hidden clause in the contract, and thus unable to keep his mouth shut. The one he'd never read, once he become so consumed with all of the literal blood on his hands. Fitz was so elated with the idea of an extra payout, that he simply couldn't contain himself in the moment. Just another example of why no one, especially Statham, ever accused Travis of being too smart. Just willing to do the shit work that kept the shrewd CEO far enough removed, whenever necessary.

~~~~~~~~~~~~~

By the end of that same week, Garner McCall would be taken completely off of Fitz's conversion initiative and put back into his regular day job. Statham's quick about-face excuse in doing so was supposedly because of how bad overall sales had become since pulling McCall out. Even telling the executive team his rationale right in front of McCall's boss at the time, either to make his boss look bad or to make Garner feel puffed up. Then again, knowing Statham, it was most likely both. As for Fitz hitting his numbers and second five million dollar payout, Garner would never know for sure. Right after the meeting in the lawyer's office and getting yanked off of the initiative with just a few weeks to go, it became quickly apparent that Fitz, Statham, Travis, and even Garner's colleague were not willing to discuss any of it with him going forward.

It's funny though how close people become when they spend weeks on end traveling together on the road. Garner and Fitz had spent months and months together no less. There had been many a glass of fine wine or scotch sipped, as Garner listened patiently to Fitz talk endlessly of his impending retirement plans, about the expensive beach condo he planned to buy, this time states-side, as well as the new fancy sports cars on his wish list. Fitz had two lists; one if he hit the second payout, and another if he missed.

The casket business is a small world. Plenty of people knew Fitz and stayed in touch. And many of those, Garner knew just as well. Within just a few months of Fitz's twelfth month window closing, it became completely apparent that he had employed his first list, meaning the full ten million dollars had been paid out. Just as interesting was how Statham and Travis had both gotten new expensive cars too, with 'ol Larry's only being new to him, of course. More telling were the rumors of how the two Miracle Casket men both upgraded their own beachfront condo's right not long after Fitz bought his own South Florida penthouse.

In the end, Garner would always wonder, given how things had mysteriously gone down, if the three men had wound up splitting the second five million dollar payout somehow. Even more curious, was why Baker Haskins had changed his tune so unexpectedly. Especially since he'd immediately shut off all connections to his lifelong friend Fitz Edmonson in the process, that was something else that never seemed on the up and up. Just like a bloated, dead corpse pulled out of a lake after weeks and weeks, the whole thing stunk to the high heavens.

~~~~~~~~~~~

CABO

It's amazing how easy it is to break and enter most residences. Witman had already dispatched Roseville Black's dirty ex-cops to the condo weeks earlier, assuming Fitz would have not had such a difficult time getting Haskins to agree to meet. Hanging out somewhere like Cabo San Lucas, for weeks on end waiting for a shake down to happen, wasn't something Witman's thugs would have ever imagined back when Arthur Black put them on the payroll. For sure, they weren't complaining. By the first week, they had the condo next door to Fitz's rented out for two months with an option on the third, and at the owner's full rate even though it was the off-season. The bugs and cameras were all in place and had been tested several times a week, just to be sure.

Regardless of their long-standing allegiance, Fitz knew Baker wasn't going to be happy hearing about his deal with Great American. He also didn't want to risk getting him to sign over his purchase commitment based upon a threat of being outed. After all, it wasn't like Fitz had any physical proof of the man's improprieties. Realizing it would just be his word against Baker's, his rationale would have to be especially convincing. He thought perhaps if he offered Baker part of his five million dollar deal payout, maybe it would show his sincerity. Although he quickly realized that the last thing in the world that Baker Haskins lacked or needed was money. The man was filthy rich as it was, especially now since his business was generating twenty thousand services a year, producing over one hundred million in

328

revenues. From which, Baker was personally netting a very tidy five percent or five million in annual earnings, each and every year. Another million or so from Fitz wasn't going to be enough to bend Baker Haskins over a barrel.

The only other option Fitz thought of, was to be honest with Baker, and then to have McCall close by in case he could get him open to the idea and willing to meet with the smooth Southern sales exec from GAC. That was the best approach he could think of as he and McCall flew down on one of the luxury Cessna's; something else he wouldn't mention to Baker.

~~~~~~~~~~~~

Baker never wasted his time and was always one to get right to the point. As soon as he and Fitz were settled in the condo, with Witman's men listening and watching from next door, the conversation about Fitz's announcement started up. Fitz had put some clever, and somewhat honest, calculated thought into his intended line of persuasion, which was how he recently experienced a major life scare. Only in this version it was health-related, but still it had caused him to decide to slow down and spend more "quality" time with family. Fitz proved to be very convincing in his storytelling, even tearing up, as the still fresh ghastly blood-soaked images from The Ranch flooded his memory. His performance proved sufficient enough in getting Baker to offer his sincerest understanding and concern, along with well wishes for a wonderful retirement. He went even further to tell Fitz how his funeral group would have never been able to grow as successfully as it had without Fitz's support over the years.

Despite Fitz's best efforts to set up his rationale and motivation, the conversation quickly went south when Baker asked about his succession plan. At first, Baker was pleased to hear that operations would continue as always without any expected interruptions. Fitz went further to spin quite a tail about meeting with all of the main line casket suppliers who had operations throughout Baker's current and intended footprint of funeral home locations. When finally pressed to cough up the name of the company he was looking to sell to, Fitz hemmed and hawed, throwing out all the reasons why he thought there was really only one good choice. Never one to play guessing games, Baker flat out demanded to know what Fitz wasn't saying.

As soon as the words "Great American" crossed Fitz's lips, the two goons next door could literally see the hair stand up on the back of the funeral man's neck, as he began to blast Fitz. "No fucking way, Fitz! Absolutely, no fucking way! You know I detest those scumbags in Bergholz! We've talked about this a hundred times, man! I can't believe you went to those guys!" "Baker, I promise you, Great American is by far the best firm for you to partner with. They put all the others to shame, I've checked them all – and I'm telling you, they're the best outfit to take care of you today and especially for how you want to grow in the future! Just let me go through it with you." Fitz implored.

To no avail, Baker said again "Absolutely not. I told my daddy and granddaddy both that I would NEVER EVER buy from Great American or that fucking, DAK Kleinmark, Fitz! And, I'm not going to, that much I can promise you! Who else you got in mind? Let's talk about your second candidate and stop

330

wasting time getting pissed off about those assholes at Great American!"

Fitz might not have been a great salesman, but like all great ones, he knew when to shut up and end a downward spiral. "Ok, ok, Baker, you're right. Let's walk down to the beach and have a beer. We just got here, so let's relax. We can talk about it later, maybe tomorrow." Fitz sheepishly conceded.

After a couple of beers in them, Baker broached the topic again, this time without so much passion and anger. "So Fitz, did you really think I'd go for Great American, really?" "To tell you the truth Baker, I really never knew anything about them, except for what I had ever heard from you. I get that you and your father had a run-in with DAK Kleinmark way back when, but I've got to tell you what I found. First off, I've never even met or spoke to DAK Kleinmark. I don't think he's been involved in the business these days, or for several years now. I guess he's pretty old at this point. The guys I talked to were by far the most professional, straight-shooters I've met; and I met with the top five casket suppliers. And only two were even interested, and Great American was, hands down, the premier firm. You know how awesome their casket quality is compared to everyone else's, Baker. I really think they're the right fit for you, if you think you can ever get past your current attitude about them." Seeing now that Baker was letting him actually state his case, without just shooting a bunch of emotional holes in everything he said, Fitz stopped to get a reaction.

Baker sat there for a few minutes, sipping his beer, and looking out at the tide coming in. Finally, he said, "So what are you proposing, Fitz? That I just switch over and start selling Great American caskets? I'm not sure I've got it in me to do that, to be honest." Finally Baker had opened the door and said the very words aloud – "start selling Great American caskets" – then Fitz knew he was coming around emotionally to the idea. In an effort to advance his interest,

Fitz replied, "Honestly Baker, I knew you would struggle with this idea. I also knew that I was probably not the right one to provide you with enough reason and information about making such a huge change. So, now please hear me out on this, I brought down one of their top sales executives to speak with you personally, but only if you're open to it. If not, then it's ok. Although honestly, I don't think you have anything to lose and perhaps a lot to gain by hearing him out. Just think on it tonight and you can decide in the morning. He's staying just down the beach, so he's here if you change your mind. Tell you what, I'm getting hungry. What do say we go get some tamales and rest for the night?"

"Rest for the night" was code for the planned knock on Baker's door that would come later in the evening. The two thugs had tried to get close enough on the beach with their long-range recording devices, but all they heard when they checked the tape back in their room later was the sound of waves crashing onto the shoreline. Despite their planning, now all they could do was to wait until the two men came back to Fitz's condo and see what else might happen.

~~~~~~~~~~~~~

332

By the time the next day dawned, the two men had all the footage Great American would likely ever need to bring Baker Haskins mercilessly to his knees and around to doing business on their terms. If for some reason Baker shot down Garner McCall, then the two heavies would be flying north to personally deliver a life-altering manila envelope to 'ol Baker. Thankfully for Fitz, Baker had ultimately caved in as they walked back after dinner, and said to go ahead and set up the meeting with the man from Great American. If all went well, then Baker and Fitz both could escape the humiliation and hard lessons of doing wrong. If not, well then Baker Haskins would learn the hard way that he too had a decision to make.

Baker had to admit to Fitz that Garner McCall was no DAK Kleinmark. He went as far to say that if Great American had made such a polished professional approach with him years earlier, that maybe he'd already be selling their caskets. The meeting had gone well, very well in fact. By the time the two hour lunch discussion concluded, Baker felt in his gut that Great American was undoubtedly the highest quality line in funeral service, at least as caskets went. Regardless, he was also honest and upfront with both Fitz and McCall that all he would promise them for now was that he would think long and hard about their offer.

Once Baker and Fitz had returned to the condo, Fitz realized that Baker had unexpectedly already packed and scheduled his taxi pickup to fly back home. Worse yet, Fitz told Garner that Baker had never said anything about leaving early, and figured it was not a good sign. All Baker said when he shook

Fitz's hand was how he appreciated and understood everything they had talked about, and how he knew everything Fitz had done was in his firm's best interest. He stressed to Fitz, just how much that meant to him and promised to follow-up with a decision real soon.

~~~~~~~~~~~~

Two days later, Baker called Fitz late in the evening. Up until then, all of their business calls took place well before eight o'clock in the morning before business hours consumed both men's attention. This time, Fitz knew Baker was calling about their discussion in Cabo concerning Great American. True to his nature of getting right to the point, Baker said, "Fitz, I've thought about little else than helping you sell to Great American. I figure they have probably made you the very best offer by far too, especially in hopes of getting my volume. But honestly, I simply cannot support you on this one Fitz. There's just no way I can go back on my word to my father and grandfather. I just can't do it. I'm sorry.

What I can do is take the business over from you and then try to find someone to buy it from me. Obviously, I'm not asking what Great American offered you, but I think I know what the business is likely worth. So I'm willing to pay you two and a half million in cash upfront for it, lock, stock, and barrel. That's the best I can do. I wanted to get back with you and let you think about it for as long as you need. Then we can talk again when you're ready." Baker offered no chance for Fitz to rebut or negotiate. He had already decided to not get into a long, drawn out back and forth over it. He was clear. Now Fitz would have to decide if his offer was good enough.

Just like that, Fitz's dream of cashing out had come crashing down. A cool ten million dollars in the bank, down the drain. He didn't know what to say to Baker in the moment, at least nothing that would make any difference. All he said was that he "understood and would give it some thought." Nothing else was said between the men.

Figuring he might as well get the next hard part over, Fitz called McCall and gave him the news. Garner was none too happy that he hadn't been able to help get Haskins over the goal line down in Cabo. Figuring they both might as well share the bad news, Fitz and McCall dialed up Travis, now very late in the night back east, waking him up with the dreaded news. Smart enough to let Statham get a good night's sleep, Travis was in the top corner office first thing the morning as the two men called Witman.

~~~~~~~~~~~~~

It wasn't even nine in the morning the following day when Witman's dirty ex-cops walked into Baker's headquarter funeral home location. Clean-cut and well-groomed in their dark suits and ties, he figured they must either be a couple of preachers or professional types. He'd be correct on the latter.

With his beaming smile and welcoming disposition, Baker gladly waved the two men back towards his office down the hallway and proceeded to sit down behind his huge desk. Quickly however, a lump began to form in his throat upon noticing how the white-headed man slowly and quietly closed his thick office door. Seconds afterward, the other man walked straight up to the front of the desk and pulled out a manila envelope, handing it to their VIC. Keeping a tight grip on the package just as Baker tried to take its possession, the man said, almost whispering under his breath, "Edmondson knows nothing about this, but other very serious people do and they think you need to change your mind. The rest is up to you. You have twenty-four hours to decide. Make a late or wrong decision, and your wife and the State Attorney will get an audio video tape version of these. It's your call." With that, the two pros walked out of Baker's office and disappeared.

It's amazing how the human body reacts to fear and stress. Sitting alone in his office behind his huge, antique, hand-carved desk, Baker sat there for several minutes just staring at the envelope he was left holding. He knew he had to open it to see what it contained, but the thought of doing so almost made him sick to his stomach. Even a fool would know that what he was about to see wasn't going to be good. Baker Haskins couldn't recall the last time he had actually been afraid of anything, but he was deathly afraid to see what the envelope hid inside. Obviously, whatever it was, those men had been deadly certain its contents would make him change his mind about something.

Within ten seconds of opening the envelope, Baker's heartbeat was pounding out of his chest. Seeing the photos he was holding in his hands, and fearing someone might walk in as often occurred, Baker jumped up and moved quickly to shut and lock the door to his huge office suite. By the end of the first minute, his shirt was completely soaked with sweat and he was ready to throw up in the fine wicker wastebasket his wife had bought for him at some high-brow furnishings store. The loving photos on the desk of his family's beautiful, trusting faces staring back made him agonize in his own wretched shame. The photos were glaring evidence of him doing all sorts of perverted things to a clearly, under aged Mexican boy and vice versa. The images of the boy, about his own youngest son's age, who had most likely either been kidnapped by gangs or sold to sex-traffickers by his own family, would now haunt him for the rest of his life. Whereas after all the other times with so many other boys, Baker Haskins had never once given any thought about them after leaving Cabo. It was safe to say, undoubtedly now, the images of his despicable acts would be indelibly marked on his memory and consciousness for the rest of his life.

~~~~~~~~~~~

As the next few months went by, Garner focused on leading the conversion effort to switch over all of Baker's locations with Great American caskets and consumer-friendly cut display rooms. Even Baker himself was astonished at the reports from his field managers about how families were spending more time than ever in the partial display rooms looking at different styles and colors. As for Great American's defensive marketing and manipulative pricing approach, Baker allowed McCall to implement them as well, although he would have never before entertained bamboozling grieving families by turning their stomachs and hearts inside out like that; of course,

337

totally discounting his own putrid brown and baby-shit green marketing philosophy.

Regardless, he was scared to death to not give in completely to everything that Great American requested. It was a complete about-face attitudinal change that absolutely confused his staff. They had long since tried in vain for years, after going to many of the industry conventions and seeing how GAC stacked up above all others, to get Baker to bring in the top quality casket line. So they were obviously elated as their boss tried to put a positive spin on the major change, and how it had all related to "his friend" Fitz wanting to retire. The message allowed Baker to save face as well as convince his staff to keep believing what a good friend and honorable man, their boss was.

Deep inside, Baker was struggling emotionally and spiritually to process the images that had burned into his brain, as well as to deal with the threat of them being used against him again. He knew it was hardly unlikely such incriminating proof wouldn't be dusted off, whenever it suited their greedy purposes. Clearly, Great American had already used it once to force him to submit to their demands. And, he knew in his heart that it was a cold, hard fact they would do it again too, if they ever needed to make him comply against his will.

~~~~~~~~~~~~

It wasn't long until Fitz had cashed out and disappeared to his new million dollar plus stateside condo. Still keeping his Northern California home, of course, especially after all the money Great American had sent his way. When Fitz exited, once the final funds hit his bank account, he bowed out completely.

That was the deal. No more state or national funeral director conventions, no contact with former clients, unless GAC ever requested such, otherwise nothing. He was finally free and clear, never once realizing how he'd been framed for murder or how his longtime associate Baker had been setup.

Funny how a few cool million can make a man sail off into the sunset and never look back or wonder how it had come so easily. One would have thought that Fitz would ask someone, at least once, what had caused Baker to abruptly change his mind, but he never did. All he ever wanted was as much cash as he could extract from the deal, and he got away with far more than he'd ever dreamed possible.

Statham's confirmation to Ren and DAK of his successful takeover and conversion of the Haskins Group of funeral homes, plus an added bonus of three thousand to boot, was enough to assure his future appointment to Chairman of the Board, once his replacement as CEO had been named. Now very elderly, but still sharp and conniving as ever, DAK was over the moon to hear how his promotion of Statham years ago had paid off again and, he relished in the fact that his great enterprise had finally prevailed, bringing another obnoxious kingpin operator in funeral service to his knees.

After privately hearing the full story of how both entrapments had played out so perfectly, as, of course, Statham had personally masterminded, old, hardened DAK told his man, "I just wish I could have been there personally to see them both knuckle under, Bill. You've done a great job on this, and I'm proud to know my firm will have you at the helm as Great

American goes into another decade. I know I can count on you to do anything necessary to make certain we get and take whatever we deem necessary to secure Great American's preeminence."

With DAK's blessing in hand, William Statham was announced to become the new Chairman of the Board, while Renford Kleinmark would transition to Chairman Emeritus. The next step in the well-planned-out puzzle would be the promotion of Statham's heir apparent, Rick Winther. Statham couldn't be more pleased with how things had come together so perfectly. As he sat on the penthouse balcony of his new and exclusive, South Florida multi-million dollar condo and sipped coffee while his wife slept in, he gloated in the shimmering silence; reflecting about his masterful manipulation of the entire sequence of events that had propelled his own success into one of the very utmost, respected, and highest paid positions in the whole deathcare industry.

Statham truly considered himself a genius. Never once considering the lives of those ruined in the process. The young wayward girl who had been strangled to death just to make Fitz believe he'd been drugged and lost his mind, while screwing around on his wife. How Baker Haskins would surely never be the same after seeing the perverted photos of him. Even thoughts of the young Mexican boy, about whom he was told, and who had been defiled in the whole scheme, Statham never allowed any of it to cross his mind. He was able to compartmentalize all of the treacherous events with the justification under the heading of, how people create their own circumstances in life, and that he had only leveraged the situations they had in fact put themselves in. It was quite extraordinary really.

By the time Winther was promoted, becoming the new rookie CEO of Great American, Statham thought the future was in a good place. A major competitor had been bought out. Another growing funeral home consolidator had been successfully coerced over to Great American. Surging West Coast operating costs were plummeting now with Haskins's volume flowing through GAC's supply chain. Already, Baker's twenty thousand new casket orders were making a positive impact on GAC's overall materials cost, despite how cremation rates continued to increase each year; plus the preplanned, annual GAC price increase strategy made sure to offset the typical negative impacts as always. All combined, the next few years looked to be smooth sailing and more profitable than ever. That's what Statham thought anyway.

~~~~~~~~~~~~~~

As Winther came into to his new role, he elected to take McCall off of the Haskins Group and make them one of GAC's top house accounts. Meaning, now the huge funeral home consolidator account would fall under Travis's umbrella. As soon as the change occurred, Garner would be forced to hold a joint conference call with Baker, Winther, and Travis to announce it to the client. To make it official, Winther and Travis would take one of the Cessna's out to meet Baker and his team. The Falcon was rarely ever available to those two pricks, especially now that DAK, Ren, and Statham all had first dibs.

The meeting with Baker went fine, or so Winther and Travis thought. McCall of course wasn't invited, since the new CEO failed to recognize how smoothly he'd handled Baker and his organization after Fitz set sail off into the wild blue yonder. The truth was, that Baker felt like he was right back to where he'd been with DAK years ago, being talked down to as if he wasn't the customer, but rather someone fortunate enough to do business with the almighty Great American Casket Company.

After the meeting concluded, he and his top leadership team marveled at how clueless the two senior GAC execs had seemed when they showed up unprepared about the smooth state of their transition and spouting off about what all GAC was planning to do "to get things moving." McCall had never approached them that way, stating the company's plan or intentions. He had always presented everything as their option, giving them the information to make a decision they were comfortable with. Most of the time, knowing full well McCall preferred a particular direction or decision. He had never once given them directives like these two assholes had done. They didn't like it one bit, as it had sounded GAC would be treating them this way going-forward. It was as if, GAC would decide what caskets they would sell, how they would price their merchandise, and how their showrooms would be setup.

One of the Haskins's younger, less tactful directors had even interrupted Winther and Travis in the middle of their long list of so-called next steps and asked, "So are you guys going to tell us how to embalm bodies and dig graves too?" Hearing this, Baker just sat back and listened, thinking how his own sins had caused him to lose complete control of his business and life. It was the worst day he'd had in funeral service after thirty years, he'd had plenty of bad days.

~~~~~~~~~~~~

Now that Garner had the Haskins Group casket sales removed from his volume totals, Winther had also informed him that his division's total revenue target would not be decreased to account for the removal of the seventeen thousand caskets from Fitz's conversion accounts. For Travis on the other hand, the windfall assignment of the additional volume into his responsibility area would guarantee him one of the best overall performance years in his career at GAC, and especially another huge bonus, just as Statham had always ensured his right-hand man received.

With the new sales year ahead of him, Garner set his sights on helping his teams grow and hit their numbers. He was well familiar with getting screwed on sales quotas, something overachievers are accustomed to, because the higher-ups know they're usually likely to step up and hit the inflated numbers, while the complacent types and slackers phone it in like always. Making up the loss of seventeen thousand caskets, plus the expected cremation hit to the market, would mean that he and his teams would need to do something extraordinary to achieve their goals. Like always, McCall and his lieutenants came up with a plan to do just that.

The core of GAC's sales had, as always, traditionally come from white-owned funeral homes. While many of the African-American owned firms around the country had an

343

account with Great American, GAC reps rarely, if ever, called on them, at least compared to the inordinate amount of time spent supporting white firms. Especially when it came to deals and promotions, whenever volume pushes were engaged to spur on needed revenue in a particular quarter or year, the company sales organization always focused on their core white-owned clients.

Garner knew that going after the black-owned accounts would definitely gin up some new found interest for access to Great American caskets. Sure, these customers had the "right" to buy from GAC, but really they had never before been given much of an incentive in terms of an attractive buying program. The vast majority of the black firms, that was, if they even had an account with Great American, had only been signed up with a basic purchase program years ago. Meaning that their programs were greatly outdated compared to normal, current terms, especially considering all of the annual price increase impacts, even for small size white firms that were far richer in terms of the discounts offered. That fact was further compounded when one stopped to think how most of the better white firms were accustomed to having their discounts increased each year to offset the latest price increase. While other non-essential white firms, and black-owned operators, paid the increased prices year after year, significantly adding to GAC's annual bottom-line. So, Garner and his managers figured that if they targeted the right, larger, black-owned firms with current, competitive buying program offers, they might very well be able to hit their inflated numbers..

The plan seemed smart and, just possibly, attainable, although their reps would have to be trained on how to effectively engage the black operators, particularly since they had ignored them for so long. The other positive aspect of the plan was how the industry had continued to remain so segregated, even after two hundred years, and on both sides. As such, Garner's team of GAC reps wouldn't expect any pushback or fallout from white-owned operators, even those selling funerals in the same city, since their clientele's largely remained separate. Once he and his managers had developed their target lists of larger black operators to go after and the reps were sufficiently trained in how to have the conversations, the plan was ready for action.

~~~~~~~~~~~~~~

Like his predecessor, Winther held regular monthly executive review meetings to gauge business performance metrics, financials, key industry movements, competitive activities, any legal issues, as well as concerning HR issues. Also, like the former CEO, Winther started out his meetings with him doing most of the talking, which in this particular session, led to him and Travis talking at length about their meeting with the Haskins Group. Both fools spoke ad nauseam about how well they had done in conveying Great American's commitment and capabilities, and especially how well their message had been received. That last dig was mostly for McCall's benefit since he had been personally managing the account since its inception. Although the intentional underlying message wasn't lost on anyone around the huge oval GAC conference table, it was clear that Winther had taken a direct shot at McCall for some reason.

Once the agenda caught up with Garner's turn to report on his division in all the critical areas, he had learned a long time ago to focus immediately on sales and margin performance. Incredibly, and rather indignantly, Winther took an immediate cheap shot at McCall about how "poorly" he was allowing his team to perform. Everyone around the table knew that Winther had taken the Haskins Group and other newly converted accounts out of McCall's numbers but left him with the inflated goal, which was the only reason his numbers were in the tank. Nonetheless, Winther continued to keep pressing McCall about his strategy and plans to "reverse and revive" his "team's downward spiral."

McCall hadn't planned to announce his team's growth initiative focused upon the black-owned funeral operators. At least, not until his teams had had a chance to explore the market reception and first had a few wins under their belt. But this was no time to tell the new CEO that his strategy was to take the same 'ol racecar, paint-trading approach as usual, where his folks would spend their wheels trying to win over more white accounts with bigger and bigger discount deals. He knew going after what was really an untapped market for GAC was a smart move. Furthermore, he thought it was the fair and ethical approach, given how many black-owned firms already bought a fair number of caskets each year, but weren't getting a similar fair shake on discounts.

After seeming to listen attentively for the first ten minutes or so, as McCall laid out his team's planned strategy and detailed how they were targeting a pickup of more than fifteen thousand caskets in a ninety-day period, Winther quickly interrupted. Despite multiple, complimentary ooh's and aah's coming from his colleagues around the oversized table, as he laid out his team's logic and plan, the new CEO jumped all over McCall's idea as "ill-conceived" and "absolutely not in the vein of Great American."

Winther further told McCall "No way in fucking hell are you going to deploy such a reckless sales strategy that would have a hugely, devastating impact on our overall profit margins. Those people buy a ton of caskets from us each year. Hell, they're our most profitable customer segment! And, here you waltz in saying you want to go give them the same kinds of deals most of our customers already get. From where I sit, while you may think you'll pick a few thousand new casket orders, your decision would lead to everyone around this table not getting a bonus; certainly not this year, and most likely not for years to come! How in the world can you stand here and say you've even thought this through?"

Detecting Winther's tirade had momentarily ceased, McCall jumped in and fired back, unnerving the rookie CEO. Being sure to make eye contact with his entire audience, versus just Winther, McCall pulled up a slide showing in detail the bottom-line financial impact to GAC from his proposed strategy. Everyone could see the plan, if successful, would indeed be very favorable financially overall to GAC.

Next, he proposed a concern that had been long rumored but never outwardly stated, which was intentionally going after the black market based upon an ethical position. Sensing the tightening of his onlookers, McCall uttered the words that many had wondered for years, "How could Great American continue to legally, if not ethically, risk not offering the same types of purchase programs to black customers as white ones?" Further elaborating his point with a phrase that was intended for its emphasis and impact, the mere mention of possible "class action retaliation" caused the already quieted crowd to become even more hushed around the table.

Closing with, "Rick, surely if just one black funeral operator ever pushed this envelope with us legally, I fear what that result might be to our precious bottom-line! I don't think it makes any sense at all, especially business sense, for the company, much less my team, to just keep going out there and raising discounts in the market to buy away competitively-held accounts. Everyone here knows full well, the only thing that will result from that tired old approach, is that our competitors will simply return the favor like always, meaning we wind up making less profit each year off of the same volume. By going after the black market, we will essentially open up a brand new sales channel that we've always left to bottom-feeder manufacturers. Plus, we all know it's the right, ethical thing to do! But, I guess that's your call, Rick." Then McCall shut up and waited to see how Winther would respond.

Not saying a word, as if to let McCall keep hanging himself with his own rope, Winther just sat back in his chair,

348

sneering with distain, for several uncomfortable seconds. Most had been expected him to interrupt again, and waited to see how the new CEO would respond to McCall's challenge. Once McCall had finished, still standing in the front of the huge presentation screen at the front of the room, Winter waited several more seconds before saying, "No way in fucking hell are you going to launch this campaign, McCall! Do you understand me?! Meeting adjourned!" With that, Winther jumped up and stormed out of the executive conference room, disappearing behind the closed door to his new corner office. Everyone had seen how he was shaken and seething with anger as he rushed out of the conference room. Winther knew they had seen it too.

After Winther's overly harsh berating of McCall, especially in front of his peers, it was obvious to everyone that the first such outburst from their new CEO was highly unusual around the revered halls of GAC, and completely unlike any of his prior behavior when he'd been positioning and politicking for the head role. Until he got the nod, that jackass had always been the most sweet and syrupy suck-up around the building, always trying extra hard to appear genuine and conscientious of all others in any meeting, especially if Statham or Ren Kleinmark were ever in attendance.

After his thrashing, all of McCall's colleagues, except for Travis, pulled him aside quietly showed their support of his planned growth initiative on the black-owned market; saying, how it was obvious the upside potential far outweighed the impact of higher discounts on the few sales GAC presently realized from the segment. Some even shared his sentiment, that

349

GAC was flat out wrong and perhaps even engaging in illegal price fixing by not fairly offering the same availability of purchase programs to all customers, regardless of race.

Nevertheless, Garner's sales growth initiative was primarily intended to save his team's chances of hitting their numbers, which also directly impacted their individual earnings opportunity, since he had to spread the reassigned seventeen thousand caskets to everyone's quota. As a result, Winther's shut down made the possibility of a good sales year and earnings opportunity they had each hoped for. The real truth was if he and his managers went out and tried to take a seventeen thousand unit share away from their primary competitors in predominantly white accounts, that the net profit loss to GAC and his division, would have been far worse, whether Winther admitted it or not.

~~~~~~~~~~~~

A few months after Winther had shown his true colors, he announced, in a specially called executive meeting, the appointment of a new executive vice president role that Tom Pittman would fill. The move conveniently allowed Winther to give one of his lifelong friends from Bergholz a big time promotion to backfill Pittman's previous role. This time, McCall wasn't even listed on the agenda, another intentional and planned swipe from the new CEO. Winther used the announcement to talk about how Pittman's role was "desperately needed to ensure Great American has a cohesive and profitable go to market strategy, while furthermore ensuring our sales and distribution teams remain consistent with the values and practices of the company." Stemming over from Winther's prior condemnation

350

of Garner's sales strategy earlier in the year, everyone knew the statement was another thinly veiled shot at McCall.

McCall on the other hand, since the blowup with Winther over his African American market strategy, had simply let it go. Figuring he had not seriously considered the whole black versus white go to market suggestion being that big of a deal after Winther had rejected it. In fact, he'd really never given it much more thought. It was no secret that GAC had always ignored the black operators and left them for the competition to go after. Mostly because, by and large, white firms purchased more, higher wholesale average units, which simply meant more profit per unit. It had never dawned on him that the company would prove to be completely uninterested in growing its business with black owners, regardless of how much incremental profit could be made. Beyond that, Statham had always allowed his execs to voice their unfiltered opinions in his roundtable sessions; and while he might shoot them down, he never seemed to hold grudges.

~~~~~~~~~~~~

Fast forward another few months when Winther was sitting comfortably in his big corner office, still pinching himself and shopping online for his own south Florida condo, when Travis walked in completely white-faced. News had reached back to Great American that Baker Haskins had unexpectedly died a couple of days earlier. Although overweight and obviously not one to exercise, Haskins was only in his late fifties at the time and in generally good health. All Travis knew was that the owner of one of GAC's largest national account customers had recently died. Figuring Great American would need to attend their customer's own funeral service, Travis and Winther called in Pittman about scheduling one of the Cessna's and flying out like big shots who really cared.

Garner had actually learned of Baker's death the day it happened, when one of the location managers called him directly. He already knew that Baker had taken his life by shooting himself in the temple, apparently while sitting in the same office chair where he'd first come face to face with the very sins that still tormented him every minute of every day. In the end, Baker Haskins could simply no longer live knowing and waiting for those photographs to resurface, and take the risk that they could be used against his family. McCall was never asked or told about Baker from his higher-ups. They had no clue he knew, much less appreciated how he could have easily learned more about what had happened and any potential fallout.

Baker had set up his business with an employee stock ownership program model. In doing so, his main family members would own the majority of the stock, while his most senior to the least junior employees would own an according representative share, based upon tenure, position, and long-term performance. As a result, and prescribed in his company's bylaws, a new executive leadership team would take control of the Haskins Group of funeral homes, now doing over twenty-five thousand services annually since Baker's final series of acquisitions. Baker had left two handwritten notes on his huge, beautiful desk; one for his family and the other for his management team.

The family note expressed the man's obvious love and forever apologies for leaving them so soon, as well as for how he had chosen to leave. Never before had he allowed his personal demeanor to change around his family or staff. Except anytime he was alone now, whether day or night, his mind immediately reverted to the photos, which caused him to begin weeping without control. Even as time had passed, and he had finally become able to control his outward moans and gut-wrenching agony, his tears of shame never stopped. Ultimately, his pain tormented him to a certain and literal death, which was the only sure way to make his anguish finally ended. Sitting alone in his office for several hours at the end of a long day, again with his door locked, all he said before pulling the trigger was "God, please forgive my sins."

~~~~~~~~~~~~~~

It was unusual to request a business meeting after a funeral, however since the top GAC executives had flown out for their boss's services, the newly, empowered executive team felt there was no reason to delay dealing with the directive in Baker's farewell note to them. Never forgiving himself for being blackmailed into going against the promise he'd made to his father and grandfather, Baker's last wish was for his top staff to try and break the Great American deal as soon as possible. Though the timing was odd, the man who Baker had tapped to be his chief operating officer, essentially placing him over all aspects of the funeral home empire, had called Winther to arrange the meeting to discuss the matter.

The five year purchase agreement that Baker had been forced to sign had the same claw back penalty in it as had all the others. If canceled before the five year term was met, all discounts and showroom investments would become immediately due and payable. Which for the Haskins Group, meant they would have to pay back Great American a total in earned discounts of more than eight million, as well as another three and a half million for selection room investments. While the eleven and a half million dollar penalty was significant, it was certainly not impossible for the Haskins Group. The only caveat Baker had left open in the final note to his staff was that since the company was now operating as an ESOP, meaning essentially they owned it as much as he had, that if the organization ultimately preferred to remain with Great American; then he would have accordingly honored their opinion. But, if the employees had not developed a close affinity for GAC quality, then his request was that they make the change.

Upon hearing the startling announcement from the Haskins' COO, the Great American execs were left shaken and wondering how to curtail the potential loss. When more than a few of the Haskins' senior team indicated how their firms had begun to underperform and experience unaddressed issues, since Garner McCall had been pulled off their account, it became more clear that GAC's position of strength had all but vaporized within the rank and file throughout the customer's organization. Winther knew though, regardless of what the customer thought, there was no way he was going to put McCall back in charge of the account, which would assuredly cause him to lose face with his own senior team and Statham.

After hearing out Baker's management team as they shared their grievances, it appeared as if their team was split on jettisoning Great American from their funeral homes' display rooms. Winther knew GAC would have one opportunity to pull the smoldering account out of the flames and asked the clients if they could all table the discussion, of course only out of a deep respect and for the sanctity of the time they were there to honor the great Baker Haskins. Taking the slick, polished CEO at his well masked words of insincerity, the COO and his two most senior officers at the table agreed to postpone any deeper discussions on the subject. Ultimately, both parties agreed to revisit the matter in a few weeks after the shock of Baker's death had subsided.

Finally, Winther assured all of the Haskins folks staring back at him that Great American most certainly did not want to lose the new found relationship with their group, especially since Baker himself had, in fact, personally endorsed it not that long ago. Acknowledging that "perhaps, given his final state of mind, Baker had reached some point of regret for whatever reason. Why, of course, no one could ever know." Nonetheless, if that was ultimately what their team decided, then of course Great American would honor and support their decision. All he asked was that both sides take some "thoughtful time" to truly assess how the new venture had been going overall, besides any minor issues that surely "any supplier could have."

Fortunately for Winther, the bullshit worked and bought him some time to confer with his mentor, Bill Statham.

~~~~~~~~~~~~~~~

When Winther and Travis reached out to the Haskins' COO a few weeks later to take their temperature on the past discussions about dissolving their supplier relationship, it was agreed that a more serious sit-down business review was a fair way to reach a final verdict. Winther offered that his top GAC executive team would of course be willing to come back out West for the session. Likewise the Haskins COO, acknowledging the GAC team had recently made the last travel effort to meet at their convenience, offered to have his team make their way to Bergholz. Now no one in their right mind would ever want to go to Bergholz, unless there's a family crisis or a paying will involved. Especially, not to do a casket deal, much less hang onto one. Even Winther was smart enough to know that, and besides, Statham had already made a much different suggestion.

Just the sound of the place, "Cabo San Lucas", was enticing enough. When Winther made the suggestion to the COO, the new Haskins' top man was a little taken back. That is, until he heard the GAC's CEO rationale. "You see, Cabo was where Baker first came around to the idea of buying from our old firm. I just thought it might be a most appropriate setting, given everything, for us all to regroup, you know, on neutral turf, and revisit our relationship. In talking to some of our team, like Garner McCall and others who had gotten to know Baker so well, they all felt like Cabo was the one place he always said he was the happiest, and perhaps where we should all meet." Of

356

course, the lying sack of shit had never spoken to McCall or anyone else, only Statham and Witman.

Expressing how he and his colleagues had always heard Baker talk so favorably about his regular trips to Cabo being so "refreshing and helping him to clear his head", the COO told Winther to let him bounce it off his two most senior counterparts, their chief marketing officer and chief sales officer. First thing the next morning, the trip was confirmed and planned for two weeks out, right in the middle of January, a nice time to escape Northern California. Of course, anytime was always a nice time to escape Bergholz!

~~~~~~~~~~~~~

Witman's thugs had already been doing their legwork on the three top Haskins's executive officers. The marketing guy was a straight-up Christian who even sang in the church choir and taught his son's Sunday school class. The sales guy, thank God they thought, was an out and out drunk. Unhappily married for years, the guy traveled incessantly, it seemed, based upon his credit card bills. Although the only vice they could find he had was an unquenchable love affair with whiskey sours. As for the COO, there was plenty to work with.

He was in his early sixties, and like his former mentor Baker, looked on the outside to be the model of propriety. As usual, those tend to make the best targets Witman explained. The COO had been married for thirty years, with four kids, and eight grandchildren. "On the surface, the man looked like a fucking saint." Witman elaborated. "However after a quick download of the browsing histories off the computers at his home and office,

357

Eureka! This guy spends more time looking at hardcore porn online than most guys in prison! He's definitely our target. Maybe the sales guy too, if we lace his drinks like 'ol Fitz, but definitely the COO."

~~~~~~~~~~~

This trip to Cabo would last for three days. The three chiefs from the Haskins Group attended, plus Winther, Travis, and Pittman from GAC. Statham also suggested pulling in Miles from an "acquisition" standpoint. Telling Winther, "You may be able to play that angle, whereas another casket company couldn't." Miles had done well in his new role since Ren and Statham funded the angle he'd been playing. Now, it seemed it just might be a perfect play for the Haskins trip.

By the time the trip was over and the Haskins's team got back to Northern California, the necessary execution had taken place as intended. Ultimately the COO would convince his fellow ESOP constituents that Great American had overall been serving their firm well. Even using the GAC provided presentation which demonstrated how each one of their funeral homes had been increasing in sales dollars and profits. The strong results in large part were due to the master merchandising plans that Baker and McCall had implemented. Plus, the new cut rooms had proved consumers were spending more time evaluating their selections, resulting in more money spent per service. There was no smoke and mirrors, at least in the data, as it had been compared directly to the original Haskins's data, pre-GAC, based upon the prior twelve months since switching over from Fitz. Ultimately the Haskins Group's decision was to stay with Great American.

As Winther would later explain in the following senior leadership review session, despite all the unresolved complaints they griped about during the original transition period, meaning under McCall's oversight, he, Travis, and Pittman had been able to pull them back from the cliff.

~~~~~~~~~~

Sitting there not saying a word, Garner McCall knew it was bullshit. For some reason, the new CEO had a hard-on for him, though he didn't know why. He figured it might have had something to do with the fact of how tight Winther and Travis had become since Statham moved up to his new lofty perch. After all, Travis surely knew he had been part of the discussions insinuating some possible wrongdoings concerning Fitz's deal and final payout. Not to mention, Travis had been Statham's right hand errand boy ever since he became CEO. Now that he was Chairman, McCall figured Statham may have cemented the relationship between his favorite used car client and replacement. So maybe with Statham removed, Winther was pushing on McCall to impress Travis somehow.

Never thinking Bill Statham would have ever sold him out, after all, why would he? He was the one who, not once but twice, begged him to take the senior promotion in the first place. Besides that, Garner knew he'd done his job extremely well, time and again. Statham knew it too. Ultimately McCall decided to chalk it up to personalities. After all, everyone doesn't hit it off.

McCall had only ever really been around Winther a handful of times. Whether it was at regular executive meetings, board meetings, or the occasional client dinner when somehow Winther had gotten invited and actually showed up. Usually he detested being around funeral home operators.

Garner recalled one huge group from Canada that he had been working to land for over a year, and finally getting them to come down for the whole dog and pony show in Bergholz, which included a swanky dinner at The Club. Garner had even gotten Statham to agree to join, though knowing full well he'd be as pompous as ever, holding court in his usual arrogant style, speaking on all things funeral-related, as if he was the most high priest of the industry. Unexpectedly, Statham had Winther attend, as part of his future CEO grooming process. That way it could be said how he'd spent so much time understanding customers and markets.

The dinner went as most did. Lots of expensive wine and food, plus McCall was always good for great cigars afterwards, for any who partook. Sitting out on the club's private terrace with some of the customers, McCall was shocked when Winther came out to join. The few times he'd ever dined with likes of lowly salesmen and inferior customers, he'd never once stayed more than five minutes past dessert. This time, he pulled up a chair, and took one of Garner's cigars, and ordered another full pour glass of wine.

As the conversation ebbed and flowed, finally some lulls and silent breaks crept in between the lines. At one such awkward moment, as a couple of the customers would often tease McCall whenever they saw him at the Canadian funeral convention or U.S. national, Winther placed his hand uncomfortably close on the back of McCall's chair. Worse yet, was how he raised his hand, thank God not the one holding the lit cigar, almost touching the back of McCall's hair, saying "Garner, man you have the most beautiful hair in the world! How do you get it like that?" Completely stunned, McCall and all the other guys sitting there just stopped and stared at the fool. Then, to break the weirdness of the moment, which a well-inebriated Winther hadn't even seemed to recognize, one of the customers began belly-laughing and said in his best, most sultry voice, "Oohh... yes Garner, please do tell us, how in the world do you account for such beautiful hair, man? Naturally making everyone burst out laughing. All McCall could do was to turn to Winther and say, "Uh thanks...Rick, you too!"

Another similarly odd exchange that McCall would later recall happening, was right after Winther first got promoted and asked to meet him for dinner at one of the little three star bistros in Bergholz. Of course, there weren't any that ever got more than three stars. It was one of the few restaurants in town, all of which closed when the small town rolled up their sidewalks each school night by eight o'clock. This was the session when Winther launched into his bullshit facade about whether or not McCall felt he was ready to take on the head sales role. For over an hour, Winther grilled the man who Statham had recruited and promoted to help fulfill his own personal greedy motives.

Once their discussions were exhausted, having realized he still had a forty-five minute drive home, McCall suggested to

361

Winther that he needed to hit the road, as he had an early, busy day, the following morning. To which, Winther amazingly suggested to McCall that perhaps he should just stay in town at one of the local motels. Even going as far to suggest, "You've had a bit to drink, perhaps I should drive you over to the hotel, if you'd like." McCall wasn't sure how to react to that one. He hadn't had that much to drink after all, and was absolutely fine to drive home. Plus, Winther had kept oddly glaring and smiling at him so much all through dinner, that it had all gotten just plain weird. After the hair episode, the last thing he'd be doing was going anywhere alone with Winther. So Garner politely declined, whatever it was that he was declining.

~~~~~~~~~~~~~~

Sitting there after being thrown under the bus once again by Winther, Garner wasn't sure if whatever was up his crawl stemmed from a simple relationship issue of not hitting it off, possibly the issue with Travis over Fitz's deal, or from not responding favorably to two awkward personal advances, if that's what they were. Maybe it was as simple as the guy can't hold his liquor and sometimes said stupid stuff. Lord knows, that's true of most. Regardless of the reason, it was clear that Winther was taking shot after shot at McCall. Worse yet, it seemed like each shot over the bow kept getting too close for comfort.

Ultimately, Garner decided not to push the envelope with Winther just yet. Perhaps things would die down, now that he had heard through the grapevine that everything had worked out with the Haskins Group down in Cabo. Meanwhile, he had a nice customer golf outing to look forward to out in sunny Palm Springs the following week, meaning he wouldn't be in the office for several glorious days. That alone would be like a wonderful slice of heaven. Although oddly, Pittman had all of a sudden somehow been invited along on the trip, which was fine enough to Garner. It would give him a chance to get to know the guy who was now over so many of the company's functions.

Better yet, McCall could do it while spending time with some great customers. Like always, the trip was the same old gag; with some baked-in, tried and true, loyal firms who would talk up how great GAC was, plus three or four huge prospects to be wrangled in. Even if they only landed one of the huge firms on a multi-year deal, all of which met the minimum four hundred casketed services per year requirement, it would prove to be another very profitable and worthwhile use of time and money, no less spent in sunny, Southern California.

For several weeks after the golf trip, everything with Winther had seemed to settle down. He was back to his old, syrupy self, even occasionally popping into McCall's office, seemingly just to shoot the shit about how the expected deals from the golf outing were coming along. Once or twice, he'd even referenced the discussion they had at the local bistro about Garner stepping up someday. Even once or twice suggesting it could be sooner than later. Garner wasn't sure how to interpret Winther's new about-face, but took it for what it was worth, and assumed like many relationships, he and Winther had finally broken the ice. He also wondered if Statham might have coached his replacement on how much better off he might be with a happier, hard-charging McCall on his side versus not. Regardless, as time would prove, the rookie CEO had taken careful clues on how to set up people from his mentor, in terms of his skills at deceitful set up and backstabbing. They both had it down to a purely, underhanded science, and like all the others, McCall never saw it coming.

~~~~~~~~~~~

UNEXPECTED ALLY

Denise and Garner began the process of putting their life back together as much as possible after getting back home from their two weeks at the beach. Each of them had always been fairly frugal when it came to money and material things. Growing up in low to middle class families, they had both worked hard to provide for their life together, always saving for a rainy day. Once all the dirty laundry and beach towels had been cleaned and put away, they knew a conversation about money and jobs needed to happen. They had been open and close about everything since marrying and this time wouldn't be any different.

Garner hoped to find another job, hopefully soon, and if lucky, back down south closer to where they considered home. However, as time and the current struggling economy would eventually prove, that would ultimately not be the case. Unfortunately, despite spending all of his waking hours every day looking and sending out resumes, it would take almost a full year for him to find the next job. The fact was there were simply a lot fewer jobs than lookers, including the high level ones, for which the applicant pipelines were overflowing. The other challenge he found was how the mere mention of "caskets" on his resume knocked him out of most initial considerations. Though he finally figured out that the term "consumer products" kept a lot more doors open longer, allowing him a greater chance to sell himself and his talents.

As the first several weeks of his adult life went by where he'd not been employed, Denise decided to sign up for her Ohio nursing license and to return to the workforce. Since they'd moved to Big Ten country she'd enjoyed not working full time for a change, instead spending her time gardening and painting. Nursing was always one of the easiest jobs to find anywhere, and thankfully she was back in R.N. mode in no time, and helping to cover their monthly expenses. As for Garner, his days were consumed with job hunting and trying to get any kind of response from Great American.

~~~~~~~~~~~~~

Don McCloud was a retired FBI agent, who after losing his wife of thirty years to breast cancer, finally befriended Garner when the first big snow storm hit after he and Denise moved into the neighborhood. Although for the longest time after the McCall's moved in next door, their neighbor had always stayed very much to himself, rarely ever saying more than a quick hello when they saw him for any brief moment. Denise always remarked how the man seemed so sad and lonely. Garner, being raised a southern gentlemen, knew well enough to not go sticking his nose into another man's business without a reason. So he gave the man his space, figuring he just wasn't the friendly sort. Then unexpectedly, one day that changed.

Looking out and seeing the new next door neighbor shoveling his long driveway by hand for the second time within a matter of just a few hours, McCloud decided to finally go over to introduce himself and offer to loan the use of his powerful snow blower. Garner would always recall being shocked just to

366

see the man walking across the imaginary boundary separating their properties, as Don came closer and closer, pulling the wonderful contraption behind him.

Ever since, the retired, grizzled agent took a huge liking to his young Southern neighbor, especially upon discovering their mutual interest in good cigars and scotch. Garner loved sitting and listening to Don talk about his many crime stories from his days with the bureau. He was a good storyteller, plus knowing they were all true made them that much more fascinating to a man who sold boring caskets for a living.

One day when the self-appointed neighborhood detective looked out his front window, he noticed that Garner's company car wasn't around any longer although he clearly was. Trusting his gut, Don decided to time his mail run and catch up with his friend when he saw him back outside. Hearing how Garner had gotten fired, especially with the whole clause aspect, Don was naturally disappointed for his friend. Garner wound up telling Don the whole story for hours, since it was the first time he'd really talked to anyone other than Denise about everything.

The whole mess pissed Don off. It was the reason he had always preferred law enforcement over corporate; "black and white laws versus political bullshit", he said. Of course the bureau had plenty of politics going on like any other large organization. However, Don stayed out of that fray and kept himself out in the field, "where the real work of catching crooks and killers happens." Now some four years later, it was easy to see that he still really missed his lifelong profession of fighting for good versus evil.

Hearing how Garner kept trying to get his former company on the phone, and electing to not yet hire an attorney to intercede, Don warned his friend of how he'd seen so many people entrapped just by saying the wrong thing, or even something quite nebulous in the wrong context that was later used against them. Always one to think in covert terms, Don ran home and came back with a small, sensitive recording device. He told Garner to use the device with his cell or landline anytime he got in touch with Great American. Saying, "You have to protect yourself, Garner. I promise you, those guys will be recording any call with you, so you need to be protected too. Record everything, every chance you get!"

~~~~~~~~~~~~~

Garner was settling into his new monotonous "work routine" of finding a job, which was a whole lot harder than actually working as he discovered while constantly researching and contacting various companies about roles every day. After doing this for weeks on end, one day his cell rang with an old familiar number originating with a Bergholz exchange. It was Tom Pittman.

Pittman said he was driving out Garner's way and asked if he could swing by to talk. Even though Garner couldn't imagine why in the world Pittman would ever want to talk to him, he figured it couldn't hurt and perhaps he'd learn something helpful to get Great American to finally respond to him. Waiting in his driveway smoking a cigar when Pittman pulled up, Garner could smell the alcohol reeking when they shook hands. He could tell Pittman had quite a bit to drink and was very nervous.

368

Accepting Garner's offer to go around back and sit on his deck, Pittman grabbed one of his own cigars from his car to enjoy and help him calm down.

Seeing that McCall wasn't going to waste time on bull like "Great to see you!" or "How have you been?" Pittman got right to the point. Flatly asking Garner, "So did you get fired with cause? That fucker, Winther, fired me with cause, can you believe that? I gotta tell you, I still can't believe it, Garner. Not after everything that goes on around there! They act like I don't know about a bunch of that shit! Hell, I've even got photos of Statham partying with young girls, that they sure as shit wouldn't want to get out!" Stopping to take a long puff on his Cohiba, Pittman waited a second to see how McCall would react.

Highly skilled in the art of behavioral selling, Garner was a master at quickly reading people and adapting to their attitudes and behaviors. Without hesitating, and intentionally looking just as anxious and pissed off, Garner told Pittman how Winther had done him the same way. Further explaining how neither of them had done anything that countless others, especially Statham and Travis, hadn't done a million times before.

Then all of a sudden, Pittman jumped up, taking a huge swig of the beer he'd brought, and began to rant and rave at how the company had screwed him "out of millions of dollars in stock grants that hadn't vested yet, over ten million in total." He went on to say "Winther had planned out the whole fucking ordeal just to get rid of me; after of course giving his buddy my old job, which I'd had for over ten years before." As they talked

369

for the next two hours, it became obvious that Pittman was just as pissed as Garner was and had been just as unsuccessful in getting the company to respond, much less reconsider, his circumstances.

Then Garner decided to push the envelope a little with the ex-COO to see what he could learn. Saying, "Yeah, I guess we're both screwed Tom! It looks like we don't have any leverage on those guys at all. Guess we both have to eat it and forget about it, huh?" Now on his fourth beer since pulling into Garner's drive, Pittman, who was prone to pacing while he ranted, said, "No fucking way, Garner, absolutely no fucking way! I can tell you that! If those assholes don't make it right by me soon, I'm going to blow the whole Cabo fiasco thing wide open! I promise you that!" Just then, Garner knew there was an opening, and it must have something to do with when Pittman, Winther, and Travis met with the Haskins Group in Cabo after Baker's suicide.

"What about Cabo, Tom? I went down there with Fitz when we first tried to get Baker to sign up. I remember it was weird. We both thought we'd hooked him when we were down there, but then two days later he called Fitz late one night to tell us he'd reconsidered and was passing on coming our way. Then out of the blue and even weirder, just two days later Fitz received the signed contract via email. Baker didn't even try to negotiate the terms. It was the damnedest thing I have ever seen. Even weirder than that was how Baker only wanted me on his accounts and cut out Fitz entirely, even though they had worked hand in hand for over a decade. I tell you what, Tom; something was never right with that whole deal."

Before he realized what he was saying out loud, Pittman blurted out, "I'll tell you what about Cabo, Garner! Those motherfuckers are fucking stupid if they think I won't go to the cops. I know everything. Who was there, who got special late night treatment, and who set it up, the whole bloody thing! I promise you that!" Just then Pittman shut up, realizing that he was saying too much. Even though Garner tried a couple more times to get him to stay, keeping drinking, and keep him talking, Pittman decided to leave. Before he did, Garner poured on his southern charm and said how great it was to see Pittman, saying how they should stay in touch, and definitely let each other know if either had made any progress with the company. Pittman agreed, before getting back into his little sports car and backing out, ever so crookedly from Garner's long driveway, almost taking out his mailbox.

Garner realized he didn't know Pittman well enough to be sure he was being truthful about the whole Cabo thing, whatever it entailed. Although, the guy had seemed pretty hot and bothered about it and came across to Garner as being legitimately pissed off and forthright that something bad had definitely happened down there. What it was, of course he wasn't clear, but just having the inkling knowledge that something had happened, might just be enough to stir Great American into a response.

With that new ammunition, Garner McCall planned out his call to Renford Kleinmark. After which, it didn't take long to finally get the quick response from Jed Malish requesting a meeting.

~~~~~~~~~~~~~~~

The meeting with Jed Malish, Great American's chief legal counsel, was finally set to happen, now several months since Garner and Denise had returned from the coast, as well as his abrupt termination "with cause." Garner had done a lot of work with Jed Malish over the ten years he'd been at GAC, coming to trust him implicitly. He had always found Malish to be, especially for a lawyer mind you, a very easy-going and straight-shooting type of individual. Garner had done numerous deals over the years that had required Malish to get involved in helping develop and approve the legalese verbiage in certain contracts that would make it comfortable enough to get a customer to sign on the dotted line, but moreover left Great American completely protected. Malish was extremely skilled at that. More so, he was always the nicest, happiest, and by far, the friendliest senior executive in the huge corporate offices in Bergholz. Like McCall, he also chose to live almost an hour away from the not-so garden spot of Northeastern Ohio. Always laughing, he would often say how he "preferred to stay happily married and drive a little farther each day!"

There had only been a total of three email series back and forth between Malish and McCall in advance of the face to face meeting. The first was to acknowledge McCall's call with Renford Kleinmark and the request to meet as soon as possible in person. This was the one Garner McCall mistook for a positive development in the company's previously consistent and complete avoidance of "his endless, annoyingly silly, attempts" to get GAC to "negotiate." The second communication was a perfunctory necessity only in confirming a date, place, and time for the meeting. Whereas, the third from Malish was to suggest how McCall might be "prepared to propose or recommend what he felt a reasonable resolution might be to settle matters between him and the company."

Just to set the stage, as if Malish especially, and even now, "on behalf of the company since some time for reflection has past", GAC's top lawyer wanted to convey in advance of their planned meeting, how "surprised and disappointed he and others had been to hear of Garner's termination; even going as far to say how "additional information had come to light in recent weeks." Regardless, Garner knew he'd been kicked to the curb. Furthermore, he fully realized at this point that those bastards had fired him knowing full well he didn't deserve it. Nor would he have ever heard from them again unless he'd made Renford Kleinmark so uncomfortable. The best thing for them to do was pay him what had been promised years ago by Statham, per his contract. If Malish didn't show up to the meeting and commit to those simple terms, then he would be forced to take more serious steps.

~~~~~~~~~~~~

The meeting place Malish had suggested in the final, warmer email, supposedly because he liked their pie, was one of those roadside chain places, complete with a huge all you can eat breakfast bar and a well-worn wait staff, which was, let's just say, on the far other ass-end of the likes ever employed by DAK or The Ranch. Mostly, it had tons of open, low-wall booths at ten o'clock on a Tuesday morning. Something else that would later dawn on McCall had been planned all along too.

To be sure he got there before Malish, Garner left extra early so he could first arrive at the spot that was about halfway between Bergholz and his and Denise's home. Walking in, Garner told the sweet, wrinkled-face woman he'd be meeting a man there soon and would like a back table, preferably in a quiet area of the restaurant if possible. Having traveled for so many years, eating hundreds if not thousands of meals on the road, Garner always tried to sit with his back to an outer wall just so he could keep an eye on his surroundings. Plus the people-watching helped entertain and pass his time eating alone so often.

Describing Malish to the old waitress, Garner said the man who would be "coming in and looking for him was bald, wore black glasses, and was always smiling. Also, he would be wearing dark dress slacks, either navy or grey, with a long sleeve, button-down, fine print shirt." As soon as the perplexed woman looked back at him as if to suggest how one man might be so well informed of another's dress habits, Garner just smiled real big and said, "I know, I know, but the man dresses the same way every day; weird huh?"

With a few minutes to spare, Garner downed more black coffee, finally having the woman leave a full pot and another cup for his "guest", as she referred to his expected dining partner. Moments later, Malish came inside the restaurant as Garner waved to get his attention. At that mid-morning hour, there were

374

only two other tables occupied with dining guests in the tired old chain restaurant. Both of those tables were up in the front part of the restaurant, whereas the lady had allowed Garner to sit was in the back closed off section. Although the rear of the frequented lunch spot would reopen in the next hour, when the famed breakfast bar magically transformed into "the world's greatest salad and dessert bar!"

As Garner saw his old colleague, Jed Malish, walking toward him, he then noticed a smaller statured, balding, man with thicker glasses following behind. That man was in a dark suit with a heavily starched white button-down shirt. Seeing that Malish was already surprising him with an unexpected participant in the meeting, Garner became somewhat nervous and leery of the whole situation. Just as the two men sat, Garner also noticed, out of the corner of his eye, that two other men, one with very white hair, also in white starched button-down shirts had come into the restaurant and sat down not too far away, near the back portion of the restaurant. Like the pasty skinned man with Malish, the two men had extremely close, military-styled haircuts. There was no doubt to McCall in that instant that the extra men were part of Malish's squad, and meant as a show of force for whatever reason. Later he figured the two extra men were there to either listen in via recording devices or were there on the off chance that some altercation broke out. While Garner McCall was completely inexperienced in the craft of espionage or spying, he nonetheless had certainly been in enough tough meeting environments to know what a setup felt like, and this was definitely not a situation to trust.

375

Never cracking his usual, ever present smile, Jed Malish said a terse hello to McCall and introduced the man to his right who was already trying too hard to smile and look especially friendly. "Garner, I want you to meet Dennis Witman. Dennis is with our outside counsel of Roseville Black in Pittsburgh. He's been extremely helpful to us as we've continued to try and unravel the events that ultimately led to your termination, particularly in light of new information that came to us afterwards." As Witman offered an outreached gesture to shake hands across the greasy tabletop, the dead cold palms of the man's unusually small, soft hands were so delicate and slimy, that it made it hard for McCall to imagine any man going through life with them.

Malish, still not smiling, continued saying, "Garner, I want you to know that we, the company, have taken this entire circumstance extremely seriously. We especially want to thank you for your call of concern to Mr. Kleinmark. I know you were, and are, only acting out of a most professional and best intended goodwill toward the company. For that, we are all very much grateful. As Witman continued to stare at McCall, as if to read his mind, it was clear in his body posture that he was there for more than just moral support to Malish. Garner may not have had any experience at espionage or surveillance, but he knew how to read people. And his read on this little fucker was that he was an absolute shit who couldn't be trusted for one iota.

Just then Witman spoke up. "Garner, is it OK if I call you Garner? You can call me Denny, that's what Jed and all the folks I work with call me." Garner never responded, rather just looked at the little snit of a man. Clearing his throat, realizing McCall had just completely ignored his feigned humility, Witman continued, "We at Roseville Black have worked with Great American as a client for a long time. Throughout the years, we have been engaged in any number of similar situations concerning termination, whereby some critical material facts came to light afterwards. We believe yours may be one of those cases." Waiting to see if and how Garner would respond or react to his opening, both Witman and Malish began to squirm a bit when their target didn't take the bait. Garner knew he was getting fed a load of bullshit, no doubt about it!

Seeing how Witman had failed to connect, Malish jumped back in to try and get Garner to show some sense of connection and interest in what they were saying. Now trying his best to smile, even if forced, Malish continued. "Garner, I guess what we're trying to say is that since you left, some additional information came to light that Rick hadn't had available to consider when you last met. Given that information, we believe there may be some accountability on the company's part in all of this." Now Malish shut up, trying to force a reaction out of McCall.

"So, Jed, what are you saying? That you brought a corporate outside attorney to our pie meeting just to tell me that new information came in that proves that I shouldn't have been fired in the first place? I guess you guys are here to tell me I'm getting my job back, correct?" The looks on the faces of the two men sitting opposite of McCall both went dark. They knew they had gone about the line of discussion the wrong way. Now they had to tell McCall, that while information came in to support that he should have never been fired in the first place, that he still wasn't getting his job back. "So what kind of information came in, Jed? Let's hear it." Just then scrawny, little Witman piped back in, saving his client from speaking more lies. "Well, unfortunately since it's an ongoing investigation, I'm afraid that we can't get into that level of detail. I'm sure you understand, Garner." again trying to look empathetic as he continued lying through his teeth. Just then Garner decided to unload on both of his adversaries.

"Look, I have already spoken with and received signed affidavits from two eye-witnesses who were in attendance in Palm Springs who can and are willing, if needed, to testify on my behalf about what occurred out there. So, it's really up to Great American how you guys want to proceed. You can either do what's right and fair, which is all I've ever asked for; or we can go to court. It's totally your call. At this point, I really don't care. I had hoped to avoid any public embarrassment for the company, but after being screwed over and ignored for months on end, I really don't fucking care. So it's however you choose to play it." In that moment, Garner had an eerie feeling come over him as if he'd just said exactly what they had hoped for. Both men all of sudden had begun to look smugly pleased with his demands.

Malish came back as he worked to reel McCall in further, "Well, that's why, Garner I suggested that you give some thought to how you saw this all playing out. Have you figured out what it is exactly that you want? Why don't you share that with us, just so Dennis and I are on the same page." Malish was referring to the third of the three email exchanges he and McCall had shared prior to the meeting. Garner had put a lot of work into the one-page word doc that outlined exactly what he had lost as a result of being fired. In very neat order and detail, the page listed each line item of salary, bonus, stock, and options that his agreement with Bill Statham had promised. He also had the email from Statham stating his joy when McCall accepted and included his reaffirming, humorous quip about his new man McCall staying on at GAC until retirement. The email ended with McCall stating his career plan to do just that.

Adding up all of those numbers, even presuming an early retirement so as not to be perceived as greedy, McCall's brief outlined a total payout due of just over five and a half million dollars. Upon seeing the bottom-line dark bolded figure, McCall could see the two men's eyes fixate upon the number. Asking if he could see the paper, taking it to hold, Malish acted as if he wanted to study it more, as if committing it to memory. Then, he asked if McCall would be willing to share the file with them via email or perhaps if they could have that copy.

Stupidly and trustingly, McCall gave them the copy. After pretending to study the document for several seconds, Malish said that obviously the figure was a very big number. "However, given the new light that has developed, as we eluded earlier Garner, what I would like to do is go back and share this file with Rick and Bill. Then, I would plan to follow-up with you. Does that sound reasonable?"

Without responding directly, still wanting to stoke the fires a bit more just so those boys could think about how they might respond to his expectations in the future, Garner asked a question instead of answering. "It sounds like you are ready to conclude our meeting, Jed. Did you not want to also hear about my information concerning the Cabo meeting with the Haskins Group? It's pretty interesting too."

Now beginning to look a little perturbed, Malish paused before responding. "Well, Garner, it's my understanding that you personally were not in Cabo at those meetings, correct?" To which, McCall admitted being correct. "With that being the case, then I'm afraid that anything you feel you know or perhaps were told would merely be considered hearsay, and not something that we, or our attorneys, like Dennis, could really give any credence to. However I can share with you, is that after your call with Renford, Bill Statham instructed me to launch a thorough and exhaustive internal investigation into those allegations. I assure you that neither Rick Winther, Larry Travis, or Tom Pittman were ever privy to our investigation or findings, other than as targeted subjects themselves; given how they each were individually investigated as part of the matter. What we ultimately found, after a long drawn-out, and rather expensive, I might add, investigation was that there was simply no truth to the allegations whatsoever. As a result, we have absolutely resigned ourselves to the fact that no wrongdoing of any kind occurred, at least by Great American employees, and have hereby closed the matter completely." After his longwinded oration, Malish paused, again not smiling, to see if McCall was buying the bullshit.

"So Jed, I'm curious, who led the investigation of GAC's top three executives? Garner asked. "I did." Witman chimed in. "Roseville Black is our primary outside firm, Garner, concerning all such matters of impropriety." Malish added. Never before had a truer statement been made about Great American and their scumbag law firm, Roseville Black.

As the meeting concluded, completely pie-free mind you, Garner remained seated as Malish and his hired prick of a lawyer got up to leave. There were no parting handshakes or well-wishes. The only thing Malish said before they turned to walk away was, "You'll hear from us Garner." Then they were gone.

Garner had kept an eye on the other two white-starched men who had seemed to be completely still in each of their booths. Then, not less than three seconds after Malish and Witman walked out of the greasy spoon restaurant, both men quickly got up and followed suit. Neither needing to stop and pay a bill at the register. Apparently goon types pay in cash at the table.

~~~~~~~~~~~~

As soon as he pulled out the restaurant chain's tired parking lot onto the main road leading back to the interstate, Garner noticed a dark sedan had followed soon after. One of the other two men from the restaurant, the one with the bright white hair, was behind the wheel and kept about three car lengths behind. Now Garner was certain the other two men had been in the restaurant for a specific reason. Speeding up and changing lanes, Garner watched through the rearview mirror, as the sedan kept up. Little did the white-headed man know that McCall was only on his way to buy a new violin to surprise Denise on her upcoming birthday. As he walked out of the music shop back to his car, Garner tried his best Bond-like move by snapping a few pictures of the vehicle and driver on his cell.

Another couple of weeks passed as Garner waited to hear a promised response from Malish. As it would turn out, that response would come in the form of a certified letter from the Pittsburgh corporate offices of the law firm of Roseville Black. The letter titled "Great American V. G. McCall", as if for effect, was authored by Dennis Witman, who stated that he was "officially representing Great American Casket Company in the matter." The letter went on to stipulate, how "in a recent meeting to reaffirm the company's rightful, and fair decision to terminate Mr. McCall with cause, based upon clear and certain evidence of wrongdoing", that "Mr. McCall then proceeded to try and extort his client for five and a half million dollars."

Immediately Garner knew that he had been hoodwinked by those jackals in the restaurant. He should have seen right through Malish, refusing to smile like normal, showing up with that little turd, Witman, and suckering him to give them the document. The very thought of how Great American was going to twist the whole thing around as if they were the ones being harmed was completely infuriating. The letter concluded with a threat to sue McCall for intimidation and extortion should any other efforts, either written or verbal, to contact his client again take place, unless through the offices of Roseville Black; and signed, "Dennis U. Witman, Esquire." Esquire, my ass!

Garner and Denise were livid at how Great American had asked for him to sum up what he thought was a fair assessment, only to use it against him and threaten him legally. Neither of them could ever have dreamt that the company he'd worked for over ten years, turn out to be that deceptive. Except the following week, when Garner got another notice of his character being besmirched.

One of his former managers called to ask Garner, if he had actually written a post online "saying all those things to absolutely to destroy GAC would come out", saying, "Man, if you did, you sure set them on fire!" Garner had no idea what his friend was even talking about, much less had ever even heard of the website before. It turned out that the site was one of those where funeral directors go on to blog about all kinds of subjects, only related to funeral service that is. Once he searched and located the post that supposedly he had written, he couldn't believe what he read. Whoever had written the salacious information had intentionally presented them self as being "the Garner McCall who used to work for Great American Casket." Besides unscrupulously impersonating him, and committing multiple felonies in the process, the statements the asshole went on to make in his or her blog were some of the most inflammatory things that anyone could imagine saying about a former employer, much less putting it in writing on the world wide web, for all to see.

As soon as he'd read the pack of lies, Garner immediately called the person listed on the website as being in charge, demanding that he in fact was the real Garner McCall and that the blog be immediately removed. Finally, getting the guy to realize that someone had taken illegal civil liberties with his site, the man agreed, and to his credit sent out a notice to all users of the site about the incident and warning them to not act in such a manner. Garner wouldn't know until later, when telling Don about it, that the computer used to post the malicious information could be easily traced down and offered to do it, promising to have his old FBI buddies handle it.

After the Witman letter and blog incident, Garner sent an email to Malish indicating his disappointment with both circumstances. Further clarifying how he had the blog site director take down the lies that someone had posted just to disparage him in the industry, from which he was barred from working in for two years after termination. As for Witman's letter sent on behalf of the company, Garner didn't acknowledge it.

~~~~~~~~~~~~~~~

Contemplating his next move, Garner decided this time to reach back out to Pittman to see if any other developments had happened with him since their last talk. Like McCall, Pittman had received a similar warning from Roseville Black, requiring any and all contact through Witman. The two agreed to meet back on Garner's deck, as Pittman favored the thought again of getting out of Bergholz for a while.

Just like before, Pittman was still extremely pissed. He said he had been putting calls into Winther and Malish every other day until it had gotten to a point of being ridiculous. None of his calls were ever returned either. Then one day recently, he had received his fuck you letter from Witman, who he called "that little prick." Turns out Pittman had some past experience with Dennis Witman before, and was not a fan by any stretch.

The second deck chat went the same. Both men updating the attempts they'd taken to get resolution, only to still be shut out. Pittman was drinking heavier than the last time and more heavily slurring his words. Garner knew it was a good time to try and learn more about the dirt in Cabo, except Pittman was still sober enough to keep his cards and secrets close. He did, as expected, get wound back up pretty good at the mere mention of the ritzy beach spot. Saying loudly, "I called that asshole, Winther, on the way over here! I told him that I was going to go to the cops and tell it all, if he didn't return my call and vest out all my fucking stock shares! I also told him to tell that fucking Statham that I have a few interesting pictures of him on some of our trips over the years, with hookers sitting on his lap too, if I ever need to draw a comparison of his past behavior with what they've accused me of! I told him, to tell that son of a bitch that I'd be happy to mail them to his little wife at home too if they didn't respond to me!"

"So you actually talked to Rick?" Garner asked. "No, no, I just left him a message from my phone in the car, driving over here. I told just you that!" he said, as if annoyed McCall wasn't paying attention. "Oh, I see, Tom." Garner replied. "Well, do

385

you think your message will get him to call you back, I mean do you think it had enough heat in it?" "Abso-fucking-lutely, I do, Garner, abso-fucking-lutely buddy!" the wound-up drunk assured. "I laid out every last illegal detail, including his! If he doesn't call me back, I'll be fucking shocked!" "Well, I hope he does so for your sake, Tom." Garner said to show support.

Garner was left still wanting to know what those devilish details were, but despite his best efforts to get Pittman to spill the beans, the man proved to hold his tongue even after six beers and two powerful, triple Maduro cigars. Miraculously though, sometimes the glorious skies open up and rain down sweet manna from heaven! About halfway through the last Maduro and seventh beer, Pittman's cell rings. "It's fucking Winther!" He shouted, obviously astonished. Then, he immediately answered.

Looking at Pittman, showing his understanding that the call should be taken in private, Garner quickly goes inside the house to allow him privacy for the call. Being sure to walk out of plain sight, since Pittman could see well into his house, Garner wanted Pittman to hopefully get into it big time with Winther. Now that fortune had smiled, all he could do was hope.

~~~~~~~~~~~~

Malish never responded to McCall's email about the blogger's libelous actions. Garner never really figured he would. He figured all he could do at this point, particularly after Witman's threatening letter, was to either let it go and forget about it or contact an attorney. He chose the latter.

The law firm of Sumner & Steed, LLC in downtown Cleveland consumed a huge, shiny skyscraper that was large enough to house the entirety of Roseville Black's old gridiron building inside their lobby. Malish and Witman both were well aware of the firm's prominent reputation for winning the overwhelming majority of its cases, mostly due to their expert due diligence on preliminary discovery preparation before ever notifying an opposing party.

When Malish read aloud the notice of McCall's intent to sue in Statham's office, the new GAC chairman and likewise CEO both knew things were spiraling out of hand. The usual efforts to flick away a pesky ex-executive were clearly not working. While they knew a call to Witman would be required, in order to apply more pressure to McCall, they decided to first try a more personal approach with their former employee to see if things could be settled. By going to such a huge firm, it was obvious that McCall was willing to spend some serious cash to wage his battle and now the notice demanded that Great American provide a copy of all documents and interviews associated with the "internal investigation that led to Mr. McCall's dismissal." Meaning that Great American would have to either manufacture the so-called evidence, or admit that actually no outside persons related to the company had been contacted to support their decision, despite McCall's verbal and written pleadings to the contrary. The legal notice also informed Great American of their "intent to depose all parties involved with the Palm Springs golf trip, including current and former employees, as well as customers of Great American, and other informed persons to the said events."

In an effort to clean up his own mess and save face with Statham, as well to keep things from getting back to Renford Kleinmark, who had asked to be kept abreast of any significant events, Winther said he would personally arrange to meet with McCall.

~~~~~~~~~~~~

Acting quickly, Winther called McCall on his cell that afternoon. As soon as the number popped up, Garner's mind raced back to the day when Winther had last called his cell, the same day he'd been fired. Winther immediately acknowledged the letter from McCall's attorney, and said he felt like he "had let things get out of hand." Even saying that he and Malish didn't know Witman was going to send the letter accusing him of trying to extort the company; saying how Malish had not authorized their outside counsel to take such a harsh action, and how they knew that Garner had never suggested something so nefarious.

Winther finally said, "Garner, I think you and I can work this out if we just sit down over a cup of coffee. It's become clear to all of us, that my decision to let you go so abruptly was entirely short-sided. I should have made sure that everyone we interviewed had been telling the truth, which later we discovered wasn't the case." I want to make this right with you, if you'll let me. I understand how pissed off you must be, but I hope we can save ourselves a lot of trouble and expense, if you'll just meet with me. Would you be willing do that, please?"

Finally, Garner felt like he'd gotten their attention. After months and months of chasing them down, being ignored, threatened, and having his reputation smeared online, now perhaps it all might come to an end. He prayed that Great American was shooting him straight this time. All he wanted them to do was to acknowledge that his termination was "without" cause and pay him according to the terms of his employment agreement. Hopefully, now that would happen.

Winther asked if they could meet the following day at the same restaurant where he and Malish had met, since it was about halfway. "So are you going to show up with a bunch of lawyers and goons too, Rick, like Malish did the last time? I guess I should also ask if someone is going to follow me home like last time, as well." Garner snarked sarcastically. "No, absolutely not, Garner. You have my word on that. It will just be me and you, I promise. I just want you and me to sit down and talk, and hopefully to find a way to work this out, that's all."

As Don heard about Garner's updates, he knew the only reason Great American was now taking the lead to reach out to him was because they were scared. "While that may make you feel good at the moment, Garner, you should know that scared people are the ones who tend to take the most dangerous risks and actions. You need to be clear that you can't trust these people!" Garner knew his friend was right.

~~~~~~~~~~~~

DANGEROUS NEGOTIATIONS

Winther had barely sat down when he placed his cell phone right in the middle of the table between himself and McCall. It was obvious that it was either to record their conversation or for the benefit of others outside listening in. As he began to talk, in his usually dreadful ad nauseam fashion, Garner quickly cut him off, thinking how there was no way he had to sit there subjecting himself to that shit any longer. "Ok, Rick, why are we here? What is it that you would like to say to me?" Garner said in a very monotone and unaffectionate manner. Despite his inability to get to the point, Winther finally hemmed and hawed his way around to say how they "all felt so bad about how things had gone" and "how we want to make it up somehow." "Which means what?" Garner shot back.

Struggling to swallow McCall's obvious and insulting darts, Winther continued. "In looking back Garner, while we still feel that your actions were inappropriate, we now know that it was mostly Pittman who was in the wrong. In light of that, we would like to offer you a full year's salary, which as I recall, was right around two hundred and eighty thousand when you left. In addition, we will change your personnel file to show that you are eligible for rehire in case any future employers call for a reference. Besides that, we would offer you an "A-Level" executive outplacement package to help you get traction in the job market, as well as, I would personally write you a glowing letter of endorsement."

Barely letting a moment rest since his last word, McCall snapped back, "Rick, why in the world would I ever want a letter of reference from your sorry ass? Are you insane? What about my contract; my lost bonuses, stocks, what about all of that, Rick? Am I just supposed to forget all that? We know for a fact you guys are a bunch of fucking dog-faced liars, and my attorney and I will prove it. You never once called the hotel or golf course manager, like I asked you in your office the day you fired me. You didn't even call the customers! Yet, you sat there on your high horse and lied straight to my face. You want to know who my lawyer's talked to, Rick? Everyone who doesn't work for Great American, that's who! It's funny too how the customers were all told that I had resigned out of the blue. What's funnier is how my contract precludes me from contacting or returning any calls or emails to any of Great American's customers for a full two year period.

We also have an FBI agent working to see who in the hell libeled me on that online blog not too long ago. Then there's Pittman. We have plenty of proof he was the one who invited those girls to show up at the hotel with the customers. He was the one who had them sit on his lap and then dance in front of everyone like they were going to strip, which, thank God they didn't! I bet you knew that too, but you're too fucking dishonest to be truthful about it.

You know Rick, what I've never understood is why you guys decided to fire me in the first place. I'm the only one in years to get a whole division to hit plan, much less year after year. At least, that is, until you fucked my whole team by taking

391

the Haskins Group's revenues out of our sales, although, you were nice enough to leave in the added quota. And don't think for a minute, that everyone in the whole sales force doesn't fully understand how you screwed my team over on their quotas and from having any chance of hitting their bonuses this year. Even the folks in other divisions are just as pissed off as mine, because they know if you did it to our team, then you'd fuck theirs too! They all have your number, Winther! More than that, not one person, in the sales group at least, has any respect whatsoever for you! I can assure you of that, and you did it to yourself!"

Now seeing that Winther was struggling to respond after being unloaded on with both barrels, Garner went in for the kill, quickly pivoting to his phone he'd just laid in the middle of the greasy table.

"I tell you what, Rick, let's table all of that crap for a moment and talk about Cabo." McCall said with the biggest kiss-my-ass grin he could manage as he stared at the snide prick sitting across from him. "What about Cabo? Malish said you'd brought that up last time. That's all hearsay as far as you're concerned, Garner, which he told you. They even investigated me over all of that just because of what you suggested to Renford Kleinmark. I don't know what you've been told but there's nothing to it, at all, I swear!" Winther said, hoping he'd be able to shoot the topic down again. "Well, I tell you what, Rick, take a listen to this, then you tell me there's nothing to it!"

At that very moment, Garner pressed play on the cell phone recording of the call between Pittman and Winther. The recording device Don had provided worked perfectly picking up every syllable from Pittman and enough to confirm Winther on the other end. Pittman had gotten blistering hot as he yelled and screamed at Winther that day on the deck, causing Winther to also thankfully scream right back at Pittman over not calling him back and the Cabo episode.

Winther squirmed when he realized that the other people sitting around could also overhear the recording as it played on. Thanks to the little, grey-haired lady, who had seated Garner the last time he was there and loved his southern accent, had made sure of, and just as he had asked her to do. Seeing him walk in again, she said how she could "tell the last time that something wasn't right about all those other men who left at the same time, and there you were left all alone. Looked like a gang up situation to me!" Then, stretching out her face's beautiful well-earned wrinkles, she smiled bigger than life, saying, "And none of those yahoos even left me a tip, much less, like the big one you left young man!"

As the recording rolled on, it provided proof of words like prostitutes, people's names, and how those who were interested in an after dinner companion received a late text message from Miles. It also captured Pittman screaming and chewing out his old boss about taking so much bloviated credit for pulling the account back from the proverbial ashes, when in truth it was only because of the fifty percent upfront, straight discount Winther had coughed up right out of the gate on day one in the first sit-down, like some nasty fur ball, when the customers postured like they weren't going to stay with Great American. Except in Winther's lack of basic sales knowledge, he

393

was too stupid to know that tactic was an upfront-given that every shrewd business man attempts at least once in a new negotiation.

Worse than that, Pittman railed how Winther inexplicably threw in the Most Favored Nations Status into the deal, which guaranteed the Haskins Group they'd be assured of always getting Great American's best trade terms, compared to any other operator, period. Pittman persisted in his raged rant, talking about how the deal-clincher had ultimately proven to be when Winther promised that Miles would be at their beck and call to help them target available accounts that the GAC sales reps flushed out all the time. Miles would work exclusively with the COO to specifically target the right large firms in the best markets, making it an almost certainty of their hard-charging growth. Between Miles and the famed tarmac meetings, which he now had down pat, plus the incredible deep discount offer, they would absolutely be able to undercut any firm anywhere with their new found ability to offer the lowest prices when and wherever they needed.

The only caveat that Great American would mandate would be that Miles would make certain that the Haskins Group no longer kept targeting only GAC firms. This way, Miles could ensure their growth meant likewise volume growth for Great American, unless, of course, a good GAC firm looked to be selling out to another operator that hated Great American. They would cover their bases there too. It was a perfect scenario that included market manipulation and price-fixing, all rolled up in less than two and a half sweet-ass minutes, right there for all the world to hear, starting with the diner's blue-collared crowd!

After reminding Winther of how stupid the deal was he had cut with the Haskins Group, Pittman began to laugh almost uncontrollably on the taped playback. Finally, Pittman landed his final verbal blow by insulting Winther on how he had made him and Travis swear to never publicize the deal's outlandish terms, so that the rest of the sales teams wouldn't think they could start jacking up discounts even higher to regular accounts, which would only leave GAC far less profitable. Reminding Winther how he said "No one outside of us, Statham, and Malish will ever hear these fucking terms!"

Hearing all of it made Winther's face turn redder than his favorite Buckeye red. Once enough of the recording had played, Garner snatched his phone and cut it off prematurely in mid-sentence of the wonderful screaming match. That was another trick his buddy Don taught him, to keep the VIC guessing what else they'd said in the heat of the moment, when they didn't know they were being secretly recorded.

Piling on, Garner launched in to his own loud rant that absolutely made Rick Winther's head explode, saying, "Looks like to me, Winther, Statham's grand plan was supposed to be pretty simple. Lord knows, you're that not fucking smart enough to figure out a brilliant ruse like this. Control which firms get to buy Great American caskets, ensure that some of the largest funeral home operators that aren't buying from GAC get invited to talk with Miles in a tarmac meeting, help the Haskins Group target and take over the biggest ones in their area, and, if

395

necessary, blackmail all of the best volume firms in the country who are looking to sell out, which in turn would ensure the Haskins Group ultimately becomes the largest corporate consolidator in the business; who, in turn, of course then only buys from Great American. Then the poor Mom & Pop firms left standing would never be able to compete fairly whenever a Haskins Group location showed up in their market. Because the new Haskins Group funeral home in town would easily be able low-ball and undercut their prices all day long! Which all makes total sense, of course, and was exactly why my reps always said their independently-owned customers were constantly bitching about whenever a Haskins firm showed up in their market. Have I got that about right, did I miss anything there, Rick?"

It was a simple plan, or so Statham thought. The only problem with the whole sorted mess was that he didn't expect his inexperienced protégé to make such a mess out of pissing off Pittman. Winther should have known better, he thought, to keep Pittman quiet, one way or another.

Winther was completely flabbergasted, and sat there staring at the tabletop as if McCall's phone was still there. Having landed his intended blows, Garner abruptly stood up, just like Winther had the day he'd been fired in the corner office, and said, "I'll tell you this, Rick. Fuck your hundred and eighty thousand, and especially, fuck you! I think the FBI and the Securities Exchange Commission would be more interested in this recording than I am, don't you think?" With that, Garner began slowly walking out of the hushed restaurant, where all of the staff and customers present had clearly overheard everything, and remained completely stunned and motionless, as he confidently exited the old, roadside diner. Before pushing open the well-worn metal and glass exit doors, Garner gave a big grin and wink to his new waitress ally, on his way out to get in his car and head home.

~~~~~~~~~~~

This time it was a black sedan that followed suit as Garner pulled onto the interstate. The driver, like before, was the same white-headed man. Apparently, per his routine technique, he stayed about three car lengths back. Fully expecting his chaser to reappear in his rearview again, Garner had planned ahead this time, asking Denise to swap cars for the day. Although not telling her why, as she would have never stood for what he was planning, much less with the likes of these guys. Thankfully she had agreed to drive his four by four to the hospital, so he could tank up and drive her high-performance, silver Porsche coupe. He and Don knew, if this panned out, it was going to be fun for sure!

Don had been parked across the street in his Tahoe as the goon set out after McCall. No doubt, whatever their signal was, Winther had sent it as "code red" while he was still sitting back at the restaurant. What Garner hadn't noticed this time was how two cars followed him. The other sedan had gotten lost in his line of sight to the traffic behind the black car, so he hadn't caught that he had two chasers. However the 'ol wily detective, Don, had definitely seen it.

Just to have some fun and see how serious they were, as soon as the road ahead cleared, Garner punched the Panamera up to about a hundred miles per hour, at first leaving the goons in the proverbial dust. Moments later, according to Don, the two sedans proved to be former cop cars with some major high-performance V-8 engines in them. Saying, "You could have outrun them for a while, Garner, but those cars wouldn't ever be too far behind." For the twenty or so miles home, Garner darted and dodged in and out of traffic, as Don watched him and the two goons break every moving violation known to man. One thing was certain, whatever the reason, those guys weren't about to lose their tail on McCall and they didn't care if he knew they were there. That was the most concerning thing to Don.

When Garner was almost home, Don called his cell to say he would hang back across the street from the neighborhood. "If one of those bastards goes into our neighborhood, the odds are high the other one won't. He'll probably either find a place to lurk around close by or go back to wherever in the fuck they hang out. Either way, I'm going to get a read on his plates and follow where he goes. You go home, pull inside your garage and don't get out of your car until the garage door closes completely, Garner. Then get your ass in the house and make sure all the doors are locked. Keep that Glock I gave you close by, and use it if you have to. And if that son of a bitch walks anywhere near your door, you put a bullet in his gut and call me!"

Garner did exactly as Don instructed, with one small exception. When the goon had the audacity to pull up and park right there on the street in front of McCall's home, obviously just to intimidate him and his family, Garner thought, "Fuck that!" and, with the Glock in hand, went out his front door and sat on

398

his front porch staring at the man and covertly taking pictures with his phone.

~~~~~~~~~~~~

Now Great American knew they had a very serious problem, and not one that another certified mailed threat could remedy. Winther lost all favor with Statham when he had to admit to the recording between him and Pittman. Still, convinced they could resolve everything, the calm and collected Statham rationalized the situation. "Look Rick, the only thing that has changed is the recording. Pittman obviously doesn't know about it. Most likely, neither does McCall's lawyer, since it would be inadmissible evidence anyway. It's pretty clear that McCall is playing both ends against the middle. Sue us if we don't pay, and blackmail to not get sued in return. I always knew he was smart, but this is smarter than I had given him credit for, I'll admit.

The fact remains that since he met with you and planned to use the tape means that he still wants to settle. The only thing we have to figure out now is how much will it take. That's what we have to find out. At this point, it is unlikely that either you or Malish could get him to trust you enough to meet again. Given that, I think the only play left, is for me to reach out and set up a final meeting to resolve this once and for all."

~~~~~~~~~~~~

Knowing the recording would come back on Pittman, Garner and Don were anxious to find out what his mood would be like if he was invited over again for more drinks and cigars. This time, however, when Garner called and got him on the phone, Pittman said he had needed to get out of Bergholz for a while and had gone down to his condo in South Florida.

To hell with all the fucking GAC execs and their condos in South Florida! Ever since Statham bought his first from DAK, it was if all of Statham's direct reports felt it necessary to own one too. At one point, so many GAC execs owned high-priced condos in South Florida, that DAK finally decided to sell his to Statham and move his winter home to Aruba. Where, he'd always said it was because of how the tiny island had been discovered by his native Netherlanders. The truth was he couldn't stand having that many GAC execs so close by, and constantly trying to suck up, by inviting him over for dinner or golf. He couldn't stand being around any of those pricks, unless he absolutely had to. So, he used his personal Falcon to fly right over their asses as his private jet hurled over the Nation's most southeasterly state, all the while, smiling and knowing he'd be over twelve hundred wonderful miles away.

Oddly now, while Pittman was still pissed off just as much as before, this time he said Great American had finally called him back. All of sudden, Jed Malish wanted to meet with him "as soon as possible" Pittman said. "When I told Malish that I wasn't around, he told me to just say where we could meet and he'd come to me, but that it had to happen soon. When I told them I was at my condo, he said he could be here tomorrow, which is today. We're supposed to meet this afternoon at my favorite cigar bar. I guess I'll see what it's all about, Garner. I'll let you know if anything comes of it." Garner wished Pittman good luck, and said, "Give'em hell Tom! Let's connect when you're back, I'd be curious to hear how it went." Pittman agreed and told McCall that he'd be back north in another two or three days. Even jokingly saying, "Hey, if it goes well, maybe I'll come back on the jet with Jed!"

~~~~~~~~~~~~~

Over the next several days, the goon in the black car stayed out front of Garner and Denise's home, intentionally to intimidate and spy on them. Little did he know that Garner had a high-powered, deer rifle set up in his front dining room window, just in case the goon ever got out of the sedan and set one foot on his property. The other goon, as Don confirmed, stayed parked down the street in view of the entrance to the neighborhood and followed either of them anytime they went somewhere. They followed Denise when she went to her hair appointment, the mall, or even to the local market when she shopped for groceries. With her, they always followed slowly and never engaged her directly. Don told Garner, "They just want you to know that she's at risk."

Whenever Garner went somewhere, the pursuit was more amped up. Now they started following closely, right on his bumper most of the time when they could. And if he ever tried to lose them or speed out of the restricted speed zones in their neighborhood, the goons gave hot pursuit just the same. One time, when Garner ran to the grocery, the white-headed man followed him inside and continued so up and down each aisle. Garner had seen the man's actions and decided to get a little braver on his own. At one point when Garner was about halfway down an aisle and the man had followed behind about a third of the way, he abruptly turned and began walking straight at the white-headed man, who he could see had the scariest eyes ever. Welcoming his prey toward him, the man raised his cell phone to his ear, most likely for effect, and said loud enough for McCall to hear, "Yeah, he's right here. He'll never know what hit him, or his little tight-ass wife for that matter. I'm ready to put an end to this shit once and for all, and soon!" Hearing every word as he strolled past within a foot of the man, Garner turned and looked him right in the eye. He didn't say anything, but he felt proud that he had at least stared him down.

Driving home, Garner called Don and asked him to come over to meet on the deck. When he told his ex-FBI buddy about the grocery store encounter, Don's face instantly turned blood red. "I'll tell you what Garner, I'm done letting these guys fuck around with you and Denise. This shit is getting serious for him to do that. Don't you worry I'm going to take care of this." Don had already followed the second car a couple of times and now knew exactly where they went whenever they left Garner's house.

It had been over four days since Garner and Pittman last spoke. Figuring his former colleague was back from Florida, Garner reached out to schedule the next cigar session. This time, he could tell that Pittman, although friendly enough, was now clearly uninterested in making the drive over to his house. Finally, agreeing to meet at a Mexican restaurant that allowed smoking outside on its patio, the two men agreed to reconnect the following day.

From the moment Garner laid eyes on Pittman, he could tell things were different. The guy's whole demeanor had changed. No longer was he pissed off and easily excitable over the mention of Great American and being fired. When Garner asked him about it, all he would say is how he had "finally realized to let it all go and just focus on the future." He even went so far to say how "life was too short to worry about money" and how "family was really only the important thing." Garner had enough experience dealing with people to know when they don't or won't look you in the eye throughout an entire conversation anytime you ask them something, that they're not being forthcoming and honest. Now, anytime Garner asked him a direct question, Pittman just looked away and gave some bullshit, philosophical response.

When Pittman never mentioned Malish's urgent trip to meet with him in South Florida, Garner flat out asked how it went and what the top company lawyer had to say. But all he got from Pittman was, "Oh, it was really nothing. He just wanted to know if I wanted to cash out what few stock options I had left and were vested. He was coming down to his condo anyway, so he thought it would convenient to swing by and ask me. That's it." "So what was so fucking urgent about that, Tom?" Garner asked. "Oh, I think I just misunderstood how Jed had put it last week, that's all." Pittman tried to explain with a straight face.

It was obvious Malish and Great American had gotten to Pittman. Whatever they did to appease him, Tom Pittman now didn't have a care in the world. He was as relaxed as Garner had ever seen the man, even though he hadn't been around him all

403

that much. Over the coming weeks, Pittman would stop returning Garner's calls. It was obvious now they no longer had anything in common to talk about. Despite Garner reaching out for drinks or cigar chats, even golf since they both had the time, Pittman would never respond after Malish's urgent visit.

It doesn't take a rocket scientist, or even a rock scientist, to figure out that Great American realized that if the recording was ever used against them, Pittman would be needed to swear that it wasn't his voice on it; nor that had he ever been to McCall's house. The fact that cell phone records could only be used to prove that the two men had a couple of brief chats, which would never prove anything. Although, if Pittman was so inclined to admit that it was him on the recording and the facts he'd screamed were indeed true, especially if ever investigated, then Great American would come under more scrutiny from the U.S. Justice Department faster than you can say "Cabo."

Now it was plain as day that Great American had made that concern go away. No doubt, they most likely paid out Pittman's ten million dollar portfolio, and allowed his unvested stock grants to be reinstated. As an ESOP managed, privately-held firm, versus a public one, they could easily do that. Regardless, Pittman would never know that he actually had Garner McCall and his FBI buddy to thank for setting him up for a cushy, early retirement and stress-free life.

It's always smart to keep your network active when you move on or retire. It only took one phone call from Don to one of his old confidential informants to put his plan in motion. It

404

would be planned to happen when the two goons switched off from sitting outside Garner's house, sending the white-headed man back to their hideout for the night. He was one of the two pricks Don said he wanted his "CI to chat with."

Don's CI, was a guy who had gone to prison after spending years with the mob, running drug and prostitution rackets. This guy's reputation was what had kept him alive in prison. In his late forties, standing at six foot four, still with virtually little body fat, which was one of the perks of working out every day in prison, this guy was mean as a snake and able to handle most any man alive. The only good news these days, since he figured out that life on the outside offered a lot more upside than being locked up, was that he turned his considerable "persuasion" talents to working for the good guys at the bureau. Don told Garner this guy was actually pretty decent once you got to know him. The only problem with that was how anyone who knew anything about him was scared to death to get too close. He had killed more pimps, pushers, and hookers than most around Cleveland, but since he'd never killed a cop or agent, he got a break for time served based upon how he could better help the law than break it.

"And just one more thing about this guy…" Don told Garner, "If he tells you his real name, don't ever call him by it, not even once. Trust me he doesn't like it too much, apparently never did; which is why I just call him "CI." His real name growing up was Clarence Ignatius Griswold, which must have been a son a bitch growing up as a kid. Supposedly his mother thought, with a middle name like Ignatius, that her son would

405

grow up and become a big important person one day, except it didn't quite turn out that way, that's for damn sure.

Turns out 'ol Clarence started in elementary school beating the crap out of anyone whoever called him names like Clare, or Ignatius, or Iggy, or Grisworm. Kids can be such mean little shits sometime. When the Feds picked him up in one of our stings, several years ago now, his playground buddies in the mob were calling him the Gris-man, for how brutal he always was with some pimp who forgot to pay on time or a hooker that ever got out of line. When I first met this dude, I don't mind telling you, I was pretty fucking scared. He's got the darkest eyes, I've ever seen, Garner. Those things will stare a black hole right through you! Anyway, I knew I sure as hell wasn't going to call him Gris-man, which is still what he went by in prison.

When we first got him in an interrogation room, after learning how some of the meaner mob guys also sometimes teased him with the whole "Iggy" thing, we thought we'd start there just to get his emotions running high. You see, by getting a perp's blood all hot and bothered like that, the psychology of it, causes them to actually open up and talk more than what they otherwise would normally, than if they kept their emotions under control.

Anyway, so we told him how we heard he likes to be called Iggy, and we called him that like a hundred times or so over the first couple of days trying to get information out of old CI. Immediately, you could see how he hated that nickname so much, as his eyes bulged out of his head and his veins coursed with rage. It was a sight to see for sure, and one that must have brought back all of those painful playground memories from his childhood. Those are always the toughest for any human to conquer in life. Once he got out of lock up, we figured he could be useful, so I decided that since he was going to be a Confidential Informant and how his first two initials were "CI", that was exactly what I was going to call him. Thank God above, that he liked it, that's all I got to say brother! Thank God!"

~~~~~~~~~~~~

After surveilling the address Don had provided, CI knew the white-headed man parked out front on the street every night when it was his turn to get some shut eye, while his associate slept with one eye open outside McCall's house. The white-headed goon's routine was the same. He went to the same diner each time, and usually sat in the same seat. Even when the seat was occupied, he'd always move to it as soon as it opened up; weird too how he'd move even if he only sat there for two minutes before leaving. Next, like clockwork, he went around the corner to a bar, where he had two drinks; no more, and no less, just two, always two. Again, it was weird. Telling Don this, CI laughed saying, "the fuck must be that dedicated to his job so that he's never hungover in case he gets a call!"

Once the VIC's routine was down to a hard pattern, the timing was right for CI to make his move. He would wait until the goon came to park on the street in front the low-rent apartment that he and the other guy were using. CI knew they switched places every so often, just in case anything or anyone ever followed them home. The guy was a creature of habit to say the least; every day the same shirt, same diner, same bar, same number of drinks, and same parking space in front of the apartment; and always the jazz. When at home, or in his car, this particular goon enjoyed an exceptional good taste in traditional jazz, the likes of Armstrong, Ellington, and Monk. Apparently the guy was a virtual expert on traditional jazz, even fancying himself a self-taught talent, who played jazz piano by ear.

On this particular evening, CI's rusty old work van, one of those without any side or rear windows, would be sitting in the VIC's preferred parking spot running with the lights on. Seeing the VIC's car pull up behind him, waiting to see if the worn out van would eventually pull away, the goon took the bait. Getting out of his car, he walked up to the driver's window, although carefully coming up from the back side of it as he'd learned from being a cop. Tapping on the window just like he'd done a thousand times back when he used to stop and harass the fine motoring citizens of Philadelphia, his intent was to find out if the driver would be moving soon or, if not, to put on his best, intimidating shit-face suggesting it would be a good idea. However when CI rolled the van's window down, he smiled his biggest, friendliest smile, saying immediately, "Oh hey there friend, I sure hope you can help me, I am so lost! I got this urgent plumbing call out here and I have no idea where the street is I'm looking for."

As if on cue, the VIC asked, "What's the street you're looking for buddy?" Allowing CI to raise the map he was looking at under the faded interior dome light. As soon as CI raised the map to the open window, pointing to it and pushing it towards the VIC, the guy took a hold of the map just as expected; which allowed CI to grab the taser gun resting from the door handle. After two highly-amped, electrocuting shots to the man's chest, he was down on the ground instantly and completely incapacitated. Seconds later he was in the back of the van, with duct tape completely wrapped around his hands, feet, as well as his head and mouth.

An hour and a half later, CI got the man chained to a rusted old metal chair in the back warehouse of a dilapidated hog rendering plant on the south side of Canton. Once everything was set up, the white-haired man's interrogation began. It would only take a few quick electrocutions, powered by a small generator, to get the VIC out of his foggy stupor. Once the VIC was sufficiently resuscitated so that the "negotiation" would be effective, then CI commenced with his well-honed tactics. Like most reputable thugs, the first approach would be the "respectable ask." Meaning CI would simply tell the VIC what he wanted to know, and as long as all of his questions were answered quickly, truthfully, and completely, then the VIC would be released unharmed. Sadly, as everyone knows from the movies, despite the most sincere offers, captors rarely ensnare VICs with such agreeable attitudes. As such, more circumstantial methods require deployment. When the VIC's only conscious acknowledgement of his captor's most generous offer, was a heartfelt "Fuck You!" well then, CI's festivities proceeded.

Over the next four hours, CI continued to ramp up his degree of torture on the white-haired VIC until learning everything that Don had said he wanted to know. After giving the goon's driver license number to Don, once he'd been tasered and duct taped, CI already knew the white-headed man had been a dirty cop back in Philly. He enjoyed reminding the man how he'd been fired from the force for helping to hide and profit from a human smuggling ring that mostly focused on minor-aged girls. The man had been caught red-handed by a federal sting operation, although it was unclear why he'd never faced prison time. Upon asking his VIC how he managed to do that, CI was met with the same snarky, two-word response that apparently the tough guy was only able to manage in the moment.

As CI turned up the abuse from blows to the chest and face, to deep cuts on the man's back with a sharp, jagged knife, the man remarkably began to get more agreeable in his responses. Once CI began to slice into the top half of the man's right ear, demanding to know who ordered the tail on McCall and who he worked for, the man began to talk. Saying, "All I know is it's one of Roseville Black's biggest clients. I don't know who. Me and the other guy work for the law firm. We just do what we're told, that's all, I swear!"

Not convinced he'd applied enough incentive for a more detailed response, CI pulled the sliced portion of the dangling ear away from the man's head, so as to let the blood exceedingly flow down his face as the sharp pain tormented and jogged his memory. "Oh, I believe you can do better than that friend. Tell you what, let me ask you this. Have you ever wondered what life would be like if you were deaf or blind? Let's start with deaf, since I need to be sure that you 'see' how serious I am, I'm not going to take your eyes out just yet. Instead, I'm going to give you one more chance to tell me the truth; otherwise the rest of your right ear is coming off. As CI tugged on the ear, as if to keep it taut and easier to slice, the man swore again that he knew nothing more, begging his tormentor to please not cut him anymore. Not believing the chained VIC for a second, CI took the rest of the ear off in one mighty downward jagged, brutal slice and aggressive rip of the knife. Screaming in agony, the VIC violently flopped around in the chair, with tons of rich, red blood draining from where his ear used to be, begging CI to not hurt him anymore, and promising to tell him anything he wanted.

Continuing his staged encouragement for truth and transparency, CI now shared with the VIC how he too loved great jazz, even selecting the downloaded genre of songs on his cell phone, and setting its speaker on high. "Ah, I have to say that Coltrane is my favorite. That's him playing there. You can hear that right? Just imagine when your other ear comes off, that could be the last jazz song you will ever hear in your fucking, miserable life. Of course, I also know how you like to play piano, so maybe we should shift the knife to your fingers next, what do you say?" Begging and screaming uncontrollably for mercy, as CI takes his left hand and begins to joke how the man won't be able to hear out of his right ear, much less play anything with his left hand's fingers cutoff, the VIC desperately pleads and promises to tell him anything he wants.

CI's final opportunity to the VIC was this, "Ok friend, I'll tell you what. I'm a fair man, so let's see if this time goes better than before. I'm going to step aside so the powerful little video camera on this smartphone can capture you in all your

411

glory. And if you promise to not waste our time here, then we could be getting close to being finished. So let's try again."

Now CI had the VIC's full, unadulterated attention. Further, CI's interrogation skills were as good as most cops, since he'd delivered plenty such sessions back in his mob days. After going through the series of questions that Don provided, CI was comfortable that the VIC was answering truthfully. Within a span of thirty minutes, the VIC regurgitated all of the criminal and violent sins that he and his partner had committed over the years on behalf of Roseville Black. The kidnapping and murder, and post-mortem mutilation of the young street walker from Pittsburgh was the first. How they drugged and framed Fitz at Great American's famed Ranch resort, and then covered it up at Statham's direction. How they later followed Fitz to Cabo, and secretly videotaped his biggest customer Baker Haskins having perverted oral and anal sex with an underage Mexican boy. How days later, the two men had traveled to Northern California to Haskins's office to blackmail him with photos of him and the boy so that he would sign up with Great American. Then finally again how they had gone back to Cabo, after Baker Haskins' suicide, and framed his top two executive officers.

When CI asked him to detail all of the last Cabo trip details, the VIC went into detail with the video rolling. Saying, "There was a guy named Miles we worked with. Apparently he runs some off-the-book company for the Kleinmark family that owns Great American, or at least most of it. Anyway he was our guy on the inside. We had done our surveillance of the three Haskins customers in attendance. One was as clean as a church

412

mouse, but the other two, their COO and Sales VP, we figured we could set them up. Sure enough, that wasn't very hard.

My partner had followed the pimp that came to pick up the young boy on the first trip, so we could see where he went and who was involved. Turns out it was all local, and set up by the woman who managed the property where Fitz owned his condo. We had rented out the one next door, and had bugs all through Fitz's condo on that first job down there. Anyway, we worked through the same woman to arrange for some young, beautiful Mexican girls to be available, you know in and around the bar area at this five-star hotel where all these guys were staying. That way we'd be able to tell if their juices got flowing on the first night. They were there for three nights in total.

Miles and this guy named Travis were the ones who whispered to the COO and VP about how gorgeous those young girls were, and they were too, even though they couldn't have been more than fourteen or fifteen. Once Miles suggested to the two VICs that the girls were available for what Great American always referred to as their famous "turn-down service," well the two guys couldn't say no. Especially if the girls were just going to show up in the middle of night with a soft knock on their hotel door; you know, so there was no chance of them getting caught. Of course, we had all the rooms bugged, even the church mouse's just in case he turned out to be into whatever. You know how most men are when their away, especially in a place like that. That guy was the real deal though. Reading his Bible every night and calling home to his wife and kids.

The other two pricks, they had their way with the girls. So did Miles and the Pittman guy. But Travis and their CEO, they were smarter than to do that with us around. They knew we had the rooms bugged too. Everything went fine, until the COO, who had a real thing for hardcore porn, became too physical with his girl. When we first saw on camera how he started to hit and knock her around, we sat back to see if he'd stop. But when he didn't, we had to rush into his room and pretend to be security guards at the hotel.

The fool was out of his mind, and was shocked that we'd walked right into his room so easily. The girl was really badly beaten up, with a broken jaw. So we yanked him out of there and got him into our room next door. I'm not sure what eventually happened to the girl, we just figured she'd be ok. Still, she was pretty badly beaten up. The COO had to be at least two hundred and twenty pounds to her one hundred. By the time we got into the room, he'd knocked her all over that room like a bloody, rag doll. We gave her back to the woman who we met on the first Cabo trip, when we set up the sting on Baker at Fitz's condo. She was deep into the sex trafficking trade down there, and helped us arrange the girls.

That's all I know, I promise. I swear I'm not lying this time. Please believe me, man. If I knew anything else, I'd tell you. Anything we ever did came to us from Arthur Black, he used to be one of the big shots at the firm, but he's dead now. Now, it's Dennis Witman. He's the one we always hear from. He tells us what to do. Most of it's always for Great American. We always gave the evidence, you know, photos and videos, to

414

Witman. Of course, what he doesn't know is how we always keep an extra copy of everything, just in case those snakes at Roseville Black ever turned on us. We have all of that hidden away. I can get it for you, if you want it."

Now CI knew he had enough information that Don McCloud would be very pleased. Turns out, while the white-haired VIC was writhing in grotesque pain after his ear had been removed, CI called Don on the burner phone, so he could listen to the taped confession. Even though everything inside of CI made him want to put a slug into the sack of shit sitting in front of him, the deal with McCloud was that he wouldn't. Instead the VIC, thinking he'd get to leave or be taken home, learned that his fate was sealed. He had just confessed to multiple crimes, while incriminating Great American and Roseville Black.

The final conversation between CI and the VIC was about how the goon wouldn't be going anywhere just yet. CI rolled over a metal stand holding an inverted three liter bottle of water and electrolytes that had a looped hose and suction tip, that when sucked on would allow water to slowly drip out. Rolling the stand near enough to the VIC, whose hands and feet were completely duct taped to the frame of rusty and bloodied chair, so that he was completely immoveable, other than his ability to swivel his neck, CI told the goon to go slow on the water. Further saying it would be days before anyone would be there to release him. Then he told him that if he died first, it wouldn't matter anyway. "Of course, you shouldn't die, friend. You just had a full dinner last night and your regular two drinks. This fluid ought to last you a few days if you go easy on it."

When the VIC asked who would be coming, all CI said before walking out the back door of the dark slaughter room was, "Friend, that's outside of my paygrade!"

~~~~~~~~~~~~~~

PAYBACK

It was the first time that Bill Statham had ever personally called to arrange a meeting with McCall. It was amusing for Garner to think the pompous ass could even manage such a task without the help of his trusty executive administrative assistant. What wasn't amusing, almost frightening really, was how Statham sounded just like he always had, upbeat, clear, and commanding. He and McCall both knew the only reason he was calling was about the recording of Pittman that Winther had relayed. It was most certainly wasn't related to Garner's gigantic law firm reaching out, that was for damn sure. It'd take a lot more than that to put the fear of God into Statham and Great American. The company would have welcomed a law suit at this point. Especially since knowing they would have it tied up for years on their home turf in Greed County. Arthur Black had seen to that certainty for DAK decades ago.

Even though he wouldn't allow his personality to submit to such a fact, this time Bill Statham was calling out of sheer desperation. Garner knew it, and Statham knew Garner knew it. "Garner, my boy, it seems we have a predicament of sorts to work out. Winther, of course, came back and told me about the recording you played for his benefit at the diner. Apparently you seem to feel fairly certain that the voices on the tape are those of Winther and Tom Pittman. While you may be right, Winther of course swears that he didn't hold such a call with Tom. As a matter of fact, he says he hasn't spoken with Pittman since the day he was terminated, which was a long time ago at this point.

417

So I guess, while it's possible that Pittman may refute what Winther told me, who knows, maybe it really is him and my new CEO is just trying to keep me from firing his ass, it is also possible that he's telling the truth. I presume you have some strong reason to believe that it was indeed Pittman on the call, perhaps you even have proof of it. I am not suggesting it is or it isn't mind you. All I'm saying Garner, is that it's time we get together and settle your grievances once and for all, and get all of this nonsense behind us. I think that is the right thing to do given where we are. Can we do that?"

Up until now, Garner had always addressed Bill Statham as "Bill" or, whenever his southern respectability came out, even calling him "Mr. Statham." This time, however, when Garner's turn came next to speak, he would forego his upbringing, only to show a profound casualness and deference of respectability to his elder. "Sure Statham, I guess one more meeting wouldn't hurt. I've already wasted my time with Malish, Witman, and Winther. So what the hell, you might as well be next! What were you thinking, sometime in a few more weeks or months from now? Obviously since I have no leverage of any concern to you and Great American, I'm sure you boys aren't in any rush. That is what you're suggesting, correct? I guess I should get down on my knees and kiss your ass for being so compassionate and kindhearted enough to reach out to some worthless, ex-executive like me. Have I got this right, Statham?" Then McCall shut up, and wondered if the phone line had gone dead with all the silence that filled the airway for the next several seconds.

McCall's blatant disrespect had thrown the man on the other end of the phone line. The venerable William Statham had all of a sudden lost his train of thought. He had become so used to never being talked back at, much less down to, that his thinly-plied ego was still processing how McCall had just rattled his cage, which was still reverberating as his mind and eyes kept twitching while taking it all in. Once his mental footing was back under him, Statham said, "Garner, I understand you are upset. From what I have heard since getting brought up to speed on everything that has transpired, which by the way has just been as of this morning so forgive me if I do not seem fully cognizant of it all, but it does sound as if my team here has royally botched up this entire matter with you.

From what I heard today Garner, which by the way, please know I got extremely upset at what I heard from Winther and Malish, I promise you, it would seem that you should not have been terminated at all. To begin with, from everything I read in detail this morning, which I fully trust as an exhaustive review, it seems perfectly clear to me that you were terminated based upon a very poor investigation. Much of the evidence, which I understand mostly came in well after the fact, clearly exonerated you of any wrongdoing whatsoever.

Given that, I cannot tell you how sorry I am Garner, I truly am. I wish I could go back in time and make everything right. Unfortunately, I cannot. What I can do is try to make the future aspect of these circumstances as right as I possibly can. That is why I have called you today and that is what I would very appreciate having the opportunity to meet with you personally about. I guess the only other thing I would say is that this has all gone on far too long. Because of that, I feel responsible, personally responsible, for my enterprise here at Great American, and have decided to get directly involved myself to make sure everything is fully rectified with you.

As you know, I was the one who personally wanted to see you hired to begin with, Garner. Then, you know I was your biggest admirer and supporter of how you were reestablishing our sales organization. That is why I wanted you promoted to a very high level in my organization. So I hope and trust we can meet very soon, even this week if possible, to remedy all of this."

Finally, Garner had become tired of Statham's voice, much less the bullshit. All he told Statham before agreeing to meet and ending the call, was that he would give him fifteen minutes the next day if he wanted to meet that bad. Waiting to see if Statham's precious and pompous ego could take the time limit blow, Garner was almost amazed when he accepted instead of hanging up. Although Statham offered to revisit the same chain restaurant that had become "negotiation central" for their opposing sides, Garner refused, demanding to meet at the firm of Sumner & Steed, LLC in downtown Cleveland. Saying, "There, I know you guys aren't going to try and secretly record me, or have some goons come inside for fear and intimidation purposes.

And one other thing, Statham, or the deal to meet is off right now. That fucking Witman had better not show up! I can tell you that if I see his scrawny little ass, or those goons anywhere around, the meeting is off and I will hand the recording over to the FBI. I don't know if it's legit or not, but I bet they could find out. Especially if your man down in Cabo was really so stupid enough to actually use cell phone transmissions back and forth by sending text messages to the customers to notify when their underage hookers were on their way up for the night. Don't you guys watch the news? Hell, even some really high-up, bad-acting, FBI agents recently got busted and fired because their bureau-issued phones weren't encrypted enough to keep from having their own deleted text messages used against them. That was pretty fucking stupid, I gotta say, even for you dumbasses!" That statement caught Statham off-guard, big time.

Winther hadn't said that the recording of Pittman mentioned anything about Miles texting the customers about the prostitutes. But, then Statham recalled how Winther had said that McCall snatched the phone away before it ended. As such, Statham just figured that McCall may have forgot about that part not playing, since Winther had remained in the restaurant for several minutes after McCall walked out, taking down copious notes while they were still fresh in his mind. Either way, the added information didn't change what Statham knew he needed to do. What it did do, was cement that McCall had them over a fucking barrel and he knew it.

~~~~~~~~~~~~

Garner and Don went in early the day of the meeting at Sumner & Steed, LLC. Garner told his "attorney" that Don was his friend and retired FBI detective, who had been coaching him through the "whole sorted mess." Don was there to help him get settled in the room, so that he was comfortable when Statham arrived. He knew full well that Statham was an old pro at the types of confrontations that were slated between them. With his expertise, Don could help him best prepare for what they thought was coming.

One of Garner's old college buddy's from down south had made partner at Sumner & Steed over the past couple years, and had been the one to write the chain-rattling letter to Great American. Despite what Statham, Winther, and Malish had surmised, Garner hadn't written some big retainer check to one of the most prestigious law firms in the country. His 'ol college buddy just did him a favor and wrote the seething narrative, and gladly after hearing how his friend had gotten shafted.

Besides their friendship, when Garner's lawyer buddy heard that Roseville Black was Great American's law firm, that was all he needed for motivation to help his friend stir the pot. He and his fellow partners, like most firms around the nation, knew the longstanding reputation of Arthur Black, and how it continued to reach back from the grave for their clients. The bottom-line was Roseville Black was extremely well-known as being the type of firm that did whatever it took, on either side of the law, to ensure their client was protected, against any and everything.

The word on the street for decades had been how they were the shadiest firm in Pittsburgh, even in the country, when it came to skirting the law. Worse than that, Arthur Black had come close multiple times over the years to almost losing his law license and having his firm shut down. Multiple times, the

422

Justice Department had investigated his firm for alleged criminal activity. Somehow though, Roseville Black had seemed to find their way out of each and every circumstance where it looked like they might go down. Amazingly though, just when the wheels of justice seemed to be turning against their favor, the fact was that any witnesses to any alleged crimes seemed to always get a permanent case of amnesia, laryngitis, or end up dead.

~~~~~~~~~~~~

Bill Statham was a lot of things, but one of them was never tardy. Accordingly, he walked into the lobby of the law offices of Sumner & Steed at exactly two o'clock the next afternoon as expected. Normally, McCall had the same penchant for his personal punctuality, but this time, he none the less made Statham sit and wait in one of the firm's elaborate conference rooms for a full fifteen minutes before going in. That was another one of Don's "old bureau tricks, called "Watch'em Squirm, that worked with almost one hundred percent certainty with corporate big shots like Statham, who usually got to where they were in life by overachieving, the early worm, and all that shit," as McCloud said. Garner knew the trick had worked too, because as soon as he walked in, Statham made a big point to look at his twenty thousand dollar Rolex, saying, "I thought our meeting was supposed to start fifteen minutes ago?"

Apologizing profusely and going on and on about how talkative his attorney had just been, "probably just to charge me more", Garner said, enjoying seeing his older nemesis swallow the acknowledgment of his own less self-importance. Catching that he had already been a dick to the one guy he was trying to keep from blowing up Great American, and himself in the process, Statham did his best to put on a smile and act friendly from there on. That was strike one!

For the next several minutes, as was the same tiring custom both he and his junior CEO successor had become known, Statham dominated the entire conversation revisiting everything the two had just discussed the day before. Fully expecting this from the arrogant and unaware executive, Garner allowed Statham's bloviating to continue until such a point, when it was a good time to abruptly jump in and shut his pontifications to the ground. Strike two in the bullseye! More than anything, Statham never tolerated being interrupted. Something else that Garner and Don had planned to attack his ego and set the right mood in the meeting, ensuring their VIC got his back up enough and would be ready to hopefully strike back at some point.

Sitting there fuming, Statham tried to not let on how livid he was at how this ex-employee was obviously disrespecting him and his importance, regardless of the matter at hand. With Statham so agitated, Garner decided to take control of the meeting by interrupting the Chairman's grandiose posturing. "Look Statham, I don't have all day. You asked me here, and here I am. I told you I would give you fifteen minutes, which you've already taken listening to the sound of your own voice. So what is that you wanted to do or say to "remedy" things as you put it the other day? How about you get busy explaining what it is you and that company of yours is going to

424

do for me? If you think you can manage to fall out of love with the sound of your own annoying voice, then I'd like to get this shit over with!"

Direct hit, strike three! Statham had had enough of McCall's insults and insubordination. If McCall thought that the Chairman of the Board of one of the largest companies in funeral service was going to sit there and keep taking his obnoxious diatribes, then he had another thing coming. When Statham began his next with "Look, McCall..." Garner knew he had gotten the arrogant man's goat for sure. It was just as Don predicted would happen if Garner kept poking the bear.

"Look McCall, I can see that you intend to make this as painful a process as possible. So let's just get to it. I think you and I both want to resolve this so here it is." Pointing to the sealed envelope, prominently embossed with the Great American logo, Statham explained what he was "prepared to offer as a final and non-negotiable settlement of their differences." Which, he said in total ignorance of the clear, undisputed fact that neither he nor Great American was in charge of this situation.

Pulling out the executive summary, Statham begrudgingly pointed how each of the individual bullet points pertaining to his original senior executive agreement would be paid out in full, as if he had been terminated "at will but without cause." Just as McCall had prepared and trustingly handed to Malish many weeks earlier, the total sum came to almost four and a half million dollars. After forcing himself to say the huge number out load, Statham said, "Well, there you go McCall. I trust that makes you feel "remedied", emphasizing the word with the most artificial insincerity possible. It was inescapable how Statham had just tried to make him feel unworthy and undeserving to be paid out according to the terms of this agreement. Regardless of how any lost salary, bonuses, stocks, and harassment pay, for the pain and suffering they had put him and Denise through over the prior year, had most certainly not been considered into their so called "goodwill decision" to forego the clause aspect of his termination.

The most insulting mistake Statham made, although it didn't matter to the plan Garner was carefully executing in the meeting, was after he'd gone through the one page overview and verbalized the painful number to be paid out to his young nemesis, how he then obnoxiously shoved the paper and envelope at McCall across the large conference table. By arrogantly shoving the envelope, especially at the one man who could possibly keep Great American's dark shadows from ever being exposed to the harsh light of truth, it proved to be just another example of Statham's bruised self-sense of greater importance, manifested in his own stupidity. Garner never budged or reached as the materials flew across the table, not once taking his eyes off Statham, who tried to close by demanding, "Are we done here? Are you satisfied now, McCall?"

Still locked in visually, Garner said, "Not yet. As for the offer, I will let you know on that in a minute. Before I get to that, I do have one question for you that none of your other fucking minions have had the balls or courageous enough to answer. I would like to know just why in the hell I was ever fired to begin with. You, Winther, Malish, and I all know that there was never a so called "internal investigation" about what happened in Palm Springs on that golf trip. To this day, I still don't understand why Pittman had even gotten invited on the trip in the first place. Lord knows Jostens wouldn't have been the one to plan it. Plus, it's clear now that Winther planned a double hit on taking me and Pittman out all along.

As for Pittman, I really don't care, although I presume it was because Rick wanted to give his 'ol Bergholz buddy a good job and look like a big shot around town after becoming CEO. Still, what I can't wrap my head around is why in the hell you guys would fire one of your best sales executives? You especially, Statham, I know nothing ever happens in Bergholz that you don't know about, much less approve. Winther is an idiot, everyone knows that, but he's not so stupid to fire me without your blessing. So, if you think you have the balls big enough to man up and tell me, then I would like to know.

I'll take the money and get past this. Lord knows I want it to be over with too. But I am really hoping that I'm finally sitting with one person who has the decency or guts, whichever, to tell me why on God's green earth was I fired to begin with." Never unlocking eye-contact, Garner rested his case and sat still waiting to see what Statham said. Figuring McCall would never walk away from a guaranteed four and a half million dollar payoff, Statham took the bait. This time he'd take another notch out of McCall, just for good measure, and he'd do it by putting his patent leather foot on the neck of the younger man once more.

427

"You want to know why we fired you, Garner? I'll tell you, I have no problem with that. As for Pittman, that had been decided long before Winther ever stepped up. That was his one condition going into the job. He hated the guy, apparently over something that went back years. I never cared to even ask why. Then, when Rick found out Pittman tried to end-around him for the CEO spot, I knew he was done for sure. All we had to do was create the right scenario and, like always, he'd do the rest. See, we knew Pittman wouldn't be able to resist staying drunk and chasing women on that trip, regardless of customers. So sending him there was like sending some fool to the front lines in war. He was certain to hang himself with "cause." Once we had Travis play that suck-up Jostens into setting up the trip and inviting Pittman, we knew he'd be toast.

As for you, Garner, there were two reasons. One was stupidity, plain 'ol stupidity! First you were stupid to stand up in an executive meeting and try to shoot down your new CEO like you did. You never do that, no matter what you may believe or feel. A shrewd business man always lives to fight another day.

The main reason, and the biggest way you fucked yourself out of my great company, was because you were so bound and determined to sell aggressively to the blacks! Where in the world do you get off trying to preach from atop your mighty high horse to the likes of me and the Kleinmarks? We run this fucking company, and if some little fucking piss-ant like you thinks they're going to decide if and when we start going after the black business, then they need to think again. We have intentionally managed for over a hundred years to avoid that

428

segment of the funeral market, rather successfully I might add. No one, and I mean no one, least of which the likes of your southern dumbass, is going to tell me that I have to approve giving them the same kinds of discounts we give white firms. Not in my lifetime, as Chairman of the Board for the Great American Casket Company!

Furthermore, as for your suggested threats of class-action litigation being taken against the great enterprise I lead, then I will close by telling you this. The best way we avoid the possibility of something like that getting stirred up is by firing stupid idiots like you who think Great American has a presumptive ethical and moral obligation to sell to a bunch of black funeral directors. We do sell to them, if they want to buy caskets with the lowest basic terms provided, regardless of how many they purchase. So there's your fucking reason, McCall! Do you understand now, do you?"

All Garner said was, "Yes, I understand. Thank you for putting it so clearly to be completely and easily understood. I think that satisfies the purposes of our discussion here today. As promised, I will get back with you after I've have a chance to read the documents. You can expect my call at five o'clock sharp tomorrow afternoon."

Seeing Garner then reach to pull the envelope toward him and presuming their meeting was finally coming to a close, Statham simply couldn't resist letting his truly malicious nature be exposed, as he took one last parting shot to intimidate McCall into signing and going away once and for all. "McCall, I would suggest you sign those right now and leave them with me so I can file them with our outside counsel. It would be a real shame if one of those guys, who have been sitting out front of your home for the past several days and following you and Denise around, were to possibly be outside now and follow you again. Especially, since you have such a long drive back. It would be awful if somehow you got into a fatal car wreck on your way home. At least if that happened, Denise would get the money promised in the offer. You should really think about that Garner before you leave and get in your car and start driving."

No sooner had Statham finished delivering his final, threatening shot at McCall, did he suddenly realize how stupid he had just been. It was completely out of character for his personal emotions to get the best of him and say something so incriminating and egregious, much less right there in McCall's own attorney's conference room. As his subconscious, brainless, action registered, causing his mind to reel with regret, Statham's face instantly transitioned from a look of sheer intimidation to one reflecting the horrified reality of what he had just said aloud. All Garner did in response was just sit there for a long, wonderful pause, smiling with absolute delight at what he'd just heard. No doubt, it was the final blow to the great Statham and the mighty Great American Casket Company!

With his mission fully accomplished, Garner slowly picked up the envelope by its corner tip and abruptly leapt out of his chair, rushing out without saying another word, which again completely caught the obnoxious Chairman off guard. Statham hadn't expected McCall's last reaction of enjoyment, much less his last nonverbal parting shot of belittlement. Not wanting to feel he'd been dissed again, Statham jumped up to follow. Except as soon as he'd gotten outside the conference room into the hallway, McCall had already disappeared back down another corridor to where his friends were waiting in his buddy's office. Don and the attorney, who had been listening in, high-fived their friend for goading Statham's ego into submission and for getting him to finally speak the very dark truth they had suspected.

~~~~~~~~~~~~~

As promised, Garner made the call to Statham the next afternoon at five o'clock sharp. Waiting on edge to receive McCall's call, Statham was sitting behind the enormous, hand-carved, dark mahogany antique desk in his office that overlooked the Great American complex in Bergholz. The desk was always the first focal point of conversation anytime some dignitary, such as a big politician, industry magnet, or on the rare off-chance an occasional funeral home operator was ever allowed to grace the highly-considered, hallowed room. Like DAK and Renford before him, Statham spun a great tale about how the first founder of the company, Helmutt Kleinmark, had been the inspiration for the magnificent furniture piece, and how DAK had sat and studied the casket business at it for years after coming to America back in the early 1900s. Everyone marveled at the enormity and majestic craftsmanship of the desk, especially Bill Statham. Ever since his first time of being invited into DAK's revered office, to be congratulated on the success that had resulted from his Miracle Casket blackmail campaign, Statham had long admired his mentor's grand desk and dreamed of taking his rightful place at it one day.

431

Sitting there now, on this day that would prove to be the most memorable in his entire career, he had no clue whatsoever about the man they called "Big Sam" who had actually designed and built the inspirational piece by hand, on his own, for his most dear, lifelong friend, Helmutt. The desk had been built long ago in secret as a gift from one man to another, to honor their lifetime of good memories and loving, respectful friendship. As hoped, the desk would ultimately live on to represent something greater about the company they had built together, and be a reminder to the art and craftsmanship that made their firm unique to any other.

~~~~~~~~~~~~

It had been a long time since Bill Statham had truly been nervous about a phone call, but no question, this time he was sitting on pins and needles. Having become completely consumed by his mental wonderings about what he might hear and how he would respond, he uncharacteristically almost jumped out of his chair when the phone finally rang. Trying quickly to gather himself, Statham answered the phone in his best confident tone manageable, given the gravity of the moment. He had been stunned how the meeting the prior day had gone, and was still in shock how McCall had acted in such defiance to him and his position; not signing the offer, which Statham considered was way more than what the lowly ex-minion ever deserved. The worst part for Statham was being forced another full twenty-four hours to get an answer. Mostly, he was still beside himself for how he had been so stupid to threaten McCall's life like that. Now he just prayed that what

432

McCall might say would finally put it all to rest. He knew they had let everything get so far out of hand, that whatever it took now, he must end it once and for all.

Statham was almost envious of how calm Garner McCall sounded when he began speaking. The instant their exchange began, he could tell something was wrong just by the solemn and determined tone in McCall's voice. When Garner told him to look out his lofty perch window that overlooked the front entrance to Great American Drive, he said Statham would see an old, rusted stock van waiting to pull out left onto the main road that led away from the company's exclusive compound. Acknowledging his sight of the van, Statham waited to hear what McCall would say next. "There is a sealed envelope, the one you gave me yesterday actually, which only has your fingerprints on it, slid under the windshield wiper of your new six hundred thousand Rolls. You need to send your admin down to get the package immediately. Trust me, I promise you do not want anyone else to grab it out of curiosity and see what's inside. I will stay on the phone while she retrieves the envelope, but you will put your receiver down, because I will say nothing else until you have it in hand. Once you have the envelope in hand, then you will pick the receiver back up to hear what's next. Keep me waiting more than two minutes on the line, and I promise I will hang up. I also promise that you don't want that to happen."

Once Statham told McCall that she had brought the envelope to him, Garner continued. "Inside you will find some disturbing photos of a white-headed man who is barely alive, but I assure you he is still very much alive. The man is an employee of the Roseville Black Law Firm. As you will hear on the computer disk enclosed, he has made a taped confession about how he and another thug, both dirty ex-cops, were instructed over the years by Arthur Black, and later Dennis Witman, to repeatedly commit numerous illegal and criminal acts on behalf of Great American. He also states how you and DAK Kleinmark authorized the brutal killing of a young girl at The Ranch to frame and set up Fitz Edmondson in order to force him to sell his casket distribution business to Great American. Then, how the girl's body was flown to a Great American customer out in Oklahoma in order to be cremated and destroy the evidence.

The man's confession also goes on to explain how Fitz was framed and photographed by the thugs. The man later details how Baker Haskins was secretly surveilled and blackmailed, after having disgusting, perverted sex with a minor-aged boy in Mexico. You will also find copies of those photos, as well as of the photos from one of the rooms at The Ranch, showing a blood-covered Fitz Edmondson when he had been drugged with GHB and convinced that he had murdered the girl. I'm sure that even you are not shocked to now realize that your hired goons really didn't destroy all those incriminating photos, Statham."

Sitting behind the most famous desk in the whole casket industry, Statham remained speechless as he tried to gather his thoughts and emotions. Garner continued, "The man went onto describe in deadly detail how your lowly minions, as you like to call them, took the Haskins Group executives down to Cabo. As you will see on the tape, he explains how two of the men enjoyed the late night sexual company of two under-age Mexican girls,

434

not more than fourteen years old. One of the men even beat one girl so badly, that her jaw was completely broken in three places. But you probably knew all of that already, Statham. What you didn't know, perhaps, was that Witman had his goons bug all the rooms of Winther, Travis, Pittman, and Miles as well, so he could get any dirt on Great American; just in case you or any of your successors ever had the notion of dropping their firm. The white-haired man also said Arthur Black had done the exact same thing to your beloved DAK Kleinmark, who never once suspected it, only later to teach the same backhanded dirty tricks to his own protégé, Witman.

Finally, the thug explained how Miles spent every night on the phone speaking with you and Renford Kleinmark about how the tarmac meetings were going and which foolish funeral operators he'd blackmailed lately. It was amazing how lucky Witman's goons were to record 'ol Miles as he actually listed each firm off by city, state, volume, and owner's name. Of course, I know how you were always a stickler for details in reporting!" Garner said snidely. After promising Statham there was way more information on the compact disc to incriminate him, DAK, Renford, and Great American of authorizing many other heinous acts and crimes, Garner paused a moment before saying, "I could keep going Statham, but I think you get the picture. I guess the thing to be decided now, is how you want to play this."

It took the great William Statham considerable more time that usual to collect himself and gather his thoughts. When Statham did finally speak, once he'd thought of what to say and how to respond, Garner was more than surprised that the weight of the information had not sufficiently scared him enough. But he never figured Statham was one to lie down quickly and give in. So Garner wasn't entirely shocked when he heard his ex-Chairman say, "So McCall, what it sounds like to me, is that somehow you have managed, illegally I might add, to get confessions out of several people who do not actually work for me or Great American; Pittman, Miles, and this white-haired guy, who you say works for Roseville Black. My guess is that if we got Witman on the phone, he would be willing to swear that he has never seen or spoken with the man once in his life. As a matter of a fact, I would make a really huge bet on that!" Thinking he'd squashed McCall's grandiose plans of bringing down the Great American Casket Company, Statham eased back in his big, expensive black leather chair, managed to restart his ear to ear grin, and waited with bated breath for his young nemesis' response.

"Well, we sort of guessed you might twist it that way. So, I tell you what Statham; let's do talk about Great American. Why don't you put that disk into your computer, and press play. What I haven't mentioned is how the video footage actually begins with your own taped confession, made just yesterday in the pristine Law Offices of Sumner & Steed, right there in downtown Cleveland. Your taped portion begins and ends with you coming into the lobby of Sumner & Steed, riding up the elevator, walking to the conference room, and then back-tracking those same steps after our little chat. I don't think I have to remind you of how you so stupidly admitted to a practice, going

436

back decades, of market manipulation, price-fixing, and multiple other unfair business practices engaged by Great American, since the great DAK Kleinmark, his brother, and you have been at the helm. I would suggest that you watch it in its entirety, and then let's talk. It's all there, in living color!"

As soon Statham quietly put the disk into his computer and pressed play, he could see his worst fears realized upon learning how he had walked right into McCall's trap the prior day. He knew the words he'd said about the company's racial discrimination practices could be easily audited if the Feds were ever notified about how they cheated black-owned funeral homes out of the same kinds of incentives, even though in many cases they bought more than white firms who got far, better deals. The information would be a certain death blow to Great American and especially to him personally.

As the former Chief Executive Officer for over twenty years, until not that long ago, and now Chairman of the Board, he knew he would be personally charged, and most likely go to prison for a long, long time. The evening news of the day was full of other stupid industry kingpins who had been tried and convicted based on less evidence, and who served a long time behind bars. Now sinking and slouching lower in his chair, Statham knew McCall had total control of the situation.

By this point, Statham knew he was out of moves to bluster and bluff McCall. His mind was reeling to even think of what to say next, as he tried to just get enough saliva to return to his dried-out cotton-mouth. The deafening silence confirmed that the great man had become, at least if only momentarily,

437

impossible to speak at all. When Statham finally did speak, albeit only with a tone of complete surrender, he muttered, "OK Garner, what's next? What do you want? Just tell me, and I promise I will make it happen. I have heard enough, OK?" Asking and almost begging the younger, smarter man, who he knew now exerted all of the control in the situation, Statham all but broke down. Now it was painfully clear that he would be held personally responsible for the most dire, serious situation that he or the company had ever faced.

"It's simple, Statham. All you have to do is give me the same deal that you gave Fitz, ten million. Except, given circumstances, I know you will want to pay me in cash. And just like Baker, you have twenty-four hours to decide and have the money delivered to the back side of an old, hog rendering plant on the south side of Canton. The address is inside the manila folder. That same old, rusty van will be parked and waiting out back. The driver won't be there, but the van will be unlocked with the back doors open. You personally will deliver the money in two large black duffle bags. Of course, even though it should go without saying, if our man finds any bugs or tracking devices on those duffle bags, I can promise that you will meet him one day soon, just like the one-eared, white-haired dirty ex-cop did. You have my personal word on that. Do you understand everything, Statham, or do you want me to repeat it all?" With that, Garner stopped and waited for Statham's final response.

"Yes, I understand, Garner. The only thing I don't know about is getting that kind of cash so quickly. Banks are already closed today as you know, so that doesn't give me very much time before tomorrow. I doubt seriously if I can come up that much cash so soon to tell you the truth." Fully expecting him to say that very thing, Garner shot back, "Oh Bill, do you seriously think the great Kleinmark men don't have that much lying around their stately mansions? You disappoint me, Statham. What you need to do Statham, is go get your fucking ass on that big Falcon and go get the money! Either way, it's up to you. Know that if the cash isn't delivered by five o'clock tomorrow, four more sets of the envelope you opened today will go out. The first one will be delivered to the U.S. Justice Department. A second will go to Roseville Black, where I just bet they long ago covered all their tracks with Great American, meaning you and the Kleinmarks will be hanging out in the wind to go down all by your lonesome. Then, the other two will be hand delivered to the personal residences of DAK and Renford Kleinmark, who both will most certainly plead complete ignorance and begin to fire a lot of people at good 'ol GAC, starting with you! So what do you think Statham, think now you can get it done? I bet an over-achiever like you has already figured it out, right? I guess time will tell. Just know there are no do-overs here, Statham." With his last assurance, Garner McCall hung up.

~~~~~~~~~~~~~

Statham wasn't so stupid to drive a six hundred thousand dollar Rolls to the back of an abandoned, old hog rendering plant. As expected, Statham himself delivered the two black duffle bags on time twenty-four hours later, with five million dollars cash in each. After CI watched the unmarked car drive off, he scanned and checked the bags for any sign of a bug or tracking device. He then drove the van into the rear freight door of the dilapidated, old hog plant and transferred the money into black hard case tubs, he'd purchased at one of those oversized do-it-yourself depot stores, and loaded them into Don's Tahoe. If there's ever a safe and secure vehicle to drive around with ten million dollars in cash inside, it's a retired FBI agent's car, for sure.

With the cash loaded, the man pulled the Tahoe out back of the deserted pig plant, which he had soaked all over in gasoline. Then CI went back to the edge of the freight door and lit a line of roman candles he had set up to shoot out dozens of flaming fire balls in every direction around the old plant. Hurrying back to the Tahoe and speeding away, he could see the broken out windows in the old rendering plant begin to bellow out the deep, dark smoke and shadows as it went up in flames, completely destroying any evidence of the white-haired man's torture and blood, as well as anything that had been planted in the two black duffle bags. When the story of the burning building hit the evening Canton news, the local fire chief reported the apparent use of the bottle rockets as the primary cause for the incineration, the prevailing presumption was how some local kids must have been goofing off and shooting off the airborne firecrackers for fun in the old run-down, fire-trap of a building.

As for the white-haired man who had been left hanging on for dear life in the old hog plant, sucking ever so judiciously on the water tube to stay alive, CI had already moved his bloody body back to his apartment. Having been shot up with several

440

high-powered doses of GHB, appropriately the goon's own personal knock-out drug of choice, the white-haired man wouldn't come to for two days. When he did finally come out of the deep stupor, he was still blood-soaked, bound and chained to the rusty metal chair, which had now been secured to some exposed metal pipes in the apartment room, such that the man could not move at all. CI had used duct tape to wrap around the man's head and mouth several times, making it impossible to speak.

Seeing that he was back inside the apartment, the man agonized whether his partner would show up at any point to free him. But his partner, having the mind of the dirty ex-cop that fueled his brain's thoughts and paranoia, was too experienced to know that his partner was either dead or long gone. Whoever walked into the apartment next, would not be coming to help, but rather to apprehend. The white-haired goon knew that, his partner knew it too well. Days later, his prediction would prove to be right.

Days earlier, CI had kept a watch on the place to see when the other goon would return. When his white-haired ally hadn't showed up as expected to relieve his lurking duties out front of the McCall house, the dirty ex-cop knew something was definitely wrong. Going back to the apartment, after himself staking it out his own residence for a day or so and not seeing anyone come or go, CI watched from the shadows across the street as the man hurried out and sped away. Following behind in his old, rusty van, CI trailed and watched as the white-haired man's partner in crime kept driving until he had crossed the state

441

line at Steubenville. CI knew the man was too smart to come back, especially once Witman confirmed not hearing anything from his partner for days on end, which was never the case before and definitely not tolerated.

The following day, only one other envelope enclosed with a manila folder full of enough evidence to incriminate Great American and Roseville Black, as well as Statham and the Kleinmarks, would be couriered to the FBI field office in Columbus, Ohio. Over the coming weeks, Statham, Winther, Malish, Witman, the two dirty ex-cops, the Haskins' COO, and Fitz would be taken into custody, causing a major national scandal that rocked the entire landscape of funeral service. The industry that had always strived so hard to play down all media attention of any kind to protect their shiny image and profit kingdom was now embroiled in one the most salacious crime and corruption stories that America had seen uncovered in decades, regardless of the industry.

As expected, Statham and Witman hired the best defense attorneys and tried denying any knowledge of wrongdoing or conspiracy, except that, the two dirty ex-cops took care of that. They were going to make sure they didn't go down alone for everything that had happened. Once they copped a plea deal with the Feds and turned over all of the evidence they'd collected and kept on GAC and Roseville Black over the last several years, including multiple taped phone calls between Witman and Statham, they were both allowed to serve out their life sentences in different minimum security prisons.

As for Statham and Witman who were both sent to a maximum security prison in Lewisburg, Pennsylvania, well let's just say, that their prison life experiences were quite different. Just like depicted in the movies, Don made sure his bureau buddies tipped off the warden and enough of the meanest and vile inmates to make sure the facility's newest guests were met with the customary treatment for those convicted of torturing and murdering children. The only instructions were to not kill either of the men, as death would have been deemed too lenient. Instead, for the next several years, both would be subjected to the same types of deviant sexual abuse and physical torture they'd often authorized to further their own careers and greedy interests.

DAK and Renford Kleinmark would of course escape any prison time, as their political connections, who had ever visited The Ranch or the Falcon, would make certain. Although they both still payed a huge price, perhaps the best for the likes of their kind, given how their reputations and massive fortunes were almost completely depleted from the resulting class-action lawsuits filed on behalf of the hundreds of black-owned funeral operators. Most of all, and especially painful to the great DAK Kleinmark, was how his company was taken away, stripping him and his brother from retaining any stock ownership shares whatsoever.

Thankfully for the many, honest, hardworking employees at Great American, DAK had set up the business as an employee-owned stock based business. In the end, many of the honest town folk of Bergholz, Ohio, who worked at the

443

company, wound up owning it outright, and ultimately hiring their own new CEO to come in and run the business for them. Given everything that had come out during the various trials which consumed the Nation and their town for over two years, the new employee board of directors thought it only fitting to hire a well-known, prominent African American to run the company.

Less than a year later when DAK finally passed away, though never tormented by any shame or regret, but from the harsh spotlight of the truth, it would only be his brother, Renford, who would stand at his graveside. The massive five million dollar Italian marble mausoleum DAK had custom-built for himself was situated at the highest lofted point in the nicest cemetery in Greed County. The impressive structured was also crested with his initials encircled by a thin elegant oval, although, it would never receive his remains. For Renford knew, from all the negative press and hatred in Bergholz for him and his late brother, the mausoleum would stand as an eternal reminder of what his beloved brother's life had finally come to represent to the town.

Not even his sister's replied to Renford's letter, telling them of DAK's passing, as the tarnished news of the great American Kleinmarks had already reached back to them in Vielsalm. From then on, Renford would move far away out West somewhere to live out his days in the mountains, trying to avoid being recognized or ever reminded again of it all.

~~~~~~~~~~~~~~~~

Samuel H. White was a well-known man and prominent corporate lawyer from Columbus, who first became familiar to the people of Bergholz when he began playing football in college for State and even getting talked about for the Heisman. He was a huge and very strong, young man who could barely be tackled by three or even four defenders much of the time, setting multiple new rushing records at his alma mater. Though he didn't win the prestigious accolade, he did go onto play in the pro's for a few years, while also going to law school.

His teammates always thought it was perfect to use Samuel's middle name for his nickname. As it turned out, Samuel White was the great-grandson of Helmutt's life-long friend, Isaac Samuelson, aka, Big Sam. Big Sam had begged his only daughter, with whom he had been blessed after remarrying in life, to please give her first born son his dearest friend's middle name. Knowing how Helmutt had never had children of his own, it was Big Sam's way to convey how Helmutt would always be part of his family, who were as good as the salt of the earth. Though she thought that "Helmutt" was a really weird name, she finally did consent to the request just to please her loving father.

Unbeknownst originally and surprisingly to the new Great American non-executive, employee-only board, was how their new CEO knew so much about the service side of the funeral business. To their dismay, as he would often share, underscoring his understanding and commitment to running a fair and honorable business, Samuel White explained, how early on in his law career, he had picked up a new, smaller client and

445

became introduced to funeral service. The new client just happened to be a funeral home owner out on the East Coast.

Though originally, Samuel never said anything to the operator about his connection to Great American, noticing the man apparently chose to sell a different brand, he would later talk about how he learned why. Which was that the local Great American sales rep would never call on the man's firm, much less return his call whenever the operator got wind that Great American was running some big incentive promotion to boost its sales.

Finally after all of the truth came out in the news of how the company had forever racially profiled its preferred customer base, then Samuel White understood why the man sold a different line all those years. Samuel no longer represented the same funeral home client years later when the truth came out. Now the man who had been his client was since deceased, and his grandson ran the business. It would be the first phone call CEO Samuel White would make from behind that huge, magnificent desk.

One day, not long after taking the helm of the company, Samuel was alone in his office, working at the desk, when he dropped his pen. Always being a little bit clumsy, it wasn't anything new for him to do. Rolling his eyes and looking over to the open door in his office, hoping no one would see their new CEO crawling around on the floor under the desk to find the pen, he happened to take note of something that neither DAK Kleinmark or Bill Statham had ever noticed. Hand-carved into the under-side of the middle pull-out drawer were two aged lines of elegant script. The first simply read, "To My Dear Friend Helmutt – Big Sam"; and the second worn line with obviously different penmanship said, "Thank You My Dearest Friend – Helmutt." Sitting there on the floor of his office under the huge, old desk, Samuel White began to tear and weep as he thought about the sheer amazement of that moment, never feeling closer to his grandfather, as all of the amazing stories his grandfather had shared with him as a little boy instantly ran through his head. He knew then, it was indeed God's work that had put him on that floor at that very moment. He also knew that his grandfather, Helmutt's Big Sam, was looking down and smiling on his grandson.

Samuel White would come to love funeral service, not just the business of it, but mostly the tremendous personal societal value that the vast majority of funeral directors delivered for grieving families every day. He saw it up close and personal time after time. He worked so hard to learn the casket business and vowed that all of its employees would represent the Great American Casket Company as ethically and professionally as they possibly could, while honorably serving all customers, regardless of race, religion, or creed.

~~~~~~~~~~~~~

Garner and Denise moved back home to their beloved South Georgia only weeks after the news broke. Using some of the money the company had rightfully owed, by breaking Garner's contract, they both retired after all the Great American drama. Denise still volunteered occasionally at the local hospitals and nursing homes, whereas Garner stuck to ranching horses and cattle, which he knew as well as anyone.

Working his own ranch now, his mind fluttered less and less over the years back to the few times he'd actually gotten to enjoy being out at The Ranch in Bergholz. It was always mostly for DAK to show off, but Garner had enjoyed whenever he'd gotten to sneak out for a late evening ride after dinner with a client, a few times over the years. Anyway these days, Garner spent his time working the cattle stock and breeding horses. He and Denise were known for their impressive stable of Texas Mustangs, Paints, and Appaloosa's. Their operations allowed folks from all around to stable their horses at the Smoke Circle Ranch, or take riding lessons regardless of age. They especially loved having children from the area orphanages come for the day to pet and ride their many ponies; never once charging them a penny. The smiles from the children were always more than payment enough.

After all the dust settled from the mess with Great American, Garner spent most of his days on a horse in jeans and boots, and always with his ever present cowboy hat. He had them in every color for any season, and each with a regular cattlemen's crease crown. From there on out, it would take a wedding or funeral to ever get him in another suit, which had always been the required work attire for the sales group at Great American. He always laughed about how donating all of his suits to charity had been a really good day.

~~~~~~~~~~

On this particular day, marking the tenth year anniversary of his last phone call with Bill Statham, Garner took the day off from working the ranch; leaving it instead, to his buddies, Don and CI to look after. After his usual three cups of hot, black coffee in the morning, Garner saddled up his favorite personal horse, a Texas Mustang he called "Statler." Statler could tell the day's ride was going to be a long one, just by the way his beloved owner settled in to the well-worn, leathered seat. Before nudging Statler to move out, Garner took his torch lighter and scorched the tip end of one of his ever present cigars. By now, after all of their time spent together, Statler knew the scent of his trusted owner's smokes just as well. With his cigar well-lit and drawing clear, Garner McCall gently pulled on Statler's reins and led his horse out to ride and survey the thousand acres he and Denise had purchased after moving home. It was beautiful land, with clean lakes and flowing streams crossing paths through it. Garner would enjoy this day. Just like every day, since hearing the white-haired man's taped confession, he would say a quiet prayer for the dead girl and the younger ones down in Mexico.

Not long after CI played the confession for them, Don and a couple of his still active FBI buddies flew down to Cabo to find the heinous woman at Fitz's old condo complex. Once CI finally convinced the woman to tell them how the children had been procured, what they found later was terribly disturbing. Knowing she had been caught and would certainly be killed herself, the woman led them to where the girls were hidden away at a dark, secret compound. After finding the compound full of

449

many other young girls and boys who were all confined in locked rooms, including the one from Baker's video, Don and his FBI cronies involved the Mexican government to swarm the villa and capture the sex trafficking operation. What they discovered were dozens of underage girls and boys, mostly of Mexican dissent but also many who had simply been kidnapped from one of the area coastal hotel beaches while they're parents were either sleeping on the beach or just not paying attention. The sex ring then used the kids to satisfy the perverted requests of some of the wealthy guests that their moles in those same hotels messengered back to the compound. They also learned that the woman's condo complex was the central location where the guests would be with the children. Apparently it had been going on for many years, sadly.

Knowing the children were now safe, Garner and Denise set up a secure trust to make sure they would never be in harm's way again and lead safe and normal lives. At least as normal as possible given all the evil they had suffered as well as all the dark shadows that would surely stay in their minds.

Back home, Garner and Denise used the money to set up a similar trust for wayward girls and boys, as well as to pay for a funeral service any time they learned of a child being murdered and having no family to pay for a proper burial and grave site. Good hearted funeral directors all over America came to work with the Yellow Scarf Foundation, named in honor of the girl the white-haired dirty ex-cop had picked up and strangled to death, just to frame Fitz. No one knew the girl's name since her only identification had been thrown into the cheap cardboard

450

cremation casket along with her body, when it was loaded up and flown out to Oklahoma. All the white-haired man had ever said to describe the girl was of the yellow scarf she wore.

Garner and Denise had always wanted children of their own, but God had other plans.

~~~~~~~~~~~~~~~~~

~~~ *Adios* ~~~

Made in the USA
Monee, IL
12 June 2020